NO PLACE FOR A WOMAN

Val Wood

BANTAM PRESS

LONDON • TORONTO • SYDNEY • AUCKLAND • JOHANNESBURG

TRANSWORLD PUBLISHERS
61–63 Uxbridge Road, London W5 5SA
www.penguin.co.uk

Transworld is part of the Penguin Random House group of companies
whose addresses can be found at global.penguinrandomhouse.com

Penguin
Random House
UK

First published in Great Britain in 2016 by Bantam Press
an imprint of Transworld Publishers

A CIP catalogue record for this book
is available from the British Library.

ISBN 9780593074336

Typeset in 11.5/14pt New Baskerville by Falcon Oast Graphic Art Ltd.
Printed and bound by Clays Ltd, Bungay, Suffolk.

Penguin Random House is committed to a sustainable
future for our business, our readers and our planet. This book
is made from Forest Stewardship Council® certified paper.

MIX
Paper from
responsible sources
FSC
www.fsc.org   FSC® C018179

1 3 5 7 9 10 8 6 4 2

In memory of Lance Corporal James Andrew Foss
(1884–1917) of the 7th Battalion, East Yorkshire
Regiment. Killed by hostile aircraft on
29 November 1917 at Passchendaele, Flanders,
Belgium, Western European theatre of war; and
in recognition of all those killed, injured or who
endured at home and abroad during the
First World War.

Nothing in life is to be feared; it is only to be understood.

Marie Curie

BOOK III

PROLOGUE

Even into her old age, which was very long indeed, she would sometimes waken, startled, unaware for a few seconds of where she was. In the space of that transient time she remembered again the screeching, shrieking sound of metal on metal, the screams of petrified passengers, the white-hot flashes and the crimson blood and her parents, her beloved mama and papa, lying still and silent with their arms wrapped protectively around her. And then oblivion; and with a deep sigh she would reach out for a comforting hand and wonder what it was that had aroused her.

PART ONE

CHAPTER ONE

July 1897

It was Saturday 10 July and a month short of Lucy's fourth birthday when she returned to the house in Baker Street, where she had been born. She had been absent for six months.

As they walked the short distance from the railway station she clung to the hand of the housekeeper, Mary Chester, who had travelled to London to accompany Lucy when her uncle William brought her home. William was returning to London the next day, and after finalizing their household arrangements would be travelling back to Hull the following week, bringing his wife Nora and her son Oswald with him.

Lucy had barely spoken on the train journey and had sat very close to Mary, tucked beneath her comforting arm. Her uncle had tried to be very jolly and point out interesting viewpoints as they steamed towards Yorkshire, but Lucy had closed her eyes and huddled into herself.

'I'm afraid 'memory might still be strong, sir,' Mary had murmured respectfully when she thought that Lucy was asleep; but she wasn't, although she didn't understand what Mary had meant, nor comprehend her uncle's reply.

'I'm inclined to agree with you, but the people who are supposed to know about the effects of these . . . *incidents* say that she is too young to bring them to mind, and that it was best to make another train journey as soon as possible. If by chance the memory is still there it will eventually fade.' He'd sighed. 'My wife thought they were right, and I agreed with her that it is also a long way to travel by road.'

Lucy was thankful to get off the train, and as they crossed the road towards Baker Street she tightened her grip on Mary's hand and looked up at her. She wanted to ask a question but felt that she didn't want to hear the answer; and she was frightened of what she might find when they reached her house.

'Nearly home, Miss Lucy,' Mary said quietly. 'All your toys are waiting for you. Your pretty dollies have had their clothes washed and ironed especially for your return.'

It wasn't enough, Mary knew, and as she put the key in the lock of the door she expected the worst as she felt the child's hand tremble in hers. She stepped inside and Lucy followed, and dropping Mary's hand ran to the foot of the wide staircase.

'*Mama*,' she shouted, with a note of keening desperation in her voice. '*Papa!* Where are you? Your little Lucy has come home.'

William Thornbury was too overcome with emotion to be of much help to the child so it was left to Mary to take her to her bedroom and hope that its familiarity would help soothe her distress.

For him, stepping into the house brought home the full measure of the tragedy that had overtaken him in the loss of his younger brother and his wife. He had been fond of Joseph, and his sister-in-law Alice had been a sweet-tempered, kind and intelligent woman.

Urgent decisions had had to be made when he was told of the train crash that had killed them both and left Lucy unconscious with a broken arm in a London hospital bed. He had visited his niece daily and decided that when she recovered, as the doctors said she would, he would take her to his own London home to live. It was the least he could do.

His wife, Nora, had agreed that he should, but were they in a position to bring her up in the manner that her parents would have expected, she had asked, and which room would she have?

14

She couldn't share Oswald's. She would have to have the attic room, or else they would have to move. They still lived in the small house that William had bought whilst a bachelor. He had heard the worry in her voice and said that he would write to his brother's lawyer, Roger Groves, and arrange a meeting; Joseph would have made provision for his child in the event of his early demise, but he wouldn't in the least have expected that he and his wife would be taken together.

'But in any case,' William said firmly, determined to do his duty by the child, 'Lucy is my niece as well as my god-daughter, and as such is under my care, unless other provisions have been made.'

He had visited Hull as soon as possible after the inquest to see the lawyer, speak to Joseph's colleagues at the Infirmary and arrange the funerals, which would take place in Hull. At the meeting with the lawyer it was confirmed that as he was the closest living relative – Lucy's mother being an only child and the whereabouts of her parents unknown, and his and Joseph's parents having died of influenza shortly after Lucy's first birthday – he had been appointed in Joseph's Will as Lucy's legal guardian until she reached the age of twenty-one, when she would receive her inheritance and the property in Baker Street. Until then a yearly allowance which William would administer was to be set out for her expenses.

'And what will happen to the property in the meantime? Whilst the child is living in my care?' he'd asked.

'The usual procedure would be that the furniture would be stored and the house rented out,' Groves told him, 'the rental going towards keeping the house in good repair.' He'd rubbed his chin thoughtfully. 'Unless, of course, you would consider living there yourself once the little girl is recovered?'

William had nodded, but didn't comment. He wondered what his wife would make of that suggestion, and then he'd been shaken to the core when Groves had remarked, 'How different things would have been, Mr Thornbury, if the child had died in the accident along with her parents rather than making such a remarkable recovery, for then you would have been the sole recipient of your brother's estate, is that not so?'

William had felt the blood drain from his face and the lawyer had apologized profusely for his insensitivity. 'You were close to your brother, I take it,' he murmured. 'You have felt his loss.'

William had wiped his face with his handkerchief and realized he was trembling. 'Yes, indeed. I was very proud of his achievements. He was a first class physician and bound for great things in the field of medicine.' Unlike me, he had thought. Just a lowly second class bank manager without ambition.

But in their parents' eyes the brothers had been equal. Their mother had come to her marriage from a prosperous family and William and Joseph, with their own salaries to keep them comfortable, had inherited sufficient wealth on their parents' early death for each to buy property. William, with his astute financial mind, had invested prudently, yet well. Now he must also invest for Lucy's future.

Lucy had run, howling, up the stairs to her top-floor bedroom. Mary, hurrying after her, found her in bed under the blanket and bedspread, still wearing her boots, coat and bonnet and refusing to take them off. After some persuasion she let Mary remove her boots but wouldn't take off her coat or bonnet.

'Shall I make you a nice cup of chocolate, Miss Lucy?' Mary asked her. 'You used to like that.'

Lucy removed her thumb from her mouth. 'Yes, please,' she whispered, and as Mary smiled and turned for the door she added, 'And ask Mama to bring it up to me.'

Mary came back, sat down on the bed and said softly, 'Miss Lucy, I'll explain to you again, though I know how much it will pain you to hear me repeat it, that I'm afraid your mama and papa will not be coming back. They were hurt in the train crash, as you were, and are now in heaven with Jesus.'

'Why didn't I go with them?'

'Because,' Mary said patiently, 'Jesus wasn't ready for you. He said because you are only a little girl there are still lots of things for you to do on this earth.'

16

'What kind of things?' Lucy spoke thickly through her thumb.

Mary shook her head. 'That's not for me to know, Miss Lucy. Jesus hasn't shared His plans with me.' And thought sorrowfully, and with more than a tinge of anger, that it must surely be an extraordinary master plan to take a child's parents away and leave her alone.

When she went downstairs again she found Mr Thornbury standing by the sitting room window looking down into the street. She asked him if he'd like a cup of tea and told him that before leaving for London she had prepared a joint of beef which they would eat cold for dinner later.

He turned towards her. 'Thank you, Mary; tea would be very nice, and I would also like to thank you for your care in helping me bring Lucy home. It must be so very difficult for her.'

'I believe it is, sir, and will continue to be so for quite some time.'

'But it is for the best, isn't it?' he asked, as if wanting assurance that his decision had been the right one. 'She will recover more easily in her own home than in London?'

'I believe it'll help, sir, for her to be in familiar surroundings.' Then she added, 'But you do understand, Mr Thornbury, that I can only stay for another month until your wife settles in. My forthcoming marriage. . . ?'

'Of course, of course, I do understand. Naturally your husband-to-be will want you to have a place of your own once you're married.' Marriage meant a different kind of life, and not for the first time he wondered if perhaps he should have remained a bachelor as he had originally intended. He still puzzled over how he had come to marry Nora, a widow with a two-year-old son: a child who wasn't his, and even now, five years later, didn't appear to like him despite his best efforts.

Mary left to go to the kitchen and he turned to the window once more, still wondering whether he had made the right decision in moving to Hull. He had discussed the lawyer's remark with his wife, and she had instantly pooh-poohed the idea as preposterous. She had lived all her life in London.

But the next day she had asked what kind of house it was and what the district was like, and was there culture in the town. Hull was the place of William's birth, where he had worked as a bank clerk until he had been offered a more lucrative position as under-manager in the up and coming Brixton area of London, so he was able to answer with confidence.

'Hull is a fine prosperous town,' he'd said. 'Ship-building and the fishing industry have made it so. There are literary institutions, museums and a good library, and the house is much larger than this one. But before we even consider it I would need to find another position. I must have employment.'

'Well,' she had answered, picking up her sewing to signal the end of their conversation, and as if the decision would be entirely hers, 'I'll think about it, and how it might affect Oswald.'

Ah, Oswald, he thought as he continued gazing down the street. Completely ruined by his mother; not surprising, I suppose, when she was the only one in his life. He seems to regard me as a usurper bent on stealing away her affection. The boy has built a protective shell around himself, much as his mother has. Yet in those early days in Brixton she told me that she would consider remarrying in order to give Oswald a father figure. It was that persuasion, and the fact that he was attracted to her, that had somehow propelled him into marriage.

He turned away from the window and sat to await his tea. He was pleased to be back in Hull. Pleased to have found the opportunity of a position in a private bank so quickly, his London experience coming in useful after all; but he somehow couldn't shake off the feeling of guilt that he would be living in his vital younger brother's house when Joseph lay dead in his grave.

But it is Lucy who must be taken care of now, he vowed. Poor child, how she must be suffering, and I must make sure that Nora and Oswald understand that she must be our priority. We must give her a full and happy life to make up for her great loss.

CHAPTER TWO

The following day William left for London on the early train, and Mary took the opportunity to explain to Lucy that she was going to be married soon. She didn't tell the child that she couldn't bear to stay on in this house with another mistress running it. She had been very fond of Dr and Mrs Thornbury, and although her amiable fiancé would have understood if she had wanted to become a daily maid instead of a live-in one, she had decided that a clean break was called for. When she had travelled to London at Mr Thornbury's request, and had met his wife for the first time, her resolve to leave as soon as possible was strengthened. Mrs William Thornbury had told her that she would be choosing her own servants when she came to live in Hull.

'An excellent idea, ma'am,' Mary had said, and tried not to sound too pleased as she went on to say that she herself would only be staying on until a new housekeeper was hired, since she was leaving to be married. She considered that she was a good judge of character and knew without a shadow of doubt that she would not wish to work for Nora Thornbury.

'May I come to your wedding?' Lucy asked Mary as she dressed her. 'I have lots of pretty frocks that I could wear.'

'Of course you can. That would be lovely! Let's tek a look in your wardrobe,' Mary said, 'and see what still fits you. You've grown so tall whilst you've been away.'

Taller and thinner is what she meant, and she hoped that a

19

new cook would look to providing the little girl with nourishing food to build her up again.

They found several dresses that still fitted, although Mary would have to let down some of the hems. Lucy asked if she could wear one of them now instead of the one that her aunt had bought her as a mourning dress, which was dark grey wool and edged on the collar and hem with black frogging. Mary didn't see why she shouldn't and was convinced that the little girl would be cheered up by wearing something more colourful.

She dressed her and brushed her dark hair and found a blue satin bow to pin in it, and was pleased to see Lucy's brown eyes light up as she looked in the mirror.

'Wouldn't Mama be happy to see me in this,' she said.

Mary swallowed hard. 'Indeed she would, Miss Lucy, and she would be more than happy to see that lovely smile on your face.'

'I'll try to smile, Mary,' Lucy said. 'It's just that sometimes I feel very sad.'

'We all feel sad sometimes, Miss Lucy,' Mary told her. 'But being happy is better and will chase 'sadness away.'

'Could we go out?' the little girl asked. 'Is it allowed?'

'Yes, it's allowed. Why wouldn't it be?'

'Aunt Nora said I wasn't well enough to go out before, because I have had a – had a . . .' She delicately patted her mouth in an unconscious mimicry of her mother that broke Mary's heart. 'A *drama* I think she said.'

'A drama?' Mary frowned as she pondered on what that meant. '*Trauma*, was it?'

'Oh, it might have been trauma. I don't know what a trauma is; perhaps it's something like a drama. But I don't think I've had one.'

Mary took a deep breath. 'I don't know what it is either,' she lied, 'so we won't bother about it and we'll tek a short walk into town.'

It was a warm and sunny day when they ventured out after Lucy had eaten breakfast, with Mary carrying an umbrella in case of rain.

'Could we go and see your house, Mary? The one you'll live in when you get married?'

Mary hesitated. The house, or room as it really was, was situated in one of the poorer districts of Hull, being the only place that she and Joe could afford. 'I haven't got the key yet, Miss Lucy,' she said at last, 'but I'll show you where it is.' It wouldn't do any harm, she thought, if the child saw how ordinary folk lived.

They walked from Baker Street into the town. Dr Thornbury and his wife had decided on that address as it was close to the General Infirmary where, had he lived, it was expected he would have eventually become a senior surgeon, but Mary took Lucy in a different direction so that she didn't see the hospital. As they went through other streets Lucy seemed to be concentrating on her white buckled shoes. She gave a few little hops. 'Did you hear that, Mary? My heels make a tapping noise when I go forward.'

Mary laughed. 'So they do,' she said, and she too hopped. 'Tap, tap, tap!'

'They're dancing shoes.' Lucy tried several different steps, and by the time they had skipped and hopped to her satisfaction they were well away from the Infirmary, cutting through narrow streets and into the town, skirting the Queen's Dock and heading towards Whitefriargate where they could look in the smart shop windows.

Hull already had some fine buildings, but in this year, when the town was to be granted the status of a city, there was much talk of change and plans of demolishing the slum courts and alleyways were under discussion; new streets and housing would be built and the imposing Venetian-styled town hall, designed by the Hull-born architect Cuthbert Brodrick, would also be knocked down and a new guildhall built to reflect the status of a city. Mary hoped that they wouldn't start demolishing just yet; some of the properties tucked down the alleyways between High Street and Lowgate, where she and Joe would live when they were married, must surely be on the list.

'What's that smell?' Lucy wrinkled her nose as they crossed

over Lowgate and through narrow Bishop Lane into High Street.

Mary knew what it was but hedged, saying, 'It could be all manner of things, Miss Lucy. There are lots of mills and factories in this area and all of 'smells mingle together. There're fish manure works and fish oil companies, and linseed and turpentine works. All manner of places. Hull is a busy industrial town, and we must put up with a few bad smells if it's to thrive.'

The overriding aroma to which Lucy was referring, which Mary hardly ever noticed any more, came from the old privies at the back of the houses where the drains, such as they were, overflowed when the rain came down, or stank during hot weather. That was another reason why the corporation was so very keen to knock down some of these ancient buildings where people no longer wanted to live.

'Why, look here,' she went on, as a man approached. 'Here's Mr Harrigan himself. Joe, what you doing down here at this time of day? Why aren't you at work?'

A solidly built man in a shabby tweed jacket and wearing a cap that he took off as soon as he drew near bent down to greet Lucy.

'This must be Miss Thornbury her very self, is it, Mary?' he said, putting his hand to his chest. 'How do you do, miss? I'm very pleased to have your acquaintance.'

'I'm very well, thank you, Mr Harrigan,' Lucy piped, and politely dipped her knee. 'And I hope that you are too? You may call me Lucy if you wish.'

'I'd be honoured, Miss Lucy,' he grinned. '*Dee-lighted.*' Then he frowned. 'But what 'you doing down here, Mary, and bringing 'young miss? That's not on at all, you know.'

'I asked you first, Joe,' Mary said. 'Why aren't you at work?'

'Short time,' he said glumly. 'I don't start till after dinner.' He shrugged. 'I thought I'd collect 'key to 'house while I'd got 'time off.'

'Oh, so I can see the house after all,' Lucy said excitedly.

Mary shook her head silently, indicating to Joe that it wasn't a good idea, and Joe, catching on, said as if reluctantly, 'I'm afraid not, Miss Lucy. It's being prepared, cleaned an' that, ready for when me and Mary gets married. Mebbe you could come after that.'

'All right,' Lucy said. 'Perhaps when you've got your own furniture and curtains?'

'We'd consider it a great honour,' Joe said. 'Wouldn't we, my Mary?'

Mary put her hand on Lucy's shoulder and gave a soft sigh. 'We would indeed.'

Joe left them and continued up High Street whilst Lucy and Mary carried on in the opposite direction until Mary halted at the top of a narrow alleyway where there were eight small houses.

'We won't go down, Miss Lucy, but 'house that me and Joe is renting is down here. This is called Narrow Passage.'

Lucy peered down and then looked up at the topmost windows. 'It is very narrow, isn't it? And rather dark,' she said. 'Won't you be afraid of walking down here on your own? Although I suppose Mr Harrigan will be with you most of the time.' She looked rather puzzled. 'Except when he's at work. What kind of work does he do?'

'Joe works on 'docks. He's a labourer,' Mary said. 'He unloads cargo off 'ships that come in.'

'I see,' Lucy said. 'I suppose that's very difficult work. He'll have to be very careful not to drop anything.'

Mary smiled. 'Oh, he's very strong is my Joe, and very careful. Come along then, Miss Lucy. Let's turn round and be getting home again.'

As they strolled back across town, Mary stopped to speak to someone else. 'This is my sister Dolly, Miss Lucy.'

They exchanged greetings, and then in a low voice Mary asked a question of her sister. When Dolly shook her head, Mary said more loudly, 'Ask her to come and see me early tomorrow morning. And then I can tell her what's what.'

Lucy laughed. 'What's what,' she said merrily as they continued, cutting through streets that Mary seemed to know very well until they arrived back in Albion Street, where many of the houses were occupied by doctors who worked at the hospital, dental surgeons, bank officials and others who didn't have any occupation but were supported by an inheritance which allowed them to live in such a superior district.

'What's what?' Mary said, turning the subject on its head as they walked on into Baker Street. 'In a few years' time, Hull will have changed. Old streets will have been knocked down and new thoroughfares built.'

'Will you still know the way, Mary?' Lucy asked. 'Or will you get lost?'

'I won't get lost,' Mary answered. 'Soon you'll be able to walk right down Prospect Street and into town without cutting through all those little streets the way we did when we came in.'

'But if their houses are knocked down,' Lucy said, 'where will all the people live?'

'Ah, well,' Mary said solemnly. 'I don't know if all those clever folk with big ideas have thought of that yet.'

The following morning, before Lucy was awake, Mary opened the back door in answer to a soft tap and let in her niece Ada, Dolly's eldest daughter.

'Ma said I should come to see you,' the girl whispered.

Mary led her into the kitchen. 'No need to whisper, there's nobody else here at 'minute. Your ma said you haven't got any work yet.'

'I haven't,' Ada said. 'I've applied for some but haven't had any luck so far. I was going to try one of 'mills, but I'd rather work in a house than a mill or a factory.'

Mary nodded. 'I'm leaving here as soon as 'new mistress gets fixed up. She wants new staff and I don't fancy working for her. I was used to my Mrs Thornbury's ways and I know this one'll be different.'

'Bit of a firecracker, is she?' Ada said perceptively.

'I might be doing her an injustice,' Mary answered, 'cos I don't really know her, but probably. Master's nice though, just like his brother. But what I'd hoped,' she lowered her voice, 'was for somebody to keep an eye on Miss Lucy. She deserves some kindness after what she's been through, and I know that you're used to looking after your sisters and brothers.'

'Surely they'll want a nursery maid, not somebody like me?' Ada said.

'Mistress'll want a maid of all work if I'm any judge, and I think you'll be right up her street if you play your cards right. Now this is what I suggest . . .'

CHAPTER THREE

A week after William Thornbury arrived back in Hull with his wife and stepson, Mary tapped on the sitting room door where Mrs Thornbury was arranging her own ornaments on the shelves and side tables and placing her predecessor's treasures in boxes ready for storage in the loft. Mary had been helping her but had been called away to answer the door.

'Begging your pardon, ma'am, there's a young woman at 'door asking if there are any positions vacant or likely to be in 'near future.'

'Good heavens. So soon? Has she come in answer to the advertisement?'

'I didn't enquire, ma'am, but I wouldn't have thought so. I only took it into 'newspaper office yesterday.'

'Well, how has she found out?'

'News travels fast in this town, ma'am.'

Mrs Thornbury humphed and huffed. 'Well, I don't think I'm quite ready to interview anyone just yet. Tell her to come back next week.'

'She seems very presentable, ma'am,' Mary offered. 'And young. Not got into any set ways yet, I wouldn't think.'

Mrs Thornbury glanced at her. 'What are you saying?'

'Just that she might easily find another position, ma'am.'

'Oh, I see. Very well; send her in and I'll talk to her.'

Mary went out and then came back again. 'Mrs Thornbury will see you now,' she said in a carrying voice, adding in a lower tone, 'Mind your p's and q's,' as Ada knocked and went in.

Nora Thornbury sat down in a chair at the side of the fireplace. There was no fire burning but a vase with palm fronds was set in the centre of the hearth.

'Name?' she said without preamble.

'Ada Morris, ma'am.' Ada dipped her knee as Mary had instructed her.

'Age?'

'Fourteen, ma'am. Last week,' she added.

'Previous employment?'

'None. Onny at home. My mother said she'd teach me everything I needed to know before sending me out to work for somebody else. But I already know about housework and can do a bit of cooking, and I help out with me brothers and sisters as well.'

'Do you? How old are they?'

'Eldest under me, our Bob, is nearly twelve, then ten, eight, six and 'youngest is nearly three.'

Mrs Thornbury gave a shudder. 'You must be pleased to be leaving home?'

'Oh, no, ma'am, they're all well behaved; my ma wouldn't have it any other way.'

'I see. Why did you think there might be a vacancy here? You can't have seen it in the newspaper?'

'We don't see 'newspaper until it's at least a week old, ma'am, but I'd heard about 'nice doctor and his poor wife and of 'little girl left an orphan an' I just kept me eyes and ears open in case there was another family coming.' She heaved a breath. 'And then I rang 'doorbell on 'off chance.'

'Well, that was very perceptive of you,' Mrs Thornbury acknowledged. 'It shows that you can act on your own initiative which is good, but I must tell you that I would expect you to comply *fully* with my orders. I know how I want things done and to the *letter*. Do you understand?'

'Oh, yes, ma'am.' Ada nodded. 'My mother said exactly 'same thing and that I might stand a chance with being young and untrained and ready to be melded to someone else's ways.'

'Your mother sounds like a very sensible woman.'

'She is. Brought us all up to be polite and – and industrious,' she added as an afterthought.

Mrs Thornbury thought of the rest of the boxes that needed unpacking and the contents arranging to replace those that were going up in the loft and knew that Mary couldn't deal with all that and look after Lucy as was expected of her. And she was also preparing food until a cook was hired. She thought that perhaps another housemaid might eventually be needed as well as a cook, for it was a much bigger house than she had expected, but if she took this girl at least it would be a start.

'Very well. I need a general maid and you seem presentable,' she said, echoing Mary's words. 'I'll give you a month's trial and if you prove to be suitable I'll take you on. Six pounds a year all found.'

Ada's expression dropped. 'Oh,' she said. 'I'm real sorry, ma'am, but I'd get more than that if I worked in one of 'mills and they're known to be miserly.' She buttoned up her coat. 'I couldn't work for less than six pounds ten shillings; all found,' she added. 'I have to give money to my ma, you see.'

Nora Thornbury had thought that she could get away with giving less to a Hull servant than she had to her London house-maid, but it seemed she was wrong.

'But surely you wouldn't want to work in a mill when you can work in pleasant surroundings in an establishment like this? With food and a uniform provided!'

'It probably sounds like a lot o' money, ma'am,' Ada explained. 'But when my ma needs help to buy food and clothing for five other bairns, six pounds doesn't go very far, especially when me father's off sick. So, I'm sorry. I really would have liked to work here,' she added regretfully. She pressed her lips together and nodded her head. 'Never mind, eh.'

'Well, wait a minute.' Mrs Thornbury pondered. A bird in the hand, she thought; she's very neat and seems intelligent, and who knows who might turn up after the advertisement has been displayed; it might be someone totally unsuitable. 'If I agree to give you six pounds ten shillings—'

'All found,' Ada said quickly, in case she'd forgotten.

Nora sighed. 'All found. With that salary I would expect you to be *on your toes* at all times!'

'Oh, yes, ma'am.' Ada unconsciously stretched herself up on tiptoe. 'It goes without saying I'll always do my best.'

Nora rose regally from her chair to indicate the interview was over. 'Very well, that's agreed then. I'd like you to start tomorrow.'

'Not tomorrow ma'am,' Ada said. 'Tomorrow I'll help my mother clean 'house and wash 'sheets so that my brother can tek my bed, then pack my things to bring wi' me. I'll come 'day after,' she said. 'That'll be Sat'day.'

Nora gave in. She had never been very good with servants. Perhaps because her own mother had never had anyone but a daily maid who, if she thought fit to turn up, did her regular chores in a morning and then left after eating a midday meal which she seemed to expect as her right. 'Saturday morning then,' she agreed. 'Eight o'clock sharp.'

'Bloomin' old skinflint,' Ada muttered as Mary let her out of the outer door. 'Talk about getting blood from a stone.'

Mary put her hand to her mouth to hide a grin. She'd been listening from the hall. 'And what's this about your da being off sick?'

Ada rolled her eyes. 'Oh, yeh! He had a sudden bout of *idle-itis*.' She laughed. 'He'll mek a good recovery, don't you worry! See you on Sat'day. Thanks, Aunt Mary. I'm going to enjoy working here.'

One day during the following week Lucy slipped into the sitting room and with her hands folded in front of her sat quietly watching her aunt pack the last of her mother's possessions into a box. There were wax flowers in a domed glass container, a pair of cut glass celery vases, two crystal decanters which her aunt put aside, two photographs in silver frames that went into the box and various pieces of silverware that Nora held up for inspection before looking about the room as if deciding whether or not to place them somewhere. It was as she was doing this that her eyes fell on Lucy.

'Good heavens,' she exclaimed. 'You startled me, Lucy. How long have you been sitting there?'

Lucy knew the numbers on the clock but hadn't yet mastered the art of telling the time, nor could she judge the length of its passing. She looked up at her aunt from dark eyes and shook her head. 'I don't know, Aunt Nora. Can I help you? Those are Mama's things.'

'I know they are,' her aunt agreed. 'I'm packing them away so that they don't get broken, and when you're a grown-up young lady you'll be able to open the boxes for yourself and put them wherever you want.'

'In this house?' Lucy asked.

'Yes, if you are still living here, which I expect you will be.'

'I asked Oswald if he would play a game with me, but he won't.'

'Well, he's older than you, Lucy, I expect that's why. He's seven already.'

'I'm nearly four,' Lucy told her. 'I'll be having a birthday soon, won't I? Will he play with me then?'

Her aunt sighed. She was no better with children than she was with servants, not even her own son; William said he thought she had spoiled Oswald, and she thought she probably had, but excused herself by saying she was trying to make up for his not remembering his father. Even though very young, Oswald hadn't taken to William and he'd kicked up a fuss when they'd moved into his house after their marriage.

'Oswald will be going to school in September,' she said, 'so he won't have much time for playing. He'll have his lessons to learn.'

'So can Ada play with me?'

Nora pressed the bell on the wall. 'I'll ask her,' she said, 'but you really must learn to entertain yourself when grown-ups are busy.'

It was Mary who answered the bell. She smiled at Lucy and looked enquiringly at her mistress. 'Yes, ma'am?'

'Can we spare Ada to look after Miss Lucy? I think she's bored.'

'She's up in 'loft moving 'boxes, Mrs Thornbury,' Mary said. She looked at the little girl sitting so forlornly. 'Could Miss Lucy come into 'kitchen wi' me and Cook? We're baking some little cakes,' she added, for Lucy's benefit more than Mrs Thornbury's, and the child's eyes lit up.

'Oh, yes, of course she can,' Nora said with some relief. 'Would you like that, Lucy?'

'Yes, please.' Lucy slid down from the chair and put her hand into Mary's. 'I'll make a cake for Uncle William's supper.'

Nora had given Ada precise instructions on what was expected of her. She would be the only maid living in after Mary left. Ada would rise at six o'clock in the morning and her first job was to see to the fires. She would riddle and relight the kitchen range so that the oven would be hot when the new cook arrived at seven, and then clear and clean the sitting room and dining room hearths and lay them for lighting later. Then she would prepare the table for Mr Thornbury's breakfast: porridge and toast that Cook would have ready for him when he came downstairs at seven thirty.

After he had left for the bank Ada would prepare the table again for the mistress and the children. Whilst they were eating she would make the beds and dust and tidy the rooms, and after they finished she would wash the dishes and prepare the vegetables for luncheon before beginning any other jobs that the mistress required. Once a week she would polish the brass, including the knocker and the bell on the front door.

'I'll see how it goes,' Ada told her aunt Mary. 'If I'm to be general maid, I'll need somebody under me to fetch and carry, chop wood and carry coal. I can't be expected to do all that myself, or who's going to mek 'beds and do 'dusting an' that?'

'I've allus had an undermaid,' Mary agreed. 'But mebbe they can't afford anybody else.'

'Well, 'mistress will have to shift herself,' Ada muttered, 'and do some of 'jobs herself.' She pondered for a minute, scratching her chin. 'Do you think they'd run to paying a lad for filling 'coal hods and chopping wood for 'fires, cos I could get our Bob to do that. He'd even clean an' polish Mr Thornbury's shoes.'

31

'Hmm,' Mary said. 'I'll mention it when 'master's at home. He'll look after 'finances, I expect.'

A few days later Mary presented herself to Mr and Mrs Thornbury as she was clearing their supper tray in the sitting room. It was always something very simple: cheese or cold meat and pickles and a small helping of bread and butter and perhaps a slice of cake or biscuits with a pot of tea or cocoa.

'I thought I might comment on how Ada and the new cook are managing their duties, as I shall be leaving you at 'end of next week.'

'Will you?' Mr Thornbury seemed surprised. 'Of course!' he exclaimed after a moment. 'You are to be married. Oh, my word. You will be sorely missed, and particularly by my niece. I do believe Lucy has come to rely on you absolutely.'

'She has, sir, but she likes Ada and Ada is very good wi' children, so I think Miss Lucy will come to terms with me not being here. I've told her that I'm leaving and she's asked if she can come to our wedding.'

'Well, and indeed why not?' He glanced at his wife. 'Someone would accompany her, wouldn't they?'

Nora drew herself up, her back rigid. 'I'm not sure if—'

Mary interrupted before Mrs Thornbury could make any objections. 'Ada said she'd bring her if you wouldn't object, ma'am. Miss Lucy has already chosen what she'd wear if she's allowed to come and it would be such a treat for her, poor little mite.'

'I quite agree,' William Thornbury boomed. 'She's had her fair share of sorrow at such a young age; a wedding would cheer her up immensely.'

'Thank you, sir.' Mary bobbed her knee. 'And if I might just mention, to get back to Ada and her duties, I wonder if it would be possible to hire a young lad to chop wood and fill 'coal hods and buckets? There's quite a lot for Ada to do, especially if she's to look after Miss Lucy as well as fulfil her other duties; if there was a lad to do 'heavier work and even 'jobs like cleaning shoes and boots and sweeping 'front of house and back yard, it would save her having to do it.'

'Has she complained?' Nora asked.

'No, never, ma'am. But she's a good worker and it would be a shame to lose her if she should decide in say a twelvemonth or so to better herself.'

Nora frowned. 'How much extra help did you have when you worked for Dr Thornbury?'

'Allus a boot boy, ma'am, and a scullery maid as well as a live-in cook.'

'We don't need a live-in cook,' William told his wife. 'My brother and Alice entertained quite frequently, much more than we are likely to.'

Mary nodded in agreement. She recalled with pleasure the merry times the doctor and his wife had when entertaining friends to dinner.

'But,' William went on, 'I quite agree we should have a lad to help out for a few mornings a week at least. We can't have that slip of a girl carrying buckets of coal or wielding an axe; oh dear no! Do you know of someone, Mary?' he asked.

'Ada's brother is of an age to be looking for work, and she'd make sure he was up to scratch and came in on time.'

'Well, there we are then. Ask her if she can arrange it. Every morning. A shilling a week, would that be about right?'

'I'll tell her, sir.' Mary bobbed her knee again. 'Thank you.'

CHAPTER FOUR

Ada dressed Lucy in her prettiest dress for Mary's wedding, which would have been a quiet affair except that so many people knew the bride and her groom that there was quite a large crowd of family and friends waiting outside St Mary's church for her arrival.

Mary had borrowed a blue two-piece costume from her sister, one that Dolly had worn for her own wedding many years before, and she had splashed out and bought a new hat with the money that Mr Thornbury had given her before she left. He had pressed a gold sovereign in her hand and thanked her for taking such care of his niece following the death of his brother and sister-in-law.

She had been quite overcome by his generosity, and although she felt she didn't want to spend the gleaming coin but keep it as a memento, reasoned that if she bought something as frivolous as a new hat for her wedding then she would always remember his kindness whenever she looked at it, even though she doubted that she would ever wear it again. The hat had cost five shillings so she had change left over, which reduced her feeling of being a spendthrift.

'Mary looks really pretty,' Lucy piped up as the bride arrived, escorted on the arm of one of her brothers.

'She does,' Ada said. 'Can you see? Shall I lift you up?' She scooped Lucy up to let her see above the crowd of onlookers, until they parted and let the little girl come through to the front to get a better view.

Mary's family then piled into the church, sisters, brothers, nephews, nieces and cousins, closely followed by friends and neighbours. Ada marched down the church holding on to Lucy's hand and sat next to her mother, who was saving her a seat at the front. Dolly lifted Lucy on to her knee to have a better view.

'Is this 'first time you've been to a wedding?' she asked in a whisper.

Lucy nodded and then gazed around the church, up at the stained glass windows and then back at the people sitting behind her, who seemed to know her as they nodded and smiled or gave her a little wave. She smiled back at them and felt the stone of sadness inside her dissolving and an uplifting surge of pleasure replacing it.

After the marriage ceremony was over, everyone followed the bride and groom outside to give their good wishes. Then another of Mary's brothers announced that they had booked a room at the Commercial Hotel in Castle Street. 'Family have all clubbed together,' he said. 'There's beef and ham and plenty o' bread and a jug or two of ale, an' cake of course, and you're all welcome to come an' share it and drink 'health of our Mary and Joe.'

'Are you coming?' Dolly asked Ada. 'You can bring 'bairn with you for an hour, can't you?'

'Yeh, I'll risk it,' Ada said, and turned to Lucy. 'Would you like to come an' have a glass o' lemonade to drink to 'health of 'bride an' groom, Miss Lucy?'

'Oh, yes please.' Lucy beamed. 'I love lemonade. Cook used to make it when . . .' Her words tailed off as she half recalled some forgotten time, and she tapped on her lips. 'I don't know – when it was.'

Mary came across to them and took hold of Lucy's hand. 'You look very pretty,' she said. 'I'm glad you could be here.'

'I'm coming with you to have some lemonade,' Lucy piped up, the uneasy memory disappearing. 'Ada says that I can.'

'Of course you can, and you'll meet our Bob and Stanley, our Joshua and Edie an' all of 'others. There's loads of us. Our Bob is starting work at your house next week to chop wood for 'fires and fill 'coal hods and do a few other jobs for your uncle.'

'Oh, goody!' Lucy breathed. 'That means I'll know a lot of people.'

There were far more cousins and relations than she would ever remember, but Ada's siblings, or *bairns* as Ada called them, Bob, Stanley, Joshua and Edie, who were all older than Lucy, scooped her up and took charge of her, sitting her at their table and making sure that she had a glass of lemonade, some bread and beef, and a slice of cake. Then there was the toddler Charlie who ran from table to table, was picked up and kissed and cuddled and then put down again. Dolly, who answered to Mam from her children, told Lucy, when she asked what she should call her, 'You can call me Auntie Dolly, if you want to.'

'Yes, please,' Lucy said. 'I'd like that. I only have one other aunt: Aunt Nora. Uncle William sometimes calls her *my dear*, but I don't think that's her name.'

All the others laughed at that and Lucy happily joined in but wasn't sure why.

'Our Bob's coming to work at your house next week,' Edie said. 'Our Ada's told him he's not to speak to you if he sees you.'

Lucy gazed at her in dismay. 'Why not?'

Edie shrugged. 'Don't know. Come on,' she said, getting down from the table. 'Let's go an' talk to 'other bairns.'

She took Lucy from table to table to meet her aunts, uncles and cousins and Lucy couldn't keep up with who belonged to whom, but it didn't seem to matter, as all the older people disciplined or praised all of the children regardless of whether or not they belonged to them, and they all called Lucy *Miss Lucy*, as if they knew her and all about her. All of the uncles took her hand and gently shook it and all the aunts smiled and some of them smoothed her hair or kissed her cheek and said 'Pleased to meet you, Miss Lucy' as if they really meant it and murmured, 'What a bonny bairn,' or else 'Poor bairn,' and she didn't really understand what they meant by that.

In what seemed to be no time at all Ada said, 'Come on, Miss Lucy, we have to be getting back now or I'll be in trouble with Mrs Thornbury.'

Lucy was sad to leave such a merry gathering but she didn't want Ada to get into trouble. 'I wish I could see Auntie Dolly and all of your bairns again, Ada. I don't know any other children.' She paused and then said, 'I remember a little boy, I think.' She shook her head. 'But I don't know who he was.'

He belonged to someone, she remembered. He'd come to their house with his father; he'd pulled her hair and she'd smacked him for it, and her mama had scolded her, *her mama*; hot tears flooded her eyes at the memory. She searched her remembrance. The boy's father had been cross with him and had said, 'That's very naughty of you, Henry. She's only a very little girl and you mustn't do that ever again.'

'Miss Lucy!' Ada was holding out her coat for Lucy to put her arms in the sleeves. 'You're miles away. Did you hear what I said?'

Lucy blinked. 'You said you'd get into trouble with Aunt Nora if we were late.'

Ada fastened up her coat and patted her on the head. 'Are you tired?' she asked. 'You look it. Will I have to give you a piggy-back home?'

Lucy giggled and asked, 'How do you do that, Ada?'

Before Ada could answer, a young man came up to her and put an arm round her shoulder. 'I'll walk you back, Ada,' he said. 'I'm going your way, and I'll give Miss Lucy a piggy-back if she needs one.'

Lucy thought that Ada looked lovely as she blushed and smiled at the young man and accepted his offer of walking back with them, but she refused to let him give Lucy a piggy-back and told him that it wouldn't be seemly. They talked to each other until they reached the top of Whitefriargate and then he left them to walk down Junction Dock where he said he worked. By then Lucy's feet were aching and they still had quite a long way to go, but Ada knew a shortcut down Savile Street and Bond Street, where she stood Lucy on a wall and told her to climb on to her back and she'd carry her, and then Lucy knew that they were almost home for the next cut-through brought them into Albion Street and then Baker Street and she was carefully put down on her feet before they reached the house.

'Hurry upstairs and wash your hands and face, Miss Lucy,' Ada whispered as they entered the hallway. 'Then put your indoor slippers on, there's a good girl, cos Cook'll have pre-pared afternoon tea and I'll have to serve it.'

They must have been late, Lucy thought, as after obeying instructions she came back downstairs again and went into the sitting room to find her aunt and Oswald waiting for their tea.

'Did you enjoy the wedding?' her aunt asked. 'You've been a long time.'

'It was lovely,' Lucy said enthusiastically. 'And then I was invited to go for a – *celebration* and I had lemonade and cake.' She turned to Oswald. 'I wish you could have come, Oswald. There were lots of children there and—'

'I don't play with children,' he scoffed. 'I'm *seven*!'

'Oh, but our Stanley is ten and our Joshua's eight so you could have played with them.'

Oswald curled his lip. 'I wouldn't want to play with *them*. They wouldn't be my sort.'

Lucy pressed her lips together and frowned. His sort?

'What Oswald means, Lucy,' her aunt explained, 'is that they are different from us. They were Mary's relatives, weren't they?'

'Yes,' Lucy agreed. 'And Ada's as well. All of those bairns are her brothers and sisters and there were lots of others there too. I don't know who they all were.'

Oswald pulled a face and his mother drew in a breath. 'So there you are,' she murmured.

Ada knocked on the door and came in with the tea tray. She had changed into a crisp white apron and a fresh cap. She put the tray down on a table and dipped her knee. 'I'll just bring in 'teapot and a jug of hot water, ma'am.'

'Miss Lucy has been telling us of Mary's wedding and the

38

celebration afterwards,' Mrs Thornbury said pointedly. 'Where was the celebration held?'

'In a hotel in Castle Street, ma'am. In a private room.' Ada instantly made it clear that the event wasn't in a public house, which was obviously what Mrs Thornbury expected. 'I didn't think you'd mind, ma'am. Mary specially asked if I'd take Miss Lucy. We didn't stay long.'

The door opened again and William came in. 'Ah!' he said. 'That was excellent timing. Yes please, Ada, I will have a cup. Have you had a nice time, Lucy, my dear? Your first wedding, I should think? Did Mary look nice?'

Ada slipped out again as Lucy got up to stand by his side and tell him. 'She bought a new hat and I was *specially* invited to go to the celebration afterwards and all the uncles and aunties were there with all their bairns.'

Her uncle laughed and fingered his moustache. 'Were they really? Well, how splendid,' he said.

'And our Bob who's coming to work here next week was there, but our Edie told me that Ada said he hasn't to speak to me when he's here.' Her bottom lip trembled. 'Why can't he?'

Uncle William shook his head. 'I can't imagine why Ada should say such a thing,' he said solemnly. 'But I'll have a word with our Bob when he gets here and tell him that he most certainly can.'

Lucy took a deep breath and smiled, instantly reassured, but wondered why her uncle raised his eyebrows as he looked across at Aunt Nora and then at Oswald.

CHAPTER FIVE

'The child is unhappy, but doesn't understand why,' William told his wife later when the two children had gone to bed. 'It's good for her to mix with others, and Oswald should too, even if you don't consider they come up to your exacting standards.'

'You don't seem to realize that we must raise her in the same manner as her parents would have done,' Nora retaliated. 'She's a sweet child, but it doesn't come easily for me to bring up a little girl with expectations who must be guided away from ne'er-do-wells and the servant classes.'

'Now you are being ridiculous,' he admonished her. 'You are trying too hard. Do you imagine that people with money or advantages are always honest and honourable and not driven by greed or avarice? Well I can tell you that it isn't always so. They can be as deceitful and unworthy as anyone else. And in general, the working classes are decent, sincere and trust-worthy people.'

Nora turned her head away. Not all of them, they weren't; she didn't voice her opinion, for he wouldn't listen, but she knew better. She knew *them* better than he did, those working class people he admired so much. They weren't all decent. She'd lived with them, been brought up by them. *Brought up,* she scoffed. Dragged up more like. By her hair sometimes. William thought he knew all about her, but he didn't. There were some things she hadn't admitted even to him; afraid that if she did, caring and honourable man though he was, he would turn away and abandon her, just as other men had done.

On the Monday evening after he had returned from his day at the bank, he brought the subject up again. 'As Lucy is going to be four next week, I think she should have a birthday tea,' he said decisively. 'She should invite two of the children she met at Mary's wedding, and,' he emphasized, 'I met a former friend of Joseph and Alice's today. Matthew Warrington. He came into the bank and introduced himself. He's a doctor at the Infirmary and has two children, a boy and a girl, both a little older than Lucy, more Oswald's age. I suggest we invite them along as well. They are both home on holiday at the moment. The boy, Henry, goes to Pocklington School and I was thinking—'

'Oh, but Oswald is too young to be sent away to school,' his wife began to object as she realized where the conversation was heading.

'I quite agree, but what I propose is that we organize a governess for Lucy for September.' Without waiting for an answer he went on, 'Oswald could take lessons too, or perhaps you'd prefer him to go to a local school. And that would prepare him to go to Pocklington, or somewhere else if you choose, when he's eight.'

She put her hands to her face. 'I don't know. I don't know.'

'You can't keep him by your side for ever, my dear,' he said quietly. 'He needs a good education if he is to succeed in life. Joseph and I both went to St Peter's in York, but I thought as Pocklington is nearer—' He saw her obvious distress. 'I am willing to do whatever I can for the boy, you know that, don't you? But the decision is yours alone.'

Lucy was delighted to hear about the promised birthday tea. Her aunt told her that she could ask Ada's sister and one brother, 'but not Bob,' she said, 'as he's too old.'

'I'm going to ask our Edie and our Joshua.' Lucy clapped her hands. 'Then Oswald can play with our Joshua if he wants to.'

'Lucy! Please will you stop saying *our* Edie and *our* Joshua and

41

our whoever else,' her aunt said in exasperation. 'They are not *your* relations, they are Ada's!'

Lucy gazed at her in bewilderment, not understanding what she meant.

'You don't say *our* unless they are brothers or sisters, and even then not always!' Her aunt huffed out a breath, knowing she hadn't explained herself properly. How difficult it was to bring up a child who wasn't hers, and to do right by her. A governess is a good idea, she thought. She can teach her so much more than I can.

'I thought they were their names,' Lucy said in a small deflated voice. 'It's what they all say to each other. Should I say our Oswald?'

'No.' Her aunt was brusque, although not really meaning to be. 'Oswald isn't related to you either.'

'Isn't he a cousin?' Lucy whispered. Then she pouted when her aunt shook her head, muttered, 'Well, I'm glad that he's not,' and rushed out of the room and ran upstairs.

The tea party was not a great success. Henry and Elizabeth Warrington hadn't wanted to come to the birthday party of a four-year-old girl they didn't know, even though their mother said they had met her before. They were brought into the hall by a maid who said she remembered Miss Lucy when she was a baby in her baby carriage. 'You were walking by then, Miss Elizabeth,' she said, smiling down at her charge, but Elizabeth didn't answer. 'I'll come back about four o'clock,' she told Ada. 'Master Henry, behave yourself. No fighting or I shall tell your father.'

'Tell-tale,' he called after her and then turned to glare at Joshua and Edie who had also just arrived at the door, but had come alone, having been given directions by Bob.

'Who 'you staring at?' Joshua asked him.

'Don't you mean *what* am I staring at?' Henry retaliated loftily. 'Because the answer would be that I don't know.'

Joshua took a step towards him, but Ada said swiftly, 'Come in, all of you. Miss Lucy and Master Oswald are waiting for you in 'sitting room.'

'I don't know who they are,' Elizabeth complained. 'I've never met them in my *life*!'

'We've met Miss Lucy,' Edie pronounced. 'She's our friend, mine and me brothers'.'

'Really?' Elizabeth said. 'How old are you?'

'Six,' Edie said, 'and our Josh is eight.'

Joshua squared his shoulders, and before they entered the sitting room he said to Henry, 'If you like fighting I'll tek you on after. I'm going to be a sodger when I'm old enough.'

'Pah!' Henry answered. 'I shall be an officer, so I shan't fight the likes of you.'

'Get inside, all of you.' Ada gave them a push towards the sitting room door. 'And you, Joshua. Behave yourself. Don't fight the young gentleman.' She looked pointedly at Henry. 'You might hurt him.'

'Do come in.' Nora greeted the doctor's children. 'You must be Master Henry and Miss Elizabeth. This is Lucy, whose birthday it is, and this is my son Oswald.'

Lucy smiled delightedly at Elizabeth but hesitated in front of Henry. 'Have you been here before?' she asked. There was something about him that brought back a hazy memory.

Elizabeth shook her head and Henry shrugged. 'Might have been,' he said nonchalantly. 'Is your father a doctor?'

Lucy's smile slipped and she looked up at her aunt, who turned to Edie and Joshua, saying, 'And you must be Ethel and Joshua?'

'It's Edith,' Edie proclaimed. 'My teacher says it's an *aynshunt* royal name and—'

'So is mine,' Elizabeth interrupted. 'Mine's a *queenly* name.'

'Mine's a kingly name,' Henry said, and looked disdainfully at Oswald, who scowled back at him.

'Would you all like some lemonade?' Nora broke in, beginning to think the party was not a good idea.

'We've got some board games to play,' Lucy said eagerly, and ran towards the window where boxed games that her uncle had bought for her birthday were waiting. 'I've got Ludo and—' She hesitated over the name on another box.

43

Edie came to look. 'That says *Tiddledy Winks*,' she said, pointing. 'We've got that at home.' She picked up a small box holding a set of cards. 'Snap,' she said. 'I know how to play this. I'll show you, Miss Lucy.'

Elizabeth heard her and came over too. 'It's best with four people,' she pronounced, 'so we'll need one more. Henry, do you want to play?'

'Do you have chess? Although who will I play with? I don't suppose you play?' Henry turned to Joshua, completely ignoring Oswald, who so far hadn't uttered a single word to any of them.

'No, but I can learn. I'm good at games – an' fightin',' Joshua responded.

'This says *Chess*,' Lucy said, holding out a box to Joshua.

'You, boy,' Elizabeth said to Oswald. 'You can make up the fourth for snap.'

'Don't want to,' Oswald muttered. 'I'm not playing with girls.'

'Please yourself,' Edie said placidly. 'We can play wi' three.'

Nora Thornbury heaved a sigh of relief when Ada came in with a tray of glasses and a jug of lemonade, but was rather disconcerted when she saw Joshua look up at his older sister and give an artful grin and cunning wink.

At four o'clock, after tea and games, the Warrington children were collected by their maid even though they only lived in the next street, and Edie and Joshua followed behind them. Later on, while Lucy was having her bath before bed, Nora sat on the sofa sipping from a glass of sherry that William had poured her.

'That was the most exhausting day I've ever had,' she moaned. 'I thought that Henry would be just the right companion for Oswald, but he didn't even speak to him!'

'Who didn't speak to whom?' William asked, sitting down in an easy chair by the window.

'Henry. He didn't speak to Oswald and Oswald didn't want to play with any of them, certainly not the girls. And as for Joshua! He wiped everyone off the board at every game they played, including chess which he had never played before.' She laughed in spite of her frustration. 'Henry was furious.'

'Smart boy,' William said, meaning Joshua, whom he had met only briefly on his return from the bank. 'I'll teach Oswald to play chess,' he murmured. 'Every boy should learn. Where is he anyway?'

'In his room reading; and I've decided that you're right about schooling. Oswald can share a governess with Lucy rather than attend a local school, and then – can we afford to send him to Pocklington?' She hadn't as yet considered Lucy's ongoing education.

'Yes, I think so,' he said quietly. 'I'll look into it. Lucy's education will be paid for out of her estate, of course, when the time comes.'

What a huge responsibility it is, looking after others' children, he reflected. It is not something I ever thought I would be contemplating; and yet Lucy seems almost like a daughter now. As for Oswald, he doesn't like me very much, or anyone else for that matter, but I must still do my duty by him.

During the rest of the month there was a mixture of weather conditions, heavy downpours of rain, blustery winds and occasional bright and warm sunny days, and on one of the good days Ada offered to take Lucy and Oswald to the public park on Beverley Road.

'In Pearson's Park children can run about and throw a ball, ma'am,' Ada told Lucy's aunt, 'and there're lots of flowers and trees to look at. We can walk there but maybe we should get 'omnibus back again. Bairns'll be tired after running about. It's a penny fare,' she added, 'although Miss Lucy might go free if she sits on my knee.'

Mrs Thornbury agreed that she could take them, although Oswald didn't want to go. He dragged his heels all the way there and it wasn't until they arrived at the gates and he saw the grass and the trees that he perked up and began chasing about trying to catch the ducks that had come ashore from the pond. Lucy loved it all, the fish in the pond, the flower beds, the trees, which were in full leaf, and she too ran about on the grass. Ada thought that if the weather held she would ask Joshua and Edie, and maybe even Stanley, who was ten, if they would like to come too. We could bring a picnic, she thought, getting carried away by the idea. We could bring a blanket to sit on and some lemonade and ask Cook to prepare some food. Miss Lucy would like that. It's good for her to mix with ordinary folk like us; otherwise her aunt will encourage her to only see rich children like the Warringtons who are not much fun at all.

'What do you think, Master Oswald? Miss Lucy, wouldn't it be nice if we brought a picnic one day? Lemonade and cake?'

Lucy clapped her hands in delight and looked at Oswald, who gazed at Ada for a moment before saying, 'I'll only come if I can play cricket and maybe ask that boy and girl you know. But not Henry, because I don't like him.'

CHAPTER SIX

The sunny weather held for the rest of August and Mr Thornbury decreed that they should all go on the picnic. He would take the afternoon off from the bank and declare it to be a holiday. 'We'll hire a wagonette to carry all we need. Is that acceptable, Ada?' he added, thinking she seemed rather crestfallen.

'I've asked my brother 'n' sister, sir. Master Oswald said he'd like to play cricket and wanted our Joshua and Edie to come, but not Master Henry.'

'Ah. Getting choosy over his companions, is he? Well, that's not a bad thing. Ask your brother and sister to be here for . . . what shall we say, twelve noon? There'll be plenty of room for everyone. Can someone bring them?'

'They know their way, sir,' Ada told him. 'It's not far.'

'Nevertheless, tell them to be careful; there are buildings being knocked down and some of the streets are not safe. I have to take a detour on the way to the bank.'

She nodded. 'I'll tell them sir, but there's no need to worry.' She had heard from various members of her extensive family that the younger boys and some of the more intrepid girls were having a great time climbing on the piles of rubble every night after the workmen had gone home, in spite of the notices that said KEEP OUT in large letters and a watchman who could never catch them.

'Good.' He rubbed his hands together. 'And we'll send *our* Bob up into the loft and see if we can find the old cricket bat, though I rather think we might need some new balls.'

On the chosen day, the sun was hot and there wasn't a cloud in the sky. Cook had made two large meat and potato pies, cooked and sliced a chicken and a small ham, hard-boiled a dozen eggs, and made a large apple tart and two fruit cakes.

'You'll never get through all of this,' she said, putting two bottles of lemonade in the picnic basket along with several glasses, plates, cutlery and table napkins.

'Bet you we will,' Ada said. 'And two more bottles if you've made enough. Our Josh can eat and drink all of that himself.'

'I'll put a loaf of bread in as well then, and they can fill up on that.' And just to be sure that there'd be enough food to go round she put a frying pan on the range and cooked two pounds of sausages.

At a quarter to twelve the front door bell rang and a grinning Joshua and Edie stood on the step. Joshua was carrying a bag with a variety of balls and Edie a brown paper parcel.

'Our mam said we had to bring some food,' Edie said, 'but we didn't have much in so I brought bread and jam. Is that all right, Ada?'

Ada ushered them in and took them to the kitchen. 'Yes, course it is, but we've got plenty for everybody,' she said, and vowed to make sure there'd be something for them to take home afterwards.

Mr Thornbury arrived five minutes later and on the stroke of midday, as they all clustered in the hall with blankets and picnic basket at their feet, the wagonette arrived. Lucy was excited at seeing Edie and Joshua again and they were all hopping about at the prospect of a ride in the wagonette.

'The bat!' Mr Thornbury gasped. 'I didn't ask Bob to look for the cricket bat! It's too late now to go up in the loft. Sorry, Oswald. Is there somewhere on the way we can buy one?'

Oswald looked angry and then as if he were going to cry, but Joshua spoke up. 'Our Stanley's bringing a bat. He wouldn't let me have a lend of it unless he came as well, so I said it would be all right.' He looked up at Mr and Mrs Thornbury. 'It will be, won't it? I said we'd see them at 'park.'

'Who else?' Ada frowned. 'Who else is coming?'

'Onny our Max,' Joshua said. 'It's his bat really. We just look after it for him.'

Ada relaxed. 'Our Max is all right, sir. He's a good lad. He and Stanley won't be a bother.'

'Well, that's all right then,' William Thornbury said heartily, whilst his wife looked decidedly pale at the idea of so many boys in tow. 'Come along. Let's be on our way.'

They drove up Beverley Road and all the children cheered when they overtook a horse tram. As they drove through the ornamental park gates, Joshua spotted the other two boys on the footpath and stood up to shout and wave at them. Edie pulled at his arm and hissed at him to sit down. 'Our mam said you had to behave,' she said, but she too waved as they passed them by and the two boys set off at a run to catch them up.

'Stop here,' Mrs Thornbury said. 'William! Tell the driver to stop here and we'll sit under that pine, where there's plenty of shade from the sun.'

The driver drew up as directed and the children piled out and immediately ran across the grass to claim the space beneath the huge tree. Joshua held out both arms as if to stop anyone else from coming there, and then Oswald copied him. Lucy giggled and held her arms out too and Edie did the same until Ada arrived with the blankets and the hamper. Mr Thornbury followed, carrying two wood and canvas chairs, and last of all came Mrs Thornbury, with the mackintoshes and umbrella she had insisted on bringing despite its being a perfect summer's day.

'This is me brother Stanley,' Joshua announced, as the other boys came across the grass, 'and that one is our cousin Max. It's his bat.'

Stanley was almost a copy of Joshua with his brown curly hair, dark eyes and cheeky grin, except that he was slightly taller and two years older. Max was taller than Stanley by half a head and looked nothing like his cousins, being fair-haired with blue eyes. He went over to Mr and Mrs Thornbury. 'I'm Max Glover, sir, Mrs Thornbury,' he told them. 'Thank you for letting me come with you today. Joshua said it would be all right. I hope that it is? I don't really mind lending my bat.'

For a moment they were both taken aback by his politeness, and then William cleared his throat. 'Of course, of course, you're very welcome, even though the numbers seem to be growing by the minute. Do you know my stepson Oswald and my niece Lucy?'

Max turned round. Oswald stared at him and was then astounded when Max came towards him and put out his hand and Oswald, mesmerized, held out his limp one.

Lucy gazed up at the blond giant who seemed to have stepped out of one of her story books and licked her lips as he bent down to speak to her. 'Hello, Miss Lucy,' he said softly. 'I saw you at Aunt Mary's wedding. It's nice to see you again.'

She unclasped her hands, which had been locked together, and still holding his gaze she held them both out in front of him. He smiled and took them in his. 'How do you do?' he murmured.

'Very well, thank you,' she whispered, and although she was only just four she decided there and then that when she was old enough she would marry Max Glover, for she loved him already.

On being questioned by William regarding his relationship to the other children, Max confirmed that he was a cousin. 'There are a lot of us,' he said. 'My mother Susan is 'eldest of three sisters and then there are four older brothers as well, and all of them are married with five or six children. I've onny got one sister, though, so there's just the two of us. Jenny's fourteen and I'm twelve.'

'And is your sister working?' Nora asked him. There was a reason behind her question; she was considering that if Ada ever left her employ then this polite boy's sister might be a possible replacement.

'She works for my father. He's a general grocer. We both work in 'shop at weekends and school holidays. Jenny helps behind

50

'counter and I'm 'errand lad. She's started full time now she's fourteen, but I've been given 'day off today.'

'How very industrious of your father,' William joked. 'To employ his children.'

'He says it's 'onny way to teach us how to mek a living. His father had 'shop before him and *his* father kept a milch cow and a pig in his back yard in order to feed his family.'

Joshua came over and stood in front of them. 'Are we going to play cricket or what?'

William got out of the picnic chair and stood up. 'Yes, come along. Let's get organized. Who wants to be captain? Shall we toss for it?'

'Max!' Stanley, Joshua and Edie all called out.

'Lads don't fall out if our Max is captain,' Edie explained. 'Cos he plays fair and doesn't cheat.'

'Max,' Lucy piped up, although not knowing what a captain did. 'Max!'

Oswald stayed silent. At his London school it had always been best not to have an opinion in case it was the wrong one, and besides, he was overawed by this boy who seemed to be in charge and yet wasn't a bully. He had hoped that it would have been just him and Joshua playing and Edie and Lucy running to fetch the ball back to them; he partly blamed his stepfather for forgetting to bring the bat for then he, Oswald, would have been in charge of it, but now, look, here was Max choosing two teams, tossing a coin and calling 'Heads'.

It wasn't fair, he fumed. He was teamed up with Stanley who he didn't know and Edie who was just a girl, and Joshua was with Max and granted they had no chance of winning because Lucy was on their team and wouldn't know how to play because she was too young as well as being a girl, but it still wasn't fair.

For Lucy it was the best day of her life. She had found her hero. All other troubles and anxieties faded that day; Max had chosen her to play on his team and told her she could throw the first ball which she did and Oswald had missed by a mile. She threw another one and he missed that too and it hit the wicket, a short tree branch stuck in the ground behind him.

51

'Out,' Uncle William called, and Oswald threw the bat on the ground and marched off in a huff to sit next to his mother.

Then it was Edie's turn to bat and she hit the ball each time, sending it flying across the grass with Joshua running after it whilst Edie ran up and down counting. Lucy didn't know what that was supposed to mean but Edie said it was a score and she'd scored six and so Lucy clapped her and said 'Well done' and her uncle laughed.

When Edie was eventually caught out, it was Stanley's turn to bat and Max took over the ball, to let Lucy have a rest, he said, and she was glad that he did as Stanley hit the ball very hard and they all had to duck and then everybody had to look for it under the bushes.

When they eventually broke up the game to eat their picnic, everyone, apart from Oswald, agreed that it was the best day they had ever had.

CHAPTER SEVEN

The arrival of the governess was a turning point for Lucy and for Oswald. Miss Goddard came to the interview with excellent references and enquired about the children's previous education before agreeing to take the position.

'Lucy is only four,' Nora Thornbury had explained to the plainly dressed young woman, 'and is able to read a little, nursery rhymes and suchlike. We haven't attempted to teach her but I understand that either her mother or father used to read to her; it's only a short time since her parents died and we didn't want to inflict lessons on her. Now, we believe it is time.'

'So she was able to read at three? That is quite unusual.'

'My son Oswald is able to read, of course,' Nora continued, 'but we wish to make him ready for next year when he will go away to school.'

Miss Goddard frowned slightly. 'Would you not prefer him to go to a local school until then? He'd be mixing with other children, which would better prepare him for boarding.'

'Oh no! Oswald is rather delicate,' Nora explained. 'And we want him to have a good grounding in the three R's so that he can keep up with the other boys.'

Miss Goddard agreed to teach them both, but each with a different curriculum. She asked Lucy to read nursery rhymes to her and discovered that she wasn't reading them but remembering, and when she saw that Lucy's lips were trembling and her eyes filling with tears she guessed that these were the very rhymes that her mother or father had taught her. So she put away those books and brought some of her own and wrote some of the more difficult words on a blackboard, explaining what they meant.

It was whilst she was doing this one morning that she noticed that Oswald was completely ignoring the blackboard and with his nose close to his exercise book was writing laboriously as she was speaking.

'Oswald,' she said, turning from the board, 'will you please read out this new word I have written and explain to Lucy what it says and means.'

Oswald squirmed in his seat and flushed. 'She has to learn for herself,' he muttered. 'I can't be expected to teach her.'

'Will you then please open a new page in your book,' she said, 'and write down the meaning.' She smiled encouragingly at the boy. 'I'll give you five minutes.'

Lucy gazed at the new word and then with the tip of her tongue between her teeth she copied it into her own exercise book and put up her hand to speak.

Miss Goddard put a finger to her lips and crossed her arms in front of her and Lucy did the same and waited. Miss Goddard waited too and when the five minutes were up went to stand by Oswald's side. The page in his book was blank. Miss Goddard put a hand on his shoulder, but said nothing.

'Lucy, will you kindly tell us what you think the word says and the meaning of it, please.'

'*Never-the-less*,' Lucy said eagerly. 'I know it because Uncle William says it.' She hesitated. 'I'm not sure what it means, though.'

Oswald's head snapped up. 'It means *anyway* or *anyhow*,' he said.

Miss Goddard clapped her hands. 'Well done, both of you,' she said. 'Very well done indeed.'

Lucy and Oswald looked at each other across the table. Oswald gave a nonchalant shrug whilst Lucy smiled from ear to ear at their success.

At the end of the afternoon, Miss Goddard sought out Mrs

Thornbury. 'I don't know if you or your husband realize that it's possible that Oswald is myopic and that the condition is holding up his education. I believe if you take him to your doctor for an examination and have him fitted with a pair of spectacles, his learning will come along in leaps and bounds.'

The Thornburys were astonished to hear this but did as Miss Goddard suggested. When Oswald came out of the oculist's surgery and stood outside the door, probably for the first time in his young life he had a smile on his face. At last, through the concave glass in his round tortoiseshell frames, he could clearly observe the world around him.

A year later, after he had gone off to his new school, Lucy rather missed him. He had become more friendly than he had once been and she missed having a companion. Miss Goddard sometimes took her out for a walk to look at buildings of interest, or new ones being built, or sometimes across town to the River Hull to watch the shipping coming in from the Humber; and when they came to the ancient High Street Lucy eagerly told her she had been here before, because it was near here that Mary now lived.

'I wish I could see Edie and Joshua again,' she told the governess. 'Last summer we all went to the park and played cricket and had a lovely time, but I suppose they're back at school now.'

Miss Goddard asked how old the children were; Lucy told her that Edie would be seven and Joshua nine. 'He won't want to play with me now,' she added rather sadly. 'He'll be too old to play with girls.'

'Perhaps we might ask if Edie could visit sometime,' Miss Goddard said. 'Maybe share a lesson with you?'

Lucy looked up at her with such joy that the governess determined to do something about it. She approached Mr Thornbury and made an unusual suggestion.

'Lucy would benefit greatly if she had a companion occasionally,' she began. 'Especially for lessons in, say, English conversation. I'm not suggesting that she should share lessons every day, but perhaps one or two days a week, if you agreed?'

William scratched at his short beard. He liked this enterprising young woman; as she had predicted, Oswald had made great strides in his education since her suggestion that he needed spectacles, but was there a catch in this latest proposal?

'Your fee . . . ?' he said hesitatingly. 'I am Lucy's legal guardian and administer her allowance only for her. I cannot under any circumstances—'

'Oh, no,' Miss Goddard interrupted. 'I wasn't suggesting that there would be extra to pay or that a fee should be charged for another child. It will not be every day in any case, and only if the parents and the school authorities allow it.' She paused. 'Lucy mentioned a little girl called Edie, a relation of your maid I understand?'

'Edie. Ah, yes.' He nodded. 'A happy, jolly child. Mmm. I suspect they live in rather straitened circumstances.'

'I gathered so, because of the area in which they live.' Miss Goddard waited.

'It's a very nice idea,' he murmured. 'And the other child would benefit too; enormously, I should think. Yes, why not,' he said with sudden conviction. 'I'll have a word with Ada; she's the child's sister. The family are all right. Good honest people.'

Dolly Morris came in person to discuss the matter early one evening when both Mr and Mrs Thornbury would be at home. She was rather suspicious of their motive in asking Edie to join Miss Lucy for lessons, even though the two girls had spent time in each other's company and become friends.

'We're not like you, sir, or you, madam.' She nodded to Mrs Thornbury, who had sat silently and apparently disapprovingly throughout the interview. 'And I wonder what advantage there'd be for my Edie?'

'Improvement in her reading and comprehension, I would suggest,' William said. 'Miss Goddard is a very enthusiastic and resourceful teacher and it was her idea. Lucy had told her about Edie and Joshua.'

'Joshua couldn't come,' his mother said firmly. 'He needs a strong male hand to keep him in check, but our Edie, she's a clever girl, very bright.' She sat with her lips clenched and looked from one to another. 'It could be 'making of her, but then what good would it do? She'd still be who she is, on 'bottom rung of 'ladder.'

Nora took a sharp intake of breath. 'Not so, Mrs Morris,' she broke in. 'We none of us know where life will take us or what's in store. Edie might well thank you one day for giving her this opportunity.'

'You think so, ma'am?' Dolly gazed at her and appeared to ponder on this for a moment. 'I like to think I do 'best I can for my bairns, but it's not much.' She stood up and William stood up too. 'Well, thank you, sir, and you, Mrs Thornbury. I'm very grateful. I'll speak to 'schoolmaster tomorrow and ask him if he'll release her.'

'And Edie?' William asked. 'Won't you ask her?'

'Won't need to,' she grinned. 'She hates school. She'll be glad to get away from it for a couple o' days a week.'

After she had gone, William turned to his wife. 'Why the sudden change of heart?' he asked. 'I thought you were against the idea.'

'I was at first,' she said after a moment's consideration. 'It was when she said, "What good would it do? She'd still be on the bottom rung of the ladder."'

'I see,' he said softly.

'Do you?' she murmured, and shook her head. 'I'm not sure if you do. I wanted to tell her that when you're on the bottom rung there's only one way to go, and that's up.'

'You're a kind woman,' he observed. 'But you always hide behind a stern demeanour.'

She gave a whimsical smile. 'It's my armour,' she said, and held out her hand, which he took. 'And you are the only one to have ever found a way through it.'

Lucy couldn't contain her excitement. Edie was to come every Wednesday and Friday for lessons with Miss Goddard. She turned up alone on the Baker Street doorstep at a quarter to nine prompt on that first morning in October with a clean scrubbed face, her thick hair contained in two long plaits and a starched white apron over her dress.

Her mother had said she was a clever girl but she stumbled over her spelling; not so with arithmetic. She was very sharp indeed with numbers, and on enquiring Miss Goddard discovered why. Edie did the household shopping for her mother most weekends; she could spot a bargain and knew the price of everything the grocer, greengrocer or butcher sold, and how much change she should receive.

The tactics that the teacher then employed were to spell out items that Edie would recognize, such as potato not *tatie*, bread not *bred*, and flour not *flower*, explaining the difference between the two last by drawing a simple daisy.

'Will I get 'cane, Miss, if I get 'em wrong?'

'If you get *them* wrong, Edie,' Miss Goddard smiled, 'you will not get the cane.'

'Will I, Miss Goddard?' Lucy asked, and then, 'What is the cane?'

How sheltered she has been, Miss Goddard thought, and how worldly Edie is. They'll be a good mix and will both learn through the other.

Edie seemed to know much more about the town than Miss Goddard did, perhaps because she lived in the heart of it. She told them one morning that fencing was being put round the old Guildhall so that it could be demolished and foundations dug for the new one.

'My da says it's a *bl— blinking* shame and a waste o' good money when there was nowt – *nothing* wrong with 'old one,' she said. 'And that 'money could have been put to better use.'

Miss Goddard put down her chalk and sat at her desk. 'Very interesting,' she said. 'Did your father suggest what else might be done with the money?'

'Well, my ma said she could do wi' some of it, and my da said there'd be no chance o' that, but he said they should use it for housing for folk like us, and give us an indoor tap and our own privy instead of having to share with half a dozen others. By.' She screwed up her face. 'Sometimes there's a right old stink.'

'Hasn't that already been discussed?' Miss Goddard asked her. 'I understood that many of the old houses were being pulled down and new housing built. I thought that was on the corporation's agenda.'

Edie's eyes narrowed. 'I haven't heard of any *adgender*,' she said. 'But I'll ask my da. He'll know if anybody does.'

'What does *adgende*r mean?' Lucy said. 'And why haven't you got an indoor tap, Edie? Do you have to go outside to wash your hands and face?'

'Yeh,' Edie said, 'we do, except on a Friday and then Ma heats up pans of water on 'fire and fills 'tin bath in front of it. I'm 'first in cos I'm 'onny girl; it used to be Ada but she gets washed here now, and then it's Charlie and then 'others scrap over who's next. *Adgender*,' she said thoughtfully. 'I suppose it's a sort of list, is it, Miss? A sort of shopping list like my ma gives me, and if there's not much money, then we have to decide what's 'most important?'

Miss Goddard felt a moment of pride and achievement. 'Quite right, Edie. It is a list or a plan. If we're ever going to do something special, it's best to make a plan and *prioritize,* just as you do when out shopping; that means making a decision about what is the most important item on the list.'

She could sense that both children were chewing this piece of information over. 'Shall I put the two words on the board?' she suggested. 'I'm so pleased that you thought to mention them. They are such important, useful words that I know you will come across them many times in your lives.'

'Yes, please, Miss,' Edie said. 'And what was that other word you said? Instead of *thing*? *Item*,' she said triumphantly. 'That's what it was.'

Miss Goddard turned to look at the girls when she had finished writing and saw that Lucy was counting the words and mouthing them. Then Lucy pressed her lips together and frowned. Suddenly her face cleared. 'There's another word, Miss Goddard,' she beamed. 'You said *decision*!'

CHAPTER EIGHT

Although she would never admit it, Nora Thornbury was pleased that she had agreed to come and live in Hull. When William had first made the suggestion of moving there to live in his brother's house for Lucy's sake she had rebutted the idea, but after apparently reconsidering had agreed.

In fact, the proposal had appealed immediately, but her nature, as she freely admitted to herself, was such that she never would, never could, appear to be compliant. Being controversial or opposing had always been her defence. She blamed her mother. At fifteen, they had locked horns when Nora realized that her mother wasn't who she claimed to be and therefore neither was she.

Her mother hadn't been a widow left with a small child struggling to survive on a low income as Nora had been led to believe, but a woman who was *kept*. Whether or not Uncle Jack, who had kept her, was Nora's father was debatable and probably unlikely, for she vaguely remembered other 'uncles' throughout her childhood, and on her mother's sudden death from a virulent attack of influenza he gave Nora her marching orders, which he surely wouldn't have done had she been his daughter. A week after the funeral she left the house with her few belongings: clothes, shoes and her mother's gold necklace which she had secreted about her person, swearing to Uncle Jack, when he demanded its return, that she hadn't seen it in years and she thought her mother had probably pawned it.

Nora had never previously had a job of work, her mother constantly encouraging her to look above her station in life and find a husband of substantial means. She didn't, however, tell her how she was to do that. To give Uncle Jack his due, he recommended her to a friend of his who ran a hostelry and needed someone to wash the glasses; she worked for him for a week whilst she gathered her thoughts as to what she would do next to keep body and soul together. She was just seventeen and a complete innocent although one with a sharp tongue and wit; these she had also inherited from her mother, the formidable Mrs Milburn.

She thought she could do better than working in a hostelry and decided to become a shop girl. The wages were poor but a uniform of black dress and jacket were provided in some of the better shops, those selling fabrics, gowns and millinery. She had gazed in the windows of John Lewis and Whiteley's and realized that she was not yet equipped for such splendour. She decided she would manage one way or another; she left the hostelry with some of the tips and takings she had found lying around and took any work she could find as long as she could earn enough to pay the rent on a room and have some small change left to buy food. She took her mother's necklace to the pawnbroker's and discovered that it wasn't gold after all and was worth nothing. Presumably Uncle Jack had wanted it back to give to the next occupant of her mother's former house.

She sat now by the window in a delightfully furnished first-floor sitting room with her sewing and a pot of coffee brought to her by the maid, and although the house didn't belong to her and William she felt as content as she thought she would ever be. Oswald was at school and had announced after a few weeks that he wouldn't come home every weekend as he'd first intended but would only come at the end of term like the other chaps. William had smiled at that and was pleased that he had settled so well.

It had been inevitable, she thought now as she turned a hem. I was so vulnerable, a young girl on my own with no visible

61

means of support. I must have been seen as a sitting target by those reprehensible men with their false promises.

Some of the work she had previously been offered when she was at rock bottom – domestic, chambermaid or barmaid – wasn't always what she had agreed to. Other duties and services were often expected and were difficult to get out of without the threat of a black eye; she took the black eye on a number of occasions and then left the establishment concerned, but a bruised face wasn't conducive to obtaining another job of anything but the kind she had just vacated.

But then she had met Jimmy, who seemed different from the rest. He offered her work looking after his office, doing some paperwork and taking in parcels. The delivery men sometimes tried to take advantage of her and she complained to Jimmy, who put his arms round her, kissed her cheek and said he'd sort them out. He told her that he'd take care of her, and she felt safe and loved.

She had heard many expletives, swear words and profanities in the life she had previously lived but she had never used them herself, except sometimes beneath her breath as now when she was reminiscing and she rained bitter and malevolent curses on Jimmy and his friend Ned. Ned, who had been charming and handsome and rotten to the core. Jimmy had said she must be nice to him, for he was the key to the future. And she thought he meant her future, hers and Jimmy's. But he didn't. He just told her to be nice to Ned and sent her to his rooms on a false errand whilst he went off to rob him of a shipment of goods being delivered at the London docks.

The front door banged, and, startled, Nora glanced at the clock on the mantelpiece. Twelve fifteen. William must have decided to come home for lunch. She heard the patter of feet on the stairs and Miss Goddard's voice as she greeted him in the hall. The door closed again and through the window she saw the young woman walking swiftly away, and then William came into the room.

'Hello, my dear,' he said. 'I thought I'd pop home for a spot of lunch. Is that all right?'

'Of course it's all right,' she said. 'Why ever not! It will be something cold, or you could have soup if you prefer?'

'I'll have whatever you're having,' he said. 'I can't stay long but I wanted to get out of the bank for a while. I might be late home tonight.'

'Why? Nothing wrong, is there?'

'I'm not sure.' He seemed anxious. 'Smithers isn't well and told me a week ago that he'd informed the head office that he's thinking of retiring.'

'Your manager? Oh, dear. What will it mean?'

'I don't know.' He rubbed at his beard. 'We're expecting some of the top men at the bank this afternoon. If Smithers does decide to retire they'll either bring someone in from elsewhere to replace him or . . .'

'Promote you?'

'Possibly.'

'Then a short lunch only,' she said, and galvanized into action pressed the bell to summon Ada. 'Change into another jacket,' she said. 'Your frock coat perhaps, and another cravat, and a top hat, not a bowler.'

'It's not about how I look,' he said, amused. 'It's whether I'm fit for the position.'

'Even so,' she fussed. 'It's also about your appearance.' She smiled. 'You're a very striking man. You make a good impression. Go.' She shooed him away. 'Get changed. I'll ask Ada to bring you a ham sandwich and a pot of coffee.'

When Ada answered the bell, she asked her to ask Cook to make Mr Thornbury a sandwich and some coffee as quickly as possible, and then asked if Bob was still there. When she said he was, she gave her sixpence from her purse.

'Give that to Bob and ask him to run and order a cab to come back here in half an hour prompt.'

'Yes, ma'am.' Ada hurried away to do her bidding.

Nora tried to compose herself.

On meeting William in the tea shop just off Brixton's major thoroughfare she had considered that at last something good had happened to her. She wasn't a customer, but a waitress;

she had her uniform, not a black dress and jacket as she had once hoped, but a black skirt and blouse, a white apron and a starched cap, and had become adept at carrying trays laden with teapots, milk jugs, cups, saucers, plates and tiered cake stands.

If she had ever given thought to the type of man who would attract her, which she rarely did, having become cynical about men in general, William wouldn't have been on the list; he was quiet and rather reserved, but he had smiled at her that day when he had given his order for tea and scones, and she, unusually, for she wasn't given to smiling much, had smiled back.

She put down her sewing and turned to look out of the window into the street. It was a quiet area with little traffic, not like the busy London streets that she had known with their constant rush of traffic, horse-drawn carriages, coal carts and delivery vans, and always a crush of people, a hum of noise, voices shouting, dogs barking and horses whinnying. Hull's Baker Street consisted of private respectable houses and some smaller buildings, dental surgeries and the like, and was adjacent to the elegant Albion Street and at the top end of Prospect Street, the main route into the centre of town. It had an air of gentility about it, and she liked that.

Her thoughts returned to the day she and William had met. He had left a generous gratuity beneath his plate and she surreptitiously pocketed it: she and the other two waitresses were supposed to share the gratuities, but they didn't; it was a rule made by the owner who had a tin where the money was kept, but none of them trusted her enough to share it out evenly.

On her way back to the room which was home to her and Oswald, she impulsively slipped into a toy shop and bought him a coloured ball. He was almost two years old and becoming too much of a handful for the thirteen-year-old neighbour who looked after him whilst she was at work. Soon she would have to make another decision about their future.

If only she'd met William sooner; if only she hadn't fabricated the story about her life, about Oswald and his so-called father, when she didn't know who his father was. Was it Jimmy or was it Ned? Whichever one it was, neither wanted to claim responsibility. They were at daggers drawn with each other and had called her all kinds of names that she didn't deserve. Both of them blamed her for her situation, even though she was given no choice.

She twisted the wedding ring on her finger. The ring that William had given her on their wedding day, not the gold-coloured tin one that had been her mother's which she had been wearing when she met him again. For he had come back to the tea shop and she'd told him the cock and bull tale of being a widow with a child. Just as her mother had once done.

'You look very dignified,' she told William when he came downstairs again. 'The sort of man to inspire confidence. Now.' She handed him a large napkin. 'Drink your coffee and eat your sandwich. I've ordered a cab to come in half an hour so you won't be late back at the bank.'

He laughed. 'Don't be too disappointed if they appoint someone else above me, will you?'

'I will! They must surely see a man of experience and gravitas.'

'I hope you are right, my dear, and thank you for your confidence in me.' He took a sip of coffee and remarked wryly, 'However did I manage without you?'

CHAPTER NINE

Edie was wearing an oversized woollen jumper and her cheeks were red with cold from the walk to Baker Street. She stood with her hands behind her back and her chin held high and looked at Miss Goddard and Lucy. 'I've been asked to inform you,' she said proudly, 'or I've been asked to – erm – *announce* . . .' She hesitated, as if remembering the order of the words, and Miss Goddard raised her eyebrows quizzically as she waited. 'That my aunt Mary has been delivered of her first bairn, a girl child,' Edie finished.

'Oh!' Lucy clasped her hands together. 'Can we go and see her?'

'I don't know your aunt,' Miss Goddard said to Edie, 'but I'm very pleased to hear of the baby's safe arrival.'

'Mary used to look after me,' Lucy explained. 'Before . . . before . . .' Her eyes took on a glazed look.

'Before Ada,' Edie finished for her.

'Yes,' Lucy said. 'Before Ada.' Her thoughts were hazy as to what had happened before Ada, but she knew she had loved Mary. 'I went to her wedding. What does delivered mean?'

Miss Goddard took a breath and asked them to sit down. She was a single woman and had a few qualms about explaining the business of giving birth to children when she had no real understanding of the matter herself.

'It's not like delivering a parcel,' Edie said. 'It means that it popped out of Aunt Mary cos it was ready. *She* was ready, I mean. The baby. She's going to be called Sally. She's got red hair, like Uncle Joe.'

Much too early to explain the facts of life to Lucy, Miss Goddard thought, and Edie probably knows them already, so she said, 'Well, perhaps as soon as Aunt Mary is able to receive visitors we can take a walk to see them.'

'Oh, she had her on Sunday, Miss Goddard,' Edie explained. 'My ma and Aunt Susan have been already and crossed Sally's hand with a silver sixpence to bring her luck. Ma said she had *tiny* little fingers that curled round 'sixpences as if she knew they were hers.'

'Oh, can we go? Can we go? Please,' Lucy said eagerly. 'I've never seen a new baby before.'

'Well,' Miss Goddard said. 'If Edie will ask if it is convenient, we could perhaps visit on Friday or one day next week.' And that will give me the opportunity to say something about bringing a child into the world, she thought. Perhaps not the actual birth process, but we could discuss nature and pollination and . . . She sighed. And other matters.

'What did you mean when you said Aunt Mary was ready?' Lucy persisted. 'Ready for what?'

Edie screwed up her face, then, enlightened, said, 'No. I said '*bairn* was ready. Ready to come out into 'world. She'd had nine months to get ready. That's how long it teks to make a baby.'

'What a long time,' Lucy said thoughtfully and was about to make another comment when Miss Goddard interrupted.

'Get your numbers books out, children, and we'll count out how many weeks there are in nine months.'

'Have you had a baby, Miss Goddard?' Lucy persisted.

'No, because I'm not married. Now we really must get on—'

'You don't have to be married, Miss,' Edie informed her. 'A girl in 'next entry to ours had a bairn and she wasn't married and nobody talked to her, but my ma does now that she's had it, because she said somebody had to help her. It was a boy,' she added. 'I've seen him; you can tell he's a boy cos he's got a little toggle.'

Lucy's eyes were like saucers and she opened her mouth to

speak. Miss Goddard took a breath. 'Enough,' she said sharply. 'Open your arithmetic books at page four and no more talking.'

On the Friday morning, Edie came back with the message that they could visit Aunt Mary that afternoon. Miss Goddard arranged with Mrs Thornbury that after lessons had finished she would take the children to see the new baby and then Edie would go home, and the governess would bring Lucy back.

'Please give Mrs Harrigan my good wishes,' Mrs Thornbury said. 'And I hope the child will thrive.' She reached for her purse and opening it took out a silver sixpence. 'Will you give this to Lucy? To cross the baby's palm.'

The governess was surprised at the gesture. 'Is it not a superstition?' she asked.

'It might well be,' Mrs Thornbury said. 'It's also an old tradition; but apart from that, a child coming into a poor household needs all the help it can get.'

Mrs Goddard nodded and wondered if perhaps Mrs Thornbury knew more about life than was apparent from her impassive and sometimes disapproving manner.

'I'll tek us on a shortcut, Miss,' Edie told the governess. 'There's a lot o' dust down Prospect Street and some of it's closed anyway cos of 'houses at 'other end being demolished.'

'I know the way too,' Lucy piped up. 'I went with Mary and with Ada and then you and I went for a walk there, Miss Goddard,' she reminded her.

'Yes, indeed we did.' Miss Goddard agreed that the two children should guide her, and she took a hand of each of them as they walked away from the house and headed in the direction of Whitefriargate, where she gave them a brief lesson on the history of the name before continuing down Silver Street and crossing over the busy road towards High Street.

'There!' Edie said triumphantly. 'Now you'll be able to do it on your own, next time, Miss.'

'Thank you, Edie.' Miss Goddard smiled. 'I will indeed.'

Joe Harrigan opened the front door to their knock, invited

them in and then excused himself and took off at speed out of the narrow court.

'Please excuse me if I don't get up, Miss,' Mary said. She was sitting on an old cracked leather chair with the mewling infant on her knee. 'Babby's hungry and she won't wait. Please tek a seat.'

'That's quite all right, Mrs Harrigan.' Miss Goddard drew up a chair and sat next to a wooden scrubbed table. 'I'm sorry if it's an inconvenient time.'

'It's not,' Mary said. 'I'm pleased that Miss Lucy wanted to come, and hasn't forgotten me.'

Lucy stood shyly in front of her and looked down at the baby now nestling in her mother's arms. 'What is she doing?'

Mary smiled. 'She's feeding. I'm giving her milk.'

Lucy looked puzzled and peered closer. 'But where do you keep it?'

'It's a special supply,' Edie interrupted. 'That's what my mam says, anyway.'

Mary loosened her shawl so that Lucy could see the baby latched on to her nipple. 'She's eating you!' Lucy squeaked. 'Does it hurt?'

'No. She hasn't any teeth yet,' Mary explained. 'When they grow it might nip a bit, but not too much.' She moved the child from her breast, patted her lightly on her back and transferred her to the other side.

'You've got two taps!' Lucy exclaimed.

Mary and Miss Goddard both laughed, Miss Goddard to conceal her embarrassment, for she had never seen a woman feeding a child before and she felt strangely moved.

When the baby had been fed, Mary discreetly covered herself again and sat the baby upright so that they could see her. Miss Goddard fumbled in her purse and took out two sixpences.

'Lucy,' she said, 'your aunt asked me to give you this so that you could give it to the new baby. It's to bring her good fortune.'

Lucy took the sixpence, a glow of delight on her face. 'Is it to cross her hand, like Edie said?'

69

'It is, and I would like to do the same, Mrs Harrigan, if I may?' The governess spoke softly. 'It's the first time I've seen such a new baby and I would consider it a great privilege.'

She felt quite choked as she spoke and saw what Mrs Thornbury had already guessed, that there was real poverty in this house. There was a low fire burning in the grate but the room was cold and bare but for a few simple pieces of furniture: a table, two chairs, and a narrow bed half hidden behind a curtain. She wondered if Mary had given birth in here, and if so where her husband had been at the time, for he surely wouldn't have been allowed to stay.

'That's very kind of you, Miss,' Mary said huskily. 'I'm sorry, I don't know your name, but it will bring Sally luck, I'm sure of it.'

'I'm Marion Goddard. Do you have plenty of food to keep up your strength?' the governess murmured as Lucy fumbled to open the baby's fingers.

'My family are very good to us and help us out,' Mary answered. 'Unfortunately Joe is still on short time at 'docks, but we manage.' She smiled weakly and Miss Goddard saw by her pale thin face that she was very tired and probably undernourished.

'There!' Lucy said, having successfully put the coin into the baby's hand. 'What do you think she'll spend it on?'

'I think she'll be guided by her mother, don't you?' Miss Goddard said, and then wished she hadn't as Lucy's face became sad. She added quickly, 'I'm going to give her a coin too. Will you show me how, please, Lucy, and then we must be going as Mrs Harrigan and baby Sally will need to rest.'

Lucy opened the fingers of the baby's other hand. 'Put it in her palm,' she said, 'and she'll close her fingers over it.'

'What a clever baby,' Miss Goddard remarked as she did as she was bid, 'and she's less than a week old.' She stood up. 'Thank you so much, Mrs Harrigan,' she said. 'I hope you both keep well. Oh, and Mrs Thornbury sends her good wishes to you and the hope that your child will thrive.'

'Did she? That's kind of her. Please give my regards to her

and Mr Thornbury. I hope they've settled in and that Ada is looking after them.'

Miss Goddard nodded and, murmuring her farewells, made a mental note to tell the Thornburys that their previous employee was living in dire conditions.

As she walked back to Baker Street with Lucy, having left Edie at the top of the entry where she lived, she reflected on her good fortune. Although she and her brother lived simply, their parents had left them sufficient capital to survive quite comfortably, providing they both kept working to pay the rent on their tidy little house.

Ada opened the door to them and Miss Goddard saw Mr Thornbury's top hat on the hallstand. She hesitated, not wanting to bother him or his wife yet wanting to tell them of Mrs Harrigan's circumstances.

'Mr Thornbury is home early, is he not?' she asked Ada in an undertone, speaking over Lucy who was telling the maid about Mary's baby. 'I was hoping to speak to them before I go home.'

'I think it will be all right to knock,' Ada answered. 'Master seems to be in a jolly mood.' She nodded significantly. 'I've tekken 'sherry decanter in.'

Whilst Lucy continued talking to Ada about Mary's baby, Miss Goddard knocked gently on the sitting room door. On hearing *Enter*, she pushed open the door and found Mr Thornbury, looking very distinguished, standing by the window with a sherry glass in his hand. His wife was sitting by the fireplace, also with a glass in her hand, and smiling.

'I'm so sorry to disturb you, sir, Mrs Thornbury, but I thought I'd report back on Mrs Harrigan and her child.'

'Come in, come in,' Mr Thornbury beckoned. He looked rather pleased with himself, she thought. 'Mrs Harrigan? Ah! Mary, of course.' He looked at his wife questioningly.

'She's been delivered of a girl,' Nora told him. 'Lucy wanted to see the new baby. Did you find them well?'

'I'm – not too sure,' Miss Goddard said haltingly. 'I'm not familiar with babies, but I thought that Mrs Harrigan looked very tired and pale and not in the best of health. It's very poor

71

accommodation I'm afraid. Just the one room, I think, and she told me that her husband was on short time at work which must mean that they haven't much money.'

'Oh, dear, I'm sorry to hear that,' William Thornbury said. 'She was a very robust young woman when she was here. Mmm.' He put his hand to his face. 'Well, thank you for telling us, Miss Goddard.' He looked again at his wife. 'We must see what we can do.'

He sat down in the chair opposite Nora after the governess had gone. 'It's the way of the world, isn't it, that one man's fortune goes up and at the same time someone else's goes down?'

'That's very true,' she said. 'But we were about to drink to your success and accomplishment. Very well done indeed, William. I'm delighted for you, but it's only what you deserve.'

'Good luck for me, but hard luck for Smithers becoming ill and deciding to retire,' he said modestly.

'You were obviously the right person for the position,' she protested.

He raised his glass and laughed. 'It was changing into my frock coat that was the deciding factor, my dear, so here's to you and your wisdom.'

They both drank the toast. 'Now,' he said. 'In view of our good fortune, what can we do for Mary?'

CHAPTER TEN

Lucy's hand was enclosed within her aunt's and they walked in silence towards the town; *city*, she reminded herself. Miss Goddard had said Hull was a city now and told her of the exciting plans the corporation had for the people who lived here.

They were on their way to Mary's. Aunt Nora had said she would like to visit her and enquire after the new baby and asked Lucy if she would like to come too. Of course Lucy had said yes, and that she knew the way. It hadn't been long since her last visit so she didn't expect that the baby would have changed much, but she still wanted to visit. Aunt Nora was carrying a basket that she said contained a few things for Mrs Harrigan.

She began to ease her hand from her aunt's but it was grasped more firmly as they crossed a road. 'Don't fidget, Lucy,' her aunt admonished her, tightening her hold as they reached the top of Whitefriargate and paused to look in some of the shop windows to make sure that Lucy stayed on the inside of the pavement and away from the traffic, which was quite heavy today as work-men were digging up some of the roads in preparation for the rails which would carry the electric trams that were replacing the horse-drawn ones.

It wasn't that Lucy objected to holding her aunt's hand; it was just that sometimes she was reminded of another hand that had held hers. A soft hand with long delicate fingers that had brushed lovingly across hers. She flexed the fingers on her

73

other hand and remembered that sometimes both hands were held at the same time, one in a bigger, firmer and stronger grasp that felt safe and comforting. She tried, time and again, to put a face to whoever was holding her hands, but the picture was always hazy; she saw dark hair and a slender body on one side and a taller, more solid one on the other. But the images made her feel sad, as if her feet were weighted down, and she put them away.

She guided them successfully to the entry, although her aunt asked more than once if she was sure this was the right way, and Lucy saw her wrinkle her nose as she did so.

'It is a bit of a stink,' Lucy said, paraphrasing Edie's comments about Hull's old housing. 'But that's because of the privies.'

Aunt Nora took out her handkerchief and covered her nose. 'Or lack of them,' she murmured. 'And Lucy, it's an odour, not a stink.'

'An odour,' Lucy mouthed. 'Yes.'

Unlike her last visit, they were not expected, and they could hear the baby crying as they approached the house. When Mary opened the door she looked flustered and ill.

'Oh, ma'am! Miss Lucy.' She pressed her lips together and then said, 'I'm afraid everything's upside down. Babby's rather fretful. But come in, please come in.'

'I'm so sorry, Mary,' Nora said. 'I hope it's not inconvenient.'

'No, ma'am. It's all right. I wasn't going anywhere. Won't you sit down?' She waited until Mrs Thornbury was seated and then picked up the baby from where she was lying in a drawer lined with a thin blanket.

'There she is.' She held the baby so that they could see her.

Mrs Thornbury nodded. She hadn't known any babies until she'd had Oswald, but she smiled at this one with her rosebud mouth and fuzz of red hair.

'She's lovely.' She turned to Lucy. 'You were quite right, Lucy. She's very pretty.'

'Would you like a cup of tea, ma'am?' Mary asked.

'No, thank you. I had a cup just before we left.' She reached down into her basket. 'But as I was drinking it, I thought that you'd be getting a lot of visitors to see the baby and you'd be sure to offer all of them a pot of your precious tea, so I've brought you some.' She took out a tin of tea and another one containing biscuits and put them on the table. 'It's astounding how much tea is consumed when visitors arrive, isn't it?'

She leaned forward. 'I was wondering also whether you could use some good quality sheets for which I have no further use? You'll remember them from your time with Dr and Mrs Thornbury. I brought our own with us, you see, and it's a pity to leave the others languishing in a cupboard. They'll make good cot sheets,' she added. 'I could make up a parcel and send it with Bob?'

Lucy saw Mary's eyes fill with tears and wondered why she would be tearful on being offered a gift; but Mary pressed her hand to her lips and murmured her thanks.

Before they left, Lucy heard her aunt whisper, 'Things are bound to get better, Mary. Keep positive. Think how lucky you are to have such a sweet child and, I hope, a good husband. I trust he'll find work soon.'

Mary nodded and wiped her eyes and wondered if she had misjudged her former employer. Kindness and understanding from Mrs Thornbury was unanticipated and it had touched her. She had previously thought her cold and unfeeling. She had been totally wrong. 'Folks are saying that things are looking up in the town. I hope they're right.'

When they got home Aunt Nora asked Lucy to find something to do until teatime as she had a headache and was going to lie down for an hour. 'Do you have a book to read, or lessons to learn before Monday? Or perhaps you'd like to draw or paint?'

'I wish Edie could come on a Saturday,' Lucy said plaintively. 'It's a long time until Wednesday.'

Nora nodded. 'I agree, it is. But doesn't she help her mother on a Saturday?'

'Yes. She goes shopping and then she helps in the house. Her mother says she's a very useful girl. Could I make some biscuits?' Lucy asked eagerly. 'Before Cook goes home?'

'If Cook agrees.' Nora put her hand to her head. 'But try not to get in her way and don't forget to wash your hands first,' she called after her as Lucy ran off towards the kitchen.

Nora eased off her shoes and then stretched out on the bed. She hadn't expected that the sight of Mary and her baby living in such dire conditions would affect her in the way it had. It had brought back painful memories, memories that she had successfully pushed to the very back of her mind since marrying William; William, so dependable, kind and caring. It was true that she had married him because she realized he could be her salvation and back then had thought she would never come to love him but would always and for ever be grateful to him; she hadn't thought she was capable of loving anyone but Oswald, the child who, when she was expecting him, she had been determined to give away, but then couldn't. She had been wrong on both counts.

She sat up and adjusted the pillows. She felt nauseous. The fish they ate at lunchtime must have been off; she could feel it churning inside her. She reached over to pour some water into a glass but pressed her hand to her mouth. She was going to be sick, and rolling off the bed felt beneath it for the chamber pot.

She retched and retched until her throat was sore and then staggered to the water closet on the landing. Thank heavens for Thomas Crapper, she thought as she pulled the chain and rinsed the pot, and thank heavens for Dr Thornbury who had spent the money and had the WC fitted.

She went back to lie down again, and recalled how sick she had been when she was expecting Oswald. She had been so young and terrified that she was going to die; it was an old man living in the next room who had heard her and knocked on her door to ask if she was all right, had looked at her and gone away, returning a few minutes later with a cup of hot water.

'Drink this,' he'd said. 'My wife always drank hot water when she was nauseous with her babies.'

She hadn't known, until he'd uttered those words, that she was pregnant. How kind he had been. She closed her eyes and breathed out; she had forgotten about him until now and couldn't even recall his name. There were some men who were kind and understanding after all.

Her eyes opened and she sat up with a start. Surely not? Not after so long! She ran her hands over her abdomen and her breasts. Her breasts had felt tender lately but she'd never considered, not for a moment . . . and, she thought, she hadn't marked her diary for months. There never seemed to be any need.

Can it be true? I think it must be. An innate sense told her it was. What will William say? Will he be pleased, or not? And Oswald, will he be jealous? Lucy will be delighted, of course. But I, what do I feel? Here I am expecting a child when Oswald will be nine next June. And, she thought, I'm living a different life. She had recently joined a women's charitable group; they had been pleased to accept her, a bank manager's wife, and with her London accent seemed to consider that she was a cut above what she knew she really was: a nobody.

Will a child fit into this new settled life? She put her head back against the pillow. She was happy. Yes, she thought. It will.

CHAPTER ELEVEN

It was decided to tell Oswald that his mother was expecting a child when he arrived home for the Christmas holidays. Then they would also tell Lucy that she was to have a cousin.

Oswald was embarrassed when he was told and didn't know what to say or how to respond. He went up to his room; William went up to see him later, knocked on his door and spoke confidentially to him.

'Look here, Oswald, I've been thinking, old fellow,' he said genially. 'I know it's been rather difficult for you over the last few years, with me coming into your life and sharing your mother. You'd only be two or three when your mother and I married, weren't you?'

'I don't know,' Oswald said, pushing his glasses up his nose. 'I don't remember.'

'Lucy doesn't recall much from when she was that age either.' William linked the two concepts to make the children equal. He sighed. 'She was three and a half when her parents died, and that's not so long ago.'

'Was she?' Oswald looked up. He frowned. 'But she's got the same name as you.'

'That's because she was my brother's daughter,' William reminded him. 'So this is what I'm proposing. When your mother has the baby it will have the name Thornbury, and I was wondering – how would you feel about changing your name from Milburn to Thornbury, so that we're all the same?' He paused. 'We can do it through adoption, so that legally you'd be my son, just as our new son or daughter will be, but if you don't want to do that, then you could simply change your name by deed poll.'

Oswald pondered and his eyes roamed from side to side of the room. 'Would I have to call you Father?'

'Only if you'd like to,' William said patiently. 'Though I would rather like it if you did. Or Pa, if you prefer; that's what my brother and I called our father. But only if you want to. But we'd have a proper grown-up relationship, wouldn't we, now that you're no longer an infant and don't have to rely on your mother any more?'

It was as if a light had been switched on and Oswald's face lit up. 'Especially as she'll be busy with the new baby,' he agreed, 'and it being sick and other smelly things.'

'*Exactly.*' William grinned. 'My thoughts precisely.'

'I expect Lucy will enjoy all that though, won't she? Being a girl.'

William laughed. 'They do seem to, don't they? We haven't told her about the baby yet, by the way. We wanted you to be the first to know and I wanted to sort out the business of the name. So, what shall we do? I mean, if you'd prefer to stay as Milburn then that's all right, but you know, if I introduced you to anyone, I'd rather like to say *Have you met my son Oswald?* What do you think? Would you like to sleep on it? You don't have to decide now.'

Oswald stood up and hesitated before speaking, biting on his thumbnail. Then he said, 'I – don't want to be left out of it, different from everybody else . . . not part of the family. So, if you don't mind, sir, I mean Pa, I'd like you to adopt me.'

William stood up too and put out his hand to shake Oswald's before holding out his arms to give him a hug. 'Splendid!' he said. 'Come on, let's go and tell your mother.'

'Can I tell Lucy?' Oswald asked eagerly. 'And tell her that we'll be sort of related cos we'll be part of the same family?'

'Yes indeed.' William smiled. 'She'll be delighted, I'm sure, just as we all are.'

79

'She will be, won't she?' Oswald drew himself up tall at the prospect. 'Splendid!'

'So does it mean I'll have two cousins when the baby comes?' Lucy asked eagerly when they explained about the baby and Oswald's change of name.

Nora and William glanced at each other. 'Yes,' they said simultaneously.

'That means I'm nearly catching up with Edie,' she said excitedly. 'She's got *hundreds* of cousins.'

'Not hundreds,' Oswald said pragmatically, and conscious of asserting his place within the family and enjoying the sense of belonging he went on: 'but she's got a lot more than us. Shall we try and add them up?' He went to the bureau to pick up his notebook and gave her a sheet from it. 'You write down how many you know and I'll write down how many I know, though I expect you'll know more than me cos you went to that wedding.'

But it turned out that Lucy could only remember Max and none of the names of any of the others so she wrote down Edie's brothers' and sister's names instead: Ada, Bob, Stanley, Joshua and Charlie.

'You've forgotten another cousin,' Nora reminded Lucy. 'You've forgotten Mary's new baby, Sally. She's a cousin of Edie and Joshua, isn't she?'

'Oh, yes,' Lucy said, and wrote down the name, and then she remembered Max's sister Jenny, whom she didn't know, but who was also a cousin of Edie's, and Oswald gloomily remarked that he didn't think they would ever catch up, whilst Nora and William glanced significantly at each other again, delighted that at last the two children were having a conversation together.

The baby was due in August and Lucy hoped that it would be born on her birthday, but it missed by two days and was born on the twelfth, when a girl with a mass of dark hair was delivered; Lucy now knew what delivered meant and much to her delight Uncle William told her that she too had had a lot of hair when she was born.

'People might think we're sisters,' she said excitedly, 'and not cousins.'

Oswald had peered down at his new half-sister and murmured, '*Mmm*. She's very small, isn't she? Look at her tiny fingers and toes and little fingernails. What do you think, Mother? Will she grow all right?'

Nora smiled. 'She will, Oswald, but we'll need to take care of her, won't we? All of us?'

He nodded solemnly, 'Oh yes, we will. I don't think I dare pick her up until she's bigger, but I'll listen out for her in case she cries.'

'Thank you, Oswald,' his mother said. 'I'm so pleased to think I can rely on you. What name shall we give her?'

'Oh, I don't know. I don't know many girls. Perhaps we should ask Lucy.'

Lucy suggested many pretty but unsuitable names and in the end it was left to William who suggested Eleanor; he smiled at his wife and said, 'Your name is a derivation of Eleanor, isn't it, so why not give our lovely daughter the same name as her beautiful mother?'

Lucy put her head on one side and wondered why it was that grown-ups cried when something nice was said about them, as Aunt Nora was doing now.

The new century was fast approaching and although there was anxiety over the second Boer War and the British military that was once again fighting against the Boers in the Transvaal, amidst great celebration the year 1900 was ushered in; the city of Hull was thriving and almost every area had electric trams to convey passengers cheaply into and out of town. There were still many horse-drawn carriages, omnibuses and delivery wagons, but now that wide new roads had been cut through old properties and many, although not all, slum properties had been demolished there were more motorized vehicles, less congestion and fewer accidents than previously.

Electric lights had been installed in the theatres, brass bands played in the parks and many of Hull's citizens developed a passion for cycling on the flat roads of the city. William, as a respected bank manager, had elected to join several charitable committees and Nora too had re-joined her women's group as soon as she felt confident about leaving Eleanor with a nursery maid.

There were others, however, such as Mary and Joe Harrigan, who were not faring as well. Nora surreptitiously suggested to Ada from time to time that she might take bread and tea and any leftover meat from a joint or a chicken to her aunt, but without indicating it had come from her. She was sure that Mary would feel she was being patronized even though she was in need. They still lived in the same room and Joe's work was never regular; Mary was also pregnant with another child and told her sister Dolly that she didn't know how they would cope.

'Honest to God, Dolly,' she wept one day. 'If I'd known how it would be, then I swear I'd have remained single all my life.'

'You'd not be without your Sally, though, would you?' Dolly commiserated. 'Such a sweet bairn.'

'Of course not.' She wiped her tears on her apron. 'But how am I going to feed another? We can't keep tekking handouts, it's not fair, and it's not right to have to rely on all of you. You've got your own bairns to feed.'

'But we'd not have you go short, our Mary,' her sister insisted. 'And once Joe gets back to full-time work you'll be able to manage.' She became thoughtful. 'Who do we know in a position to help you?'

'Nobody,' Mary said. 'And I wouldn't ask if I did. I onny want what we can work for.'

'Aye, that's right. Course you do,' Dolly said. 'It's what we all want. But there's one rule for us who have nowt and another for those who have everything.'

It was the beginning of July and William pondered over his Saturday paper as he drank his coffee. He'd claimed his brother's study off the hall as his own, and often thought of him as he sat in the deep leather armchair. This morning, though, he was troubled by the disturbing news he was reading.

During his various meetings he and his peers often discussed the topics of equality and the unfair distribution of wealth and success, and as a bank manager he was frequently asked for his opinion. There were also many hushed conversations and anxieties over what the new century might bring; conversations that the gentlemen didn't take home to their wives. The Boer War was still giving rise to great concern and although it was looking increasingly likely that Britain would win, the methods employed against the South African farmers and their families were considered unworthy.

Increasingly, though, William was noticing the dissent throughout Europe as new challengers – Germany, Italy and Russia – battled for possession of lands held by the old colonial and imperial powers of Britain, France, the Netherlands and Spain; and in Germany in particular there were rumblings of nationalism and more worryingly anti-Semitism.

There were many in Britain unaware of the mobilization of troops, the crumbling of old alliances and the creation of new as their concern was concentrated on South Africa, but increasingly over the last few years Britain had found itself becoming isolated, and it was this in particular that was disturbing William as he considered the implications. Then, too, there was great concern over the queen's health: it was rumoured that she was failing.

Nora had noticed on re-joining the women's group that there were some individuals among them who were more keen to promote the cause of women's suffrage than to support charitable concerns such as helping the local poor with their soup kitchens or speaking to councillors in charge of rehousing on behalf of those who had lost their homes as the city was bulldozed and modernized.

She knew she was one of the lucky ones who had escaped poverty and destitution and so could empathize with women who had been less fortunate, but as for voting rights, it wasn't something she had ever considered. What she had thought about before she met William was how to keep body and soul together; but now she was beginning to consider the importance of the subject as she heard of women who were kept in subjugation by their husbands and allowed no say in the control of their lives or those of their children, let alone the choice of who should be in power.

She sat in an easy chair across from William's and asked his opinion on whether women should be given the vote. 'The oddest thing ever is that we have a queen on the throne and yet her female subjects are not allowed a voice.'

'I have heard that her opinion is not in favour of the suffragettes,' he said, 'but like all monarchs she has no choice in the matter, as they do not have a vote.'

'It's an unfair world,' Nora complained, and William agreed with her that it probably was.

'But you made choices, didn't you?' he said. 'You worked to keep yourself and your child and,' he added, 'agreed to marry me when I might have turned out to be a terrible husband, for we hadn't known each other very long.'

She shook her head. 'Working wasn't a choice,' she said. 'It was a necessity. And I suppose when I met you I knew in my heart that you were a very honourable man.' She hesitated; was it now time to be completely honest? 'There are many men who are not, and I had known some of them.'

'Including the father of Oswald?' he asked softly.

She gazed at him through soulful eyes. 'Yes,' she whispered. 'Even so. William, I should tell you—'

'No.' He stopped her. 'There's no need.'

'But there is. Especially now that we have a daughter of our own.'

'We have a son too. Oswald is legally mine as much as he's yours.'

'But you don't understand,' she said weakly. 'I lied to you. I wanted to be seen as respectable so I told everyone I met that I was a widow with a son.'

'I know,' he murmured.

'I knew I wouldn't get work or a room if I said I was unmarried with a child, so— Wh-what do you mean?'

He got up from his chair, and going over to her he took her

hands and drew her to her feet. 'I have always known. Since the day I went to arrange our wedding and you gave me your birth certificate as you professed you couldn't find your marriage one.' He smiled teasingly. 'Milburn was your name *before* your so-called marriage. You forgot about that, didn't you?'

She screwed her eyes up tight and opened them as he put his arms round her. 'Yes,' she whispered. 'I did. So – so you've known all this time and you never said?'

He kissed the tip of her nose. 'What was there to say? I had asked you and I wasn't going to change my mind just because of a piece of paper. Besides . . .' He hesitated. 'I suppose in a way I thought I would be an absolute heel to back out when I guessed what you'd been through, bringing up a child on your own. I thought it showed great strength of character and determination on your part. Don't cry,' he begged as she began to sob.

'I just wish I had had the strength to say something before,' she wept. 'But I was afraid to.'

'I know,' he said, and smiled over the top of her head as he saw the door slowly open. Oswald, who was home for the spring holiday, stood there with a look of disgust on his face as he saw them locked in an embrace and quickly closed the door again.

CHAPTER TWELVE

Dolly Morris took it upon herself to approach the Thornburys regarding Mary's situation, although she knew that her proud sister would have raised objections had she known. But Dolly believed that if you knew someone who might be able to make a difference, then it didn't do any harm to ask; after all, they could only refuse, and on the other hand they might not.

Nora listened quietly to what Mrs Morris had to say and promised that she'd bring the matter up at her next women's meeting. She often felt contrite about her behaviour towards Mary when they'd first met, and now realized that the reason behind her false superior manner was the fear of her own inadequacies coming to light. Now that she knew that William had known the truth about her all along and that it hadn't made any difference to him, she felt that she could hold her head high, that there was no further need to pretend; she was as good as anyone. Or almost anyone. There were some women in her group who were decidedly superior and one of these was Mrs Warrington, mother of Henry and Elizabeth.

She had discussed Mary's situation with William and told him that she wanted to ask for opinions from the women's group. If there was no encouragement from that quarter, perhaps he might have some ideas of what could be done.

'Mary won't want any handouts from us, and of course she doesn't know about her sister's intervention, but isn't it wonderful how they help each other? It's such a close-knit family.'

He agreed that it was. 'People without much do tend to help those with even less. Ask the ladies by all means. There already are charitable organizations helping out the poor, but there are some people, like Mary, who wouldn't dream of asking for help even though they need it.'

She was very nervous of standing up and speaking to the assembled women. Her previous fear had been that she'd be considered unqualified to have a worthwhile opinion, but that was the old Nora; now she could speak out with knowledge and experience of what life could really be like.

When Mrs Warrington, the chairwoman and natural leader of the group, asked if there were any issues to be discussed, Nora stood up. She was trembling, but soon got into her stride as she told of a family who had been brought to her attention, who because of lack of work for the husband and unsuitable housing were finding it very difficult to manage. 'With one child and expecting another, there is not enough money for both rent and food.'

Before she could go on to ask for suggestions or opinions, Mrs Warrington interrupted. 'There are adequate soup kitchens in the town, and facilities are available when a child is sick. I don't think we can do anything further about an individual family. We are living in the twentieth century now, and there has been much improvement in all our lives. The Junction Street scheme to form a square for her majesty's statue has been started, and there are new reading rooms and lecture rooms which are open to women as well as men.' She took a breath and Nora interrupted her, as she had been interrupted.

'I wasn't speaking of facilities,' she said plainly. 'I know of those. I was speaking on the subject of poor housing and lack of work for some in our *affluent* society. It is strange, is it not, that the two subjects often go together?' She looked round the group of women, some of whom shuffled in embarrassment or found something interesting to look at in their laps; it was rare for anyone to disagree with Mrs Warrington, who had returned to her seat as if the subject were closed.

'And so, ladies, to conclude,' Nora continued: 'in order that we do not waste the committee's precious time, if any of you would care to approach me during our tea break with suggestions or recommendations on this contentious issue of the *have-nots*, I would be very pleased to discuss them.'

She was fuming, and felt that steam was coming out of her ears as she sat down. Mrs Warrington stood up again with a face like thunder.

'Mrs Thornbury,' she said icily, 'you are perhaps unaware or have forgotten that all suggestions and recommendations must come through the committee, who will then make a decision.' She glanced round the room and challenged any opposition. 'Any more business? No? Then I suggest we break for tea.'

So that's that, Nora thought as she sipped her tea. Her first impulse was to take her leave immediately, but then she considered that if she did that she wouldn't ever feel like returning, and on the whole she enjoyed the company of most of these dozen or so women. She was pleased, therefore, when a young woman sidled up to her and said she would like to speak to her outside when the meeting was over; and then another, older woman, Mrs Walker, also came to talk to her, discussing generalities until Mrs Warrington called the meeting to order. Before returning to her seat, Mrs Walker murmured, 'If I might have a word later, I have a suggestion about the family of whom you were speaking.'

Nora heaved a breath. She felt that she had won a battle, but kept her face straight so as not to show how delighted she was.

When Mrs Warrington finally declared the meeting closed, the young woman who was new to the group told Nora her name was Georgina Kemp and said hastily, 'Sorry to rush off, but I have young children at home. I just wanted to say that my husband works for the railway and he's told me that they're about to have an employment drive; seemingly they are short of suitable porters. If the man of whom you told us applies now, he may get to the front of the queue, so to speak, before a queue actually starts.'

She dashed off, waving away Nora's thanks, leaving her to speak to Mrs Walker. 'May we talk on our way out, Mrs Walker?'

Mrs Walker nodded and they left together, walking away from the building towards Albion Street.

'That woman considers herself so superior,' Mrs Walker said without preamble. 'She was a nurse, and is now a doctor's wife, so she must feel that she has gone up in the world. Not that there is anything wrong with being a nurse,' she added, 'not at all. An excellent band of women.'

'You mean Mrs Warrington?' Nora asked, hedging. 'I don't know her very well, but I must say I was rather surprised at her response. I thought that helping families in distress was the main purpose of the group.'

'And so it was to begin with,' Mrs Walker sighed. 'But now that Mrs Warrington has reorganized the committee the direction appears to have changed. However,' she went on briskly. 'This family of whom you spoke. My husband is on the housing committee and interviews those who are in need of more appropriate accommodation. Ask the woman in question to go along and ask for an appointment with Mr Walker; tell her to take her child with her and say that her husband is out looking for work and can't come himself. My husband will be sympathetic, especially if I discuss the situation with him first, which I will do this evening. What is the name of the family?'

'Harrigan,' Nora said. 'I can't thank you enough.'

'Not at all,' Mrs Walker said. 'We must do what we can; and but for the grace of God, it could be us! We mustn't forget that.'

'Indeed we mustn't,' Nora fervently agreed. 'How fortunate we are.'

She hurried home and asked Oswald and Lucy if they'd like to take a walk to High Street to see Mary. Oswald said he was too busy catching up with work he had to take back to school the following week but Lucy eagerly said she would and ran upstairs to change her shoes and get a coat.

'We'll see a change in Sally,' Nora told her as they set off, 'and Mary's expecting another baby this year. Imagine that. A new baby in a new century.'

'Are you going to have another baby, Aunt Nora?' Lucy asked.

'Erm, I hadn't planned to.' Nora smiled. The child was so direct; there was a time when it had irritated her, but now she found it refreshing and honest. 'But sometimes they come along unexpectedly.'

Lucy sighed and frowned. 'I can't work out how it happens.'

'There's no need to try,' Nora answered. 'It will all be revealed in due course. Not for a few years, but eventually.'

'Does Oswald know?'

Nora hesitated. Who would explain the intricacies to Oswald when the time was right? She hoped that William would. 'No, I don't think he does, but it's not a subject that girls should discuss with boys, *ever*.'

'Because it's got nothing to do with them?' Lucy asked, and Nora quickly took her hand to cross the road and avoid answering.

Mary was home and Sally, who was walking but not yet talking much, hid behind her mother's skirts until Lucy enticed her out by playing peek-a-boo.

'Joe's working today, I think, as he's not come back home,' Mary told Nora when she explained why she'd come. 'He goes to 'docks early every morning to try and get tekken on; but I'll tell him to go straight to 'station yard tomorrow morning.' She clasped her hands together. 'I can't thank you enough, Mrs Thornbury.'

When Nora then told her of the link with the housing committee Mary was ecstatic and started to weep. 'This room was supposed to be a bright start to our married life, but it's awful. I'm constantly worried about Sally: she's always got a cough and I'm sure it's because it's so damp; we've no inside tap and we share a privy. It's no way to bring up children; it's not what I'm used to. My family were allus poor, but it was never like this, *never*!'

'I'm so sorry, Mary. You might think that when I say I understand I really don't, but although I—' Nora hesitated. 'Well, when I was alone with Oswald, before I met Mr Thornbury, I often went without food in order to feed him. The little I earned just didn't go far enough, so I genuinely do understand.'

Mary wiped her eyes and gazed at her in astonishment. 'Really? How – how did you manage to work when you had a child?'

'I left Oswald with a child minder; she was thirteen, one of a family of six. It was a risk and I wasn't happy about it, but I had no other option.' Nora couldn't believe that she was confiding in such a manner, but she was dismayed that so little had altered in almost ten years. 'It isn't right,' she said. 'It's time for change.'

'Mary!' Lucy was screwing up her nose. 'Sally has made a big smell.'

A week later Ada opened the door to Mary. 'Can I have a quick word with Mrs Thornbury?' the older woman asked. 'You can tell her I won't keep her long.'

Ada raised her eyebrows and, grinning, she dipped her knee. 'Come in, ma'am,' she said, and Mary gave her a nudge and then waited in the hall.

'Hello, Mary.' Nora came down the stairs. 'Has something happened?'

Mary gave a huge smile. 'Yes,' she said. 'My Joe has been offered a job as a railway porter! Regular hours and a uniform provided. He starts tomorrow – and . . .' She took a deep breath. 'I've been told that I can have a look at a place off Mason Street. Man I saw said that it's on 'list to be pulled down eventually but it's in better condition than 'one we're in now; it's on 'ground floor with an inside tap and our own privy and a cooking range, and if we tek it we'll be next in line for a new house when they're available.'

'Mason Street? That's not far from here, is it?'

'That's right, ma'am.' Mary beamed. 'Keep going up Albion Street and it's right at 'top, near to 'fire station. It's where our Dolly's moved to and hers is very cosy, though she's due to be rehoused as well.'

'So you'll take it?'

'I will,' she said. 'It'll be so nice to be near Dolly and not far from Charles Street where my sister Susan's husband has opened another shop.' She sighed, and then smiled. 'It'll be so nice to be close to everybody again.'

CHAPTER THIRTEEN

In January 1901 Queen Victoria died and her son Edward became king. Lucy cried and cried over Queen Victoria. She said tearfully that she'd thought of her as a kind of grandmother, one that she never saw except in the newspapers. She had never known her own; she had asked Uncle William about them, but he said he hadn't known her mother's parents and his own had both died when Lucy was a baby.

'My father was a surgeon,' he told her one Sunday as they were relaxing after luncheon. 'A medical man, which was probably why your papa became a doctor.'

'I might be a doctor,' Lucy said; she was undressing and re-dressing a doll. 'Or maybe a nurse; or work in a flower shop. Or else,' she went on eagerly, 'I might be a baby minder and look after other people's babies until I'm old enough to have some myself. *Then*, I'm going to have six girls and Edie's going to have six boys and they'll get married to each other when they're grown up. I thought I might marry Josh, but he said I can't because he and Stanley are going to be soldiers and fight in South Africa as soon as they're old enough so I expect they'll be too busy. I'll probably marry Max, because he'll stay at home to mind his father's shop and won't go away like Josh or Stanley.'

'It's manners to wait until you're asked,' Nora remarked mildly. 'That's the usual way of things.' She was sitting contentedly in an easy chair with a sleeping Eleanor on her lap.

'Edie said that Josh or Stanley wouldn't be able to marry me anyway, because they won't have enough money to keep me, but Max will.' She frowned. 'I don't know why Edie said that, because I don't spend much money, do I, Uncle William? I don't buy groceries the way Edie does for her mother on a Saturday.'

William smiled. 'No, my dear, you don't. But I shouldn't worry about it just yet; there are a lot of years between now and then. All of you have got a lot of growing up to do; you've all got a life to lead before you need to think about marriage and babies.'

He cast a glance at Nora. The subject of Lucy's marriage had only vaguely entered his consciousness, for she was still only seven, but he supposed that her parents would have eventually steered her in the direction of suitable marriage prospects, and certainly not the young friends whose company she enjoyed now. He sighed. Perhaps it had been inappropriate for him to encourage the friendship of these playmates, but they were such delightful children, full of life and spark, bright and intelligent. It was no crime to be born on the wrong side of the class divide.

He wondered whether Lucy should go away to school to mix with children of her own set, and said, 'When does Edie finish school? National school, I mean?'

Lucy gazed at him blankly, but Nora shook her head. 'She's only ten. She can stay on two more years I believe, and then she will leave. Are we having the same thoughts?'

'I rather think we might be.' He shifted in his chair. 'Oswald is settled at boarding school. Enjoying the companionship of his fellows, wouldn't you say?'

'It's different for boys,' Nora pointed out. 'They need to be taught independence,' and then reflected that she herself had learned it at an early age. It was all dependent on where and to whom you were born in the rank and class of the social scale.

'True,' William commented. 'Boys have to be taught to stand on their own feet, to defend themselves, get a few knocks, that sort of thing; that's what Joseph and I had to learn.'

'Oswald knew how to stand up before he went away, Uncle

William,' Lucy murmured as she fiddled with the tiny buttons on her doll's dress. 'He was eight, remember?'

Nora hid a smile. 'Piano lessons could begin, I think,' she said, 'and in a few years' time, lessons in deportment and the art of conversation. I think that's what is expected.'

'Yes, and French too,' William went on, continuing the conversation over Lucy's head. 'We should plan ahead. I suppose it's never too soon. Can Miss Goddard cope, do you think?'

Nora looked down at her sleeping daughter. Would Eleanor have the same advantages as Lucy, she wondered. Oswald was certainly having a better start in life than she had ever envisaged, and there was no reason at all why a daughter shouldn't be offered the same chances as a son. The world was changing: young women were thinking for themselves and some becoming quite vociferous in their demands. Mrs Pankhurst and her daughters were forever lobbying Parliament on behalf of the movement for women's suffrage.

'I'll ask her,' she answered. 'She'll probably know someone if she can't.'

Miss Goddard spoke reasonable French, but in answer to Nora's query said that her brother was fluent in the language and would be a more suitable tutor, and so it was arranged that after Easter he would come every Monday morning for an hour to begin teaching Lucy basic French. She also knew of an excellent piano teacher, so Nora arranged for lessons to be started.

'Good,' William said to his wife. 'Well done, my dear. That's real progress.'

The Boer War was declared over in the May of the following year. Stanley Morris was very disappointed to have missed it but joined the military as a boy soldier anyway. It was what he had always wanted, as Josh did too.

In the summer of 1903 Edie left school and went to work for her uncle in his grocery shop for three days a week. He was trying her out, she told Lucy, so she still came for lessons in Baker Street on the other two days. She was so quick and useful, however, that within a month her uncle offered her full-time work serving in the shop with her cousin Jenny, whilst her brother Josh delivered grocery boxes to the customers and waited impatiently to grow up and join his brother as a soldier. Max was in charge of the ordering of supplies from the whole-salers, leaving his father to sit back and take it easy, except that he didn't, but considered opening yet another shop in another part of town as he had such a willing band of assistants among all his nephews and nieces.

'I'm really sorry, Lucy,' Edie said, 'but I have to work. We all have. Mam and Da can't afford to keep us all, not now that we're nearly all grown up, and we're lucky to have an uncle who can employ us.'

Lucy tried hard not to cry but tears were not far away when she said, 'I won't have any friends to talk to now.' She would miss Edie so much, not only as a friend and companion but as a fount of all knowledge, even more so than Miss Goddard, for Lucy now had a smattering of understanding about the intricacies of how babies came to be inside their mother's bodies and how they got there, which she thought disgusting, and also about the horror of what was to come with her own body when she was old enough, and this she had promised, on pain of death, never to reveal to any other girl under the age of ten. She had promised this with a finger-slash across her throat and a spit.

'I'll come and see you every Sunday,' Edie said. 'Honest to God I will. We'll be friends for ever,' and she too made the same vow.

As Lucy's tenth birthday was almost here, her aunt asked her if she'd like to go out for tea somewhere. Lucy shook her head. 'No thank you, Aunt Nora,' she said sadly. 'Not unless I could have it on the Sunday, and invite Edie to come. Then it would be a real party, and Eleanor could share it too.' Her little cousin was turning four and was a proper chatterbox who adored Lucy.

'What a lovely idea. We'll all come, Uncle William and Oswald too. Would you like to write an invitation to Edie?'

'Yes, please,' she said, cheering up at the prospect. 'I'll go and do it straight away.'

'Just a moment, Lucy. Uncle William and I were discussing . . .' Nora began, 'well, we were wondering – would you like to go to school? We've been trying to find a suitable day school in Hull but haven't succeeded yet.' There were many national board schools in the city and good private ones for boys, but private establishments for girls appeared to teach social behaviour and little else.

'However,' her aunt went on, 'I have had a recommendation for one in York where you could be a weekly boarder.'

It was Mrs Walker who had recommended it. Her own daughters had been pupils there and one had gone on to teacher training college while the younger girl was studying science in her final year with a view to attending university. Mrs Walker was most impressed by their progress. 'I always knew that women could do most things that men can if they put their minds to it.'

'Providing they have a brain,' Nora had said decisively. 'I know that I couldn't do it.'

'Nor I, if I'm honest,' Mrs Walker admitted, 'but it's all about being given the chance.'

'So what do you think, Lucy?' Nora asked now. 'I realize how much you miss Edie, but you would make new friends at school.'

'And could I come home every weekend as Oswald used to?'

'Of course, and there'll be lots of holidays. We could ask Uncle William to take us to see it if you'd like, before you decide.'

And so they did, and although there were no children there in the summer holidays Lucy immediately liked the atmosphere of the red brick building and the grounds, which were close by a section of the city wall. It wasn't long before the start of the autumn term, but the headmistress agreed to take her even at such short notice.

'You'll be all right here, Lucy,' said Oswald, who had come with them for the tour of inspection. 'They've got a good library and a common room as well as a games room, and only forty pupils so you won't be swamped. And,' he added, as at thirteen he was very well informed about most things, 'I expect you'll be allowed to walk on the city walls and look at the historic buildings and the Minster and everything.'

Lucy began to smile. It would be like an adventure. She had been very nervous at the thought of leaving home, and as they'd journeyed on the train to York had had a strange sensation of having once before set off on a journey that had changed her life, but the memory was somewhere in the distant past and she couldn't quite bring it to mind.

She clutched William's hand and nodded. 'Yes,' she said. 'I'd like to come, but if I don't like it I can come home, can't I?'

'Of course you can, my dear, but my worry is that we'll all miss you so much that *we'll* want to bring *you* home.'

CHAPTER FOURTEEN

1911

Lucy had made some good friends in York and renewed her acquaintance with Elizabeth Warrington, who had left school a year earlier than Lucy for finishing school in France. Lucy had been pleased to see her depart as she thought her very snooty and arrogant, tending to brush off anyone she considered unworthy of belonging to her set.

Jane Woodall and Primrose Chambers, both country girls, and Celia Marriot from Harrogate had become Lucy's special friends, and on their last day at school they had all promised to keep in touch, each in her heart wondering if she would ever see the others again. Their lives had been about to change and each was taking a separate path. Jane and Primrose had been returning to their parents' respective country estates whilst Celia was going on to finishing school in the Swiss Alps. 'Not,' she had emphasized, 'anywhere near Elizabeth Warrington. I shall be in the mountains above Interlaken, and if you happen to be holidaying in the district do come and see me. My parents know someone whose daughter went there and she recommended it highly.'

Jane and Primrose had said they might, but Lucy had shaken her head. She had other ideas that she hadn't shared with them, but she had mentioned them to Oswald. She knew she would get a straight answer and opinion from him.

'So what are you going to do, Lucy?' Celia had asked her. 'Wait for someone rich and handsome to ask for your hand?'

'You can't possibly be serious?' Primrose had laughed. 'We all know that Lucy is a suffragette and not looking for a husband!'

'I am *not* a suffragette,' Lucy had defended herself. 'I believe that women should have the right to vote, but I am not opposed to men in general and if someone rich and handsome and with half a brain comes along then I might consider him.'

'I'd have your handsome cousin,' Jane had sighed. 'Those *dreamy* grey eyes behind his glasses!'

'Oh, me too!' Primrose had agreed. 'Like a shot.' She too had sighed. 'That strong square chin . . .'

Lucy had bristled. How dare they be so personal? She and the other girls had been in York on a half-day shopping trip the previous year before leaving for the summer holidays, and quite by chance they had met Oswald and two friends who had come into the city from Pocklington. It had been Oswald's final term at school and he was waiting for his university application results to come through. She had introduced him to her friends and he had introduced his and they'd all gone off to have tea together. Oswald hadn't spoken much; he was still inclined to be quiet with people he didn't know, although his friends had chatted volubly, showing off in front of the young ladies and trying too hard to make a good impression.

'His eyes are grey-blue,' she had reluctantly agreed. 'And I suppose he might be considered handsome, but it's difficult for me to judge as I've known him most of my life; in fact he's more like a brother than a cousin. He's not rich but he is extremely clever and expected to do well at Cambridge, and that's much more important,' she had added, in an offhand kind of way.

Oswald had been determined on studying science and physics and to his amazement had obtained a place at the prestigious university; his school tutors had been convinced he would embark on a brilliant career once he obtained his degree.

'They didn't tell me what kind of brilliant career it would be,' he'd told Lucy when he heard he had been accepted. 'What will I be fit for?'

'Anything and everything,' she said enthusiastically. 'You'll have people scrabbling at your feet to offer you the world!'

He'd laughed. 'I don't think so. And what about you, Lucy? What will you do when you've finished at York? I suppose you won't need to do anything, but of course you'll want to. You'll take up a charitable cause or something, won't you?'

She had hesitated; she was only just sixteen and so far hadn't shared her thoughts with anyone as she wasn't sure that she could achieve what she dreamed of. But Oswald would listen seriously. He wasn't the negative young boy he had once been, and she had become convinced, once she was old enough to consider the matter, that the change in him had happened when he had adopted the name of Thornbury and become a completely integrated part of the family.

'Not charitable exactly,' she'd answered. 'Although I'm in favour of supporting those who can't support themselves, whatever the reason. But I'd like to be a woman with a purpose.'

He'd cast a questioning glance at her but didn't speak, which was typical of him, she'd thought. If there was a pause in a conversation he would wait for the person who had started the subject to fill the gap before commenting.

She'd heaved a breath. 'I'd rather you didn't mention it to Uncle William or your mother, not until I've thought it through.'

'So are you sure you want to discuss it? This purpose that you haven't thought through? You don't have to say anything now,' he said. 'You can tell me when you're ready, if you want to,' he added.

The house was quiet. They had both been in the sitting room, Oswald stretched out on the floor reading a newspaper and Lucy on the sofa mending one of her stockings. Uncle William was at the bank and Aunt Nora was out with Eleanor. Lucy was almost ready to go back to school the following week and Oswald had finished sorting out the books that he would need to take with him to university and was wondering how to fill the rest of his time before then.

It was, Lucy had thought, as good a time as any. 'You won't laugh, will you?'

'Why would I laugh?'

'Well,' she said hesitatingly, biting her bottom lip. 'It's a big ambition, although I feel that I can apply myself.'

He had sat up and hooked his arms around his knees. He was very tall now and his long hair flopped over his forehead, and he was trying to grow a moustache. 'I won't laugh.'

'I want to study medicine. I want to be a doctor.'

He leaned forward. 'Lucy,' he'd said on a breath. 'How *wonderful*! How absolutely inspiring. Such an aspiration.'

'But can I do it?' she said, encouraged by his enthusiasm. 'I'm doing well at school, but can I hope to achieve such an ambition?'

He jumped to his feet and sat beside her on the sofa. 'If you work hard of course you can. You'll probably have to matriculate at university first before being accepted at medical school but you won't be the first female to apply, if that's what's worrying you. This is what you should do. Speak to the school. Make an appointment to speak to the head.'

'I don't need to do that,' she said breathlessly. 'It's a very progressive modern school. I can just knock on her door.'

'Then you must do that as soon as you start term. Tell her that's what you want and ask her to suggest what you should do next.'

Lucy licked her lips. 'I'm studying maths, art and sciences already. And human biology,' she added, 'but I didn't tell Uncle William in case he didn't think it a suitable subject.'

He laughed. 'He's no fuddy-duddy, you know.'

Her cheeks burned pink. 'I do know really; it's just that I feel embarrassed that he might be – well, embarrassed.'

'He won't be,' he had said quietly. 'I feel that I know him very well now and I can say unequivocally that he's the most liberal and understanding man that I've ever met. Tell them as you've told me.'

She had done as he suggested and he had been right. Her uncle and aunt had been delighted, as were her teachers, who warned her however of the rigid and exacting course work that was entailed, some of which she would have to study elsewhere in order to matriculate. She had completed her final year in York; then, inspired in some part by the death of Florence Nightingale at the age of ninety, she had taken a first aid and nursing course, volunteered at a local hospital as an orderly, and been accepted at Cheltenham Ladies' College for one further year of study in mathematics, science, classics and French. She was now awaiting her final exam results and to find out if her application for an interview at the London School of Medicine for Women had been successful.

At home one morning she kicked her heels, unable to unwind after all the work she had been studying. Oswald, who had celebrated his twenty-first birthday last month, had been given a job as runner at William's bank as he wanted to earn some money during the summer holidays, so he wasn't at home, and Aunt Nora had taken Eleanor out to buy some new clothes as she was growing so rapidly. Lucy decided to visit Edie, who was still working in her uncle's grocery shop.

She was bored with wearing school clothes of navy skirts and white shirts and pushed these to the back of her wardrobe, bringing out instead a slim fitted cream dress with the skirt cut on a flared bias that kicked out just above her ankles. Next she chose a large blue hat trimmed with a flower and a froth of cream lace. She tried it on this way and that and then took her hairbrush, swept up and pinned her thick hair away from her face and angled the hat firmly over one ear.

Finally she slipped on a three-quarter loose coat and cream shoes, smiled at her reflection in the mirror and went downstairs. Ada was crossing the hall and looked up.

'You look nice, Miss Lucy,' she said. 'Where 'you off to?'

'To see your sister.'

'Our Edie? Oh, say hello to her from me,' Ada said, 'and tell her I'll be popping in to see her and Mam on my next day off.'

'I'll tell her,' Lucy said, and thought how different this household was from those of some of her friends. To be friendly with the domestic staff – although Ada was now the housekeeper, with a live-in scullery maid and a daily maid beneath her – and for Ada's sister to be Lucy's best friend.

She and Edie hadn't seen much of each other whilst Lucy had been away at boarding school and college, although she always visited when she came home. Edie worked full time at the shop, which stayed open until late, and although they sometimes went out together for coffee and a chat after closing time, Edie was often so tired she had to go straight home to bed. 'My uncle is such a slave-driver,' she'd grumble. 'He always reminds me that he was the first to give me a job.'

She was behind the counter when Lucy called and was serving a woman with a pound of butter that she scooped out of a barrel. She looked rather fed up, Lucy thought, and said so when the customer had gone.

'I am,' Edie agreed. 'I'd like to leave and do something else, but my ma seems to think I'd be letting my uncle down.'

'Doesn't his daughter still work here? Or Max?' Lucy asked.

'Jenny does.' She lowered her voice and tossed her head to indicate the back room. 'She's just gone home for her dinner, but Max seems to think he's above serving in the shop and reckons he's too busy doing the ordering and accounts to serve. I often catch him with his feet up on the desk reading a newspaper.'

'So can you come out for half an hour?' Lucy began, before Max himself came out of the back room and just as they had when she was a child his good looks and charm made her heart skip a beat.

'Lucy!' He had long since stopped calling her Miss Lucy. 'How lovely to see you. You look nice. Are you home for the holidays?' Although he was wearing a brown cotton grocer's coat she noticed that beneath it he wore a crisp white shirt and a blue necktie with dark blue trousers.

'Home for good until . . . well, it depends on my exam results where I'll go next.'

He smiled. 'Good. We shall see more of you then?'

'Lucy just said it depends on her exam results,' Edie said sharply. 'She's got a brain, you know.'

104

He nodded, virtually ignoring Edie. 'I know,' he said, 'and I'm sure she'll put it to good use.' He raised an eyebrow. 'As long as you don't join those awful suffragettes who are always on 'rampage.'

Lucy bridled. 'Well I just might,' she said. 'Someone has to speak up for women.'

He laughed, rather too heartily she thought. 'Believe me, all the women in our family know how to speak up for themselves. They don't need a band of militants to speak for them.'

'It's not only about the vote,' she told him. 'And it's the suffragists who are prominent in Hull, not the suffragettes, and they are not militant. They speak on behalf of all women who don't have the same opportunities as men do, or the same wages for doing the same work.'

'That they don't,' Edie said cynically.

'My word,' Max parried, 'I'd never have put you down as a bluestocking, Lucy. So that's what boarding school does to such a sweet young lady!'

'That expression went out in the last century, Max,' she remarked, but didn't say more as his sister Jenny came in just then and greeted her. She was furious with him none the less, and thought his attitude deplorable.

'Right, I'm off for my dinner.' Edie took off her long white apron and was round the other side of the counter before either of her cousins could object. 'Back in half an hour.'

'Goodbye.' Lucy turned at the door and she could tell by Max's regretful expression that he knew he had gone too far.

'Come on.' Edie took Lucy's arm and steered her towards Market Place. 'I know a place where we can get a sandwich and a pot of coffee and it won't cost much. It belongs to a friend of one of my cousins.'

Lucy laughed. 'Having a big family must be a great advantage.'

'Not always,' Edie said. 'I'm fed up with working for Uncle Sam, I can tell you. He hasn't given me a raise in wages in two years and I'm doing more hours than I used to.'

She pushed open a door, setting off a tinkling bell in a café that had gingham tablecloths on the half a dozen or so tables, some occupied, and a counter with delicious-looking cakes covered with muslin.

'Hello, Edie.' A bright-faced middle-aged woman greeted them. 'Come to eat?'

'Please, Annie. What are you going to have, Lucy? Treat's on me.'

'Oh, just coffee please. I've had something already.'

Edie ordered a ham sandwich for herself and a pot of coffee for two, calling to Annie to put plenty of mustard on the ham. Then she put her elbows on the table and faced Lucy. 'Yes, Max was right. You do look nice. Very elegant. So what's happening? After your exam results, I mean. What are you planning?'

She was always direct, Lucy thought, pressing her lips together. 'I haven't spread the news, but I've applied for a place at the London School of Medicine for Women.' She looked at Edie, whose jaw had dropped. 'It's at the Royal Free Hospital in Hampstead, which is just outside London. I've been studying really hard because they don't have many places.' She lowered her voice. 'Have you heard of Dr Mary Murdoch?'

Edie shook her head, listening avidly.

'She became house surgeon at the Hull Victoria Hospital for Sick Children when she graduated,' Lucy continued, 'and only last year she was appointed as Hull's *first* female general practitioner! She's *inspirational*, and she's also a leading light in the women's suffrage movement in Hull.'

Edie swallowed. 'Golly,' she croaked. 'Lucy! You're going to be a doctor? I can't believe it! How – oh, I'm lost for words. I don't know what to say, except how exciting and wonderful and amazing and oh, I'm *so* proud of you.' Her eyes filled with tears and she snuffled. 'So very proud.'

'I haven't got in yet,' Lucy pointed out, though she was very touched by Edie's support. 'It will depend on the results.'

'Pooh, you'll get in easy,' Edie said airily. 'Hey, that's one in the eye for our Max, isn't it?'

'What was wrong with him?' Lucy asked. 'I never thought that Max would be so disparaging.'

'You took a shine to him when you were little, didn't you?' Edie smiled. 'Our Josh always said so. But I'm afraid he's got a bit above himself lately. He was walking out with someone but then she joined the Women's Union or suffragettes or something and he took the huff. That's why he said what he did.'

'That will be the suffrage group I meant,' Lucy said thoughtfully, and then asked, 'How are Josh and Stanley and Bob and Charlie?'

'Josh and Stanley are still soldiering. They're both in 'regular army now so they don't get home much. Ma misses them and so does Charlie. He's going to be a boy soldier as soon as they'll have him. So there'll be no bairns at home, not even our Bob. He works for 'railway and he's hardly a bairn any more, since he got married in May.'

Edie paused and then sighed. 'I've been considering leaving my uncle's shop. There's no future in it and I don't want to wait for someone to snap me up and then live a life like my ma or Aunt Mary. Ada's seriously courting, did you know?' she added. 'Everybody thought she was left on 'shelf, but she's just very particular. She seems serious about this one. She onny sees him on her days off, though. I don't think your aunt knows.'

'She doesn't,' Lucy said. 'She would have mentioned it. So, what are you thinking of, Edie? What are you going to do?'

Edie gave a big grin that lit up her face. 'Well, you might be very surprised to hear this, and bearing in mind that I'm nowhere near as clever or as brilliant as you, but . . .' She leaned back in her chair and waited a few minutes while Annie brought the coffee and a plate of sandwiches before she whispered, 'I thought I'd train to be a nurse!'

CHAPTER FIFTEEN

It was Lucy's turn to be thrilled. She gave a huge shrug of delight. 'Wonderful!' she exclaimed. 'And you *are* clever, Edie, Miss Goddard always thought you were, and even though you haven't had the benefit of my extra education you're so bright and sharp. You'll get to be a nurse before I'm a doctor . . . always supposing I'm accepted,' she added gloomily. 'It's not as difficult to qualify as it once was, but women still can't get an educational degree like the male students.'

Edie nodded and bit into her sandwich. 'I can work and learn.' She chewed and swallowed. 'I've been reading up about it. If I'm willing to leave home I can apply to the London Hospital in London; that's a teaching hospital too. But I don't know if I can afford to go. I'll write and ask.'

'Oh,' Lucy breathed. 'If only we could be in London at the same time – if I get a place,' she added again.

'And if I do, too,' Edie answered. Then she gave a huge beaming grin and said passionately, 'Isn't it marvellous, Lucy? I'm so excited now that I know what you're going to do.' She lifted a clenched fist. 'I feel – *strong, energetic*, as if I can do anything!'

Lucy laughed and clenched her fist too. '*We can!* We most certainly can. What is there to stop us?'

They talked for a while and then Edie glanced at the clock on the wall. 'I'm late! Max will have something to say, but do I care?'

'Don't tell him about me, will you?' Lucy said. 'I don't want to tell anyone until, and if, it happens.'

'I won't, no fear. But it will happen,' Edie assured her. 'Believe in yourself. Got to rush. Let me know, won't you, the very minute you hear?'

Lucy promised she would and Edie dashed out of the door only to run back in again. 'Forgot to pay,' she laughed.

'I'll pay, you go. Your turn next time.' Lucy sat back and, breathing deeply, closed her eyes as Edie left. Then she opened them and poured another cup of coffee.

'That girl!' Annie came over and collected Edie's empty cup. 'She's so full of energy. I wish she'd come and work for me. I'd pay her more than her miserly uncle does. Can I get you anything else, miss?'

'Yes, please. I'll have a slice of that lovely chocolate cake, as a treat!'

After she had finished the cake she wiped her mouth free of crumbs, paid Annie and left the café. In no hurry, she sauntered back towards Whitefriargate and home; there wasn't anything pressing to do when she got back, no studying or reading for exams, which, she thought, was a very odd sensation. A disturbing thought came to her: if she didn't gain entry to the school of medicine, then what on earth would she do?

I could train to be a nurse like Edie and work in a military hospital, that might be an option. I think I'd get in there all right. I'd join the Queen Alexandra nurses but I'm not old enough, and Edie won't be either.

She had felt so confident whilst talking with Edie. Her friend's exuberance had infected her and she had felt she could do anything; now she wasn't so sure. She glanced in a shop window as she passed and saw her reflection: a smart young woman wearing a lovely hat, but also someone *very* young, someone just out of school pretending to be grown up and ready to face the world when really she wasn't.

Edie was already grown up; she was experienced in life, having worked all these years for her uncle. Any teaching hospital would be pleased to have her; she was a woman, and she'd be able to cope with sick people or soldiers' injuries.

She sighed and walked on, lost in thought, and then just

ahead of her she saw Aunt Nora and Eleanor, struggling with parcels. She hurried towards them.

'Aunt Nora,' she called, when she was almost up to them. 'Can I help with those? Goodness, Eleanor. Did you leave anything for anyone else?'

Eleanor was excited. 'I've got a new coat, hat and gloves *and* a new dress,' she said, 'and this is as well as the school clothes Mother's ordered from the outfitters.'

Eleanor was starting at the same York school that Lucy had attended, and Lucy thought she could have eased her way in had she still been there, but Eleanor was looking forward to it. She wasn't in the least shy, and besides, she had been several times with her parents when they'd visited Lucy and said she couldn't wait to be there too.

'Mrs Thornbury!'

Mrs Warrington was bearing down on them, accompanied by a young woman, a young man in uniform and Dr Warrington wearing a top hat.

Lucy dipped her knee to Mrs Warrington and then turned to the young woman. 'Elizabeth, how are you?'

Elizabeth nodded graciously to Nora, and then said, 'Lucy Thornbury! I would never have recognized you. Can this really be you?'

'Well, it's no one else,' Lucy said brightly. 'Have you finished your studies in France?'

'Oh, yes indeed,' Elizabeth answered airily. 'What about you? Are you done with school?'

'College. Yes, I have, just,' Lucy said. 'I shall miss it.'

'Really?' Elizabeth seemed astonished. 'I hated the school in York, so few people one would wish to associate with.'

Before Lucy could reply, Elizabeth's father leaned forward. 'Miss Thornbury,' he said, his voice quiet, unlike his wife's or daughter's. 'You won't remember me at all, but I was a good friend of your father's. We worked together at the Hull Infirmary.' He smiled. 'You most definitely have a look of your mother; she was a beautiful, elegant woman. They were a most handsome couple.'

She was quite taken aback. Apart from Uncle William and Mary, no one had ever really spoken about her parents. Tears sprang to her eyes.

'How very kind of you to say so,' she said huskily. 'I wish I could remember them, but I don't, not in the least. Each time I try to recall what they looked like, I only see a fleeting image and nothing else that I can catch hold of.'

'Perhaps because you suffered an emotional shock,' he suggested softly. 'Thinking of them might bring back that distressing day and your memory is blocking it out.'

'I hadn't thought of that,' she murmured. 'I can remember them holding my hands . . .'

'Taking care of you,' he murmured. 'That's a good memory to keep.'

His son came towards her too. He was smartly dressed in army uniform; an officer, she guessed. 'I don't suppose you remember me, Miss Thornbury,' he said. 'Henry? Elizabeth and I came to a birthday party at your house.'

'I vaguely recall. Was I four?' She turned to Nora. 'Aunt?'

'Yes you were, and you played card games,' Nora reminded her.

Lucy laughed. 'Snap! And didn't you and Josh play chess?' she asked Henry.

Henry looked uncomfortable and she wondered why. 'I think I remember that,' he murmured. 'It would be nice if we could get together again. I'm returning to my regiment in a day or two, but perhaps we could arrange something next time I come home on leave. We could do that, couldn't we, Elizabeth?'

'Of course! Why not,' his sister responded. 'There's nothing much happening until the Season begins. I'm dawdling around at home for the moment. You won't be out yet, are you, Lucy?'

'I'm not, nor likely to be,' Lucy said firmly. 'I have no intention whatsoever of attending London balls and parties.'

'Oh dear,' Mrs Warrington murmured. 'Do we have a rebel on our hands, Mrs Thornbury?'

Nora raised her eyebrows. 'Lucy has had an excellent education and will decide for herself what she would like to do. Her uncle and I know that is what her parents would have approved of.'

'Hear, hear!' Dr Warrington said approvingly. 'I quite agree, Mrs Thornbury. Although the parties and balls must be great fun, there are far more important matters to think about.' He touched his hat to Nora and Lucy and gave a friendly nod to Eleanor. 'Please forgive us, but we have an appointment in Parliament Street and then I'm on duty at the hospital.' He turned again to Lucy. 'If ever there is anything I can do for you, please don't hesitate to ask.'

She gave him a wide smile. How fortunate to meet him. 'I won't, Dr Warrington. Thank you. Thank you very much indeed.'

Lucy and her aunt walked in silence to Baker Street, only half listening to Eleanor's chatter, which didn't require any response.

Ada opened the door to them and exclaimed what a spend-thrift Eleanor had been, and Eleanor went through a litany of what they'd bought.

Lucy unpinned her hat and saw a letter waiting on the hall table. It must have come in the afternoon post. She casually walked towards it, picked it up and saw it was for her, and with a sudden quickening in her throat reached for the paper knife to open it.

'I was thinking, Lucy,' her aunt was saying, 'about the *Season*.' She took a deep breath. 'I'm sorry to say that I haven't the least idea of how that could be achieved, nor do I know anyone who could arrange it. I have never mixed in such circles, but although you said that you wouldn't be interested in any case I wonder if perhaps I should have made enquiries. But where or to whom I don't know—'

She stopped as Lucy turned to her, waving a piece of paper in the air. 'I'm not going to have time for such frivolous things,' she laughed, her face one great beam of happiness as she spun round and round in joy. 'I've got an interview. Cross your fingers, Aunt. I just might be going to study to be a doctor!'

CHAPTER SIXTEEN

'Oh, how *wonderful*!' Nora clapped her hands. 'What does it say?' Her face was flushed with excitement. 'Oh, my dear Lucy, I'm so proud of you.'

'Well, it's an interview of course, not a guarantee, but . . .' Lucy glanced down at the letter, which she hadn't yet read in full. 'Oh, shall we go and sit down and I'll read it again?'

She slipped off her coat. Nora did the same and draped them both over the banister. 'Ada,' she called after the housekeeper, who was following on Eleanor's heels carrying the parcels upstairs.

'It's all right, ma'am,' Ada called back. 'Leave 'coats there and I'll see to them in a minute.'

Lucy gasped as she took a seat in the small sitting room downstairs and began to read the letter again. 'Oh, my goodness, I can't believe it. It seems,' she murmured, 'that Miss Benson at Cheltenham highly recommends me, and says that as I have received such *high grades* in my exams and shown my diligence and commitment, she would *wholeheartedly* endorse an application for study in medicine! Oh!' she breathed. 'How very kind.'

'I'm sure that what she said she most sincerely meant, Lucy,' her aunt declared. 'I do believe that you have worked very hard.'

'It's what I want to do, Aunt, more than anything else.'

'And you wouldn't want to go to balls and be presented to

the queen even if we could find some way of arranging it?'

Lucy laughed. 'I'd love to meet Queen Mary, but not attend her ball. I'd liked to have met Queen Victoria,' she said. 'Do you remember how I cried when she died?'

'I do.' Nora smiled. 'But maybe one day you'll meet the queen, and King George too.'

'Who knows?' Lucy said, clasping her hands together. 'But I don't want to be part of any Season. Oh, I'm so excited, but maybe I won't tell anyone else just yet in case they don't accept me. Although I'd like to tell Edie. She's got a secret too.'

'Has she? But you'll tell your uncle William and Oswald about the letter, won't you?'

'Oh, yes, of course. I meant I wouldn't tell the Warringtons. I feel that Elizabeth might be rather scornful.' She paused. 'Her father was very nice and he did say if ever he could help me . . .' Her voice trailed away. 'Perhaps I could ask him what kind of questions I might be asked at the interview.'

'I think that's an excellent idea, Lucy,' her aunt agreed. 'Perhaps you could write to him and make an appointment to discuss a private matter; then he won't mention it at home.'

'Yes!' Lucy said fervently. 'I think I will.'

Her uncle William was delighted to hear her news when he arrived home that evening, and so was Oswald when he came in an hour later. He whooped enthusiastically, and said, 'That's marvellous, Lucy. When? When is the interview?'

'Oh, erm,' Lucy looked again at the letter, 'oh! Next week! Goodness.' She gazed round at everyone. 'So soon.'

'Shall I come with you?' Oswald asked. 'I don't mean to the interview, but to London? I remember how nervous I was when I went to Cambridge the first time.' He glanced at William. 'I know you offered to come with me, Pa, but I was so sure I could manage on my own. Then on catching the train home again I was desperate to talk to someone and tell them all about it.'

'Yes, *please*, Oswald,' Lucy said. 'I wish you would. It will be so busy in London so soon after the coronation; you could come with me to the interview too, because I'm sure I'll never be able to find the right corridor or interview room on my own.'

'You will,' he said. 'But I'll sit outside and wait to pick you up when you fall over in your excitement at being accepted.'

'Well, that's settled then,' William said. 'Otherwise I'd have taken time away from the bank to come with you myself. Do you have to reply immediately?'

She glanced again at the letter. 'Yes,' she said. 'I'd better do it now.'

'Write it now and I'll put it in the bank mail sack in the morning,' her uncle said. 'Then it will be there by the afternoon.' He gave a broad smile. 'Such exciting times. We're very proud of you, Lucy.' He looked at Oswald. 'Of both of you.'

Lucy slipped a letter addressed to Dr Warrington into his home letter box that evening and was pleased and surprised to receive one in return the next afternoon to ask if she would like to call at the Infirmary at about five o'clock that day, as he had an hour free.

The hospital was an imposing building with stone columns on either side of the double doors, and as she entered the great hall in front of her she was overtaken by a sensation of having been there before, although she couldn't recall ever having done so. Unless, she thought, I came here with my father?

A porter directed her up the curved staircase and at the top she enquired of a nurse in a plain grey dress with white cuffs, a pristine starched apron and a white headdress that looked like a crown where she might find Dr Warrington.

'Do you have an appointment, miss?'

'I do,' she said. 'Dr Warrington is expecting me.'

She found the door and knocked. Dr Warrington came to open it and invited her to take a seat.

'It's very good of you to see me, Dr Warrington,' she began, but her thanks were brushed away.

'I gather this is a private matter and not a medical one,' he said, leaning over his desk towards her. 'How can I help you, Miss Thornbury?'

'It's Lucy,' she said, smiling. 'And I wanted to tell you something in confidence and ask your advice, if I may. I have an interview next week at the London School of Medicine for

Women,' she took a breath, 'to see whether I might be suitable to train as a doctor.'

She couldn't help but expand her smile even wider as she said it. It was still amazing to her that she was to be interviewed, but it was the astonished expression on Dr Warrington's face that made her want to laugh outright.

'My word,' he said. 'What excellent news. Your father would have been so thrilled, he really would; and your mother too, of course.'

'Would he? Would they really?' She suddenly felt emotional.

He got up from his desk and came to where she was sitting and took both of her hands in his. 'Indeed yes. Yes indeed!' and he gave her hands a little shake.

'Have I been here before?' she asked. 'In the Infirmary?'

He frowned a little and then straightening up ran a hand over his dark beard. 'I'm not sure,' he said. 'You might have been. When we go out we'll ask the porter. He's been here for many years and has a most prodigious memory.'

He went back to his chair, and asked, 'So what would you like to know?'

She asked him what kind of questions she might expect so that she could prepare herself, and he reassured her that they wouldn't ask her anything about medicine as that would be what she would be taught if she were accepted, and then he said, 'If you *are* accepted you should speak to Dr Mary Murdoch. Have you heard of her?'

She said that she had, but didn't know her.

'I'll write you a letter of introduction,' he said. 'She'll be able to tell you more than I can about women in medicine. She's a grand woman, a first class doctor and rather a firebrand.'

Lucy nodded. 'I had heard that,' she said. She bit her lip. 'I'll make an appointment to see her if – if – when I come back from London, I mean.'

'Believe in yourself,' he said. 'Tell them that your father was a doctor and they'll understand that you are very serious about it and know what it will entail.'

116

She shook her head. 'But I don't know,' she said. 'I don't know anything at all.'

'You will,' he said kindly. 'Eventually. You'll make your family very proud. I wish . . .' He hesitated. 'I wish one of my offspring would have followed me into the profession, but Henry has always had his heart set on the army and I'm afraid that Elizabeth . . .' He smiled rather ruefully. 'Well, I'm afraid she's only interested in the latest fashion and catching a rich suitor.'

Lucy vaguely recalled that Josh had offered to fight Henry during her birthday party, and Henry had refused because he said he was going to be an officer. Both young men were soldiers now and she wondered whether their paths had ever crossed. She thought too that Dr Warrington was right about Elizabeth; she had always seemed intent on making a good marriage.

The doctor walked with her down the wide staircase and once again she felt the sensation of having been there before; nurses and other staff were crossing the hall and the porter she had spoken to on her arrival was still there, directing someone towards a corridor.

'Isaac,' Dr Warrington called to him. 'Can you spare a minute?'

'Certainly can, doctor.' The porter came across to them.

'This is Miss Lucy Thornbury,' the doctor said. 'Dr Thornbury's daughter.'

The man's eyes opened wide. 'Not that bonny little bairn? Nay, it can't be, it's not that long since . . .' His voice trailed away. 'Well,' he murmured. 'How 'years do pass and here you are a beautiful young woman. I remember when—'

'You carried me down the stairs,' Lucy said, with a catch in her voice.

'Aye, I did. It was that last weekend afore – afore you all went off to London to visit some relatives. Dr Thornbury had brought you in with him, to show you off I expect, and I carried you down cos he was piled high with paperwork.'

Lucy's eyes streamed with tears. She didn't recall why the porter had carried her down but she remembered the dark shaggy eyebrows he had wiggled at her and his wispy moustache that was now grey.

'Thank you so much, Isaac,' she whispered. 'For unlocking that memory,' and she turned and looked back up at the staircase and saw now, as she had done those fifteen years ago, looking over Isaac's shoulder, her father laughing at her as he followed them down the stairs.

CHAPTER SEVENTEEN

Lucy was tense during train travel and on the journey to London she jumped each time the haunting whistle blew, or the huffing and puffing of the engine turned into a hissing clanking racket of brakes or screeching wheels on the line; several times she cringed back into her seat as great clouds of steam rushed past the windows or they were plunged into the darkness of a tunnel.

Oswald took hold of her hand and tucked her arm under his. 'You're quite safe, Lucy,' he murmured.

She nodded gratefully. 'There is a buried fear,' she said. 'Perhaps one day I'll conquer it.'

William had booked them rooms in a hotel on Gray's Inn Road and they arrived in the late afternoon on the day before the interview.

'The training will be at the Royal Free Hospital,' Lucy told Oswald as they waited at the reception desk in the small hotel. 'But they're conducting interviews at the Gray's Inn hospital as the teaching hospital is being renovated.'

'Getting ready for your arrival,' he joked. 'Making sure it's spick and span.'

They booked in and were shown up to their rooms and Oswald suggested they went out to dinner somewhere. 'We can catch an omnibus or a tram,' he told her. 'We don't have to stay around here. We can go somewhere more central.'

'Do you know where to go?'

'More or less,' he said. 'I've been to London a few times with some of the chaps at weekends. But I don't want to tire you out by walking miles. I know; why don't we hop on a tram and look out for a nice restaurant nearby and then after we have eaten we can walk back to the hotel and you can have an early night.'

'All right,' she agreed. 'I am rather tired, or maybe it's because I'm nervous, and it's so noisy in London, isn't it? And so busy.'

They only rode a few stops before Oswald saw an Italian restaurant on a street corner. 'Come on,' he said. 'Let's try this one.'

Lucy laughed and took his arm as they walked back towards it. 'This is so exciting, so different from Hull or York.'

Over the restaurant door was the name *Ristorante Francesco*. It was small and nicely appointed in the Italian style, with candles on the tables and a buzz of Italian voices coming from the kitchen. There was a table free by the window where they could look out at the road. Oswald ordered a glass of wine for them both whilst they studied the menu.

'I wonder if I'll ever get used to it,' Lucy commented. 'The clamour of people, the traffic, and so on. If I get in, of course,' she added.

'Oh, Lucy. Don't be negative,' he admonished her, pushing his glasses up his nose and looking at her. 'They wouldn't have asked you to come if they weren't ninety-nine per cent sure already.'

'Well, you're the one studying mathematics, but I have to say it.' She laughed. 'It's rather like crossing fingers for luck. What?' She touched her face as she noticed his scrutiny. 'Have I got soot on my nose?'

He shook his head and smiled. 'No. No, you haven't.' He turned to the menu. 'What are you going to have?'

A waiter sidled up to them. He was decidedly Italian with his dark hair and dark eyes. 'Have you decided, signore? Signora?'

'I think so,' Oswald said, with a questioning glance at Lucy, who nodded.

Lucy chose salad with pecorino cheese and thin slices of

prosciutto drizzled with olive oil for a starter and as she pondered over her main course, Oswald chose tomato and bread soup, adding, 'and Tuscan pork liver with fennel on bruschetta for my main course.'

'And for your beautiful wife?' The waiter stood poised with notebook and pencil.

They both stared at him and then laughed. 'Sister!' Oswald said. 'Cousin!' Lucy said simultaneously, and they both laughed again whilst the waiter stood with incredulous eyebrows, then put his finger to his lips and murmured, 'I won't tell.'

Lucy, still smiling, ordered ravioli stuffed with spinach and ricotta for her main course. She leaned back in her chair after the waiter had left and commented, 'We can't possibly put a name to our relationship.'

'Because we haven't got one,' Oswald agreed. 'Our only link is through Eleanor and that's not a bloodline. Step-something or other?' His grey eyes twinkled behind his glasses and she was reminded of something Jane – or was it Primrose? – had said about his lovely eyes.

'Do you remember when I was little and you came to live in Hull?' she asked.

Oswald nodded and took a sip of wine. 'I was an awful brat, wasn't I?'

'I didn't think you liked me; you wouldn't play games.'

'I didn't like anybody,' he murmured. 'I wasn't much more than a baby, two and a bit or something, when Mother married William – Pa; and yet I can remember that I didn't like him. I thought he was taking her away from me. There'd only been the two of us until then.'

'And then I turned up a few years later and made it worse.'

'I was jealous, I think, because Mother had to look after you. She told me you'd been ill, but I didn't believe her. It wasn't just you, though,' he admitted. 'I didn't like any of the boys at my London school, or the teachers, and I was always in trouble for not knowing my lessons.' He paused. 'My mother hadn't had much of a life, you know, until she met and married Pa. I wasn't aware of it, of course, not then, I was too young; but I think

121

she'd always been anxious and that must have rubbed off on me. It wasn't until we came to Hull that things gradually began to change for the better.'

'Strange, isn't it?' Lucy murmured, toying with a fork. 'We both had a bad start in life and yet here we are on the cusp of a much better one. We're lucky, aren't we?'

Oswald raised his glass. 'Let's drink a toast to those who made it happen.'

It was almost ten o'clock when arm in arm they strolled back to the hotel. It was a lovely evening, warm and rather sultry. 'I'm so pleased you came with me, Oswald,' she told him. 'I've enjoyed this evening and I don't feel nervous now, but rather looking forward to tomorrow.'

He squeezed her arm. 'Good. We'll leave plenty of time to walk there. It's not far – I looked it up on the map.'

They collected their room keys and walked up the stairs together. Lucy was on the first floor and Oswald on the second. He escorted her to her door and kissed her cheek. 'Good night, Lucy. Sleep well.'

'Thank you, Oswald. I hope you do too.' She smiled. 'I'll see you at breakfast.'

She closed her door behind her and he walked on up the next flight of stairs, unlocked his door, took off his jacket and shoes and stretched out on the bed, his arms behind his head. 'Well, well,' he murmured. 'Little Lucy.' He lay there for a few more minutes and then heaved out a breath. 'Now there's a thing.'

The next morning they made their way to the hospital and Lucy was collected by a female clerk who escorted her to the inter-view room and asked her to wait. After a few minutes the door opened again and two women came in, one of whom, slightly senior and of a serious countenance, introduced herself as Dr Anna Cavendish and her colleague as Dr Olga Schultz.

The interview lasted about thirty minutes and although not gruelling was intensive as they asked about her aspirations and ambitions as well as her education. She felt exhausted at the end of it but thought she had answered as truthfully as possible.

Dr Cavendish closed up her folder and said, 'Your examination results have been excellent, Miss Thornbury, and I think we have everything.'

Dr Schultz thanked Lucy for coming and gave her a complicit smile as she rose to indicate the interview was over.

'I'll see Miss Thornbury out,' Dr Cavendish said. 'This place is quite a warren.'

Lucy noticed the look of surprise on Dr Schultz's face, though the other woman said nothing except goodbye, and then Dr Cavendish was opening the door and they stepped outside into the long corridor. As they walked along it towards the stairs Dr Cavendish cleared her throat and said, 'I remember your father, Miss Thornbury.'

A small gasp escaped Lucy's lips and she turned her gaze to Dr Cavendish. 'Really?'

'Yes. He was in his final year, I believe, and I in my third. Female students rarely had the chance of meeting young men in those days, and many of them were hostile to us, but just occasionally there were social events where we were given the opportunity to mix. Sounds so archaic, doesn't it, and yet it wasn't so long ago.'

Lucy felt very emotional; it seemed that lately a picture of her father was building up, but not of her mother.

'We were very serious young women, determined to overcome any obstacles and moreover to prove ourselves.' Dr Cavendish gave a swift smile. 'But that didn't mean that we didn't recognize a handsome young man when we saw one. Your father was at King's, wasn't he?' Without waiting for a reply, she went on, 'He had a good friend there too – erm – Matthew Warrington. They were the idols of many a young woman and not only because they supported the rights of female students! However, I seem to recall your father only had eyes for one female student. What happened to him?' she asked abruptly. 'You said in your letter he *was* a doctor.'

Lucy's mouth trembled and her voice shook slightly as she spoke. 'He and my mother were both killed in a train crash

123

when I was very young. They – we – were coming to London to visit his brother – my uncle, now my guardian. I was one of the survivors; concussion and a broken arm. I – I don't – I hardly remember them.'

'I'm so sorry, my dear.' Dr Cavendish paused in her stride. 'So very sorry. Such a loss. What was your mother's name?'

'Alice,' she said softly.

'Alice!' Dr Cavendish gave a winsome smile that lit up her plain features. 'That was it. Many of the young women used to say that he would marry Alice one day.'

'My mother was here?' Lucy was astonished. 'As a student? Training to be a doctor? I didn't know!' As they continued down the stairs to the floor below she saw Oswald sitting on a chair, absorbed in a magazine.

'I don't recall seeing her more than a few times and I didn't know her,' the doctor was saying. 'I think she was in her first or second year, and we were all very engrossed in our studies. Determined to do well.' She seemed pensive. 'Such a waste,' she said. 'They would have had good professional lives ahead of them.'

'My father was a doctor at the Hull Infirmary,' Lucy told her. 'As is Dr Warrington. I saw him just before I came here. No one has ever told me that my mother was also a doctor.'

Dr Cavendish heaved out a breath. 'Perhaps she didn't continue. It was very hard then, particularly for women; as it still is,' she added. 'Please give Dr Warrington my kindest regards, although I don't think for a moment he will remember me – Anna Cavendish.'

Oswald looked up as they approached. He rose to his feet and gave Lucy a questioning look.

'Dr Cavendish,' Lucy said, 'may I introduce my cousin Oswald Thornbury? Oswald, this is Dr Cavendish.'

They shook hands, and Dr Cavendish glanced at the magazine that he was still holding. 'Are you also interested in the medical profession, Mr Thornbury?'

'Erm, no, at least, *yes*, very interested, because of Lucy, not as a profession for myself.'

'Ah, and so you are – where?'

'Cambridge, doctor. Reading science – maths and physics.'

'Most impressive,' she said, before turning to Lucy. 'We are always interested to hear about our students' friends and relatives,' she said. 'It helps to build up a broader picture.'

'I see.' Lucy was beginning to feel overwhelmed. 'Of course.'

Dr Cavendish smiled and held out her hand. 'I look forward to seeing you again at your next interview, Miss Thornbury, when you will also meet the dean. Thank you for coming.'

Lucy shook her hand and they went their separate ways. 'May I hold on to your arm, Oswald?' she said breathlessly. 'I think I might fall over after all.'

They stepped outside into the sunshine and walked a few steps away from the door, then Oswald let out a whoop, picked Lucy up and swung her off her feet.

'Oh, how clever you are!' he exclaimed.

'What?' she said, holding on to her hat. 'Didn't you hear what she said? I've to come back for another interview.'

'Yes, I did, and I also heard her say that they liked to hear about their *students'* friends and relatives, not *prospective* students!'

'Oh!' Lucy said. 'She knew my father, Oswald, can you believe it? And she told me that my mother was also a student here!'

It was his turn to be astonished. 'Really? Come on, I'm going to buy you lunch, out of my own pocket, not the money Pa gave us to spend, and you can tell me all about it.'

She laughed and took his arm again and they walked away from the building. Dr Cavendish, looking out from a window which she always did after an interview when the students were not aware of her presence, watched with an intent and questioning gaze.

125

CHAPTER EIGHTEEN

Lucy's aunt and uncle were delighted with what she told them and both were enthusiastic about her almost certain acceptance at the next interview. Later, Lucy asked William how much he knew about her mother.

'I was astonished to hear that Mama had been a medical student at the same time as my father,' she said. 'Dr Cavendish, who interviewed me, said that she remembered her being there although she didn't know her.'

William drew in a breath. 'I hadn't met her in those early days, and we were all very surprised when Joseph announced that he was getting married. Our parents were worried that he would find it difficult financially to begin a medical career and maintain a wife.'

'And my mother wouldn't have been allowed to continue her medical training once she was married,' Lucy said thought-fully. 'It seems to me that a woman has to be very determined in order to join the profession.'

He smiled. 'Indeed. It has to be a very special woman with perseverance and passion to be able to succeed.'

It was a week later when Lucy received an official letter inviting her to return for a final interview when she would be considered as a possible candidate to study medicine. She shook with nerves; she was on the cusp of her eighteenth birthday and wondered if they would think her too young. Still, she pondered. They know my age already so surely they would have said so at the first interview.

She wrote again to Dr Warrington, telling him of the letter and asking him if he would be kind enough to write to Dr Mary Murdoch as he had offered, in the hope that she might meet her before she was due to go back for the final interview.

As good as his word, he had written to Dr Murdoch offering, if she agreed, to take Lucy to see her, and very soon he was able to tell Lucy that a meeting had been arranged for the following week.

'We can walk if you like,' he suggested. 'She only lives on Beverley Road so it's not very far at all.' He called for her and they talked as they walked, he telling her of his admiration for Dr Murdoch, who had campaigned so hard for women in the medical profession and for women's suffrage in particular.

'I'll join the campaign,' Lucy said emphatically. 'I read about it whilst at school and also when I was at Cheltenham, but my excuse was that there was such a lot of study that I never had time to do anything about it.'

'There will be even more if your application is successful,' he told her. 'If you thought study hard then, you will find it even harder once you begin medical school. Yet those pioneering women fought to become doctors on an equal footing with men *and* campaigned for the rights of women at the same time. Alas,' he added, 'they are still lagging behind in medicine and it is the hostile men who are holding them back: some older men, my age, who won't relinquish their power and even some younger men who really should know better.'

She nodded. She had read accounts of the hostility of some of the male students and even of a riot in Scotland when seven women were once excluded from a final exam.

She mentioned this to Dr Warrington and he answered, 'Yes, they were known as the Edinburgh Seven and became quite famous. But that was over forty years ago and there has been much improvement since then. Here we are,' he said, opening a gate to the footpath of a house. 'Don't be nervous. She'll be delighted to meet you.'

A housekeeper showed them into a small sitting room and told them that Dr Murdoch would be along shortly and asked would they like tea. Both refused, Lucy because she thought she would be too nervous to drink it and would spill it all over herself and the carpet. But her nerves disappeared when the doctor appeared followed by another younger woman, and she stood up to greet them.

Dr Murdoch shook hands with Lucy and Dr Warrington and then introduced them to Dr Louisa Martindale, who also shook hands and said, 'I'm afraid I can't stay as I must get back to the hospital, but I wanted to meet you, Miss Thornbury, and wish you every success.'

Lucy thanked her and said how nice it was to meet her too.

Louisa Martindale gazed at her for a moment. 'How young you are. And yet I was just as young when I decided I wanted to be a doctor. It is a long, hard road, but opportunities are opening up for women in medicine, thanks to people like Dr Murdoch.' She shook hands again with Lucy, and wished her good luck.

They were asked to be seated and Dr Murdoch explained that she had brought Dr Martindale to work alongside her at the children's hospital as she had exceptional talent, but that she would eventually go on to carve her own career.

'You need to have stamina, Miss Thornbury,' she said. 'Trust in what you believe in, and more than anything believe in yourself. I must warn you, however, that medicine is not for the faint-hearted. Dr Warrington has perhaps warned you of that already?'

Lucy nodded. 'He has explained how much more study I can expect, more than I have already experienced.'

'Indeed,' Dr Murdoch said. 'It is hard, and although I say it again, you must have exceptional talent to succeed. You must be better than you think you are and you must expect, no matter how clever, to be marked down as lower academically than your male colleagues.' She smiled at Lucy's astonished expression and added, 'Even if you know you are superior.'

After more discussion, Lucy left the house, giving Dr Murdoch her grateful thanks. Her thoughts were whirling. She had answered the doctor's questions as honestly as she could and had asked many herself, although as she walked back with

Dr Warrington she thought of many more that she might have asked.

Dr Warrington swung his cane as they walked back to town. 'Well, are you of the same mind? Do you still want to enter the profession, given what you have heard?'

Lucy paused for a second before answering. 'I do. I might not succeed, though I won't know that unless I try. But first of all I have to get through the next interview.'

She discussed everything she had learned from Dr Murdoch with her aunt, her uncle and Oswald, but didn't tell them the full extent of the amount of study she would have to do. She knew that she wouldn't have to explain to Oswald, as he would know already how much work lay ahead of her, and William had studied mathematics at university before going into banking, but Nora had not had a university education, or any education worth mentioning.

William had drawn her to one side and said that if she succeeded in the interview and was accepted, then he would like to speak to her about finances. It wasn't something she had considered, but he assured her that everything was in hand and that there were no monetary worries.

This time she travelled alone to London. She had said that if she was going to be independent then the time to start was now. Her aunt saw her off at the railway station; her uncle had reserved a seat in the ladies' carriage from Hull and there would be a change of trains in York.

She was nervous as always, but in the carriage there were two other young women travelling alone and one travelling with her mother. The mother looked at the three unaccompanied young women and sniffed rather disparagingly, but her daughter, who was probably about Lucy's age, seemed to be gazing enviously at all three of them.

When they arrived in York, the mother and daughter left the station and the daughter turned round to watch them; Lucy gave her a little wave and followed the others towards the London train.

'That poor girl,' one of the others said as together they entered the ladies' carriage. She was a tall broad-shouldered young woman, probably in her late twenties. 'Imagine having to have your mama with you all the time.' She smiled brightly at Lucy and the other young woman. 'Are you going to the rally?'

'Which rally is that?' Lucy asked.

'The suffragettes, of course. I thought as you were travelling alone . . .'

'I'm visiting relatives in London,' the other girl said. 'I didn't know there was a rally.'

'Really? Don't you keep up with the news?' the first young woman said patronizingly, then turned her attention to Lucy.

'I'm attending an interview,' Lucy said quietly, adding, 'Do you have to go as far as London for a rally? Don't you support the Hull suffragist movement?' She gave a questioning lift of her eyebrows. 'Or perhaps you are more militant than your Hull compatriots?'

The woman looked taken aback. 'I, erm, I don't know if there is a rally in Hull. I haven't read about there being one.'

'So you don't belong to the national women's union? The one headed by Dr Mary Murdoch?' Lucy was annoyed by the other woman's condescending manner and was determined to bring her down a peg. She succeeded, as the woman muttered something to the effect that she hadn't had time to join as yet, and opened up a magazine to read.

The other girl came across and sat next to her. 'My name's Millicent Thomas,' she whispered. 'Milly, my friends call me. Are you going to be a teacher? That's what I want to be eventually, or a governess if I don't pass the examination.'

Lucy shook her head. 'No,' she whispered back. 'A doctor.' She smiled. 'And I'll have to pass examinations too.'

Milly Thomas gazed at her in awe and heaved a breath. 'Goodness,' she murmured. 'How wonderful; how very clever of you.' She clasped her hands together. 'I'll mention you in my prayers and wish you good luck too.' She bent towards Lucy and lowered her voice further. 'I have to work; otherwise I'll

130

be dependent on my brother, poor lamb, who is struggling to support our mother and me until I'm old enough to earn a living. I'm only just seventeen, you see, and I'm visiting our uncle, my mother's brother, to ask if he can increase Mother's allowance until then.' She sighed. 'I've written to him but he doesn't seem to understand how difficult it has been since Father died, so I'm going to ask him to his face. I think he will help, providing his wife doesn't object.' She sighed again as she sat back against the seat and sadly shook her head.

Lucy felt very sorry for her and thought how hard it must be for someone so young, a year younger than she was, to be beset with worries over money, and how lucky she was to be so well provided for. Then her cogitations moved on to her uncle William, who had been so kind and thoughtful, becoming a surrogate father and guardian of her assets.

She wondered if he struggled at all with his own finances; he was providing for Oswald as well as his wife and daughter and she decided that, when they discussed her finances as he had said he wanted to on her return, she would ask if it would be possible for her to assist Oswald with his university fees.

She had no idea at all how she stood financially, or how her father had provided for her. She knew the house was hers, or would be when she reached twenty-one, but surely, she thought now, whatever monies had been left to her fourteen years ago must have dwindled considerably over the years. Perhaps, she mused, I am not as affluent as I have believed myself to be.

King's Cross station was much busier than when Lucy had come last time and she and Milly Thomas walked together towards the exit.

'I'm going to Euston Road,' Milly said, 'so I'm going on the Metropolitan line – the underground track,' she added. 'I was very frightened the first time I did it; I thought it would be very dark, but it turned out to be quite exciting. Do you think all those ladies are going to the suffragette rally?' She pointed to a group of women. 'Like the other girl said?'

'Yes, I think they might be. Look,' Lucy said. 'Over there. Someone is unfurling a banner.'

131

Milly Thomas narrowed her eyes. 'What does it say? I can't read it from here.'

'*Votes For Women*,' Lucy said. 'I wonder where the rally is going to be held?'

'Will you go?' her companion asked. 'I don't think I dare, at least not this time. I would hate to be arrested; whatever would my mother think? And I wouldn't want my uncle to hear of it. I believe he thinks that women should stay at home, get married and have children. He's very Victorian. Nothing wrong with getting married and having a family, but some women would like a career. I expect that's what you'd like?' She looked up at Lucy. 'If you have a brain you should be allowed to use it.'

'Yes,' Lucy said. 'I want to be a doctor and although now women can be, if they pass the exams, we're still in a minority.' She looked across the concourse where groups of women were gathering. 'But these women also want to have a say in how the country is run. They want to be able to vote just as men can, though even some working class men are still excluded because of their lack of income.'

They said goodbye then. Milly gave Lucy a wave and wished her good luck and left the station and Lucy went to the cab stand to be taken once more to the same hotel as last time.

'You going to the rally with them other mad women, miss?' the cab driver asked her.

'No,' she said, not wanting any altercation to upset her positive state of mind or risk his refusing to drive her. 'I'm here visiting relatives.'

CHAPTER NINETEEN

When Lucy booked in at the hotel, the reception clerk remembered her and asked if her companion would be joining her. Lucy frowned a little as she pondered his question. 'Mr Thornbury? No, he is not.' She gazed dubiously at him. 'Why do you ask?'

He gave her a sceptical glance. 'We don't get many young ladies staying alone.'

'Why not?' she faltered. 'Is this not a safe place for young women on their own? If it is not then I will cancel my reservation and go elsewhere.'

'Oh no,' he flustered, and a moment later she understood why his manner had changed. The manager was standing behind her.

'Good afternoon, madam,' he said courteously. 'Is there some difficulty with your reservation?'

'I don't know,' she said, turning to him. 'Perhaps there might be. Your desk clerk tells me that you don't often have young women putting up here. I was enquiring if the hotel is a safe place to stay.'

The manager's face turned pink and the clerk's puce as he realized his error.

'I have stayed here before,' Lucy went on. 'But if it is not suitable I will go elsewhere.'

The manager positively grovelled. 'It is perfectly safe, I assure you, madam, and I don't know why Grayson should think it otherwise; we have never had any trouble here.'

'Well, if you're sure,' Lucy said, 'then I'll stay. My uncle booked this visit as he did the last time, having been assured of your establishment's excellence, and he will expect me to report back if it doesn't come up to his exacting expectations.'

The manager assured her that they would fall over backwards to make sure she had a pleasant stay, and carried her small bag upstairs himself. Ten minutes later a complimentary tray of tea and biscuits was brought to her room.

I can see that it is going to be a different life here, she pondered as she sipped her tea, and I'm going to have to be more self-assured and demanding than is my nature.

She ate in the hotel that evening; Grayson the clerk wasn't behind the desk when she came down for dinner, having been replaced by a woman who turned out to be the manager's wife, and she wondered if he had been sent home. She was given a table in a quiet corner of the dining room and although the food wasn't as good as the Italian food she had enjoyed on her last visit she scarcely noticed, being tired after her journey and intent on an early night. Nevertheless, she didn't sleep well, her jumbled thoughts concentrating on the next day. So much depended on the interview, and if it proved to be successful she would be invited to visit the Royal Free Hospital where her medical training would take place.

Lucy's interview was arranged for ten thirty, and when she came down for breakfast she asked the manager's wife, Mrs Saunders, if she would order her a cab; then she enquired after the whereabouts of the desk clerk.

'Gone,' Mrs Saunders said. 'Can't have him upsetting our visitors.'

'Oh, I'm so sorry.' Lucy was conscience-stricken. 'Please don't dismiss him on my account. Perhaps I took his comment the wrong way. Perhaps he didn't mean it to sound the way it did.'

Mrs Saunders slowly nodded her head. 'He did,' she said. 'He didn't like me being here. He wouldn't have minded if I cleaned the rooms, but he didn't like the fact that I look after the books and assist in the management of the hotel. Don't you worry, miss. I know how to deal with his sort, and, well, I'll tell you honestly, I was looking for a reason to get rid of him.'

And that gave Lucy no comfort at all, but it did at least give her something else to think about over breakfast rather than the impending interview.

She was ten minutes early at the Gray's Inn Road hospital and was ushered into a room which was already occupied by another young woman, perhaps in her late twenties, who was also there for an interview. 'I'm an hour early,' she murmured to Lucy, 'but I was so nervous about being late I thought I'd come and just wait.'

The door opened again to admit another young woman who sat down and didn't speak but just acknowledged them by a nod of her head and anxious eyes.

At precisely ten thirty the door opened and Dr Schultz came in. 'Lucy Thornbury? Ah – Miss Thornbury, hello again. Will you come with me, please?

'Did you have a good journey?' she asked as they walked down the corridor, past wards and orderly rooms. 'You weren't held up by the suffragette rally, were you?'

'No,' Lucy said. 'I wasn't. I travelled yesterday. I saw quite a lot of women supporters gathering at King's Cross station and many of them were carrying banners.'

'Mmm. I do hope there isn't any trouble,' Dr Schultz murmured. 'We can do without that. Dr Louisa Garrett Anderson is speaking, so large crowds are expected.'

'Oh, is she really?' Lucy had heard of Dr Anderson, the suffragette and social reformer.

'Her mother was the very first female doctor, did you know?' Dr Schultz asked her, 'and co-founder of the London School of Medicine for Women,' and Lucy, not knowing if she was being questioned on her knowledge of women in medicine or if Dr Schultz was merely chatting to put her at ease, answered that she had heard of the eminent doctor, and had read up on women in medicine.

'You'll probably get to meet her if you should be invited to the Royal Free,' Dr Schultz said casually and Lucy's heart thumped.

'I'd be honoured,' she murmured, and said no more as they approached the interview room.

Dr Schultz paused before opening the door. She smiled at Lucy. 'Don't be nervous,' she whispered. 'You're in with a good chance. Dr Cavendish is here again, with the dean, and Dr Chadburn, who is another senior doctor. Good luck!'

Lucy murmured her thanks and entered. 'Good morning, doctors,' she greeted them quietly, looking at each woman in turn. 'Thank you very much indeed for inviting me to return.'

The questions were far more searching than last time and Lucy answered to the best of her ability; one such question was from the dean, a stern-looking woman dressed in a severe grey gown.

'Miss Thornbury,' she said, 'if perchance you should enter the medical profession, would you expect to attend only women and children or would you consider the treatment of sick or injured men?'

Without a pause Lucy answered, 'I would consider that men were just as deserving of my learning and experience as women. I wouldn't exclude them in any way but attempt to alleviate their illness, distress or injury.'

She sensed a twitching of lips on the dean's face and a muted smile on the faces of the other two doctors. Dr Cavendish then asked her how she would feel about marriage before qualifying.

'I haven't given marriage a single thought, Dr Cavendish,' she replied. 'I haven't any experience of young men apart from my cousin and childhood friends.' She smiled. 'There is no romance or prospect of marriage in my life.' Then she thought for a second and said, 'If there had been, then I'm afraid it would – or will – have to wait. Medicine is my dream and I would like to think I can make it a reality.'

Dr Cavendish nodded approvingly. 'We've received a letter from Dr Mary Murdoch, whom we all know very well. You have recently spoken to her, I understand?'

'Yes,' Lucy answered. 'She was kind enough to give me some

of her time, and encouragement for which I was very grateful.'

'Well.' Dr Cavendish picked up a letter from the desk. 'Although naturally she cannot recommend you as she doesn't know of your capabilities, she gives a very favourable character reference on your intellect and understanding of what is entailed in becoming a doctor. Praise indeed from Dr Murdoch.'

She looked at her colleagues and they seemed to have reached some kind of conclusion, for she then reached for a handbell on the desk and rang it three times. 'If you would kindly go with Dr Schultz, Miss Thornbury, and wait again in the waiting room; I'm sure she will send someone along to offer you a pot of coffee or tea and we will see you again shortly.'

Lucy followed Dr Schultz to another room, one which reminded her of her old common room at school with its battered but comfy sofas and easy chairs and low tables with magazines on them.

'Would you like coffee or tea, Lucy?' Dr Schultz asked her. She was much less formal than the other doctors. 'You might have to wait a while so do make yourself comfortable.'

'I'll have coffee, please, if it's no bother,' she answered and suddenly felt drained of energy.

'It's no bother at all. I'll send someone along.' The doctor smiled. 'Excuse me now, for I must take the next applicant along for her interview.'

'Of course,' Lucy said, relieved her session was over and wondering which of the two young ladies it would be. 'Wish them good luck from me,' she added.

Dr Schultz looked a little surprised but said that she would.

Within minutes a housekeeper arrived and asked her if she would like something to eat with her coffee. 'You'd be as well to have something, miss,' she said, and repeated Dr Schultz's words: 'You'll have to wait, and if you're chosen to go along to the Royal Free this afternoon you might get hungry.'

'Oh.' Lucy felt fluttery again. 'Yes, thank you. A sandwich, or anything at all really, will be very welcome.'

As she sat waiting, she wondered why it was that Dr Schultz was taking the applicants in and out of the interview room when on the last occasion she was one of the examiners. Was it to put the applicants at their ease on seeing a familiar face? Was she in fact checking on whether they were able to cope with the pressure and anxiety of a further interview? It would make sense, she considered. There must be many burdens put upon doctors: the life-saving decisions they had to make, the relieving of their patients' pain or discomfort.

Will I be able to deal with such circumstances? Will I be able to offer hope to those who are sick or injured? She sat back and closing her eyes put her hand to her forehead as doubts crept in. I don't know, she thought. I would hope that I can but I've never had to deal with such situations.

But then other voices came rushing in from her past; other images filled her head. Loud noise and commotion of people screaming and shouting; impressions and sensations of being picked up and carried in a stranger's arms, a stranger who uttered soothing words of comfort and said repeatedly what a brave girl she was; and she knew then that she had, after all, been in comparable circumstances.

Tears sprang to her eyes. Was that what had happened on that fateful train journey? Who was that unknown person who had comforted her? Had that incident been imprinted on her mind and made her who she was? And then she remembered Uncle William; Uncle William being constantly by her hospital bedside, holding her hand and assuring her that he would always look after her, that she would be in his care for ever and need never be afraid again. She blew her nose. And she hadn't been afraid; she had trusted him absolutely throughout her childhood and he it was who had made her brave.

CHAPTER TWENTY

Lucy ate her sandwich and drank the coffee, and as no one else came in to disturb her she slipped off her shoes, put her feet up on the sofa and closed her eyes again. She must have fallen asleep, for the next thing she knew Dr Schultz was leaning over her and gently shaking her arm.

'Oh, I'm so sorry,' Lucy apologized, swinging her feet down to the floor. 'I closed my eyes for a moment; such a comfy sofa—'

'It's all right,' the doctor said. 'Taking a short nap is very beneficial. Would you like to freshen up, and then I'll take you back to meet the doctors again.'

Lucy thanked her and in a nearby washroom she washed her hands, rinsed her face and combed her hair, which had become disarranged while she slept. Then once more she walked along the corridor with Dr Schultz, who didn't chat this time but kept her eyes in front. When they reached the interview room Lucy was invited to be seated, and Dr Schultz took a chair at the end of the long table with the other doctors.

'How are you feeling, Miss Thornbury?' Dr Cavendish asked.

'Rather strange now that it's all over,' she answered honestly.

Dr Cavendish gave her a questioning glance. 'Why do you think it might be over?'

Lucy licked her lips. 'I, erm, I hardly dare dream that I – might have been successful,' she said softly.

'And yet you said that medicine was your dream,' Dr Cavendish reminded her.

'It is,' she said fervently, 'and if I haven't been successful this time I will keep studying and in another year or two, if it is possible, I will apply again.'

'I really don't think that will be necessary, Miss Thornbury,' Dr Cavendish said calmly. 'Not necessary at all to put you through this again. My colleagues and I have come to the unanimous decision that you will be a welcome asset to our profession. You are very young, but we do not think your youth will be a liability.'

Lucy put her finger to her right ear and pressed it to clear the ringing. Were they saying – what were they saying? But yes, they were all smiling, even the sombre dean, and they were all standing up waiting for her to say something. She looked at Dr Schultz, who was smiling broadly and beckoning to her.

'Come along, Lucy,' she said. 'The good doctors are waiting to shake you by the hand.'

She shook hands with them all; her heart was hammering and she was so overcome that she could barely speak and a few tears trickled down her cheeks. When they asked her if she would be prepared to stay overnight as there was a visit planned that afternoon to the Royal Free Hospital in Hampstead where she would be given a tour, she stammered that she had booked a second night at her hotel in the fervent hope that she would be invited.

The dean nodded and said that they liked to see a positive attitude in their students.

Dr Schultz took her back to the comfortable waiting room and said she would order her another drink and that it would be about an hour before she and another doctor would be ready to take her to Hampstead.

'Perhaps I could step outside for a few minutes?' Lucy asked her. 'And then when I come back in the door it will be as a medical student.'

Dr Schultz laughed. 'Of course, and if you wish to send your family a telegram with the good news, there's a telegraph office just a hundred yards away where you can do that.'

'Oh! How wonderful. Yes please, thank you, I would love to do that, thank you, thank you very much.' Impulsively she reached up and kissed the doctor's cheek. Dr Schultz looked very surprised, but gratified. 'You have been so very kind,' Lucy said by way of explanation of her reckless behaviour.

'I remember how nervous I was when I came for my first interview and so I like to help a little if I can.' A little smile touched Dr Schultz's lips. 'However, I will tell you that I will be one of your tutors and I may not always be kind, although I hope that I am always fair. Now,' she said briskly. 'Off you go. Be back in half an hour.'

Lucy stood outside for a second taking deep breaths and absorbing the sounds and sights of the road. Electric trams zinged past and horse-drawn drays and wagons rattled along accompanied by the phut-phut and sharp explosive bangs of motorized cars, of which there were far more in London than she had ever seen in Hull. She looked up and down and then set off as directed towards the telegraph office.

On a slip given to her by a clerk she wrote out a brief message home. *Success Stop* she wrote. *Home tomorrow Stop Celebrate Stop.*

'Is that all, miss?' the clerk asked her as she pushed the slip towards him and fumbled in her purse.

She smiled. 'Yes,' she said happily. 'For the time being.'

Another pot of coffee and a slice of cake were brought to her and Lucy sat again and waited, and pondered on what had happened to the other two applicants. Perhaps it was their first interview. Maybe if they are successful I will see them again. But she didn't like to ask Dr Schultz when she came back again to say there was a cab waiting for them.

'It will take about an hour to get there,' the doctor said, walking briskly to the door. 'We'll take a tour of the hospital wards and I'll show you the lecture room and the theatre if it isn't occupied, just to give you an idea of the layout of the hospital and introduce you to some of the medical staff.'

'H-how many other students will be there?' Lucy asked hesitantly.

'Of those starting in October only six, that is if the next two interviewees come up to standard. This will be a preliminary induction only to find out how you shape up.'

'I'm rather nervous,' Lucy told her.

'I would expect you to be,' Dr Schultz said. 'This is a very big and important step you are taking.'

Dr Schultz introduced her to Dr Rose Mason who was waiting for them by the hansom cab and the three of them squashed into the vehicle to make the journey to Hampstead and the hospital.

'Do you know this part of London, Miss Thornbury?' Dr Mason asked her.

'No, I don't know London very well at all,' Lucy answered. 'It seems very exciting to me, bustling with traffic and people, much busier than Hull.'

'I remember your mother,' Dr Mason said. 'She was from the south of England as I was; I recall teasing her when she said she was leaving London for the north.' Then she fell silent and glanced at Dr Schultz, who was giving a little shake of her head.

Lucy was taken aback. 'I – was she?' Why did I assume she was from Hull? Uncle William has often talked of when he and my father were young, although he did once say that he hadn't known Mama's parents; if they were not from Hull that must have been why. 'I thought my mother was from Hull, as my father was.'

She briefly thought of Aunt Nora; when she was a child she had once asked her why she said 'Go with Ada for your *barth*' instead of bath, and she and Uncle William had both laughed.

'Berkshire,' Dr Mason said quietly. 'I'm so sorry. I thought you would have known.'

'No,' Lucy said softly. 'I know very little about her. I wish I knew more.'

142

Dr Mason again glanced at Dr Schultz and then murmured, 'Perhaps when you are settled in we might have a chat about her.'

'I'd like that,' Lucy began, but was interrupted by Dr Schultz who said something about students having little time for chatting. Lucy said no more, but privately she was determined that she would at some time in the future approach Dr Mason and ask her to tell her all she knew about her mother.

At the hospital she was given a white cap and gown to wear and led to a washroom where they all soaped and washed their hands. Lucy looked at herself in the mirror and thought she looked more like a nurse than a doctor; neither Dr Schultz nor Dr Mason wore any additional garment over their plain dresses.

Lucy was taken on a tour of the wards with another young woman, Leila Stockton, who was also to undertake medical training. She said, indifferently, that she was familiar with hospital wards as her father was a doctor. Lucy spoke to some of the female patients – those who were well enough to sit up in bed – and said she hoped they were making a good recovery. Leila Stockton didn't speak to any of them but picked up their notes and looked over them, much to the disapproval of Dr Schultz, who removed them from her, saying that they were private and for medical eyes only. The surgical theatre was occupied and so they were not allowed to enter.

They were shown the room where patient files were kept, the hospital laundry and a room where medication was under lock and key; they saw a large room with wooden chairs and a long table which was where they would attend lectures or study, and then they were taken to the nurses' rest room where a young nursing student offered them a cup of tea. Lucy thanked her but refused as she had seen how busy the nurses were as they flitted from patient to patient, and she then thought of Edie and determined to visit her as soon as she got home to find out if she had got any further with her thoughts on nursing.

Lucy was fired up with enthusiasm. She felt that she couldn't wait to start her professional training for a career which she knew would be long in coming and extremely difficult to attain, no matter how determined she was to achieve her goal; but, she thought decisively, I *will* attain it.

CHAPTER TWENTY-ONE

When Lucy stepped down from the train at Paragon station she was surprised to find Oswald waiting to greet her. He picked her up and swung her round which seemed to be becoming his usual form of greeting.

'How did you know which train I would be on?' she asked. 'I didn't give a time in my telegram.'

'I know,' he said, picking up her bag and ushering her towards the exit. 'I've met every train in since midday. I worked out that it couldn't possibly be before lunch and more likely teatime or later.' He put an arm round her shoulder. 'We're all so excited and thrilled for you, Lucy. Pa is cock o' hoop; he says you're fulfilling your parents' dreams.'

'Really?' She smiled. 'I'm so happy, even though I know it's going to be very hard, but I don't mind that. And I realize it will take years and years; it's still very difficult for women, you know – I don't mean the work is more difficult than it is for men, but there are many male doctors who don't want women in the profession. Isn't that just so ridiculous!'

She chatted on, wanting to describe all she had done and seen, the doctors she had met, the hospital visit, the suffragette women who had congregated on King's Cross station both going and coming back, and particularly to tell him that she had met someone else who had known her mother.

'I find it so strange that I didn't know that my mother was training to be a doctor,' she said, a frown wrinkling her brow.

'Do you think that Uncle William knew? He said he didn't meet her in the early days, but surely my father would have told him about his wife-to-be?'

Oswald didn't answer, but pressed his lips together; they dodged the traffic and crossed Prospect Street into Baker Street. Then he murmured, 'I think it's as well not to enquire too far into our family's history, Lucy; certainly *my* mother wouldn't thank me for enquiring into hers.'

Lucy turned to look at him. 'But surely you want to know about your father's profession? Perhaps even follow in his footsteps?'

He looked down at her quizzically. 'No, I do not! My father's life has no bearing whatsoever on what I do with mine. I don't remember him and my mother was always reluctant to talk about him. Your uncle – *Pa* – is the only man who has had any influence on my life and upbringing and I shall be eternally grateful to him. It's not only about blood relationship and kin, Lucy; it's about those who have taken care of us. They are the ones who have formed us, who have made us what we are.'

She nodded. He had mirrored her thoughts exactly.

William was home early from the bank and both he and Nora were waiting for them with Eleanor, wreathed in smiles and uttering congratulations.

'We are so proud,' William said. 'So very proud of you,' whilst Nora said that she had never visited a woman doctor but that she was going to try Dr Mary Murdoch if ever anyone became ill, at least until Lucy qualified.

Lucy laughed and said it would be a long wait until then. 'Years and years,' she said, just as she'd said to Oswald.

'We're going to host a dinner for you,' Nora told her. 'Not tonight, as we thought you might be tired, and besides we want to have you to ourselves to talk about your news, but we thought you might like to invite Dr and Mrs Warrington. He was very helpful, wasn't he? And perhaps Edie? And maybe that very polite cousin of hers, Max, was it? The grocer's son.'

William cleared his throat. 'It's a nice idea, my dear, but Lucy should choose whom she should invite as her guests.'

'Oh yes, of course,' Nora said, flustered. 'I was only suggesting—'

'It's so kind of you to think of that, Aunt Nora,' Lucy said, 'but actually I'd rather make it a birthday party and just invite Edie and any of her brothers who are at home and all of you.' She put her hand to her mouth, suddenly overcome with emotion. 'You are all so special to me. But I'll write to Dr Warrington and to Dr Murdoch tomorrow and thank them for their support and consideration.'

She told them that Dr Murdoch had written to the examiners and told them about their meeting, 'and she gave me a good character reference. Wasn't that kind of her?'

Later, when the four of them were sitting quietly by the fire-side after Eleanor had gone to bed, Lucy said, 'Uncle William, whilst I was in London I met another woman doctor who knew my mother. She recognized the name. Do you know why she gave up her medical training? Was it because she wanted to marry my father?'

Nora got up from her chair. 'Excuse me for a moment,' she said. 'I must just have a word with Ada.'

'Will you excuse me too?' Oswald said, unfolding his long legs from the sofa. 'I've just remembered I have a letter to write.'

Lucy and her uncle looked up at them as they left and then looked at each other. Lucy laughed. 'Was it something I said?'

'As a matter of fact I think it might have been.' William carefully and neatly folded up the newspaper he'd been holding. 'They are being diplomatic.'

'But why?' she asked. 'It was a straightforward question.'

'But there's not a straightforward answer.' William stretched out his legs and sighed. 'Your aunt is aware of a little about your parents, though not in great detail, and I told her that I proposed to discuss the matter with you when you arrived home.' He smiled. 'Oswald is a very discerning young man and I suspect took the prompt from his mother, for he hasn't been told anything. I conjectured when you went to your first interview that you might meet someone who remembered your mother, but I didn't know her during her time there.

147

In fact, I didn't meet her until your parents' wedding day.'

'Ah,' she said. 'So it *was* because of my father that she abandoned her career.'

He hesitated. 'In a way. It was then and I understand still is impossible for a woman to continue medical training if she gets married, although I imagine that after they qualify there is nothing to stop them from marrying whenever they like.'

'So why didn't they wait?' Lucy said. 'They would both have had wonderful professions in front of them, although of course . . .' She fell silent and gazed into the distance. 'It is strange, isn't it, when you think about it, how life sometimes steers you in a different direction.' She caught her breath. 'They wouldn't have been on that train and I wouldn't have been there either.'

'No,' he said quietly. 'They wouldn't, and you and I wouldn't be having this conversation.'

Lucy brought her gaze back to her uncle and found him looking tenderly at her.

'I wouldn't have had the pleasure of seeing you grow up and becoming like a daughter to me, a daughter loved just as much as my own Eleanor. But there is more, Lucy,' he went on, 'and now as you plan your new life it is perhaps time for an explanation.'

She waited as he appeared to prepare his thoughts before he slowly began.

'As I understand it, because as I said before I didn't know her then, your mother was a brilliant student, much more so than your father or any of the other young women trainees, and great things were expected of her in spite of her being so young, younger even than you are now, Lucy. Her father had taught her – she was an only child – and she was reading the classics, ahead of most adults in mathematics, and fluent in several languages including French and German when she was only twelve.

'Her father was apparently determined that she would succeed in mathematics and science and become the most educated woman in England and beyond, but she was very determined to plough her own furrow, so to speak, and said she wanted to study medicine. It was a very expensive profession to get into but finally her father agreed and she passed all the necessary exams without any trouble at all when she was just seventeen.'

'Goodness!' Lucy breathed. 'How incredible.'

William nodded and continued. 'She began her tutelage under Dr Elizabeth Garrett Anderson.'

'Oh,' Lucy breathed again. 'Her daughter Louisa . . .'

'Yes, the same,' he said. 'Both inspiring women. I understand that your mother was expected to succeed on all fronts, notwithstanding the difficulties that women had to endure.' He hesitated. 'And then at some time in her second year, I think it was, she met your father.'

'And fell in love!' Lucy murmured.

'Indeed.'

'And they didn't want to wait? She gave it all up for the love of my father?'

He gazed at her. 'She gave it up for you, Lucy,' he said quietly. 'They were impetuous young people, not thinking of the consequences, but only of their love and desire.'

Lucy stared at her uncle, lost for words. Then her cheeks flushed as she whispered, 'For me? You mean . . .'

He nodded again. 'Your father was lucky not to lose his place at King's, but he had by then passed his exams with excellent results and needed only to finish his final hospital training before qualifying and no one, not his fellow students nor his tutors, breathed a word, even though some of them must have known.'

'But not so for Mama,' she murmured. 'Everyone would have found out that she was carrying a child. I see; so she had to give up her ambition, her dream.'

'Impossible to conceal, but she had to give it up in any case,' he said. 'As soon as her parents heard she was banned from their presence and her home, as if in some early Victorian melodrama.' His voice was sharp and angry. 'Her father cut her off without a penny, only the clothes on her back, and she never saw them again. To my knowledge they never enquired about her or the child, their grandchild. I tried to contact them after the accident, but there was no response.'

'And what of Papa? What did he do?'

'He brought her home to our parents; they had a house on the Beverley Road, and they somehow understood, although of course they were shocked and disappointed. They packed Joseph off to London again and Alice stayed with them until the marriage was arranged. Which was when I came home to be your father's witness and met your mother for the first time.'

He took a deep breath and then exhaled as if he had been holding it and all his emotions inside for many a year. Then he smiled. 'They made a very handsome couple. Your mother was beautiful, Lucy – you are very much like her – and they were very happy together, even though for only a few short years.'

'She must have had some regrets,' Lucy said sorrowfully. 'To give everything up.'

'Perhaps, but I never saw any trace of it,' he said. 'They had you, their love child, and adored you; her dreams must have changed.'

Lucy fought back tears. 'I must fulfil her hopes and vision.' Her voice trembled. 'I will try to make her sacrifice worthwhile.'

CHAPTER TWENTY-TWO

Lucy called at the grocery shop to talk to Edie the next morning, but a rather surly Jenny broke off from stacking the shelves to tell her that she had left.

'Max is here if you want to talk to him?' she added as an afterthought.

'It's all right,' Lucy said. 'I'll drop in to see Edie at home.'

Max came out of the back room when he heard voices. 'Edie's not working here any more,' he said, as Jenny had. 'She wasn't pulling her weight, asked for time off and wouldn't say why, so she had to go.'

'Really? Good gracious,' Lucy protested. 'After all the years she's worked here you mean to say she couldn't ask for any time off?'

He shook his head. 'If it had been an hour or so and she'd said why, then I might have done. But she wanted two days and wouldn't say where she was going so I had to make a decision.' His cheeks flushed as he spoke and Lucy guessed that he realized he'd acted hastily.

She shrugged. 'Oh, well, she'll get another job easily enough I expect, an energetic young woman with her experience.'

'Not without a reference she won't,' he said caustically.

She gazed at him witheringly but didn't answer and simply turned on her heel and left the shop.

What a nerve! She marched away in the direction of Edie's home. No wonder women are joining the suffragettes. Would he have done that to a man? Just dismissed him without a reference? Her former admiration of Max was lessening, such was her fury at his behaviour. She rapped on Mrs Morris's door, still feeling cross, and was surprised when Edie opened the door with a huge smile on her face.

'Oh, just 'person I was hoping to see,' Edie exclaimed. 'Come in. Come in.'

Dolly Morris's rooms were very cosy and welcoming, even though the furniture was shabby and worn and the place was now filled to overflowing with people. Lucy exclaimed when she saw two soldiers, Josh and Stanley, and young Charlie, who was now of course no longer a child but a strapping boy of about sixteen. Their mother was sitting contentedly by a low fire.

'Cup o' tea?' Edie asked. 'I'm just about to mek a pot.'

'Yes, please.' Lucy took the chair vacated by Charlie. All three of the young men had got up from their seats when she came into the house. 'How good it is to see you all together,' she said. 'It's such a long time since we all met.'

'We don't get home as often as we'd like,' Stanley told her. 'We're allus off somewhere or other.'

Lucy thought how handsome the two older boys were, very much alike with their dark hair and eyes; Stanley was quieter and more serious than Josh, who was always fooling around. Charlie was fair-haired and blue-eyed like Edie and not quite as sure of himself as his brothers.

'How long are you on leave?' she asked. 'Because it's my birthday next week and I'd like you all to come to lunch.'

'We've got till next weekend,' Josh said. He turned to Stanley. 'That would be good, wouldn't it? Is Oswald at home?' He and Oswald had kept in touch from time to time.

She told him that he was and then Charlie said, 'I can't come, Miss Lucy. I'm working on 'railway as a porter and I'm on shifts. I've tekken on our Bob's job. He's going to be an engine driver.'

'Is he?' Lucy was delighted. 'I didn't know.'

'He's onny just heard,' Dolly said. 'He wanted a better job now that he's wed. We're that proud.' She beamed, then added

152

quickly, 'Of all of 'em. But I'll let our Edie tell you her bit o' news.'

'I went to the shop,' Lucy said, taking the cup of tea from Edie. 'I saw Max and he said . . .' She hesitated, wondering if Edie had told her mother.

'He told you he'd sacked me, did he?' Edie interrupted. 'He was peeved cos I wouldn't tell him why I wanted 'time off.'

'I'll have summat to say when I see him,' her mother said grimly. 'It was nowt to do wi' him why she wanted time off. He'll not find a better worker than our Edie; not that she'll need him now.' Then her face broke into a grin. 'Go on, tell her,' she said. 'Tell Miss Lucy what you're going to do.'

Edie couldn't hold back her wide grin. 'Lucy knows what I was planning. We had a discussion about our futures, didn't we, Lucy?'

Lucy nodded. She almost knew what was coming next. 'Don't keep me in suspense, Edie.'

'I went to see Dr Murdoch like you suggested, and she said I was just 'right calibre of woman they wanted as nurses. She gave me a reference and I'm to go for an interview at 'London Hospital to be considered for training.' Edie gave out the information on one long breath. 'Week after next.'

'And if ever we're injured and our Edie's in a military hospital we'll run or stagger to another one,' Josh grinned. 'We know what she's like for bandaging scabby knees.'

'Oh, that's marvellous!' Lucy resolved not to tell Edie her own news just yet as she didn't want to take the shine away from her.

'But I'll need to find a job, just to tide me over for 'time being, you know,' Edie said.

'We'll manage,' her mother interrupted. 'Don't go worrying about that.'

Stanley broke in. 'We'll all chip in to help, Edie. Like Ma says, we'll manage. Don't worry.'

'I know who'll have you,' Lucy said. 'Annie at the café. She told me that she wished you worked for her.'

'Did she?' Edie's face brightened. 'What time is it? I'll go straight away and see her. But first,' she paused and held up both her hands, 'first we want to know what Miss Lucy Thornbury has been up to.'

Lucy took a sip from the cup. 'Oh, you know, this and that,' and looked down into her lap, then lifted her eyes to Edie.

'Come on then,' Edie pleaded. 'I can't be 'onny one wi' a story to tell. Let's be hearing what you've been up to for 'last few days.'

Lucy lifted her head and glanced from one to the other. 'I've been to London,' she said quietly. 'I got back yesterday. I'm going to begin training too.' She could feel laughter and joy bubbling up inside her. 'As a medical student. I'm going to be a doctor.'

Lucy and Aunt Nora agreed that Lucy should have her birthday luncheon on the actual day, 10 August, so that Stanley and Joshua could come before leaving to go back to their regiment at the weekend.

They decided that roast pork and a joint of beef, with apple sauce and horseradish relish as accompaniments, would satisfy the appetites of three young men, and even though the weather was warm and sunny they would also have Yorkshire pudding, roast potatoes and various vegetables, with apple pie and custard and a syllabub for dessert.

Uncle William took the day off and gave permission for Oswald to do the same, except that he must make up the time in the following week. William expected and received full commitment from Oswald whilst he was working at the bank.

Before the day came, Lucy asked her aunt and uncle if she might be able to help Edie financially if she should be accepted for nursing training. She knew that Edie's family had little money and she hated to think that her friend would be barred from doing something she wanted to do because of lack of funds. 'Can I afford to?' she asked anxiously and was relieved when her uncle gave her a gentle nod and said he would arrange it for her.

They hatched a plan between them. Nora suggested that

she herself should approach Edie's mother and intimate that William's bank would be willing to advance a low interest loan towards Edie's expenses. She believed that a woman to woman discussion would satisfy Mrs Morris, but she wouldn't tell her that the funding of the loan would come from Lucy's bank account.

'And Edie won't find out?' Lucy asked anxiously. 'Because I know she wouldn't like it. She's very independent.'

'Leave it to me,' Nora said, relishing a little intrigue. 'I'll speak to Mrs Morris and we'll arrange it between us. She might well suspect something but she won't say. She's a woman who wants the best for her children. As we all do,' she added.

For the birthday luncheon Josh and Stanley were both in uniform and each was bearing a gift. Josh brought Lucy a posy of flowers and Stanley came with a box of Turkish Delight.

'I didn't expect presents,' she exclaimed. 'Your company was what I was really looking forward to.'

'You don't want this box of bon-bons then?' Edie clutched them to her chest. 'Good, cos they're my favourite.'

Lucy laughed. 'I'll force myself to eat them.'

Eleanor, dressed in her prettiest dress, had embroidered her some dainty handkerchiefs and Oswald had already given her his gift in the morning: a leather-bound anthology of Lord Byron's and Wordsworth's poetry with tooled bookmarks in two pages that he said marked his own special favourites. When she read the two chosen poems, she smiled and murmured, 'I hadn't thought of you as a Romantic, Oswald. I am seeing another side of you.' When he laughed, she wondered if he had fallen in love with someone, as each poem described a dark-haired beauty.

They sat down to eat. Ada carried in the plates of pork and beef for William to carve and gave a wink and a grin to her brothers and sister sitting as honoured guests at her employer's table. When Cook had brought in the Yorkshire pudding and vegetables and returned to the kitchen, William asked Ada to stay and have a glass of wine with them.

'You've known Lucy for many years, Ada,' he said. 'We would very much like you to.'

And although Ada wasn't a young woman accustomed to blushing, she did so now as she thanked him and wished Lucy a happy birthday.

'I was thinking that it would have been nice to have invited Elizabeth and Henry Warrington,' Lucy murmured. 'We all met here as children on another birthday. It was remiss of me not to think of it.'

'I was thinking it would have been nice too,' Oswald agreed. 'Although I didn't really take to either of them at the time. I'm sure they were all right, but I was a self-righteous killjoy back then!'

'You were,' Lucy, laughing, agreed. 'You wouldn't play games with anybody.'

'I heard only yesterday that Elizabeth's engagement to be married is about to be announced,' Nora told them, 'and Henry has gone abroad with his regiment, so they wouldn't have been able to come.'

'Oh, I've missed my chance with Miss Warrington then,' Josh said mournfully, 'and I can't fight Henry as I once wanted to as he's my superior officer!'

'Do you remember when Edie said her name was royal,' Oswald reminded them, 'and Elizabeth and Henry both said theirs were too, and I was really mad because I thought that mine wasn't?'

Lucy shook her head. She couldn't recall it at all, but both Edie and Joshua said they did, and Oswald went on, 'Then later when I started at Pocklington school I discovered King Oswald of Northumbria and I desperately wanted to tell Henry that my royal name was much older than his.'

They all laughed, and then William stood up to make a toast. 'As this is my niece's special day and in the autumn she will be leaving us to begin a professional career, I would like to wish her health and happiness throughout the rest of her life, wherever it takes her.' He paused. 'And I would like to link that toast to all of you young people on the threshold of your lives.

May you be kept safe and free from harm wherever life and circumstances take you. I wish you good health and strength in the years to come, and that you always have love in your lives.'

Lucy found it hard to swallow as she looked at her uncle and then round the table at her good friends as they all raised their glasses. Her eyes caught Oswald's; he was gazing at her with a smile on his lips and in his soft grey eyes. They had all been laughing and jesting and making merry, but now, to Lucy, the scene seemed to still, caught in an ethereal bubble of portentous significance as if all their destinies were entwined together in a haunting and prophetic moment of a lifetime.

PART TWO

CHAPTER TWENTY-THREE

1914

By the beginning of 1914 Lucy was firmly and resolutely entrenched in her medical studies. It had been much harder than she had foreseen, even though she had accepted right from the first that the work would be difficult and perhaps even incomprehensible at times. There were occasions when she had doubted her own intellect or capacity for understanding, and she remarked to Oswald on one of their rare meetings that it must be like learning a new language, Chinese, Japanese or Arabic perhaps, where none of the sounds or symbols made any sense to our Western ears.

She had also been cajoled into attending some of the suffragette meetings with Dr Schultz, who was a keen supporter; and after seeing photographs in the newspapers of women chained to railings in their attempt to bring the discrimination to public notice, and quite by chance when out in the streets one day, witnessing the horrific spectacle of women being roughly hauled off into police vans, she was convinced that the activists had justice on their side. She had been told of the cruel and degrading forced feeding when the prisoners went on hunger strikes, and of the poor conditions they were subjected to in Holloway and other women's prisons.

She was annoyed and infuriated that women had to be so vocal to justify their claim to what should be theirs by right, but in spite of her empathy for them she did not join the cause, being intent on continuing with her vocation and considering that in doing so she too was proving her worth as a woman.

On several occasions she had been sharply informed by intelligent young men who she considered should have known better that she ought to be at home tending a husband and children, or at most, if she was hell bent on a medical career, should become a midwife, which they claimed was a right and proper role for a woman. She was furious and told them that she would do whatever she considered was important and didn't need to take advice from an immature and uninformed sub-species, which had startled and silenced them. This made her even more sympathetic to the suffragettes' cause, but nevertheless she felt that without becoming an agitator she could fight back for what she believed in by continuing her medical studies and becoming a doctor to battle in her own way against all physical and humanitarian ills.

She had become even more positive when in the June of 1913, to draw attention to the suffragettes' purpose, Emily Davison had thrown herself in front of the king's horse at the Derby. Such a waste, Lucy had thought when she read of her death in the newspapers. I doubt that it will change the minds of any of those who regard women as second class citizens.

While Lucy was studying at the all-female Hampstead hospital, she could concentrate wholly on her training without disturbance, but on several occasions she had been sent to other London hospitals to observe their procedures in comparison with those at the Royal Free. She was not made welcome, was totally ignored by the senior male surgeons and not invited to watch theatre surgery. When questions were invited from the students, hers were not answered even though they were valid points.

In one hospital she was unaccountably befriended by a young male student who asked if he might sit at her table when she had gone, dejected, for a lunch break. He was handsome and knew it and very friendly, and after chatting for a while almost caught her out by asking her if the studying was very difficult for her.

162

'You must find it very challenging,' he said sympathetically. 'Not what you expected?' He reached for her hand and murmured, 'Though I imagine you have a lovely bedside manner!'

She had snatched her hand away, offended by his suggestive remark, and retorted, 'Do not patronize me. I find the study no more challenging than you do; the most demanding part of my training is dealing with schoolboys such as you. Now kindly leave my table before I report you for troubling me.'

As he left she saw a group of other male students watching, and by their faces knew he had been dared to come over. She had wondered afterwards if she had been sent to these hospitals deliberately by her female senior tutors to assess her ability to cope with such provoking and confrontational demands.

Oswald was in his final year of a master's degree and had set his mind to working in medical research. He had become increasingly interested in biology and natural sciences as his course progressed, particularly in the field of medicine, and he had explained to Lucy and his parents that the interest had begun from the time he had casually picked up a medical magazine whilst waiting for Lucy at her first interview at the Gray's Inn hospital. Lucy had been thrilled at his choice of chosen subjects as it meant that there was always someone who understood exactly what she was doing.

He was already making plans for a possible career and had applied to Burroughs Wellcome & Company to work as a research scientist in their London pharmaceutical laboratories. He received a personal letter from the head of research to say he would look forward to granting Oswald an interview once he had heard the results of his master's degree.

'You're bound to succeed,' Lucy told him, having great faith in his superior ability and knowledge. 'I don't know of anyone quite as clever as you.'

Lucy and Edie managed to meet up on occasions as Edie was in London too and making great strides in her training; 'like a duck to water,' her mother had told Nora when they had chanced to meet one day. 'I can't tell you how proud I am of her, and in some part, ma'am, it's down to you and Mr Thornbury

163

for your encouragement when she was just a bairn and giving her that grounding in edication wi' Miss Lucy.'

Nora had shaken her head. 'We can't take any credit,' she said. 'Edie's a natural. She would have succeeded without us.'

Unlike Lucy, Edie was almost ready to begin hospital work; she had completed a probationary period and was expecting to start as a nurse in a few months' time.

'I had thought I'd go back to Hull,' she told Lucy. 'Mebbe work in 'children's hospital, and perhaps I will one day, but I love it here at St Thomas's. God bless Florence Nightingale,' she added, 'and Dr Mary Murdoch. I'll allus remember them in my prayers, but I love having my independence here in London and I can live in at 'nurses' home and still send money back to my ma even though we've paid off 'loan.' She was still the caring thoughtful daughter she had always been, and had no idea that the bank loan had come from Lucy.

Unlike Lucy's, Edie's coming of age had been and gone without any fuss or acknowledgement, whereas when Lucy came of age this year she would be independent of her uncle and able to claim her inheritance. During the New Year holidays, William had taken her to one side to ask what she would like to happen once August arrived.

'Aunt Nora and I have been looking at properties in preparation for this,' he said. 'You may have plans for what you'd like to do with the house, either live in it when you have finished your studies or rent it out; either way it will be your choice.'

Lucy had looked at him blankly as if she didn't understand, and then her eyes had filled with tears. 'Do you mean that you'll be leaving? Am I to live alone?'

'It's your property, my dear,' he said gently. 'Your inheritance to do with as you wish. Come August you will have full control over your life and income without referring to me.'

'B-but,' she stammered, 'is that what you want? This has been your home too. Do you really want to leave and live somewhere else – without me?'

He took hold of her hand. 'Lucy,' he said gently, 'I told you many years ago that you were like a daughter to me and nothing has changed; I am still of that same mind. But it is your house and as such the decision is yours. No, we do not want to leave, in fact it will break our hearts, mine and your aunt's and Eleanor's too I should think, although we haven't told her yet. This has been our home and we have been happy here, in spite of the tragic circumstances that brought us to Hull.'

'Then *please* stay,' she implored him. 'I don't want you to leave. I want to know that you'll be here whenever I come home; why would I want to come back to an empty house?'

An image from many years before of returning and finding her parents were not there emerged from the shadowy recesses of her memory, and she knew that she didn't ever want to know a time like that again.

'All right.' He took a breath as if a great weight had been lifted from his shoulders. 'But maybe one day, after you are qualified, you might choose to use the house as a surgery or perhaps marry and raise a family here. We are living in difficult times. Who knows what is in store for any of us?'

'That's so far into the future, Uncle William,' she laughed and wiped her face of tears, 'that I can't think so far ahead.'

William patted her shoulder and murmured something comforting and she knew that, as always, he had been thinking of her. His consideration of her feelings and desires had always been resolute, as steadfast as those for his own daughter and Oswald. She thought how lucky she had been.

But although William was pleased to know that they would be staying in Baker Street, he suggested to Nora that perhaps they should buy a small house as an investment, with a view to his retirement. 'It's still difficult for women doctors,' he said, 'and although at the moment Lucy has no money worries, who knows what the future holds. If we purchase a house for ourselves we can rent it out for an income until such time as we might need it. After all, one day there will be just the two of us if Eleanor should marry.' He sighed and murmured that their family was growing up far too fast.

Nora pointed out practically that Eleanor was a long way

from being of an age to marry as she was not yet fifteen, and Lucy would not marry until after she had qualified. 'She's wholeheartedly committed to becoming a doctor,' she said, but she agreed with him that it was a good idea that they should look for a house of their own. There was no hurry to purchase, but they kept a keen eye on the properties for sale, including one in Pearson Park which overlooked the delightful gardens and lake.

William, however, also had other matters on his mind. As a man who always kept abreast of what was happening in the British business world and of European events too, he was not happy about what was going on politically in many countries abroad. Of particular concern was the unrest in the various alliances that had sprung up over many decades as great nations sought to expand their territories. Britain and Germany had begun a fevered arms race to build more ships and become the supreme naval power, and Britain, to protect itself, allied with Russia and France in opposition to the triple union of the German, Austro-Hungarian and Italian treaty, an association which had begun to unravel when Italy signed a secret treaty with France.

'It's not looking healthy,' William had debated with his fellows at his club. 'I don't like the look of it at all. It only needs a spark from some hot-headed imperialist or nationalist, you can take your pick which one, and conflagration will occur across the whole of the European continent and we'll be drawn in too.'

Some of the more prosaic gentlemen disagreed and remarked to one another that he was a brooding pessimist, saying that if other countries wanted to fight then let them but that Britain needn't; others, more rational and far-seeing, agreed with William that Britain would inevitably be drawn into a European conflict.

'Why are we building so many ships if it's not to prepare ourselves?' one of the men asked during a heated debate. 'We are an island nation and in a vulnerable position, ripe for attack on our shores. We should prepare for every eventuality.'

'Nonsense,' barked another. 'The Balkan question has been

settled; the only worries we have now are with the damned Scots and Irish, and the unions,' he added tetchily, 'and those hysterical suffragette women who deserve a damned whipping if you ask me.'

Nobody did ask him, however, and the meeting broke up leaving many disgruntled but many more anxious for the future, including William, who had set the ball rolling in the debate.

Both Lucy and Oswald were home for the weekend of 27 and 28 June. The weather was glorious and the four of them – for Eleanor was still away at school – took a walk in Pearson Park on the Sunday. William and Nora showed Lucy and Oswald the house they were thinking of buying for William's eventual retirement, as he explained it to Lucy, who glanced sideways at her uncle and shook her head at the mere thought of it.

'But it does look very nice,' she agreed. 'And how lovely to have the lake and the grass and flower beds right there in front of your window.'

'And no work to do in it,' Oswald remarked. 'No digging or grass cutting. The park gardener will do it for you.'

'Exactly!' William said, whilst Nora said she wouldn't mind planting a few bulbs and shrubs in the small front garden.

'You should buy it, then, Uncle, if you really like it,' Lucy said. 'Aunt Nora likes it, don't you?'

'I do,' Nora said, 'but we're looking to the future, not for now.'

'Hmm,' William murmured. 'Whatever the future brings.'

Lucy and Oswald were to take the same train to Leeds on the Monday morning for the first part of their journey, before continuing on their separate journeys. Oswald dashed away to buy a newspaper from the seller who was standing outside the Paragon concourse shouting hoarsely, 'Read all about it! Archduke assassinated!' whilst around him many men were clustered, all speaking animatedly.

'What's happening?' Lucy asked when he came back reading

167

the front page of his paper. 'Why are there so many people buying the newspapers?'

Oswald didn't answer for a minute; then he looked up, opened his mouth and took a breath. He took her elbow and said, 'Something momentous has happened. Come on, or we'll miss the train. We'll read it once we're aboard.'

The train was packed with passengers, mainly men in their business suits and top hats or bowlers, but many women too; Lucy and Oswald managed to obtain seats together. Many of the men were carrying newspapers and mutterings and exclamations were being exchanged. Those without a newspaper were leaning over the shoulders of those who had.

'*The heir to the throne of Austria-Hungary, Archduke Franz Ferdinand, and his wife Sophie have been killed during a visit to the Bosnian city of Sarajevo,*' Oswald read out in a low voice. '*The assassin, who was immediately captured and arrested, was Bosnian-Serb patriot Gavrilo Princip, aged nineteen.* That's his life over and done with, and who knows what can of worms has been opened?'

'Why were they killed?' Lucy asked. 'Why were they in Sarajevo anyway?'

'He was meant to be inspecting the troops, so it says,' he murmured, reading on. 'The country is annexed to the Austrian empire, yet both Bosnia and Serbia want to form their own Balkan state. It's a troubled state of affairs that has been simmering for years.' He turned to her. 'If Austria retaliates over this atrocity and Germany goes to their assistance, the whole thing will escalate; Serbia will call on Russia for help and before we realize it . . .'

Lucy frowned. 'We'll be at war,' she murmured. 'We'll be totally involved.'

Oswald took off his spectacles and rubbed his eyes before answering. 'I rather think so,' he said softly. 'If Germany joins forces with Austria, France will retaliate.' They looked at one another and both nodded in total agreement. 'And unless a solution is agreed on we'll be duty bound to support them.'

CHAPTER TWENTY-FOUR

William, not a man who normally used obscenities, never-theless swore beneath his breath, as exactly a month after the assassinations he read in the following day's *Telegraph* that the Austria-Hungary alliance had declared war on Serbia.

'It's going to be all-out war, mark my words,' he told Nora and Eleanor at breakfast. 'We'll all be involved sooner or later.'

'Papa?' Eleanor spoke across the table. 'If there's a war I won't have to leave school, will I? I really want to stay on and finish my art studies.'

Eleanor was developing into an accomplished artist, designer and seamstress and had said she would like to continue with art as a career. She was turning out to be a positive young woman.

Nora paused with a coffee cup in her hand. 'Surely we won't be affected?' she objected. 'It's nothing to do with us.'

'I'm afraid that it will be, my dear,' William told her. 'If France and our other allies become involved, which to me seems in–evitable, then so will we be, together with our colonies. I've seen this coming for some time now. Why didn't our men in power see it?' He gave a cynical grimace and muttered, 'Maybe they did. But no,' he added directly to Eleanor, 'of course you won't have to leave school.' He smiled. 'We want you to achieve success as much as you do.'

A few days later Lucy wrote to say she'd decided not to celebrate her birthday. *It doesn't seem appropriate, having heard the latest news*, she wrote. *My birthday falls on a Monday so if I can*

*get home for the Friday prior to that, I'll travel back to London on the
Sunday. Could we just have a small tea for the family and perhaps
Eleanor and I can once more share our birthdays?*

Eleanor was delighted with the idea; she adored Lucy and
regarded her more as a sister than a cousin.

Rather reluctantly, William and Nora agreed, but it turned out
to be fitting, as in less than a week Germany and the Ottoman
Empire had formed an alliance and a British naval vessel was
sunk by German mines in the North Sea; Germany declared
war on France and invaded Britain's ally Belgium, taking the
city of Liège, and leaving Britain no option but to declare war
with Germany. The Austrian army invaded Poland and on the
Eastern Front the Russian army began to advance.

The speed of events left everyone breathless. Within days they
heard that hundreds of troops were arriving on the east coast
and being billeted in the villages of Kilnsea and Easington, east
of Hull, with the sole purpose of protecting the Spurn Point
headland from attack by sea, whilst the small market town of
Hedon became a garrison town for men and horses.

'I'm very worried,' Nora told her friend and confidante Sarah
Walker. 'I'm afraid for my son; will he have to join the military?
He's a scientist, not a soldier!'

'I shouldn't think so for a moment,' Mrs Walker replied,
patting her arm. 'Don't worry about it. I read in the newspaper
that it's a flash in the pan, a lot of hotheads talking about war,
and that it will all be resolved by Christmas.'

William shook his head when Nora told him this. 'She's
mistaken. It's happening,' he told his wife in a voice devoid of
emotion as he read the headlines. He looked up. 'I didn't tell
you before, but I cut down Bond Street on my way home from
the bank the other evening. A troop of East Yorkshire Cavalry
were waiting on horseback outside Kayes' tool shop. I stopped
to enquire why they were there.' He took a short sharp breath.
'One of the men said they were waiting to have their bayonets
and swords sharpened.'

Nora put her hands to her mouth and waited for him to
continue.

170

'They were all in a very cheerful mood. The soldier who was speaking to me said they couldn't wait to go and fight the Hun, and as soon as the sharpening was finished they were heading off down to the docks to board a ship to take them on their way to Flanders. God help them,' he muttered. 'The tentacles of war are spreading wider and wider. I might be considered to be a purveyor of gloom' – he shook his head – 'but believe me, the world is well and truly at war.'

Oswald had come home to Hull to celebrate Lucy's and Eleanor's birthdays. He brought Eleanor a box of pastels, which thrilled her, and for Lucy a posy of silk flowers. 'They'll never die,' he told her. 'The colours might fade but the petals will never fall.' He'd kissed her cheek as he said it and she felt moved to tears.

'You're an independent young woman now,' her uncle said, and symbolically handed her a key. 'You can do whatever you've a mind to without asking permission; providing it's legal,' he added jovially.

'I know,' she said solemnly, 'but I don't ever remember being restricted before in whatever I wanted to do. I've been guided so kindly and well, and I thank you for that, both of you.' She included Nora in her little speech. 'I've been blessed.'

She took the time to visit Edie's mother whilst she was home and found her beset by worries over her sons; both Stanley and Joshua were already abroad with their regiment. Stanley had gone to Serbia, but she didn't know where Josh was. Charlie badly wanted to join up too, but both his parents were doing their best to persuade him to stay with the railway company and train as an engine driver like his brother Bob.

'I wish our Edie would come home,' Dolly said, wiping her eyes as they filled with tears. 'She could get a job at 'Infirmary easy as can be. She's done so well with all her exams. I don't want her to be away wi' all what's going on. I can do nowt about my lads, but I don't want our Edie to be away as well.'

'You've still got Ada here,' Lucy said gently. 'I know she's not living at home, but at least you know where she is.'

'Ah. Yes, Miss Lucy, I do know, but, well, she hasn't told your

171

auntie yet but she's going to get married soon, and . . . well, who knows?' She ran out of other things to worry about.

Lucy clapped her hands. 'Ada's getting married? That's wonderful news – it's a reason to celebrate, isn't it? There might be additions to the family in due course.'

Dolly nodded and then blew her nose. 'Aye, you're right, o' course. And our Bob's wife's expecting, did you know? Don't tell our Edie that I'm in a state, will you?'

Lucy said that she wouldn't but decided that she would write to Edie when she got back to London and ask her to send her mother a cheerful letter as she was worried about them all.

Oswald had secured employment at Burroughs Wellcome & Company as a research scientist; he had obtained a Medical Laboratory Scientist degree and found some decent lodgings. He too was concerned about the state of affairs abroad and discussed privately with William, though not his mother, whether it would affect his work situation.

'I doubt that you'll be called up,' William said. 'I'm fairly sure you'll be exempt.'

'I doubt they'd take me anyway, with my poor eyesight,' Oswald remarked. 'But still,' he said earnestly, 'I wonder . . .' and left the rest of his sentence dangling in thin air.

Lucy and Oswald returned to London together; it had been only a short weekend but she had much work to do and could study better at the hospital with its vast library than she could at home, particularly when everyone was on tenterhooks awaiting the next news bulletin.

Before they left, Eleanor presented them each with a pastel sketch, a delightfully caught image of Lucy dressed in pale blue which contrasted with the darkness of her hair, with her hand on her cheek and her eyelids lowered as she read a book on her lap. Oswald she had captured with his hair flopping over his forehead gazing whimsically over the top of his spectacles as if interrupted by the artist as he too sat with a book in his hand.

They were both astonished at how well she had caught their likenesses and Oswald asked, 'Oh, can we swap, Lucy? I'll have

172

the one of you and you have mine. And dearest clever sister, will you draw one of yourself and send it to me?'

'Oh, yes, and one for me too, Eleanor, please,' Lucy agreed. 'How talented you are. You must sign them too, as you are sure to be famous one day.'

They wrapped them carefully and put them in their suitcases, and Lucy wondered what her room-mate would say if she put a picture of her cousin on the wall.

On 23 August came an official announcement which, although expected, filled everyone with fear and dread as the struggle soon to be named the battle of Mons began with the British army's first engagement in France.

Oswald wrote to Lucy after he read of the British soldiers who were now fighting on French soil, asking if they could meet one Sunday if she had the time. He suggested that he could come to the hospital to meet her and they could take a walk on Hampstead Heath.

It was a soft September Sunday when they met and set off for the heath. There were many people of the same mind, walking up the hills or by the ponds; some were swimming, others just sitting on the grass enjoying a picnic. Any thought of war seemed to have disappeared as children flew kites high in the sky or fed the ducks.

'Let's sit, shall we?' Oswald said when they reached the top of a rise, and they sat on a bench overlooking Hampstead and the city of London. He put his hand in his jacket pocket and drew out a bar of chocolate for them to share.

'Do you remember when we were children and visited Pearson Park for the first time?' Lucy said, gazing wistfully down over the green grass. 'We were all there, Edie and her brothers, your mother and Pa and you and me; we took a picnic and played cricket.'

He laughed. 'Yes! I was furious with Pa for forgetting the cricket bat and we had to use Stanley's.'

'It belonged to Max,' she corrected him. 'He came too because it was his bat! Funny, isn't it – the odd things we remember.'

Oswald put his head back and his face up to the sun as he remembered. 'That's right.' He turned to gaze at her. 'I was going to be a sworn enemy of everybody because I was the first to be out!'

'What fun it was,' she said reminiscently. 'And I fell in love with Max because I thought him so handsome and he chose me for his team.'

'Did he? Did you?' He seemed astonished.

She nodded. 'I was only young, wasn't I?'

'You were; we all were. Are you still?'

'Am I still what?' She pointed up at the sky as a blue and yellow kite battled with a green one, both being flown by young men and not children. 'Young?'

'In love with Max?' he murmured.

She looked at him and laughed. 'No! The last time I met him, which was quite some time ago, I thought him arrogant and egotistical. Neither did he have a very good opinion of women. Did you know that he sacked Edie for asking for time off? I was furious on her behalf!'

'Oh, my word,' he said in mock fright. 'I must try never to upset you.'

'You never do,' she said thoughtfully. 'Max always seemed to be such a polite caring sort, but I don't know if it was really genuine. I think perhaps he'd cultivated it for their shop customers or to impress people. I remember your mother saying how polite he was.'

'Mmm,' he commented. 'Are you studying behavioural characteristics during your training or is this something that you have naturally acquired?'

Lucy glanced at him to see if he was teasing, but he wasn't, he was looking at her very seriously. She hesitated before answering, touching her mouth with her fingers, and his eyes followed the movement.

'Lucy?'

'Erm, it's part of our reading matter, yes,' she murmured. 'But I find it a very interesting subject.'

Oswald turned his gaze down the hill and sighed. Changing

the subject, he asked, 'Do you know if Edie knows where Josh and Stanley are? Have they been sent abroad with their regiment?'

She noticed a small dark cloud hovering to the west and thought that the atmosphere between them had also changed. 'She receives letters from them,' she said. 'As their mother does, of course. The last I heard was that Stanley was in Serbia but was expected home to help in the recruiting drive. She didn't mention Josh. I suppose he'll have been sent abroad. Why do you ask?'

'It's just that I've heard from one or two of the chaps I made friends with at Cambridge.' He hesitated, and then went on, 'They tell me that they're going to join the military, and asked if I would join them.'

Aghast, she put her hands to her face. 'And will you? Surely you won't. Oswald, say that you won't!'

'It wasn't part of my plan,' he pointed out. 'I'm a pacifist at heart and I won't enlist voluntarily, but if conscription is brought in then I'll have to. I'll play my part, but not as an officer. I'd join the troops.'

'I do hope it doesn't come to that, Oswald.' Her voice wavered as she spoke. 'I'd be so afraid for you, and your mother would be too.'

'All mothers will be afraid,' he said gently. 'And wives and sweethearts as well.'

She nodded. 'And sisters and cousins too.'

He gave a wry smile. 'Yes,' he said. 'Those too.'

His reason for asking about Joshua and Stanley had been that he'd thought he would write to them and find out which regiment they were in, so that if the worst came to the worst he could try to join them. But there was something else troubling him. He would, he was sure, enjoy his work once he had settled in to something specific, but it seemed to him that there were things happening that he wasn't privy to; official-looking groups of men were constantly coming and going, being closeted with senior management for hours at a time, and even the researchers who had been there for many years didn't know, or if they did were not saying, what was going on.

'Come on,' he said, standing up and taking her arm. 'Let's go. It's looking like rain. Let's find a café and have a cup of tea before I catch my train back.'

They walked arm in arm down towards Hampstead village. Neither said much, both busy with uneasy thoughts; there had been a change in atmosphere, a cold wind blowing and rain clouds overhead. Life was going to be different, not only for them but for everyone; no one would escape whatever was coming, not the smiling young couple pushing a baby in a perambulator up the hill towards them, not the young errand lad, whistling as he cycled by, not the man up a ladder painting window frames or the young woman in the café who served them tea from a china teapot. This was to be a time of change and both were anxious and rather afraid.

CHAPTER TWENTY-FIVE

In the years since Nora had come to live in Hull, she had felt very much at home there and had become an integral part of a circle of friends. Sarah Walker was her closest friend but there were others too, and Nora had over time asked these friends to tea and then, plucking up courage, and at William's instigation, invited one couple at a time for dinner.

Sarah Walker and her husband had been the first, and although William hadn't approved of all James Walker's opinions, on the whole they had had a pleasant evening. Next to come was the younger woman Georgina Kemp and her husband Anthony; both lively, well intentioned and informed and with a young family. Georgina had said that she was of a mind to create another women's group with different ideals and direction from Mrs Warrington's.

Interested, Nora had invited the two couples together and Sarah and Nora had agreed that they would like to join her if they could find some more members; this they did, and with the enthusiasm of the women and the support of all the husbands they set up a group of women from all strata of social standing, who wanted to help others whether they were experiencing some temporary difficulty or suffering chronic hardship because of illness or poverty.

Their membership had increased over time, eventually reaching fifty, at which point they closed the group and set up a waiting list. They invited speakers, including the eminent

Dr Mary Murdoch whose talk on the difficulties that women had to overcome in order to undertake medical studies led Nora to a greater understanding of what Lucy must be enduring; another woman came and told them why she supported women's suffrage, and then Dolly Morris was persuaded by Nora to speak about her early married life with a clutch of small children, a husband who was out of work and no money coming in, and how she had coped with shortage of food and no means of paying the rent; she told them how she had come through this period, and how proud she was now of her six children, two of whom were serving soldiers, one a nurse and one a housekeeper, one an engine driver and the youngest yet to make up his mind. She received the greatest ovation of all, and because she was so elated by her success afterwards asked Nora if she might be permitted to join the group, which was unanimously agreed, as was her election on to the committee as she was so sensible and level-headed.

'I've been thinking,' Nora said to Sarah Walker one day when they met for coffee. 'I think we should have a contingency plan in view of the present situation.'

'*What* kind of plan?' Sarah asked; she was a little hard of hearing.

'Contingency,' Nora repeated. 'In case of an emergency. Because of the war. There'll be women with husbands and sons joining the army and in need of support.'

'That's true,' her friend agreed, 'and we could perhaps knit socks and scarves for soldiers to keep them warm in winter.'

'We could,' Nora said, 'but what I was thinking was that we could try to raise money for wives in difficulties if their husbands are away and there are children to be fed and clothed. William has read of groups of country women in Canada who have founded a women's charitable institution, and there's talk of setting up something on those lines in Britain. But I was thinking of women in towns and cities with no means of producing their own food, who might need help if this war really does take hold.' She still didn't want to think that the war across the water would affect anyone in Britain, except for the military, but was increasingly beginning to accept that this was a false hope.

By mid-October she knew that her fears were being realized when the women's suffrage movement announced that they were delaying their militant campaign because of the war. Women were being called to munitions factories and brick factories, and as postal and railway workers, to replace the men who had answered Lord Kitchener's call to arms.

Ada knocked on Nora's sitting room door one afternoon and asked if she could have a word, and Nora half guessed what was coming.

'I'm going to be married, ma'am,' Ada told her. 'I've dithered about it for long enough, but my Isaac has told me that he's going to join 'army and if I don't marry him now he won't ask me again, so I've said yes.'

She blushed as she spoke. 'It's not that I don't care for him, I do, but I didn't want 'same kind of life that my ma had when she was first married. I can still remember being cold and hungry when I was just a little bairn.'

Nora asked her to sit down. 'It will be different for you. You could still keep on working here,' she said. 'You don't have to live in; you could come in daily.'

'Ah, but Isaac won't agree to that, you see. You know what men are like; he doesn't want his wife to keep on working is what he said, but now this war has changed everything and all women'll have to work if their men are away.' She hesitated. 'Well, after we're wed, I'm sorry but I'll still be leaving. I'm going to work in one of 'factories or on 'railway as a ticket collector. I haven't told him yet. He thinks I'll be living at home twiddling me thumbs, when we find a place that is, but I won't,' she said defiantly. 'As soon as he's settled into 'army I'll get a job and then tell him.'

'Oh, dear!' Nora said. 'We'll miss you, Ada. You've been here such a long time,' and with a start she realized that Ada was no longer a young girl. She was fourteen when she had first arrived at their door.

'I have, ma'am, and I never expected to be here so long.'

She nodded. 'But I liked it once I'd settled in and it was like running my own house, except better than I could ever afford. But Isaac's been very patient wi' me and I don't want to miss my chance wi' him.'

'He sounds like a good man,' Nora said gently. 'Don't risk losing him. And,' she added, 'if you ever want to come back, you only have to ask.'

'I will, Mrs Thornbury. That I will.'

Nora recalled when Mary, Ada's aunt, had married and how thrilled Lucy had been to be invited to the wedding, and she wondered if Ada would ask Eleanor to her wedding, for Ada had looked after her just as Mary had Lucy. But Ada was leaving in just over a fortnight and Eleanor was back at school, and Ada told Nora that only her mother, father and two brothers, if they could get time off from the railway, would attend the hastily arranged ceremony, as Isaac had already volunteered and expected to be called up very soon.

'I'm sorry, ma'am, that it's all a bit of a rush, and I'm sorry too that Miss Eleanor won't be there either, but I hope I'll see her when she's next home.'

'She'll be sorry to miss your wedding, Ada, and I think she would have wanted to make your dress; she's very good, you know, has great flair. She says she'd like to leave school next year and apply to work for Madame Clapham as an apprentice dress designer.'

'Is that – that salon in Kingston Square, ma'am? That lady who designs for royalty?' Ada took an astonished breath when Nora nodded and said yes, it was, and Madame Clapham was indeed a Court dressmaker.

'*Ooh.*' Ada rolled her eyes. 'How lovely that would be if Miss Eleanor was able to do that. Would you mind? I mean, your daughter working? Mrs Warrington's daughter has married a toff, so I hear, so she'll never have to work.'

'I'd like to think that Eleanor will do something that will satisfy her, just as Lucy is doing,' Nora replied. 'Life is changing for women, Ada, and we must grasp every opportunity.'

'You're right. Just look at my ma, speaking at one of your

meetings! Mark you, she allus did have 'gift of the gab. Better get on,' she added. 'Things to do. I'll mek sure everything looks nice 'n' tidy afore I leave.'

Nora laughed softly when she had left the room. Ada obviously didn't realize that she had all of her mother's attributes, including the gift of the gab. She knew how to stick up for herself and Nora remembered how, when Ada first came as a maid, she had successfully persuaded her that she should have more wages than she was offering. If she goes to work in a factory, she thought, amused, she'll become the forewoman in a matter of weeks.

Nora received a hurried reply from Eleanor following her letter to tell her about Ada's leaving to be married.

Please will you tell Ada that I'm making her a hat, she wrote. *The girls who are in my art and design class are submitting designs and I shall choose the one that I can adapt to suit Ada, but will you ask her what colour she'd like? I thought a deep rose colour would look nice on her and in the material cupboard there is a lovely silk moiré that the mistress says I may have. Answer immediately, please, Mama. I'm almost sure of her head size.*

Love and kisses, Eleanor.

'I'm having a designer hat?' Ada exclaimed, and put her hand to her mouth. 'Oh, how lovely. And can Miss Eleanor mek it in time?'

'Apparently so,' Nora smiled. 'So is the colour all right? It sounds beautiful.'

'What does moiré mean?' Ada asked. 'It sounds sort of French.'

'It is French,' Nora told her. 'It's sometimes called watered silk, because the pattern looks like water.'

'Oh, how lovely,' Ada repeated. 'Rose moiré,' she whispered. 'I can't wait to tell my ma!'

A hat box arrived three days before Ada was due to leave and as she was gingerly opening it in front of Mrs Thornbury, she said, 'Do you know, ma'am, when I told my ma and my aunt Mary about the hat, Aunt Mary told me that when she left here to get married Mr Thornbury gave her a sovereign, and she said she'd been very frivolous and spent some of 'money on a wedding hat. She told me that if Miss Eleanor hadn't said she was making me one she was going to offer me a lend of it.'

She heaved a breath, as Nora did too, as she unwrapped the tissue paper and drew out a concoction of silk and roses and short spotted veil. 'But now I have my very own. Oh, it's beautiful. Will you and Mr Thornbury come to see me in 'church and then write to Miss Eleanor and tell her?'

'Of course we will,' Nora said, not quite believing her daughter's talent, and not revealing either that Eleanor had been given leave of absence to attend the wedding where her very first designer hat was being worn.

CHAPTER TWENTY-SIX

At the beginning of November Oswald dropped Lucy a post-card to say he was going home that weekend; was there any chance that she would be going too? She'd replied briefly that she wasn't as she was busy with practical exam work in one of the hospitals, and added, *Give everyone my love and I hope to see you all at Christmas.*

Mmm, he thought dully. So shall I go or not? Yes, perhaps I will, otherwise my mother will think I only go to see them when Lucy is with me, which is generally true, but when I'm alone Mother will keep asking me questions relating to young women and have I met anyone nice, and *no* I have *not*, Mother! Well yes, lots, but not anyone I would want to spend my whole life with which is really what she's asking.

Besides, he pondered glumly as he packed an overnight bag, the way the troubles of the world and the war are progressing, what kind of life can anyone look forward to?

The next morning there was such a lot of traffic that he had to hurry to catch his train and began to run down the platform when he saw the engine was already building up steam. Other passengers were doing the same and he came abreast of a young woman in a nurse's uniform and cloak also rushing to catch it. A carriage door was swinging open and he grabbed it and turned to the nurse and said, 'Come on, quick!'

Then they both laughed. 'Edie!' he said.

'Oswald!' she chuckled. 'Fancy seeing you.'

'Oh, it's good to see you, Edie,' he said, scrambling in behind her. 'And here I was thinking that it was going to be a long and boring journey home.'

'It still might be,' she said breathlessly, flopping down on a seat as Oswald took her bag from her and put it with his on the overhead shelf. 'I'm so exhausted I might fall asleep, but please don't think it's because of your conversation.' She unbuttoned the high neck of her blue-grey cloak but kept it on, as she also did the small white cap perched on her head. 'I'm so lucky to get this particular weekend off. Have you heard that Ada is getting married on Monday? Although I can't stay for the wedding, I wanted to see her before she took the final plunge.'

'My mother did mention it,' he said. 'But she didn't say when.'

'Done in a rush seemingly.' She grinned. 'And not for 'usual reason you might imagine, but because her fiancé has joined up and he said if she didn't say yes this time he wouldn't ever ask her again!'

'What about you?' he asked, leaning back in his seat and crossing his legs. 'Is there a man in your life?'

She shook her head. 'I'm in 'same situation as Lucy,' she smiled. 'Can't continue in my profession if I marry.'

'Ridiculous, isn't it? We're in the twentieth century.' Oswald glimpsed the short blue-grey shoulder cape half hidden beneath her cloak. He glanced at the other two elderly passengers in the carriage and lowered his voice. 'Is that a sister's uniform?'

She shook her head again. 'Staff nurse; the uniform is similar except for the badge. I'm not ready yet to be a sister.'

'Staff Nurse Morris! Well done. I imagine it's hard work. Have you finished all your training?'

'I have for 'time being, but there'll be more.' She too glanced at their travelling companions, and leaning towards him whispered, 'I'm going abroad in January.'

'France?' he mouthed and she nodded.

'QAIMNS,' she said quietly, under the sound of the guard's piercing whistle and the jolting clanking of the engine as they got under way. Oswald immediately understood what she meant, and also knew that the uninitiated wouldn't. Queen Alexandra's Imperial Military Nursing Service. Edie was going to war.

'That's why I'm going home now,' she continued, still speaking softly. 'I won't be able to come for Christmas. I'm going to work in another London hospital for further instruction before embarkation. I'm thrilled to be accepted, but a bit scared too.'

'*Scared?*' he said, in a semi-mocking manner. '*Edie Morris?* Scared! I don't believe that for one minute.' He looked at her admiringly. 'I'm proud to know you, Edie. How brave you are.'

She denied it forcibly. 'Well, we'll see how brave I am once I'm over there, but as two of my brothers have gone I thought I could do 'same. I always tried to keep up with them when we were little bairns, and . . .' She paused, and her expression became anxious. 'I just thought that – well, if something awful happened to either of them, I'd be there, wouldn't I? On 'same side of 'water.'

'Oh, Edie!' He reached over and grasped her hands and the elderly couple looked their way, the woman looking scandalized over the top of her spectacles and the gentleman harrumphing loudly. Oswald disregarded them and said softly, 'I understand your meaning, but try to be positive.'

He withdrew his hands and Edie took a deep breath and nodded. 'I will,' she whispered. 'I will.'

She told him about the hospitals that had been or were soon to be opened for injured soldiers all over the country, including Hull. 'Reckitt's are opening one at their factory, to be ready if 'situation worsens,' she murmured, 'and 'Red Cross is setting up another, and then there's a building in Bowlalley Lane that's looking after Belgian refugees. My mother told me that she's been helping out there. Folk in Hull are always ready to give a helping hand.'

They said goodbye at the Hull railway station and Oswald wished her God speed and Keep safe and as she walked briskly away in the other direction, her cloak swinging about her ankles, he watched her with some restlessness. There were groups of young men standing around, chatting and laughing together, some in army uniform, some in their working clothes, and he wondered if they were in or had just enlisted in one of the Hull pals battalions that had recently been formed. Pasted up on the wall of the station entrance was a recruitment poster with an image of Lord Kitchener eloquently indicating to young men that Britain needed them, and this, added to his admiration of Edie brought on by her news of her mission abroad, brought to the fore a disquiet that had been festering for some time.

His mother opened the door to him. 'Hello, Mater,' he said jovially, and kissed her cheek as he stepped inside. 'I gather you might have lost your precious Ada and have to answer the door yourself, until she's back again!'

'She's left,' Nora said mournfully, closing the door behind him. 'She's getting married on Monday and not coming back. Come on up. Pa and Eleanor will be home in an hour. He went to fetch her as she's been given permission to attend the wedding – she's made Ada a hat.'

'Really?' He laughed. 'And is that reason enough for that expensive school to allow her out?'

'It is an absolutely *wonderful* hat,' Nora told him. 'I'm really quite envious, and as it's Eleanor's very first garment made specifically for someone the school made an exception. We were surprised too.'

He dumped his bag in the hall and dropped his coat on top of it. 'Eleanor probably told them it was a relative's wedding,' he joked, 'and forgot to tell them that she was the family housekeeper!'

'Ada has been here so long that she seems like a relative,' his mother mused. 'I don't know how I'm going to manage without her.' She laughed. 'I never thought that I'd say such a thing.'

'You'll find someone else, won't you?' He followed her upstairs to the sitting room, where he took off his jacket and flopped on to the sofa.

'I don't know if I will. It seems that so many young men have enlisted that women are taking their jobs now. They don't want to do housework.'

186

'I travelled back with Edie,' he remarked. 'She's come home to see Ada, though she can't stay for the wedding. Will you go?'

'Oh, yes. I'll go with Eleanor,' Nora said. 'Ada asked if we would. Pa can't go, of course, as it's a weekday. What about you, can you stay?'

'Sorry, Ma,' he said. 'I've to go back tomorrow. We're really busy at the lab. Oh, and Lucy sends her love and is sorry that she couldn't get home this weekend.'

'Have you seen her?'

'No. Not recently. She dropped me a postcard and said she hopes to be home at Christmas. I suppose it all depends on this dratted war,' he added.

She was silent for a moment, and then said, 'Yes, of course. I suppose she might be on duty, like Edie?'

It wasn't quite a question, but he took it to be a kind of enquiry. 'Yes, I expect so,' he answered, and decided not to tell her that Edie was going abroad to work in an army hospital, in case she got it into her head that Lucy might do the same, which, he thought with a considerable amount of concern, she might if a request came.

He took a stroll into town that afternoon and wondered why it was so busy; groups of young men like those he had seen at the railway station were heading towards Queen Victoria Square, and out of curiosity he followed them. Outside the city hall was a military recruiting lorry and an omnibus, each with a queue of young men and boys, some looking as if they were still of school age. They were all grinning and joking and it struck him that most wouldn't realize the seriousness of war; to them it would be merely a great and glorious adventure.

Standing at a table by the bus was a sergeant taking details and directing some of the men towards another queue, whilst the very young boys he waved away, shaking his head. Oswald narrowed his eyes. The sergeant was Stanley Morris.

It was two weeks later that the reality of war came home to those who had said that it wouldn't last, the doubters who claimed that

187

it was just a flash in the pan fomented by ambitious politicians and the military who were spoiling for a fight.

William came home from the bank extremely restless and carrying a well-read crumpled newspaper.

'Cup of tea?' Nora suggested. 'Or something stronger? Have you had a hectic day?'

'The latest war news has finally brought doubters to their senses and crowds of people have been into the bank to draw out their savings,' he said wearily. 'The clerks have notified quite a run on cash, which I suppose some might think is safer under their beds than in the bank vaults. Yes, a cup of tea would be nice, thank you.' He smiled. 'I'm sure that it is as effective at calming nerves as alcohol.'

'Why, what's happened?' She sat down opposite him, rather than going to make tea.

He handed her the newspaper. 'German battleships attacked Scarborough early yesterday morning. God damn them,' he said vehemently. 'There are less than thirty-five thousand inhabitants living in the town; what kind of threat could they have been to the Germans? People have been killed in their beds and hundreds injured!'

Nora gazed at the front page, which showed photographs of the damaged buildings and houses with the fronts blown out and tattered curtains hanging in shreds from glassless windows. She read on silently. Eighteen people had been killed including a baby, and newly recruited Territorials had been sent on their first war effort to help with the many injured.

She glanced up at him. 'It says that the battleships went on to Whitby and fired on the town,' she said. 'Why? Why these small places? Is it because they knew they would be unprepared? Or is it,' she went on slowly as the reality became clear, 'because they are practising for something bigger? A port city like Hull? A city with rail links?'

He nodded. 'I think you are right. Apparently there was a bombardment in Hartlepool too, so they've planned for the east coast. It's the first onslaught on British soil since the war began.' He sighed deeply. 'And I'm very much afraid it won't be the last. We must prepare ourselves. I know that many people might think I'm a pessimist, but I am not! I am a realist and we must be ready for what is to come.'

When Nora came back with a tray of tea, he got up and paced about and then went to the window and gazed out. 'I feel as if I should be doing something,' he muttered. 'But I'm too old to enlist.'

Nora stared at him. 'Well, thank goodness you are,' she said. 'The way things are moving on so quickly it's likely that Oswald will be conscripted and I'm worried enough about him without having to worry about you as well!'

He turned to face her. 'Oswald is doing important scientific work,' he assured her. 'It's doubtful that he'll be conscripted. Besides,' he said wryly, 'if he lost his spectacles he'd be unable to tell if the person in front of him was friend or foe!'

He sat down to drink his tea. That last remark was true, at least, he thought, but Oswald had indicated to him on his last visit that he too felt that he should be doing something, even though he was against war in principle and wouldn't want to take up arms. He had also told him in confidence of the rumours flying around amongst the scientists he knew, that the Germans were working on a secret destructive process that they were preparing to use. 'It will be devastating, Pa,' he'd said. 'Chemical warfare; and if what we hear is true, we should all be afraid.'

CHAPTER TWENTY-SEVEN

Although Lucy and Oswald managed to get home for Christmas, they were both restless; Lucy because she felt she ought to be on duty in one of the hospitals. There were more and more injured soldiers coming back to home shores to be patched up before being sent back abroad when it was decided they were ready once more for active service. She was already doing far more than she would normally have been considered ready for, but these were not normal times and she reflected that her superiors obviously had confidence in her ability to perform the duties of a more experienced doctor; she wasn't confined only to taking temperatures or listening for a heartbeat, or standing alongside a fully qualified doctor to watch and learn, but was regularly in theatre helping with surgical procedures and bonesetting.

Oswald, on the other hand, was bothered that he should be undertaking more important work than he was currently doing at the pharmaceutical laboratory, and through the recommendation of a former fellow graduate had received an offer of a more senior position with another company.

'I'm seriously debating whether to accept,' he told Lucy. 'Even though I feel that I should be at the front.'

'You can't possibly go to the front!' Lucy replied. They were setting the dining table for Christmas lunch whilst Nora was in the kitchen helping Cook prepare it. 'Can you actually *see* the letters on the optical wall chart?'

'What?' he said in mock surprise, pausing before opening a bottle of red wine. 'Which letters? Which wall chart?'

She laughed, but he put the wine bottle on the dresser and frowned. 'The news coming out of France is not good,' he said. 'They need more men than are enlisting.'

'You haven't had any papers though, have you?'

He shook his head. 'No, and when I do I know for sure that they won't want me. But do you know what? One of the young errand lads at Wellcome was handed a white feather a couple of weeks ago. He's only sixteen and was really upset about it. He told his mother and she said he should lie about his age.'

'His mother wants him to volunteer!'

Lucy was aghast at the idea, but Oswald went on, 'His brother, who's not quite eighteen, was accepted and his mother thinks young Joe would be too. She said she'd never be able to hold up her head again if he didn't volunteer.' He pondered for a moment before adding, 'He'll never make it home again if he does go. He's scarcely big enough to hold a rifle. He's just a skinny little kid.'

'Things are very serious if they'll take such young boys,' Lucy murmured. 'Do you think the Germans or the French are doing the same?'

Oswald took a deep breath. 'Yes,' he said. 'I imagine so.'

Cook went home after she'd finished cooking. William had gone to the kitchen to thank her and give her a Christmas box. She'd offered to cook lunch for them, telling Nora that she would be cooking a Christmas dinner for an elderly aunt who liked to eat at seven o'clock prompt and afterwards always fell asleep by the fire. 'I'd rather be here cooking for you who appreciates it,' she said, 'than Aunt Nell who considers it my duty as I'm 'onny niece left.'

She was still a comparatively young woman and Nora had an uneasy feeling that sooner rather than later she would up sticks and leave, probably to run a canteen or something similar.

Lucy and her aunt washed up the dishes after they'd finished lunch, which had had a forced jollity about it, and Eleanor put everything away in the cupboards. When they'd finished,

Oswald came into the kitchen and insisted they all went to sit down and he'd make the coffee. He grinned. 'Pa's asleep by the fire. That second helping of Christmas pudding and brandy has done him in,' he said in a mock Cockney voice.

'I'll help you,' Lucy said, picking up a saucepan to warm some milk on the stove. Eleanor dashed away, and then Nora said she'd join William by the fire and would Oswald bring some biscuits from the biscuit barrel.

Lucy turned to get cups and saucers down from the cupboards.

'Here, let me,' he said, reaching above her, his hand resting momentarily on her shoulder. He looked down at her. 'You smell nice,' he murmured.

She smiled. 'Antiseptic?'

He put his nose to her thick hair and breathed in. 'Definitely not antiseptic,' he said softly, and ran a strand through his fingers. 'More like roses.'

She shrugged away from him. 'If you knew how long it took to arrange my hair this morning,' she admonished him. 'It's the perfume your mother gave me,' she added awkwardly. 'Attar of roses.' She cleared her throat. 'Rose oil.'

Oswald gazed at her. 'Yes. Sorry. I mean— Oh!' He gave a start. 'The milk!'

Both reached for the saucepan to save the milk from boiling over.

'Idiot,' he muttered, and saw Lucy's eyebrows shoot up. 'Me, I mean, not you.' He gazed round the kitchen. 'I've forgotten where everything is kept. Where will I find the coffee beans?'

Where had the awkwardness come from, Lucy wondered as she drank her coffee and idly turned the pages of one of her aunt's magazines. She and Oswald had always talked easily together, or at least since they were young adults and had got over their sibling rivalry.

But something had changed and she couldn't quite put her finger on when it had begun. It wasn't just now in the kitchen as he'd commented on her perfume, and perhaps she was reading more into his gesture of fingering her hair than he had intended, but there was a stillness about him, a pause in time as his lingering soft-focused gaze had held hers. Neither, she thought, was it the first time.

You're being ridiculous, she thought, dropping the magazine on the floor. Be careful or you'll lose his friendship – his companionship, she silently chided herself, but then she wondered why he had excused himself after serving everyone with coffee and biscuits and had taken his up to his room.

On Boxing Day after lunch, when they had eaten left-over turkey and a casserole of vegetables, followed by trifle, mince pies and cream, Lucy said she was going to take a walk and thought she'd drop in on Mary to ask how everyone was. 'It's ages since I last saw her,' she said. 'And their daughters, what are they doing now?'

'Both working,' Nora said. She and Eleanor were busily knitting. 'Sally works in one of her uncle's shops, and I can't recall what Daisy does.'

'I'll come too, if I may,' Oswald said. 'I could do with stretching my legs after all that food. Mary lives near her sister, doesn't she? I'll call in on Dolly and ask if there's any news of Josh or Stanley.'

'Stanley has been home recruiting but has gone again, and the last time I saw Dolly she was waiting for a letter from Josh.' Nora counted her stitches. 'She gets very anxious.'

'Do you want to come for a walk, Eleanor?' Lucy asked.

'No fear,' Eleanor said. 'It's too cold for me.' She grinned up at them. 'I'm a hothouse flower. I'm going to get a job in a glass-house when I leave school.'

'I thought you were going to be a fashion designer?' Oswald stood up and stretched.

'I was. Perhaps I might still be,' she answered blithely. 'But I'm rethinking my options because of the war.'

'We're all having to do that,' her father said.

'You too, Pa?' Oswald said. 'Surely you won't leave the bank?'

'No, I won't do that, but I've applied to join the boards of some hospitals and first aid units. There are two wards at the Infirmary that are being earmarked for the military, and then there's a refugee centre just round the corner from the bank where I could maybe be of practical help, you know.'

'Edie mentioned that when I last saw her,' Oswald remarked as he headed towards the door to get his coat. 'She said her mother was helping out there.'

Nora looked up. 'Why don't we both do that, William?' she said. 'It's all very well knitting socks, but I can do that at any time.'

Eleanor cast off her work and said, 'There. That's twelve pairs of mittens since Christmas Eve!'

'Twelve pairs of mittens?' Oswald echoed.

'Well, fingerless gloves,' she said. 'The fingers are free so that the soldier can fire when holding a rifle. Look.' She turned one inside out. 'I've put a kiss in a different colour inside.' She giggled. 'I thought it might cheer up a homesick soldier who's missing his wife or fiancée. I've already taken some into the York recruiting office, but these can go to the Hull one.'

'What a lovely idea, Eleanor,' Lucy said. 'Not firing at anyone, but seeing the kiss inside.'

'I thought I could make shirts too,' Eleanor said, casting on more stitches. 'But I suppose they'd have to be regulation flannel or something and I'd need a bigger sewing machine than the one I've got now.'

She continued knitting and Lucy ran upstairs to get her coat and hat.

'Of course, what I could do, Papa,' Eleanor concentrated on her knitting as if her life depended upon it, 'is leave school and set up a small business making shirts and – what do they call those long pieces of cloth that soldiers wrap round their calves?'

Her father sat up straight and looked at her. 'Puttees,' he said. 'What *are* you talking about, Eleanor?'

Her mother put her knitting down too, and they all heard Lucy call out, 'We won't be long.'

'I'm talking about doing something for the war effort, Papa,'

Eleanor said. 'I'm very good at designing and sewing and knitting. I'm not as clever academically as Lucy or Oswald, although I'm not bad at maths, and staying on at school for another year or two is not going to make any difference to my education. There are other women – girls – like me who could do that kind of thing just as well as working in a factory or being postwomen. They might even prefer it,' she added.

Her father and mother looked at each other. 'Well!' her mother said, and her father sat back again in the chair and folded his arms, which Eleanor took as a very bad sign, but after a long silence he pursed his lips and rubbed his beard, and said thoughtfully, 'Perhaps – let's think it over for a day or two. I'm not saying yes or no at this point, but it needs seriously thinking through. What did you say you'd need? Bigger sewing machines – you'd need more than one – and where would you open this little workshop? You realize it would have to come up to a satisfactory standard for the military to be a proper profitable business?'

Eleanor's mouth dropped open. Not in a million years had she thought her father would take her seriously, but he was thinking about it . . . and then, as she smiled, she began to think of even bigger opportunities for when this awful war was over. She would forget about working for Madame Clapham, the Court dressmaker, because by then she would be experienced enough to start a fashion house of her own.

Lucy and Oswald walked silently side by side, no cosy arm in arm as they often did, but with a gap between them.

'The war is changing everything, isn't it?' he said as they reached the top of Baker Street and turned towards Albion Street. 'Everyone is affected by it. Imagine Pa thinking of what else he might do that would make a difference.'

'Yes,' she murmured, 'and Eleanor thinking of making shirts for soldiers.'

'I've decided to take that offer at the other lab,' he said abruptly. 'I'll be involved in more research according to the schedule I've seen, and if I still think I'm not doing enough after say six months or so, I might apply to enlist. There must be something I can do.' There was a note of desperation in his voice. 'I'm a pacifist,' he said, 'not a conscientious objector!'

'Nobody thinks you are,' she said softly. 'And as a pacifist you could be a stretcher bearer or something like that if you really thought you should.'

'I know,' he muttered. 'But it still doesn't seem enough.'

They walked on without talking until they reached Mason Street. 'I'm not sure if I remember which house it is,' Lucy murmured. 'Dolly lives on the front but Mary is through one of these arches. This one.' She pointed. 'Grotto Square.'

They knocked on the door of one of the houses down the dark and narrow street but there was no answer, so they turned away. 'Perhaps they visit their relatives on Boxing Day, or are out for a walk, like us,' Oswald suggested. 'Shall we try Mrs Morris?'

They retraced their steps to Mason Street, found the house number and climbed the steps to the door, where there were several bells, for this was a whole house with three floors and a basement divided up into apartments. Dolly Morris, her husband and their youngest son lived in three rooms upstairs, and when they knocked on the door it was opened by Mary.

'Mary!' Lucy said gleefully. 'We've just been to your house. I'm so glad that we've found you.'

'Come in, Miss Lucy,' Mary said. 'Hello, *Master* Oswald.' She looked up at him, so tall above her, and smiled. 'Mind your head!'

He ducked through the doorway. 'Hello, Mary. It's nice to see you.'

'Me and 'girls have come round to cheer our Dolly up,' Mary whispered. 'She's a bit down with it being Christmas and her lads being away. Even Charlie's working today, same as my Joe. They can't afford to turn down a bit of extra on Boxing Day.' She lowered her voice still further. 'But they're worrying over Stanley and they've onny just heard from Josh.'

'Stop whispering, Mary, and bring 'visitors in,' Dolly called out. 'You're letting 'heat out.'

196

They all looked at each other wryly and went in to greet Dolly and her husband Tom, and Mary's two daughters. Dolly was holding a letter in her hand.

After the usual season's greetings had been exchanged, Lucy and Oswald perched on chair arms as there were not enough chairs to go round and they'd both refused to take Tom's or Dolly's.

'Can't stay long,' Lucy explained, 'but we wanted to come and see you before we go back to London.'

'You're lucky to get home,' Dolly said in a gloomy voice. 'Our Edie's been on duty all of Christmas. Says she'll come home at 'beginning of January for a couple of days.'

Oswald nodded, remembering that Edie had told him she'd be going abroad in January; the visit home might be her last for quite some time.

'What do Stan and Josh have to say, Mrs Morris?' he asked. 'Are they both all right?'

'They say so, but are they telling 'truth? There's no way of us knowing, and on onny one page they can't say much.'

She handed him the crumpled paper she'd been holding. 'You can read it if you like; this one came from Josh before Christmas.'

He took it and quickly scanned it. It was true, Josh wasn't saying much, but then he'd be under orders not to otherwise some of it would be deleted.

Dear Mam, Da and everybody, we're just settling down for the night and hoping for a quiet one and that Fritz is as well. I'm quite well but a bit damp and muddy cos we're in the trenches but quite safe. I haven't seen Stanley since he got back from Blighty and he'll be further up the line I expect, but we'll catch up soon. I'll tell him to write as soon as he can. Please give my best to Bob and his wife and Charlie and everybody, and Ada, tell her I'm sorry we didn't make it to the wedding, and I hope everybody's in good spirits. Your loving son. Joshua. PS A slice of Christmas cake would be just the ticket. Ha ha!

'He sounds to be in good spirits,' Oswald said, handing the letter back to her and including Mr Morris in his comment.

She looked down at the letter again. 'He does, doesn't he?' she

197

muttered. 'But he wouldn't say even if he wasn't!' She looked up at him. 'And what about you, young man? Are you in uniform? Our Charlie comes home from work all mucky in his greasy overalls so that folk won't think he's avoiding conscription and give him a white feather.'

'No, I'm not in uniform. I'm a scientist.' He hesitated. 'I hope I'm working to make life a little easier for those at the front. We're looking at how to combat infections such as trench foot and fever and typhoid; providing tetanus injections against—' He wanted to say injuries from barbed wire, but he didn't; he'd seen photographs of the damage it could do and wouldn't want to share it with the mother of two soldiers. 'Against – cuts and other wounds, and researching into types of mobile X-ray machines that can be transported to areas where they're needed.'

He wanted to tell them more, but thought perhaps it wasn't appropriate; he would have liked to talk about the scientist Marie Curie, who had been personally involved in arranging to have army trucks adapted as X-ray units that could be driven to the battlefields so they were quickly on hand to assess injured French soldiers. It would take more than just a quick visit to explain everything; all the urgency of having critical medicine and equipment ready and available for use in the war that was consuming Europe.

'I see.' She nodded slowly. 'Important work, then? But nobody who sees you would know that, would they, lad?'

When he didn't answer she said softly, 'So has anybody given you a white feather?'

Lucy turned to look at him as without flinching he said quietly, 'Yes, as a matter of fact, they have.'

198

CHAPTER TWENTY-EIGHT

Edie went home in the first week of January 1915. She was sorry to have missed Lucy and Oswald but none of them were masters of their own destiny any more and had to snatch home leave whenever they could.

As she stepped off the train at the Paragon railway station the platforms were full of servicemen both arriving and departing and the station was full of steam and noise. Some of those arriving looked as if they had come from the war zone; others were energetic and enthusiastic after completing their basic training, whilst the raw recruits waiting to depart, young men not yet in their twenties, were rowdy and exuberant, slapping friends heartily on their shoulders in greeting whilst their relatives, mothers in particular, were trying to hold back tears. Hull had raised four battalions of Hull Pals, each with over a thousand men, and with a reserve battalion of replacements, the 4th East Yorkshires. They had trained in the streets, parks and playing fields of the city and considered themselves ready for anything.

Edie fought to hold back her own concern that she might see some of them again when she arrived in the French hospital, but then, she told herself sternly, if she did, it would mean that they had survived death, even though sustaining injuries. She and her nursing colleagues, hand-picked to travel abroad, had been left in no doubt that they would see some distressing sights that women were not generally accustomed to.

As she walked down Albion Street towards her parents' home in Mason Street she followed an officer in a very well cut uniform, one made by a tailor, she surmised. Some of the graduates she had met who had enlisted straight from university were not always as well kitted out as this one appeared to be and she wondered who he might be; he would be with an East Yorkshire regiment, that was for sure, but as his steps slowed and he paused before glancing down into the basement of one of the houses and then turning towards the steps, she knew or thought she knew who it must be, even though she hadn't seen him in many years.

Some sixth sense made him glance over his shoulder as he took the first step, and seeing her nurse's cloak he nodded and touched his cap. 'Good afternoon, nurse,' he said. 'Are you off duty too?'

'I am, captain. Henry,' she added.

His eyebrows shot up and he took off his peaked cap. 'Lieutenant,' he corrected her. 'Have we met?'

She laughed. 'A long, long, time ago and I wouldn't expect you to remember. We met when we were children. You and your sister were at Lucy Thornbury's birthday party and I was there with my brother Josh. I think I was six.' She smiled again and dimples appeared in her cheeks.

'Great heavens!' He came back down the step to the pavement. 'Imagine you remembering. Was I pretty awful back then? Is that why you remember?'

'I don't think so,' she said. 'But I recall my brother offering to fight you.'

He put his head back and laughed and she thought admiringly how handsome he had become. 'Josh!' he said. 'Yes! I was most put out, because didn't he win every game we played?'

'I expect he did,' she said, smiling. 'He usually does.'

'What's he doing now? Has he enlisted?'

'He and my brother Stanley are regular soldiers. Stanley's a sergeant, Josh a corporal. They both joined the army before the war began.'

'So did I,' he said. 'I always wanted to be a soldier. Do you see anything of Lucy Thornbury? I met her by chance a few years back when I was on leave.'

'Yes, we're still good friends. We meet from time to time. We're both in London. She's almost finished her medical training.'

'Has she really? Good for her,' he said. 'And her brother, a quiet fellow back then?' He gave a little frown as he tried to recall. 'What was his name?'

'Oswald, but he isn't her brother, they're – sort of cousins. He's a scientist. He works in London too,' she added, and then said, 'Well, it's been nice to see you again. I must be off home.' She gave a little shrug. 'It's only a short leave and I have to break some news to them.'

'Ah, getting married or something?'

'No!' she exclaimed. 'Certainly not. I'd have to give up nursing if I did.'

She saw his eyebrows lift again. Crikey, she thought, he is so good-looking. He had a thin fair moustache above an attractive smiling mouth. 'No,' she said again, more seriously. 'Erm, I'm not supposed to talk about it but I'm allowed to tell my family.'

His face dropped, as did his next words. 'You're taking a holiday abroad?'

'Yes,' she said softly. 'I am. I hope 'weather's better than here!'

He shook his head. 'It won't be,' he said. 'So take care.' He took a step towards her. 'It's Edie, isn't it? It just came to me.' He remembered then her cheeky grin from when she was a child. He put out his hand and she extended hers and he clasped it firmly and held it. 'I mean it,' he said. 'Some of those holiday destinations can be rather precarious.'

She nodded. 'So I believe, but yes, I will. Goodbye, lieutenant. Nice to see you again,' she repeated. 'And you take care too.' And she felt a great lump of anguish in her chest for all the young men who were risking their lives to defend their country and thought that if she could help to save just one of them it would be worth her small risk in being there.

201

'Henry,' he corrected her. 'Where are you nursing now, Edie?'

'At St Thomas's,' she said, knowing that he would have heard of it.

He nodded. 'Sterling work done there, I've heard,' and giving her hand another gentle squeeze he smiled at her and turned away.

His mother had been watching from the window, waiting for him to arrive. She opened the door to him. 'Darling Henry.' She put up her cheek to let him kiss her. 'Who was that nurse I saw you flirting with?' she said coyly.

'I wasn't flirting, Mother. It was someone I met a long time ago.' Though I might have done, he thought, if circumstances had been different. 'She's a very brave young woman.'

Edie's mother took the news of her impending journey well and proudly, her father not so.

'It'll be dangerous out there for a young woman,' he asserted. 'It shouldn't be allowed. It's no place for women!'

'I'm not going to be fighting, Da,' she said. 'Nurses are needed! And it's a pity that 'British authorities don't realize it too,' she said hotly, 'instead of leaving it to the French.'

'What d'ya mean?' He scowled at her.

'I mean that I'll be working in a French hospital run by English women and treating mostly French soldiers because 'English authorities won't allow their nurses to travel abroad, which means in turn that our wounded soldiers have to be transported back to this country to be treated here rather than on the spot where they were injured.'

He was silenced for a moment whilst he contemplated this piece of information. 'So, you mean, they've got to be brought overland to 'French coast and then shipped home?'

'Yes,' she said simply. 'And some of them need serious surgery where time is essential.'

She couldn't explain further as she didn't want them to worry even more about Stanley and Joshua than they were doing already. Her mother had turned away, clearly affected by the thought of the consequences if either of her sons should be injured.

'Ah, well,' Tom relented, glancing at her. 'I suppose, in that case, even though I've no love for 'French . . .'

She knew he'd want to have the last word, but couldn't resist saying wryly, 'And how many French folk do you know, Da?'

'I don't know any,' he admitted, 'but I've heard tales about 'em. They're a funny lot, so you just watch out!'

She let it go; he was worried about her, she knew that, and it was his way of telling her to be careful.

'I suppose you'll have to learn to speak French then, will you?' her mother asked. 'You'll have to learn 'lingo.'

Edie smiled and glanced at her father who had settled back into his easy chair. 'Oh, just a few words to get me by,' she said. 'I'll find some handsome Frenchman to teach me.' She saw her father turn and scowl at her and laughed. 'Onny kidding, Da.'

She visited as many of her relatives as she could during that weekend. Her newly married sister Ada; Bob and his wife; Mary and Joe and her cousins. Aunt Susan, who was working in one of the family shops. Her cousin Jenny who was managing the one in Charles Street since Max had enlisted. He'd applied for officer training but hadn't been accepted. Running a grocer's shop didn't give him the credentials that were needed and so he'd joined the Hull Pals Commercial battalion with many of the men he remembered from his schooldays.

'They'll all be in it together,' Jenny said as she and Edie chatted and she surreptitiously weighed in an extra slice of bacon and winked at Edie as she handed it over for her mother. 'You should have seen 'queue of lads at 'recruiting bus outside city hall. Some of them looked so young, barely out of school. I bet their mothers didn't know they were there.' She gave a pout. 'There'll be no eligible young men left in town,' she said gloomily. 'Have you met anybody special yet, Edie?'

Edie shook her head. 'I meet plenty of young men,' she said, thinking of the many badly injured soldiers brought to St Thomas's. 'But I don't intend marrying, not yet anyway; our Ada waited, didn't she? She was in no hurry . . .' She left her words hanging for a moment. 'I'm sorry that I wasn't there to see her wed.'

'It's a risk though, isn't it?' Jenny folded her arms. 'Isaac's gone off to war now. What if he doesn't come back?'

Edie took a breath. 'Well, she'll be in 'same situation as she was before, won't she? Except she'll be a married woman instead of a single one!'

She thought of the handsome officer, Henry Warrington. She could fall for him, she thought, but what would be the point in that? He was way above her socially and she could imagine his sister Elizabeth's scathing comments. Of course, she might have changed too from the pretentious child she used to be; just as we all have, she thought with a sigh. We're none of us the same as we once were.

CHAPTER TWENTY-NINE

Lucy was kept up to date with what was happening in Hull by letters from her uncle, who told her about the Hull fishermen in their trawlers who were minesweeping and dropping depth charges in their effort to search for and destroy submarines. He also said that he had had a telephone installed at the house, and was thinking of buying a motor car. Her aunt Nora described the women's groups who were helping out the families of many soldiers who had been sent abroad, and Eleanor was planning on leaving school at Easter and keen to tell her about her proposed project of making shirts for the military.

S.F.S. Eleanor wrote. *Shirts For Soldiers. Of course we'll make puttees and other things too if we get the contracts. Papa has done all the paperwork and worked out how much it will cost to buy sewing machines and I've sent a sample of my work so that they can see that I'm up to it, and if we do get the go-ahead Mama suggested we use the Pearson Park house as a temporary workplace. I'm so excited,* she finished. *I'll be devastated if they turn us down.*

Lucy smiled as she read the letter, the exuberance and enthusiasm showing through Eleanor's written words.

Edie had also written to say she was about to set off to France in a few days' time and would try to keep in touch. *I hope I'm doing the right thing,* she declared. *I was really thrilled when Dr Louisa Garrett Anderson herself spoke to me and thanked me for my decision to join the Women's Hospital Corps as she says they really need experienced nurses, just as much as doctors. The hospital is an important medical centre, and somewhere on the coast, near Calais, so I'll get plenty of fresh air, come summer.*

I hope all is well with you, my dear friend, and with Oswald too. Please give him my kind regards next time you see him. You'll probably be a fully qualified doctor by the time we meet again, so I'll send my congratulations in advance. By the way, you'll never guess who I saw on my visit home. Henry Warrington! We had a short conversation. He's grown very handsome and seems a thoroughly nice sort.

Much love from your old friend, Edie.

Lucy gave a pensive sigh. So much was happening, so many changes, and she would soon have news of her own to impart about moving to Endell Street Hospital along with Dr Olga Schultz and Dr Rose Mason, both of whom had become good friends despite the difference in their ages.

There would be more practical work for her at the military hospital, which was run entirely by female surgeons and doctors, many of whom had been suffragists. The hospital had been opened only recently to treat head and femoral injuries sustained in the war, and was a direct result of the success of French hospitals like the one in Wimereux that Dr Louisa Garrett Anderson and Dr Flora Murray had founded in direct opposition to the English medical fraternity and the War Office, neither of whom appeared to understand the logic of having a specialist military hospital in London.

Perhaps I'll eventually go abroad too, she thought, if this dreadful war doesn't end soon. But there didn't seem to be any end in sight; there were ongoing battles at Ypres with many casualties and as the year progressed into February and through to April thousands of British, French and Australian troops landed in Gallipoli to confront the Turkish army fighting alongside Germany.

'Dr Thornbury.'

Lucy turned her head. Strictly speaking she had not yet finally qualified as a doctor, but that is how everyone spoke of her. She had had much more experience than she would have had in normal times, and was about to make a ward visit.

'Yes, Dr Schultz? Can I do something for you?'

'A word if you please?' Dr Schultz looked tired, and there were dark rings beneath her eyes.

'Are you unwell, doctor?' Lucy asked her, following her into a small room at the end of the ward where the medical staff took an occasional rest whenever they had the opportunity.

'No,' she said wearily. 'Just tired, as we all are. Sit down a minute, Lucy. I want to tell you something.'

'Is something wrong?' Lucy interrupted anxiously. 'Can I help?'

Olga Schultz smiled. 'It's good that you ask if you can help. You're a true doctor, Lucy. But no, in this instance you can't.' She paused. 'You know that I was due to work at Endell Street with you and Dr Rose?' She paused again as if gathering her words together. 'Well, now it seems that I'm not. I'm being transferred to a convalescent hospital somewhere in the country. It's still important war work, for the aim is to get soldiers well enough to be sent back to the killing fields,' she added bitterly. 'But I will not be trusted with a scalpel as I would be in Endell Street.'

'But why?' Lucy asked. 'You're one of the best surgeons here.'

Dr Schultz gazed at her pensively. 'Have you noticed that I have a German name? I am British born, as is my mother, but my father was born in Germany. He came to England – arriving by ship in your home city of Hull, by the way – when he was three years old and has been dead for fifteen years, but it seems,' she said, with a catch in her voice, 'it seems that the War Office authorities consider that because I have a German name I might be perceived as a threat to this country that has always been my home.'

'But that's ridiculous,' Lucy began, and then remembered what Uncle William had told her in one of his letters, that there had been a demonstration by an angry and threatening mob outside a pork butcher's shop in Hull. The unfortunate butcher had a German name.

'Would you be willing to change your name?' she asked hesitantly.

The doctor nodded. 'That is what I am going to do,' she said miserably. 'If I want to continue with my work, then I must. I'm going to be Olive Spence.'

They sat quietly for a short time and then Dr Schultz, soon to be Dr Spence, said, 'I'll miss working with you, Lucy, and most of all with Rose. We have worked side by side for a long time, as well as being such very good friends. So there you have it,' she said with a sigh. 'This war is changing everyone's lives. None of us can escape the consequences of it.'

She was gone by the following week, and Lucy and Dr Mason were looking for lodgings near Endell Street. This was a very run-down area of London and finding somewhere suitable to live where a landlady didn't object to their coming and going at unsuitable hours wasn't easy, but eventually they found two rooms in the same house in Covent Garden where they could have the use of the kitchen to make a hot drink whenever they wanted, providing they supplied their own tea, coffee and milk. For breakfast, lunch and supper they ate in the hospital refectory.

'It's such a pity that Olga – Olive can't be with us,' Dr Mason remarked. 'The hospital is run by suffragists and there is no one keener than her on rights for women. In fact she was asked to come by Dr Anderson herself; she wants all of her doctors to be of the same mind.'

'Oh! Does she?' Lucy said, and wondering why she had been chosen she determined to make an appointment to speak to either Dr Anderson or Dr Murray as soon as possible.

Endell Street was a very new hospital, the War Office on this occasion having decided to turn a blind eye to the fact that many of the doctors and the nurses had been militant members of the suffragettes and suffragists campaigns; it was, however, within a very old building, a former workhouse, and there was much work required to bring it up to the exacting require-ments of Dr Anderson and Dr Murray, who were often at odds with the Royal Army Medical Corps. In addition to the doctors, clinical research scientists would be moving in too, with the aim of advancing the understanding of medicine and surgery.

'Dr Thornbury,' Dr Anderson said, inviting her to sit down. 'Are you settling in? We're rather topsy-turvy at the moment, but soon everything will be spick and span. The beds and medicines and equipment that we need are starting to arrive, and the staff too, and we are expecting to receive many seriously injured military patients who are in much need of our expertise. I'm so pleased,' she added, with a smile that lit her rather plain features, 'that you felt able to join us even though you are only just on the threshold of your profession.'

Lucy licked her lips. It was at times like this, in the company of someone like the estimable doctor and militant campaigner, that she felt totally inadequate, but she decided to be as true to herself as possible and outline her fears.

'I'm really pleased to be here, Dr Anderson,' she said, 'and I hope I can justify your faith in me.' Dr Anderson's calm gaze did not waver, and she continued, 'It's because I'm at the beginning of my professional life that I asked to speak to you, as I have a slight worry.'

She hesitated and swallowed. 'I am, of course, on the side of all women who want the same opportunities as men, but I feel I should tell you that I am not a militant campaigner, as most of the doctors and nurses here at Endell Street are.'

'Of course we know that already, Dr Thornbury, but I appreciate your honesty.' Dr Anderson gave another small smile. 'We vet our potential medical staff very thoroughly and we have had excellent reports of you, medically speaking, and understand, we think, that your inclination is to concentrate on your true calling rather than becoming involved in politics. Perhaps one day when you are fully qualified and without hindrance you might join us, but for the time being we at Endell Street would rather you focused on your studies and your work here to help the injured soldiers who need our care so much.'

Lucy was so relieved she wanted to weep, but she held back her tears. She was a doctor, or almost, and didn't cry, but must remain detached. 'Thank you,' she said, with just the merest break in her voice. 'Thank you so much.'

They were inundated with wounded men, and it was much harder than she ever imagined it would be; there were times in theatre when she was on the verge of passing out, but she didn't. She pinched her thigh or her arm to help her concentrate and tried not to think that the raw and bloody flesh beneath the surgeon's knife belonged to someone's son or husband. With her apron covered in blood she would hold a severed limb and know that the soldier who had lost it now had at least a chance of survival.

Lucy thought of the first time she had seen a naked man. They had had to strip his sodden uniform from him to attend to his injuries, and even though horribly wounded he had tried to cover himself when he saw that it was women who were tending him.

'Oh, miss,' he had wept, as he attempted to conceal himself and his injuries. 'Such sights are not for your eyes.'

'It's all right, soldier,' she had said gently. 'Don't be embarrassed. I'm not in the least,' and she had a fleeting, cherished memory of Edie when they were children explaining how to tell if a new baby was a boy.

She made a point of visiting the patients who were back on the recovery ward and sometimes the surgeon would ask her to explain to them the procedures that they had been through. 'Where are you from?' she always asked, and often said, 'Your family will be relieved to know you are safe.'

Once, when she asked the question, the soldier replied, 'I'm from Hull, wi' Hull Pals.'

'I'm from Hull too,' she said. 'Whereabouts do you live?'

'Mason Street.' He looked up at her from pained, bloodshot eyes.

'I know it,' she said. 'It's not far from where I live. Do you know Joshua and Stanley Morris? They're with Hull Pals too.'

'Aye, I do. They're wi' a different unit though. Hope they've made it.'

He tried to say something else but was growing drowsy as his medication took effect, so she patted his hand and murmured, 'So do I.'

CHAPTER THIRTY

France, 1915

Dear Mam, Father and everybody,

I'm sorry it's tekken so long for me to reply to your last letter. We've been rather busy of late and though I was expecting a week off it was cancelled as they wanted us to move somewhere else. You know don't you that I can't tell you where? Anyway, these are not bad digs so mustn't grumble, better than the last ones which were a bit damp. I still haven't seen our Stanley, but ran into a school pal who said he had, and he's fine. Being a sergeant he won't have as much time as me for letter writing, and let me tell you a secret. I'm due for promotion (another stripe), but I expect to stay with this unit for a bit.

Have to close now as it's getting late and the lights are not good enough to write by. I hope everybody's all right and that good old Hull is surviving without me, bet all the lasses miss me. Ha ha! Thanks for the last parcel, especially the cake. I shared it with a mate and we both enjoyed it. I'll write again as soon as I can, but don't worry if you don't hear for a bit as we're allus busy, but I'm fine and hope you all are too.

From your loving son, Josh.

Josh addressed the envelope and tucked in the flap so that it could be read and censored. How much of the news he gave his family they would believe was debatable, but to give too much away about the conditions or their position would mean a stern reprimand and maybe even lose him the chance of another stripe.

He scratched and scratched at his back and legs and under his arms and in his groin, swearing beneath his breath and wishing he could have a hot bath to kill off the lice. His biggest fear was not the Germans' fire, but catching trench fever caused by infection from the lice, which could put him into hospital as it had his brother.

Stanley had had it and had been very ill and taken to hospital, but they hadn't told anyone at home. Now that he was better he'd been moved further up the line to another unit, replacing one of the sergeants who had been killed along with some of the other men. The school pal that he'd mentioned in his letter had been in hospital at the same time and had brought back a message from Stanley to say he'd written home, but hadn't told them about the trench fever or the hospital and for Josh not to either.

Josh took off his damp socks one by one and examined his toes as best he could in the fading light, then rubbed them dry with a piece of flannel that he kept for the purpose, massaging both feet to warm them and keep the circulation going before reaching into his pack for the talcum powder and liberally dusting his feet before putting on clean and fairly dry socks. He was meticulous about this routine, something he had learned in the days when he'd been a boy soldier. Out here, nothing was really bone dry, but at least the weather was warmer than it had been and there was only a thin layer of caked mud at the base of the trench, unlike the last one where they'd been ankle deep in the stuff, and it wasn't only mud.

Fritz wouldn't attack tonight, it was getting too late and it had been a quiet and boring day, although he and his pals were always listening and on the lookout, even when, as now, the enemy was far enough away not to be an immediate threat. He pulled up his collar and wrapped a scarf round his neck and ears, folded his arms, closed his eyes and silently, as he had been taught to do as a youngster, said a few prayers asking God to take care of his family and especially his brother Stanley who was in a very dangerous place. As an afterthought, he implored, 'And please, dear God, please don't let this war get worse before it gets better.'

Dolly Morris gave Joshua's letter to her sister Mary to read. 'He doesn't say much, does he?' she said, taking a handkerchief out of her apron pocket to wipe her eyes. 'We got one from our Stanley just 'other day and he was 'same. He did say though that he'd had a few days off, which was why he'd had time to write.'

'They can't say, can they?' Mary said after reading it. 'But he doesn't sound worried and if he's got better digs that's a good sign, isn't it? Though I can't quite think what he means by digs.' She frowned. 'I thought they were in 'trenches?'

'They are,' Dolly said impassively. 'He's onny saying that so we don't worry about him and Stanley. Still,' she drew herself up with a sigh, 'it'll be warmer now that we've got to June and mebbe,' she said thoughtfully, 'mebbe America might come in now after that big ship of theirs was sunk. *Lusitania*, wasn't it?' She sighed again. 'All those women and children. Terrible loss of life, and almost on home shores.'

She shook her head and changed the subject. 'Our Josh didn't say if he'd got those mittens that Miss Eleanor give me to send.' She gave a little laugh that didn't convince Mary that she wasn't worried. 'Mebbe 'cake I sent was more acceptable!'

'They've taken on our Sally,' Mary told her. 'When Mrs Thornbury told me about 'factory starting up, I put Sally's name down straight away. She's a right good seamstress and she'll like being there more than 'munitions factory, but our Daisy is hoping to be a tram driver. She applied a fortnight ago and has got an interview lined up.' She laughed. 'These youngsters! They'll try anything, but rather her than me!'

'So what'll you do?' Dolly asked. 'You'll need to do summat wi' your time when everybody's out all day.'

'I know, and Joe doesn't get in till late most nights.' Mary bit her lip. 'I hate to be idle and I need to earn some extra money, but I only know about housekeeping.'

'And cooking,' Dolly said. 'You're a good cook. You could try for a job in a canteen.'

214

Mary nodded, but wasn't convinced. She'd never been used to working with a lot of women and didn't relish the thought of it.

'I'll tell you what I'm going to do,' Dolly said. 'If that young miss can start up a business, I don't see why I can't and I won't need any bank loan.'

'What?' Mary said, intrigued as always by her sister's schemes. Dolly would never ever believe that she couldn't do anything she set her mind to.

'Well, with all these women going out to work, who's going to do their washing? I'll tell you who.' She didn't wait for an answer but simply pointed a finger at herself. 'Me, that's who! I've written out some posters to push through doors.' She reached over to a pile of papers on her sideboard and showed one to Mary.

'I've bought some old sacks from 'flour mill – Tom got 'em cheap for me – and I've washed 'em three times to mek sure they're clean. We've got an old wheelbarrow that Tom says he'll scrub out and paint for me and I'll do a delivery service as well.' She sat back triumphantly as she saw the astonished look on Mary's face.

'I'll pick 'dirty washing up and every house'll have its own laundry sack. I'll wash and dry 'clothes at wash house and then tek them back, or if they want them ironed, then that'll be extra.' She leaned towards Mary. 'If you want to join me, we can do twice as much and split 'profit.'

Mary laughed. She wasn't sure she had her older sister's energy. 'You're a marvel, Doll. I'll have a think about it, and don't forget to approach some of 'bigger houses. They'll be short on staff cos all 'young girls are going into 'factories instead of into 'service. Like your Ada.'

Dolly nodded her head, and put up her thumb. 'Course,' she said. 'I hadn't thought of that.'

The next morning Mary received a visitor. 'Mrs Thornbury!'

Nora twitched her nose. 'Mmm. A good smell, Mary.'

'It's onny bread,' Mary said. 'I've always made my own bread, and I have a good oven in this house, unlike the old one where there wasn't an oven at all.'

'So what did you do?'

'I used to make it at home and then take it to 'baker's shop where he baked it for me. Charged, of course, but fair enough.'

'I was wondering, Mary . . . erm, are you working anywhere at the moment?'

Mary shook her head and lifted the kettle over the fire to make tea for them both. 'I was onny saying to Dolly yesterday that I must find work of some kind. Joe is out all day and sometimes at night as well now that he's a fireman on 'trains, and both girls are working, so I can't sit about doing nothing.'

'Ah!' Nora said. 'Well, I have a proposition for you if it appeals. Eleanor will be starting up the factory very shortly. Clearance has been given, as you know, and we're taking on five seamstresses including your Sally. Eleanor will oversee the finished results and do the pattern cutting.'

'My word!' Mary poured hot water into the teapot, swilled it round to warm it and poured it down the sink before putting in the tea leaves. 'She's remarkable for such a young girl.'

'She is,' Nora agreed. 'We're very proud of her, but I sit in with her on the interviews so that it's seen as a family business and so that no one takes advantage of her youth; not that I think she'd let them,' she added. 'But it's as well to be cautious.'

Mary poured the tea and handed a cup to Nora. 'I'd better tell you now that I'm not much good with a needle apart from 'usual make do and mend, or turning a collar and darning,' she said. 'Like we were all taught by our mothers.'

Nora sipped her tea. 'Better than I am, then,' she said. 'My mother taught me nothing useful, I'm afraid. But no, I'm not thinking of the new business, nothing like that. You're very good at housekeeping and cooking, as I know from when you worked for us that brief time before you married.'

They both smiled, each recalling that they didn't start off very well all those years ago.

Mary nodded. 'I like cooking and baking, the simple kind.

I couldn't cook for a supper party I don't think, not like 'old cook used to, but as for housekeeping, yes, I loved seeing 'house polished and tidy.' She thought wistfully back to the days of Lucy's parents and remembered too that she sometimes helped Cook in the kitchen when Dr Thornbury and his wife had guests for supper. Had she been too hasty in leaving, she wondered.

'You mustn't be embarrassed by my suggestion, and if you don't agree, or don't want to, then it's perfectly all right.' Nora put her teacup on the table and took a breath. 'I'm going to need someone to look after the house in Baker Street, because I'll be spending most of the day helping Eleanor set up, keeping time sheets and so on; and ideally I'd like someone who can also prepare food that I can just pop into the oven when Eleanor and I come home in the evenings.'

She paused. 'But I must have someone I can trust to leave on their own to manage the house. I couldn't possibly take on someone I didn't know and you know it so well, Mary. If you would consider it? Nothing much has changed since you were there.' She gave a little shrug. 'Well, we couldn't, could we? It isn't our house to do with as we wish, not that we have wanted to. It's such a lovely house in any case.'

It hadn't occurred to Mary that the house didn't belong to her and Mr Thornbury, and the penny suddenly dropped. It must have been willed to Miss Lucy after her parents' death, which meant that the Thornburys had given up their own home to live with the desolate little girl. No wonder, she thought, that Nora Thornbury had been so irritable when she first arrived; she was probably apprehensive, coming to a new area and looking after a child who wasn't hers.

'Oh, I'd love to come back, Mrs Thornbury. I've such happy memories of being there when Miss Lucy was little and before – well, before such sad times came along, and I'm grateful that you thought well enough of me to ask.' Mary smiled, confident now that they would get along all right. 'But what about your present cook? Will she mind someone else helping in the kitchen?'

217

'She's leaving at the end of the week. She's obtained a new position as a cook in a munitions canteen. What a relief,' Nora said happily. 'When can you start?'

'Tomorrow,' Mary said at once. 'And I can arrange for the washing to be done too if you'd like? Someone I can highly recommend!'

CHAPTER THIRTY-ONE

June 1915

Everyone who read newspapers had seen photographs of the effects of Zeppelin raids on London and the south of England, many of them intended for other targets when the aircraft was blown off course. The attacks were therefore haphazard in the extreme, with the deadly bombs landing where least expected.

Nora woke up on the first Sunday in June at about midnight, disturbed by a strange noise and shouting out in the street. She nudged William, who was fast asleep by her side. 'William,' she said, and then jumped out of bed and ran to the window as she heard the shrill shriek of a warning buzzer.

'What?' William grunted.

'It's the attack buzzer,' she said, lifting the curtain. 'Get up!'

He turned over. 'Another false alarm,' he grumbled. 'Come back to bed. We have to be up early in the morning.'

'No!' she said. 'There are people out in the street.'

Reluctantly he got out of bed and put on his dressing gown, and joined her by the window just as she cried out, 'Listen! You can hear them. They're dropping bombs on the city!'

'Good heavens!' he exclaimed. 'The war has come to us! Quickly. Put on your dressing gown and I'll wake Eleanor.'

But there was no need. 'What's happening?' Their daughter appeared at the bedroom door. 'What's that noise?'

William hurried them downstairs, then turned back to pick

up a coverlet from the bed. Nora unlocked and opened the front door and they went outside. 'Look!' She pointed towards the town centre, where the sky was ablaze.

'That's High Street,' William said, 'and over there' – a blazing trail in the sky headed out of town – 'that's somewhere near the railway station. It's a Zeppelin. It followed the Humber and now it's following the railway line!'

A small crowd had gathered at the junction with Percy Street, all looking up at the reddened sky. 'I saw it,' one man said. 'I thought I was seeing things. It was lit up like a silver cigar, and then it opened up and dropped its bombs. People have been hurt tonight,' he said angrily. 'Somebody's got to pay for this!'

'Somebody already is doing,' a woman broke in. 'My lad's over there doing his bit. Now we're getting a taste of it.'

A man was running towards them; he was coming from the direction of town, cutting over Albion Street and through Percy Street. 'It's bad,' he shouted as he reached them. 'Holy Trinity's been hit, it's on fire, and some houses in Porter Street so I've heard. You can see by 'colour of sky that it's been a massive attack.' He uttered an oath, and then said, 'Can't stop. Must see if everybody's all right at home.'

'They will be,' William muttered to no one in particular. 'It hasn't reached over here. It'll head back towards the Humber; there are only so many bombs a Zeppelin can hold. Come on.' He wrapped the counterpane around the shoulders of his womenfolk who were both shivering, even though it wasn't a cold night. 'There's nothing we can do. We've been caught napping all right. We weren't expecting this. Totally unprepared,' he muttered. 'We're not exempt from danger after all.'

The next day the city was buzzing with rumours and tales of the night's events, and the reported number of persons killed varied wildly. The local paper gave the full story, with photographs of the houses in Porter Street that had sustained serious damage and details of the casualties, including children, who were caught by flying glass or burned to death.

A pall of despair hung over the town and many people

said that now they really knew what the soldiers were going through.

'I feel as if I've joined the war,' Dolly said to Mary. 'I'm going through it wi' my lads, instead of onny reading about it in their letters home.'

Eleanor, starting up in business and not yet sixteen, having been really frightened on the night of the raid, stood in front of her new staff and told them that they must work hard and well to get the shirts and puttees ready as quickly as possible to send out to the troops.

'And,' she said, 'if you want to put your own discreet mark on the inside of the shirts, such as your initial, then please do so, so that the soldiers will know that someone was thinking of them whilst they were making them and they were not simply coming off a production line.'

Nora felt a lump in her throat as she listened to her daughter. So many young people, young men in particular, but girls too, were having to grow up fast in these uncertain times, with this great threat of war hanging over them. The Great War indeed, as it was now named.

Lucy heard of the Zeppelin raids over Hull from Aunt Nora's letter and she truly commiserated. She had seen some of the results from the attacks on London. By the time August came round, the war had been going on for a year and she wondered at the speed of it. They had been desperately busy at the hospital, so much so that she almost missed her own birthday; it was only the pile of letters, cards and parcels that was waiting on her return to her lodgings that night that reminded her what date it was and also that Eleanor's birthday was coming up in two days' time.

There were cards from home and one with a foreign stamp from Edie, and she wondered vaguely how her friend had managed to be so accurate with the date. Of the parcels, one was from Oswald containing a pretty silk scarf in a deep rose colour, a card, and a letter saying how he missed seeing her and asking her to let him know when she had some time off; the other parcels held a boxed set of perfume and talcum powder from her aunt and uncle, and from Eleanor six large machine-sewn white cotton handkerchiefs with her initial embroidered in one corner.

Just what I need, she thought, how very practical, and tucked one immediately into her pocket. She had so little time to find a present for Eleanor that she bought a yellow rose from Covent Garden and pressed it between two pieces of card and wrote a brief note inside.

Dearest Eleanor,

Please accept this huge bouquet at your door on the occasion of your sixteenth birthday. We are all so very proud of you and I am truly amazed when I think of myself at the same age, a mere schoolgirl, and here you are, a young businesswoman. I hope you have the loveliest of days and wish that I could be with you.

Sent with fondest love from your sister-cousin, Lucy.

She was due two days off on the following Saturday and Sunday and had written to Oswald to ask if he were free on the Sunday. On the Friday night she went to bed at eleven and slept until six, her usual time, then turned over and slept again until nine o'clock. She went down to the kitchen to make a cup of cocoa and took it back to bed, then slid down under the covers again until two o'clock.

All day she slept, getting up from time to time to make a drink or go to the bathroom and climbing straight back into bed. When she woke again, the sun was shining through her curtains, making patterns on the opposite wall, and she debated whether or not to get up and make another drink. She heard the peal of the front door bell and Mrs Peck's footsteps on the hall tiles and snuggled down once more, closing her eyes.

She jumped when someone knocked briskly on her door. 'Dr Thornbury?' It was Mrs Peck's voice. 'Are you in?'

Lucy sat up. 'Yes,' she croaked. 'What is it?'

'There's a young man asking for you. Says he's your cousin.'

My cousin? she mouthed. Oh! Golly. Oswald! I'd forgotten. Is it Sunday already?

'Just a minute,' she called, grabbing her dressing gown.

'He can't come up, cousin or not,' Mrs Peck said. 'I've told him. Those are my rules.'

'He wouldn't want to, Mrs Peck.' Lucy tied the belt around her. 'He's a respectable young man! Please tell him I'll be down in a minute.'

She pulled a hairbrush through her hair, trying to separate the tangles, and then went to the door. Mrs Peck might maintain that visitors couldn't come up, but nowhere did it say that she couldn't go down, and Oswald had seen her in her dressing gown often enough.

He was standing waiting in the small vestibule and turned when he heard her run down the stairs. Mrs Peck had returned to her domain at the back of the house, having delivered her message.

'Oswald, I'm so sorry.' She reached up for him to kiss her cheek. 'You've grown a beard. I have no idea what time it is. I've slept and slept. Did I know you were coming?'

He raised his eyebrows. 'Probably not if you haven't opened your post!' He nodded towards the mirrored hallstand where there were several unopened envelopes.

'Oh, goodness.' She ran her fingers through her hair. 'Are you able to wait whilst I wash and get dressed? Shall we go out for breakfast?'

He gazed at her flushed face and tangled hair and wanted to say that he'd wait for ever, but couldn't, considering the time and place.

'Lunch, I think.' He took out his watch from his jacket pocket and showed her the time. 'Eleven o'clock!'

She closed her eyes and exhaled, flinging her head back. 'I can't believe I've slept so long.' She opened her eyes. 'Sit down, do. Give me ten minutes and I'll be ready.'

'Ten minutes! I'll bet. Go on then.' He'd been out with young ladies who had taken twice as long just to visit a powder room. But for Lucy it was a challenge and she hitched up her robe and raced up the stairs. 'Don't fall!' he called after her and then grinned. She was no longer his young cousin to admonish or advise.

Ten minutes later exactly she came down the stairs, wearing a cotton two-piece outfit of short-sleeved jacket and ankle-length skirt and a pretty hat on her well brushed hair. She didn't seem in the least rushed, and gave him a questioning glance.

'I'm impressed.' He got up, and offering his arm said, 'Shall we?'

'Just one minute,' she said, and walking to the end of the narrow hall she knocked on a door. 'Mrs Peck,' she called, 'I'd like a bath later. Will you make sure there's plenty of hot water, please?'

She listened to the answer and called back, 'Well, I'm sorry, but it is essential for tonight. I don't know when I'll be back again. There is a war on, you know. Yes, thank you.' She smiled at Oswald as they went through the door. 'For a landlady who thinks cleanliness is above godliness she's remarkably mean with her hot water!'

They laughed as they walked along the street and he put his arm round her shoulder and she leaned into him. 'I'm sorry I've been so lax in writing,' she said. 'For the short time the hospital has been open it's been just crazy. We've worked flat out with no time off. Those poor boys! So many injuries.'

He gave a little frown. 'Don't think about it now. Enjoy the day. You'll be back soon enough. Are you hungry?'

'Famished!' she said. 'Shall we go into Covent Garden? There are some nice cafés where we can eat and they won't be too busy today as the market is closed. Then we can take a walk afterwards, if you like?'

'Perfect,' he said, taking her hand as they crossed the road.

There was a strong smell of vegetables – onions, leeks and cabbage – but also an underlying aroma of flowers: cosmos, nicotiana, stocks and phlox, all mingling and merging with the vegetable scents despite the stalls' being empty of any plants or produce.

Lucy breathed in. 'I love it in here,' she said. 'I must take a huge bunch of flowers to Aunt Nora the next time I go home.'

They found a small café just off the Garden with tables out-side and Lucy said, 'How very continental!' Then she sighed.

'Although I don't suppose anyone in France is enjoying eating out just now. Should we feel guilty?'

'No,' he said. 'We've already seen the effects of the war in England, including poor old Hull. The Zeppelin raids have really scared everyone, according to Pa, and you must be sure to take cover, Lucy, if you ever hear or see one. The Zepps are something that no one had ever seen before, and they bomb so indiscriminately. We never thought, did we, that we would ever be attacked from the air?'

She shook her head. 'Neither did we ever think that an enemy could be so callous as to attack with gas; it is unethical!' She lowered her voice to a whisper, as there were people at the next table. 'I've seen soldiers blinded by poison gas, as well as suffering terrible skin blisters.'

'Mustard gas, or perhaps chlorine,' he murmured. 'The rumour is that other types of gas are also being used and as yet there's no antidote, only water if it's available to swill off the gas before blisters appear.'

'The difficulty,' Lucy observed, 'is that such treatment is virtually impossible whilst they're in the trenches or on the battlefield.'

They stopped speaking to order their food and coffee. 'Don't think about it,' he said again. 'Today we must enjoy ourselves.'

'But first,' she said quickly, 'can I ask what are you working on with the new company? Is it to do with the war?'

He nodded and lowered his voice. 'Solutions to what we've been discussing. There's a scientist, John Scott Haldane, the best in his field; he's working on a better kind of respirator than the one they have now, as well as discovering more about the gas compound the Germans are using. But have you heard that Britain is retaliating with the same kind of warfare?' He shook his head. 'It doesn't bear thinking about.'

'No,' she whispered. 'It doesn't.' She looked up at him. 'Will life ever be the same again?'

He smiled, his eyes crinkling, and she thought how handsome he looked with his new trim beard. 'No,' he said. 'It will be different, but not necessarily worse for everyone.'

'Ever the optimist,' she said, pleased to be off the subject of war.

'You'll be a fully fledged doctor by then,' he said. 'Where will you be, do you think?'

'In Hull; where else? What about you?'

Oswald gave a droll shrug. He wanted to say *Wherever you are*, but life was so uncertain and besides, he didn't want to disturb or upset her composure when there were so many greater issues to consider. Neither did he dare risk losing her affection. What ever would she think of him, the cousin she had known most of her life, declaring his constant and enduring love?

'Who knows?' he said flippantly. 'It's in the lap of the gods!'

CHAPTER THIRTY-TWO

Edie had been very nervous when she had stepped off the troop ship into the darkness of the spring evening and heard the chatter of a foreign language, none of which she understood. She'd been tense on the ship too, wondering constantly if they would arrive safely or if they'd be blown up by a mine. It was her first sea voyage and as they drew away from the docks in Dover she thought of the Hull fishermen whose livelihood had been destroyed by the war; her mother had written to say there was no fish to be had in Hull. Many trawlers had been converted into minesweepers and the trawler men retrained to carry out searches in the North Sea and the English Channel. It was dangerous work and many of them had perished.

There were countless young soldiers on the ship, full of optimism and bravado, and she guessed that this was probably their first venture towards the war zone. The officers asked them to keep their voices down as sound carried across water, and they immediately spoke in whispers. Other soldiers were much more sombre and these she guessed were returning from home leave or convalescence and knew what to expect.

Other nurses were also on board, a few in the QAIMNS uniform: staff nurses and one sister like herself, for to her great joy she had been promoted before leaving England. Some of them kept themselves separate from those who wore the Territorial Force Nursing Service uniform, which was quite similar except for the badge.

Edie thought it quite ridiculous; although the QAIMNS were professional nurses, they would have to work alongside the territorial nurses who had volunteered to work abroad, for once they arrived at the hospital all would be desperately needed.

A motor bus was waiting to convey them to the hospital, which they had been told was only a few miles away. Edie climbed aboard and sat down next to a young nurse who smiled at her in greeting.

'Hello,' Edie said. 'Nearly there!'

'Thank goodness,' her companion said. 'I'm not a very good traveller. Have you worked here before?'

'No, it's my first time.' Edie shook her head. 'I'm Edie Morris,' she said. 'I'm with the QAIMNS.'

'Milly Thomas,' the girl said. 'How do you do? I'm with the TFNS. We were told that the QAIMNS nurses might not speak to us. I'm so glad that it isn't true.'

Edie leaned towards her. 'It might be,' she whispered. 'But you can speak to me, and remember that your job is just as important as ours, even if we've been nursing for longer.'

'Thank you. And some of us are highly trained,' she added. 'I've been working as a nurse for over three years and I was asked if I'd volunteer to come abroad, which I'm really glad to. My brother enlisted and is somewhere in France, so I thought I might as well. Originally I'd thought of becoming a teacher or a governess, but then my mother was ill and needed me at home.'

She sighed. 'After she died I thought that I might make a better nurse than a teacher. I met a young woman a few years ago who was hoping to become a doctor and I was so impressed by her. And although I couldn't possibly do that, I think I'm probably a good nurse.'

Edie suppressed a yawn. She probably was. She'd certainly cheer up a patient with her lively chit-chat, but she hoped she had good powers of concentration too.

'What rank are you, Edie? May I call you Edie?' Milly asked. 'I was promoted to staff nurse before I came out.'

'Sister,' Edie said. 'So you'll have to give me my title when we're in the hospital, Milly. Those are the rules, I'm afraid.'

Milly put her hand to her mouth. 'Oh, sorry, Sister. Listen to me, rabbiting on. My tongue always moves faster than my brain.'

Edie smiled. She liked this young nurse and hoped that they might work alongside each other. They were a long way from home; they would need as many friends as possible in the coming months of what would be a difficult time.

They were allocated accommodation in the hospital, the QAIMNS situated in a separate section from the TFNS, or the Tiffins as they were quickly named. Edie shared with the other sister, who huffed and puffed about not being given their own rooms.

'I doubt we'll be on duty at 'same time,' Edie said prosaically as she placed her few belongings in a chest of drawers. 'So you'll mostly have the room to yourself, but if we do have to spend the night together you needn't worry. I'm a good sleeper and I don't snore!'

'Well, I didn't mean—' The sister was obviously embarrassed by her thoughtlessness, but Edie shrugged it off.

'I'm Edie Morris,' she said. 'Formerly from Hull. I've been working at Endell Street.'

'Margaret Connors,' the other woman answered. 'Manchester. I volunteered to come abroad, did you?'

'No, I was asked if I would come.' Edie smiled to herself. 'Hand-picked,' she added. 'By Dr Anderson. Because of my experience.' So put that in your pipe and smoke it, she thought. Not usually one to blow her own trumpet, she thought that in this instance it was perfectly all right to do so.

She slept well that night in spite of feeling as if she was still bobbing along on the sea, and the next morning was called to a meeting by the matron.

'I'm very pleased to welcome you, Sister Morris,' Matron said in English with a delightful French accent. 'I have received a very good account of you from Dr Anderson and so I will make you senior sister above the others. I am putting you in charge of the receiving wards so that you can ascertain which patients are

most urgent. You will be answerable to me and the surgeons.'
She paused. 'You will have heard of the military expression the
triage?'

Edie said that she had. It was a system of prioritizing. Those
injured on the battlefield who had a good chance of survival
after treatment were seen to first. Those whose injuries were
not life-threatening came next in line and those who would not
survive came last.

'We believe that all our patients are important,' Matron
continued. 'Even those who will not survive deserve our care.'

'I quite agree,' Edie said quietly. 'I'd like to think if either of
my brothers suffered injury there would be somebody there to
hold their hand.'

Matron nodded. 'Have you met any nurses that you would
like on your wards?'

'I've only met one so far and that is Staff Nurse Thomas.
She told me she has had three years' training with TFNS; she's
very cheerful and I'd like to try her out and see how she shapes
up.'

'Very well,' Matron got to her feet. 'That's a good start. Thank
you, Sister.'

They were overrun by casualties from the second battle of
Ypres which lasted from April until the end of May. The gas
attacks had been the most terrifying that anyone had ever
encountered and there was worldwide condemnation. Even the
German military generals had been taken aback by the ferocity
of its effect. The soldiers who had survived with their lives
were often blinded, their lungs and throats damaged beyond
repair.

Edie had set up a small ward for the patients who she felt
might not reach home and she had put Staff Nurse Thomas
in charge of it. 'They're far from their loved ones,' she said.
'Reassure them, stay by their side so that they feel cared for,'
and Milly had nodded and said that she would.

She came back to Edie one day and asked if she would come.
'I don't think this soldier is going to survive for much longer,'

she whispered. 'He was with the Hull Pals. He was caught in a gas attack.'

Edie came to the ward immediately. The patient was heavily bandaged about his head and throat, with just his mouth showing, and appeared to be asleep. She picked up his notes. He had been blinded by the gas, which had also attacked his larynx. The injury that was causing the greatest concern was a deep chest wound from a grenade. Before she spoke to him, she glanced at the name on his case notes. It was her cousin Max.

She took a deep breath to steady herself and asked Milly to bring her some water. Then, drawing up a chair, she sat next to the bed.

'Hey, Max,' she said softly. 'Fancy meeting you here. It's your cousin Edie. Remember me?'

Slowly he turned his head to where her voice was coming from. 'Edie?' His voice was harsh and croaky and his breathing difficult. 'Are – you a nurse then?'

'I certainly am,' she said as cheerfully as she could, although she wanted to weep to see her once handsome, charismatic cousin brought so low. 'It seems that I was sent here specially to look after you. All 'other nurses are mad wi' jealousy.'

He made a little croaking sound which she interpreted as a laugh. 'I bet,' he croaked. 'Am I – going to make it – out of here, Edie?'

She took hold of his hand, the one that wasn't bandaged; the other was missing several fingers and covered by a bloody bandage. 'I'm hoping so, Max.' She bent closer so that he would hear. 'It'll be a black mark against me if you let me down.'

'If I don't – make it –' It was as if he hadn't heard her. He coughed and gasped in pain. 'Will you write – to my mam and dad – and our Jenny and say – I'm sorry. I was – hoping they'd be pr-proud o' me.'

Tears trickled down Edie's cheeks and she could barely speak. 'They're proud of you already, Max. My mother says your mam never stops talking about you, and how you're winning 'war all on your own.'

His mouth twisted into a smile. 'You were always good – at

231

telling a tale, Edie.' He took another shallow breath. 'Will you – stay wi' me?'

She gently stroked his hand. 'Course I will. For as long as it teks. Now, try to sleep and that's an order, cos I'm senior to you, corporal.' She gulped down some water to ease her tight throat. 'And we'll see what tomorrow brings.'

He nodded and sighed. 'Thanks, Edie,' he whispered. 'You're – a pal. You always were.'

CHAPTER THIRTY-THREE

At the end of August Lucy had been called in to a meeting at the hospital. 'What's it about, Rose?' she asked Dr Mason, who was also asked to attend.

She shook her head. 'No idea, but all the senior doctors have been invited.'

Lucy didn't consider she was yet a senior doctor even though she had had nearly four years of training, and wondered why she had been included.

Dr Anderson was chairing the meeting; her colleague Dr Flora Murray was by her side. Dr Anderson was brief. 'I don't want to keep you from your essential work, for which I congratulate you.' She took a breath before continuing. 'Your work here is crucial and I wanted to tell you that we now have absolute clearance from the War Office. Now that hostilities are spreading throughout Turkey, Serbia, Russia, Africa and practically every country in the world, they have at last realized just how vital our military hospitals are, and have agreed, in conjunction with the RAMC, that injured personnel can be brought straight here from the battlefields and to other English military hospitals – including those that are being run by women!'

A great cheer went up. 'Success,' one doctor called out. 'Well done Dr Anderson and Dr Murray!'

Dr Murray took on the speaking role. 'We will be recruiting more female doctors and nurses and those who are presently working abroad will be invited back if they wish to come. Some of the French hospitals will then be closed at the end of the year.'

Dr Murray asked Rose and Lucy if they would remain behind after everyone else began to leave. Neither could guess why; they were invited to take a seat and Dr Murray then explained that although the hospitals they had founded abroad would be closed, there were others that would remain open, including one in Abbeville, the casualty clearing stations in Marseilles, and the field hospitals, or *ambulances* as they were sometimes called, throughout France and Belgium.

'The field hospitals are often close to the front,' she told them, 'and are temporary and moveable so as to assist those in immediate need of care. This is not an order and will be entirely your choice, but good and reliable doctors are required to assist the RAMC and we immediately thought of both of you. However, Dr Thornbury cannot go alone at present. If you wish to do this, Dr Thornbury, a senior doctor will be required to accompany you.'

Lucy took a breath and looked at her friend. I would go, she thought. But I mustn't put pressure on Rose. It's a very big undertaking. But Rose looked back at her and raised a quizzical eyebrow before turning her gaze back to Dr Murray.

'I'm willing, if Dr Thornbury is,' she said. 'She's still young but utterly reliable and I would trust her with any patient, but she should consider very carefully that the work there will be dangerous.'

'I do realize that,' Lucy broke in. 'I am not saying yes out of bravado, but simply because I'd like to play a part. Not that we don't do that already at Endell Street, because obviously we do.' She paused and considered her next words. 'But I'd like to think that by being closer to the front line we might stand a better chance of saving more lives.'

Dr Murray smiled. 'That's what we were hoping you would say. But there's no rush. Think it over for a few days.'

They all stood up and shook hands. It's done, Lucy thought. It's considered. She smiled at Rose. It's what we want to do.

*

Letters were always late, often crossed, and were frequently out of sync, as was the one Edie received from her mother.

At last! Dolly wrote. *We've had a letter from our Stanley. He says he's had a spell in hospital with a touch of flu but he's now very well and glad to be back with his mates. It's good isn't it that the army looks after our lads so well. Our Susan is anxious that she hasn't heard from their Max for a couple of weeks, but I telled her no news is good news, as I've found out for myself. We're all right at home but we've had a few scares over Hull with the Zepps and heard that a trawler was blown up while it was minesweeping. Somebody will be weeping over them, poor lads.*

Write to us when you can, though we know how busy you'll be. God bless. From your loving mam and da and everybody.

Edie sighed and rubbed her eyes. She was so tired she felt she could sleep for a week. Aunt Susan couldn't have yet heard officially about Max and she had held back on her own letter until she was fairly sure that she would have. The family would react badly on losing their golden boy, the apple of his mother's eye.

She too had received a letter from Stanley, and another from Josh had arrived on the same day. Stanley told her he'd had a bad dose of scabies and had spent some time in hospital, but didn't stipulate where. He was about to go back to the front line. *If I don't make it back home, Edie,* he wrote, *tell everyone not to worry about me as I'll be safe in heaven. I know for a fact that I won't go to the other place because I've been there several times already and expect to go again afore this war is over.*

Tek great care of yourself. I hope you have a good and long life.

Your loving brother, Stanley.

He sounded very depressed, she thought, and wondered if he was suffering from battle shock, a newly diagnosed symptom of the war that she'd heard about recently. Josh's letter was much more positive but he hadn't been on the front line yet, although they'd been under fire. All the brothers were close, Bob being the oldest boy they had all looked up to, whilst Charlie was the baby of the family and able to get away with anything. But Stanley and Josh had had a special bond and Josh had always followed in Stanley's footsteps.

Josh's letters were jokey, as if the war was a game, yet she suspected this was sheer bravado and meant to reassure his family that the two of them were having a great time, so they didn't worry. Edie hadn't yet told either of them about their cousin Max, as he too had been a hero to them when they were young.

Someone knocked on her door and she sat up. Her hour off had passed so quickly. 'Come in?' she said.

It was Matron. Edie got to her feet.

'No, please sit down. I wanted to speak to you.'

Before complying with what felt very much like an order, Edie cleared her chair of books so that her senior might sit down as well.

'I have received some news,' Matron said. 'And I am sorry to impart it.'

Edie drew in a breath and put her hand to her chest. Not her brothers!

'Not personal; please don't worry,' Matron continued. 'It is about the hospital. I have received word that we will close.'

'Close! But we've only just started here.'

'I know, but it seems that the British government have agreed that military hospitals can now operate freely in England, and the doctors and nurses working abroad can return and apply for positions at home. It has been a most complicated arrangement. However, what they haven't made completely clear is that there are other military hospitals in France that need staff and that those working here can transfer to those.'

'Oh,' Edie folded her arms. 'Then that's what I'll do; they'll still be taking casualties from 'war zone.'

'Of course,' Matron gave a wry smile, 'it is not only the British army personnel who are injured!'

'No, I didn't mean . . .' Edie began. 'I—'

'I know what you meant, and of course we treat all nationalities. But I have a suggestion for you. You are a good nurse and also have a strong constitution, not afraid of blood or mangled bones; you keep your head.'

'I try to,' Edie murmured, and didn't tell her that whenever a badly injured soldier was brought in she kept her soldier brothers in her mind as she tried to save him.

'The casualty clearing stations,' Matron said. 'The nursing staff can't work in front line conditions for long; it would be a short term contract, then a long leave before returning to the front again. The conditions for the medical and nursing staff are not what you might expect, but the patients are well looked after. Sometimes the nurses have to live in tents or temporary accommodation.'

'I'll do it,' Edie said without preamble. 'That's why I'm here.'

CHAPTER THIRTY-FOUR

I don't know whether I'll mek it out of here, Stanley wrote to Josh from hospital, *though I'll do my best. I think I might have used up most of my nine lives in this caper. Tomorrow I'm going back to front line hell again, proper treat that'll be. I don't think. I've had a real bad dose of scabies and trench foot again, thought I'd be driven mad with itching and I can't feel my toes, but I've seen much worse in here. Some of the lads that have been gassed are in a worse state than me. Some of them were shot at as they ran to get away from the poison gas cloud. It's not proper soldiering, not fair and square. I bet the German soldiers don't like it any more than us. I've had a letter from our Bob and one from Charlie. Mebbe they had the right idea about working on the railway, though I know that Charlie was keen on soldiering to begin with. Anyway, tek care of yourself.*

Fondest regards, from your brother Stanley.

Josh tucked the letter into his battledress pocket and took out a bent and wet cigarette. He looked at it and rolled it between his fingers and then put it back in his pocket. Daren't risk the smoke being seen. What was all that about, he thought. It's not like our Stanley to be such a pessimist. Is he warning me, knowing that I'll be moving up to 'front any day now? Preparing me, that's what he's doing. He allus did look after me, just as I did wi' our Charlie.

He shifted his feet and felt the mud slurping and sucking beneath them. They'd had a deluge of rain over the last couple of days and there was really no place to keep dry. He stepped on to the ladder and peered through the periscope. Seemed quiet but you couldn't be sure, couldn't let your guard slip for a second.

He glanced down the trench. Some of the lads were snatching a spot of shut-eye in the func holes – just narrow slits that were dug into the sides of the trench; you had to sleep whenever you could. It had been a vicious few days. Fritz hadn't let up, not even at night. They'd endured hours of artillery fire. He'd heard one of the young lads sobbing. It wasn't right sending such young bairns out here when they should be at home with their mothers.

There was a low light burning in the dugout which served as the officers' mess, where the field telephone sat on a makeshift table made out of planks and the reports were written. He saw Captain Warrington looking his way and he touched his finger to his helmet in a casual acknowledgement. He'd say one thing, and that was that the captain didn't ask any man to do something he wouldn't do himself. He was a proper soldier, as Stanley would say.

Josh began to hum beneath his breath. *It's a long way to Tipperary. It's a long way to go.* Where the hell was Tipperary anyway? Sounds Irish. Some Irish fellow wanting to go home, just like we all do. Hope he made it.

He ducked as a cacophony of noise, shell explosions and a racket of rapid firing rocked him off his feet. He blew his whistle and shouted an order as he jumped up, grabbed his rifle and gas mask and felt on his back-webbing to make sure his sharpened helve was in place. He felt his heart hammering. God! That was close. His new stripe felt heavy on his sleeve. 'All right, lads,' he shouted. 'On your feet. Watch out for grenades. Lob 'em back to where they've come from if you can. Come on. Keep your heads down. Let's go.'

Henry Warrington, now in truth the captain Edie had called him, had been watching the sergeant. He appeared to be relaxed but by his movements Henry could tell that he was as aware as a cat on a night-time prowl. He watched as he read his letter and tucked it safely away, examined his roll-up but didn't light it. Henry's mouth lifted at the corners in a wry grin as he recalled his first meeting with Joshua Morris and his offer to fight him. What cocky little blighters we were back then. I thought I knew everything. I know this much, I'm glad he's on my side rather than on the enemy's, he was thinking, when the whistle went and ferocious hell came to visit them again.

Lucy was on her way home for some leave before preparing for her journey to France. She doubted that she would be back again before Christmas. She'd written to Edie to tell her that she would be heading for a casualty clearing station in France early in the New Year. *It wasn't an order*, she explained, *I volunteered. I don't know what they'll say at home and I know that Oswald will be furious with me, but I believe I should go. If I find that it's intolerable then I can leave and go back to a hospital, unlike the poor soldiers who have no choice where they will be sent. There seems to be no end in sight of this dreadful war, and for what? It seems that there has been little to gain; every few yards that are won are lost elsewhere. The German soldiers must be as sick of it as we are. Keep well and safe, dearest Edie. With love from Lucy.*

Her aunt and uncle were understandably worried when she told them, but neither of them tried to dissuade her and she was pleased that she had arrived home a day earlier than Oswald, who was expected late on Friday night. She hadn't rung the bell on her arrival but had let herself in and found that no one was home but Mary, who she could hear moving about in the kitchen. Lucy stood for a moment in the quiet hall and revelled in the silence; the melodic ticking of the grandfather clock was no more than a comforting heartbeat, and God knows, she thought, I've sought and fought for many of those.

How peaceful it seemed. No one would guess in this quiet house that such turmoil and anguish was going on elsewhere. Yet everyone did know; she'd taken a longer route home from the railway station to Baker Street than usual and it was as if a pall of sorrow hung over the city. People were going about their business but speaking in low tones to one another. The errand lads on their bicycles seemed younger than they used to be, too young to go to war, and even they were not whistling, aware perhaps that it wouldn't be fitting.

She'd called in at a newsagent's for a newspaper and noticed a rack of postcards. Amongst the flowery birthday cards there were some with photographs of soldiers standing or kneeling by their wives or sweethearts, saying goodbye before going off to war. Below them were verses from a well-known song, 'Goodbye Dolly Gray', sung during the Boer War and reintroduced for this one. There were other cards too, one depicting a child at a post office asking if he might send a letter to his soldier father in heaven.

Lucy turned away. Were they meant to bring comfort to those left at home, she wondered, and thought of some of the images in her own head: bloodied limbs and torn bodies that couldn't be healed. Yes, she thought. Those real images should not be seen. Better by far for their loved ones to remember the picture they had in their heads, of patriotic smiling men in their pristine uniforms marching off and whistling 'Pack Up Your Troubles in Your Old Kit-Bag', or 'Keep the Home-Fires Burning'. That, she thought, is how they should remember them.

She called to Mary to let her know she had arrived and put her arms around her when she came out of the kitchen, her apron dusty with flour; seeing Mary always gave her a feeling of refuge, of safety, and to know that she had come back to the house in Baker Street especially so. She sat at the kitchen table whilst Mary fussed over her, bringing out the biscuit tin and filling the kettle to make tea, and felt like a child again.

'We've had a sad time of it lately, Miss Lucy,' Mary said. She hesitated. 'I don't think you'll have heard; we've lost our Max.' She took out a handkerchief from her apron pocket and wiped her eyes. 'We're all devastated. Especially his mam and da – and Jenny, well, she never stops crying.'

'Oh, no!' Lucy was shocked and upset. She had seen death so many times, but – not Max. Tears filled her eyes. She had had a childish crush on him, and the last time she had seen him, when she hadn't liked his attitude, faded into insignificance.

'I'm so very sorry,' she murmured, her voice choked. 'He was a special young man.' As they all are, she thought. 'When did they hear?'

'Onny recently. They had a telegram.' She swallowed hard. 'Onny consolation they've had, and they were so grateful for it, was that our Edie was with him.'

'Really?' Lucy whispered.

Mary took out her hanky again and blew her nose, then turned her back to go to the sink and wash her hands. 'Yes.' She took a deep breath. 'She wrote to say she'd stayed with him until 'very end. She said that they'd had a laugh and talked about home and 'tricks they got up to when they were bairns.' She sniffled. 'And that he'd simply gone to sleep and wasn't in any pain.'

Tears rolled down Lucy's cheeks. This was the worst part of the war; it wasn't out on the battlefield or trenches and that was bad enough, it wasn't about the medical team trying to save lives. It was the gaping hole left behind, the vacant space that could never be filled for those who were sitting at home knowing that their sons or husbands wouldn't return.

As she had predicted, Oswald was furious with her for agreeing to go off to France. 'I can understand that you'd go to a military hospital abroad, but *no*, not out near the battlefields, Lucy. It's so dangerous; medical staff have been killed! A stray bomb or shell – and now there's air power, and the pilots and gunners are not so accurate with their targets on a bombing mission that they can avoid a tented hospital! And besides,' he went on in full fury, 'they're not necessarily hospitals as you might imagine them to be; they're casualty clearing stations and even nearer to the front.'

She let him rant on; she understood his concern, but did he not realize that she knew all that he was telling her? Details had been given to her and she didn't think for one minute that she would be as close to the front as he was describing.

'Stop!' she said at last. He had waited until his parents and

Eleanor had gone up to bed before letting forth with his tirade, and Lucy wanted to go to her own bed. '*Stop. Stop. Stop*! I can hear you. I'm not a little girl any more, Oswald. I know what happens and I will take care.'

'You can't take care if a grenade or a shell is heading towards you,' he persisted.

Lucy got up from her chair. 'I'm going to bed,' she said. 'You're giving me a headache.'

He got up too. 'Lucy! He put out a hand to pacify her. 'I'm sorry. It's just that—' He shrugged. 'I'm worried about you.'

She turned to face him. 'I'm worried about me too, but I have to do this. I feel the need and I'm not being foolhardy; other women, doctors and nurses, are out there, and,' she paused, 'I believe I'm ready.'

He looked miserably at her and knew he had lost this battle. He could only pray that she didn't lose the next one. He shook his head and turned away.

'Oswald?'

'Yes,' he said. 'I heard you.' When he heard the door click behind her he sat down in the chair she had vacated; he sighed and leaned forward, his elbows on his knees and his hands dangling between.

Well, there's only one thing to do, he thought. I'll never get a moment's peace if I don't.

He rose early the next morning, put on his dressing gown and went downstairs, hoping to catch Pa and have a quiet word before he left for the bank, but he'd forgotten that William was now the proud owner of a motor car and sometimes drove Eleanor to Pearson Park, which was what he was going to do this morning. Eleanor was in the kitchen having her breakfast, so when Oswald said he had something he wanted to discuss, William suggested he come through into the study. As they went in, Lucy was coming down the stairs, also in her dressing gown, in search of a cup of tea.

'What's Oswald doing?' she asked Eleanor.

Eleanor shrugged and shook her head. She picked up her

cup. 'Asked if he could have a word. Hope they don't take long.' She looked up at the clock. 'Ten minutes and we have to be off.'

Lucy smiled. 'What a busy young woman you are. Are you enjoying the challenge?'

'Oh, yes, I am. I love it! But I've been thinking, Lucy; when the war is over I'd like to keep the business going. I'll produce women's clothing, cotton dresses and skirts and blouses, clothes that people can afford, because I'd guess that there won't be much money about, and then once it's established I'll put Sally in charge and I'll take an intensive course in designer fashion and design and make clothes for the better off. Not for royalty or society ladies, like Madame Clapham, but for those who can afford something a little better and like something with style.'

Lucy was amazed at her young cousin; she seemed to have her life mapped out. She sighed. If only it were so easy.

When Eleanor and her father had left, Lucy continued sitting at the kitchen table drinking tea. How nice it was, she thought, to just relax without having to rush off to the wards or surgery. She loved her vocation but hadn't realized just how tired she had become. She wondered whether to go back to bed again; it was only eight o'clock and she hadn't slept well. The argument with Oswald had unnerved her.

She was getting up from her chair when he came in; he hadn't dressed yet either. 'There's tea in the pot.' She cleared her throat. 'It's still hot.'

'Thanks,' he said, and reached into a cupboard for a cup and saucer.

'I'll leave you to it,' she said awkwardly. 'When do you go back?'

'Tomorrow. Late afternoon. We've got a lot on just now.'

'I'll see you later, then,' she said. 'I'm going back to bed for an hour.'

'Righty ho!' He concentrated on pouring the tea, but then looked up. 'Lucy?'

She turned. 'What?'

'Don't let's fall out.' His soft grey eyes without his spectacles

244

looked larger and tender. 'You've made your decision and I'll abide by it.'

'I don't want us to fall out,' she said miserably. 'We never do. This is the first time ever, since we were adults anyway. I can't bear it when you're cross with me.'

'I'm not cross.' He put down the cup and went towards her. 'How could I be cross with you? I'm just concerned about you being out there.' He put out his arms. 'Come here. Let's make up; be friends again.'

Lucy felt her eyes smart and tears not far away as she went towards him. What on earth was wrong with her? She'd seen so much and thought she'd been hardened, and here she was about to weep over a disagreement.

He put his arms round her and kissed her cheek. 'We're the best of friends, aren't we?' he said softly, and she nodded and returned his kiss.

'Of course we are.' She looked up at him and saw something in his gaze that told her they were more than that, and as he bent his head to kiss her once more the door quietly opened and his mother came in.

She murmured, 'Good morning,' but had quite clearly comprehended that there was a charge in the air and that her son and her niece had been about to embrace.

CHAPTER THIRTY-FIVE

Lucy sat on the side of her bed; she was confused and rather bewildered. I misread Oswald's intention, that's all, she considered. How silly of me. I thought for a moment that he was going to kiss my lips. She touched her mouth. But of course he wasn't; he wouldn't . . . would he? They were cousins, sister and brother almost – and yet neither of those. And then Aunt Nora walking in as she did; whatever did she think? She seemed astounded and confused, just as I am, though she covered it very well.

I mustn't let Oswald think I'm embarrassed, because I'm not, of course I'm not, and I don't want him to feel awkward. We've had a good relationship throughout our lives, mostly anyway, although there have been times when – I don't know quite how to put my finger on it, but I've felt changes in him from time to time when we have met.

She sighed and decided that she wouldn't go back to bed after all. She was wide awake anyway. She'd get dressed and go out and ask Oswald if he wanted to come, just so that he would know that everything was all right between them. Because it is!

But still she lingered. The illogical thing is, she contemplated, that although I realize now that his intention was not to kiss my lips but my cheek as he always does – her fingers strayed to her mouth once more and she swallowed – I actually wanted him to.

She came downstairs again, dressed to go out and carrying her coat.

'You haven't had breakfast, Lucy,' Nora said, as if nothing out of the ordinary had happened. 'Do have something, or we can have an early lunch if you'd prefer. I have to do some shopping this afternoon. Eleanor has run out of a particular cotton thread that she needs and I said I'd get it from the haberdasher's. Would you like to come or have you something else planned?'

'I'll just have some toast for now, Aunt, thank you. Can I smell coffee? *Mmm*, yes, please.' She sat down at the kitchen table. 'I thought that I'd visit Max's parents. I don't know them, but I know Jenny, so I thought I'd drop in and offer my condolences. Do you suppose their shops will be open?'

'So Mary said. She doesn't really approve of Max's father. He only shut the shops for one day apparently after they'd been given the news about Max. So very sad. I recall him as such a polite boy, and so handsome.'

'Yes,' Lucy murmured. 'He was.' Her lips lifted in a gentle smile. 'I fell in love with him when we went on that first picnic, do you remember? I decided that I was going to marry him.' She laughed softly.

Nora shook her head and said she couldn't recall and Lucy silently thought of Josh and Stanley in France or Flanders, and then of Henry Warrington. Where was he? Edie said she'd met him when she was last at home. She pressed her lips together, fervently hoping that this dreadful war would end soon, before it devastated more families by taking the lives of more young men.

She looked up as she felt Oswald's hand on her shoulder. He gently patted it and she wondered how long he'd been standing there.

'I thought I'd walk across to see Max Glover's family,' she told him, 'and then Dolly Morris. Would you like to come?'

They were interrupted by Mary, who bustled into the kitchen. 'Sorry I'm so late,' she said breathlessly. 'I've just seen somebody who told me about another of 'Hull Pals being killed. I don't know him, but then she went on to say . . .' She raised her eyebrows and went on quickly. 'Well, she's a proper bearer of bad news is Mrs Thompson, but she told me that Dr Warrington's son-in-law – Miss Elizabeth's husband, I don't remember his name – is missing.'

They all three put a hand on their chests; all had thought for a split second that she was going to say Henry's name.

'It upsets everyone, doesn't it?' Nora murmured. 'Especially those with loved ones fighting.' She gazed at Oswald and then turned away as if to busy herself.

'Yes,' Oswald said quietly to Lucy. 'I'll come with you, though I might not be welcome. People expect every man they meet to be in uniform.'

They passed by the Warrington house but did not call, thinking that it was perhaps too soon. The blinds at the windows were drawn closed.

'I don't know if Elizabeth and her husband ever lived here,' Lucy said as they passed by. 'He's from somewhere in the south, I seem to recall.'

'Let's take a detour,' Oswald said, steering her across the road towards Bond Street. 'Let's go to the old town and see the Zeppelin damage for ourselves.'

'We'll go to Holy Trinity,' she agreed, 'and see how badly it was hit. Mary told me that it was going to cost hundreds of thousands of pounds to repair it. Thank goodness she moved out to Mason Street when she did. She told me the old properties along High Street have been badly damaged and that there was a huge crater in the middle of the street.'

The ancient church was covered in scaffolding and the stained glass windows were boarded up; random damage had been done to other buildings and a bomb had fallen on a nearby store, causing a great conflagration that had damaged nearby properties.

Oswald gazed around Market Place; some of the shops were still in the process of repair. 'There's nowhere for people to shelter,' he muttered. 'And little warning is given until it's too late.'

248

'The Big Lizzie, the warning siren is called,' Lucy said. 'It can be heard all over the city, apparently.'

'Yes, I dare say,' Oswald said. 'But where do you run to when you hear it? Hull is a sitting target.' He contemplated. 'Hundreds of people have been killed or injured. I'm just wondering if Ma and Pa would consider moving out to Pearson Park until the war is over.'

Lucy gasped. 'Are you serious? Do you really believe that the bombing of civilian targets will worsen?'

'I do and it will,' he said fervently. 'Hull and other east coast towns are prime objectives, not only when enemy aircraft are coming in to English air space but also when they leave. They don't want to carry unnecessary weight when flying back home so they ditch their lethal cargo before they reach the sea. And besides,' he said gloomily, 'one of their aims is to terrorize the civilians, and they're certainly succeeding in that!'

'How is it that you know all these things?' she asked.

He tapped the side of his nose and said wryly, 'Can't say, but I hear talk. Sometimes we have eminent scientists visiting us – I told you about Dr Haldane?'

Lucy nodded.

'Well, for example,' he went on, 'some distinguished experts, including Haldane, come to discuss the properties of different types of poison gas, or the type of respirator that the military should carry.'

He could have told her more, but he didn't. For one thing, much of the research he was working on was top secret, and for another it would be grossly repugnant to anyone, even an intelligent, professional young woman like Lucy, to comprehend that any nation would choose to inflict such a grotesque weapon of war on another. He struggled with the understanding of it himself.

'Did I tell you,' he said, as an afterthought, 'that I met the king?'

'No!' she said in astonishment. 'Really? How?'

'King George gets about a bit you know,' he teased. 'He likes to know what's happening. I forgot to tell my mother, too.' He grinned again. 'Remind me when we get back, will you? I know she'll be impressed!'

They walked on towards Queen Street, and he suggested they stopped for coffee before moving on towards the pier to have a look at the Humber before turning back. Lucy recommended the café she had been to with Edie, where they could have a slice of delicious cake too.

As they waited for the coffee, Oswald tried to decide whether to tell Lucy what he had decided to do after talking it over with William. Perhaps it would be better to wait until she'd left for France and then tell her by letter. He was going to apply to the RAMC, and would be almost certain to be sent abroad if he were accepted. There would be no certainty, of course, but if I put in a request to be with the Hull Pals who I know are in France . . . but then they're in Flanders too, and of course Lucy herself could be sent anywhere . . . He let out a breath of frustration. Life was so uncertain.

He saw the questioning look on Lucy's face, as if she knew he was chewing something over, but fortunately the coffee and cake were brought just then and he forced a big smile to avoid any questions; and, he thought with some relief, at least she didn't seem at all embarrassed about being caught in his arms and about to be kissed most inappropriately. A lapse of judgement on my part, and what a blessing that my mother walked in when she did. Though heaven knows what she made of it.

They walked to the pier after finishing their coffee, past the boarded up damaged buildings, and then turned to head back through High Street and across town to Charles Street.

They soon found the Glovers' grocery shop, where a queue of women with shopping baskets were waiting patiently to be served. Lucy saw Jenny behind the counter and a woman whom she took to be her mother; both were pale-faced and there was no banter between them and the customers, but she noticed that after handing over their money many of the women gave Jenny and her mother a gentle pat on their hands; a small demonstration of understanding.

They waited in the queue until they reached the front. Mrs Glover had gone into the back room so it was Jenny who looked up. 'Yes, miss?'

'Do you remember me, Jenny? I'm Lucy Thornbury, Edie's friend.'

'Oh.' Jenny's face lifted in a hesitant smile. 'Of course! Sorry. It's been ages.'

'It has.' Lucy was relieved not to have to explain herself. She turned to introduce Oswald. 'This is my cousin Oswald. I don't think you've met. We – we heard about Max and are so terribly sorry. We both wanted to come and give you our . . .' She suddenly felt the tears begin to fall and put her hand to her mouth, unable to express the words of comfort that she wanted to give. Childhood memories came to the fore and they would be all that was left; there was no chance of Max's fulfilling any dreams or ambitions that he might have had; no long life with a wife and family. Everything gone.

'Thank you.' Jenny took out a handkerchief to stem her own tears. 'We are finding it so hard, my mother and me; my father won't talk about it. He's hardly said a word since we heard the news, but he insists we keep the shops open as if nothing's happened.'

'It's his way of coping,' Oswald said softly, putting his hand on Lucy's shoulder. 'He doesn't want to acknowledge it; and deep down he's angry and hurt. Sooner or later it will hit him hard and he'll need your comfort.'

'That's what Mam says.' Jenny choked back her tears. 'But we need time to grieve, and think about what we'll do without our Max, not keep on serving groceries.'

Just then her mother came back into the shop and looked at them all. 'What's this?'

'Lucy Thornbury,' Lucy introduced herself. 'And this is my cousin Oswald. We're friends of Edie and Josh and Stanley, and we both knew Max when we were children.'

She hesitated and Oswald took over. 'We heard about Max, Mrs Glover, and came to say how sorry we were.' He shook his head. 'I didn't know him well, but I remember being jealous of him when we were children, because he was so positive and amiable. A very special person.'

'He was, wasn't he?' Susan Glover gave a wistful smile. 'Nothing daunted him; he was very confident.' She swallowed. 'Edie wrote to us. She was with him at the end, you know. It's as if it was fate that she was in the hospital where he was taken. She said how lovely it was, clean sheets and blankets an' that, and 'sound of 'sea outside 'windows, cos that was worrying me.' There was a catch in her voice. 'That he would be comfortable at the end and not lost somewhere in all that mud that we keep hearing about.'

'He would have been comfortable, Mrs Glover.' Lucy strived to retain her professional demeanour. 'I understand that Edie sat with him all night, as soon as she was told he was there. She would have cheered him up. You know Edie!'

Mrs Glover nodded. 'That's something we can hang on to, isn't it?' She began to weep. 'Knowing that he wasn't alone.'

CHAPTER THIRTY-SIX

Both William and Nora were busy with various activities. William was on several hospital committees and Nora had joined the Voluntary Aid Detachment organized by Lady Nunburnholme. The headquarters were in Peel Street on Spring Bank, within easy walking distance for Nora. She didn't train as a VAD nurse but was involved in fundraising, clerical work and dispatching parcels and gifts to the troops of East Yorkshire units.

'At last I feel as if I'm helping to make a difference and bringing some small comfort to our soldiers,' she told Lucy. 'We've raised money for thousands of parcels.'

'How wonderful!' Lucy said. 'They'll know that they haven't been forgotten when they open a parcel sent from their own county; their own people.'

'That's what everyone is hoping,' Nora agreed. 'There are hundreds of little cottage industries all over Hull, women knitting socks and scarves or sewing handkerchiefs or making up something they call a *housewife*; it's a kind of fabric package that contains needles and thread, darning wool and scissors, and goes into the parcels with sweets and chocolate and biscuits for the soldiers.'

Everyone is trying to do something, Lucy thought. Doing their bit, as we all say. But the news constantly filtering through wasn't good. The enemy had committed further atrocities in Ypres and thousands of men had been killed or injured, including many of the Hull Pals. Everyone had heard about

253

the sinking of the *Lusitania* when she had been packed with American and British passengers, but not everyone knew that she was also carrying a secret cargo of munitions for the British war effort. The hope had been that America might now come in to the war, but so far no commitment had been agreed.

Oswald returned to London the next day, relieved to think that he and Lucy had got back to something like their normal relationship. He'd asked her if she'd try persuading William and Nora to move to Pearson Park; she'd said that she would but didn't think they'd agree to it.

'Perhaps Eleanor could stay there, though,' Lucy had suggested. 'Sally might stay with her so she wouldn't be alone.'

'Good idea,' he enthused, 'and maybe Ma and Pa would go at the weekends; that would be a compromise, at least. I think Pa's worried about leaving the Baker Street house empty.'

'Perhaps he is,' Lucy said thoughtfully. 'But the Zeppelins have dropped bombs all over the city, not just the centre.'

'This is just a taste of what's to come,' he said. 'Those in the know are saying that this is the war to end all wars.'

Which sounds very ominous, she considered as she travelled back to London a few days later. She hadn't been successful in persuading her uncle and aunt to move to the Pearson Park house; Eleanor had wanted to and had asked Sally if she would join her, but that hadn't been allowed either. 'Certainly not,' Nora had said. 'Two young women on their own! I'd never have a minute's peace.'

Before Lucy left, she'd told her uncle and aunt that she doubted she would get home again for some time. Nora had put her arms round her and held her close. 'Take great care, Lucy,' she'd whispered. 'You know, don't you, that you are very precious to us? Our much loved eldest daughter?'

Lucy gave her a hug, and then, with an unsteady voice and a quavering smile that embraced them both, murmured, 'And you have both cared for me as well as any parent would have.' She kissed William on his whiskery cheek. 'Take care, Pa,' she said, using Oswald's chosen name for his adoptive father, which seemed so fitting for her too; he had been her father in practically every sense of the term. 'Of yourself, as much as everyone else,' she added, and with tears in his eyes, and too choked with worry for words, he'd simply nodded.

When she arrived back at the Endell Street hospital she found that everyone was in a sombre mood. News had been released of the execution for treason of Nurse Edith Cavell by a German firing squad, despite appeals by international voices, including Americans, for a reprieve. They had also had a huge influx of injured personnel, and this, along with the news of Cavell's death, made her feel guilty for having been away.

'Nonsense,' Rose said when she told her this. 'You need respite as much as anyone else; no point in having a sick doctor.'

She too had taken a few days off and had been to see Olive Spence. 'It seemed odd calling her Olive instead of Olga,' she said, 'but she said she'd got used to it now.'

'How was she?' Lucy asked.

'Very well. She seemed quite happy, and said the work was less stressful than at Endell Street. The men they are treating, those who will be going home at least, are pleased to be out of the war, but of course there are many who will be going back to join their units once their injuries have healed.'

Then she shook her head and lowered her voice. 'But some have injuries that can't be seen. They've been affected mentally by what they've gone through, and if the authorities think that a few weeks' convalescence is going to make them fit to be sent back to the front again, then I'm afraid they are very much mistaken!'

Lucy wondered how she would cope in France nearer the battlefields. She voiced her fears to Rose.

'We'll cope, Lucy,' the older woman said. 'But if you have any real fears, then you don't have to go.'

'It's not that I don't want to,' Lucy explained. 'It's whether or not I'll be found wanting, whether or not I'll be good enough.'

Rose smiled. 'You will be good enough. Do not doubt yourself, Dr Thornbury. We all have great faith in you.'

*

It was March 1916 before they were given orders to prepare to leave in three days' time. They were given a day off to go back to their lodging house to pack what they needed, write home and give notice to their landlady.

Neither had much to take: a valise with changes of clothing, a spare jacket and two extra plain skirts, two white coats, and their medical bags. They had been told there would be facilities for washing laundry within the unit.

Lucy wrote a quick postcard to Oswald as soon as she heard to advise him that their orders had come, and then wrote a letter to William and Nora to say that she would write once she was in France and give them her address. She sent her love to all of them, especially Eleanor. *Please try not to worry about me,* she wrote. *I will not be near the front line and the casualty clearing station – it's called a CCS – is a well-equipped medical facility. I am so pleased to be going at last.*

I love you all very much. Lucy.

She looked round the room that had been only a temporary home, a mere resting place. She was leaving nothing behind. She heard someone banging on the front door, and then raised voices and someone running up the stairs.

It was Oswald. 'Thank God you haven't left.' He was breathless. 'I thought I might be too late!'

She opened her door wider to let him in. She realized that her landlady must have been shouting at him for coming upstairs.

He put his arms on her shoulders and held her away from him. 'That dragon downstairs said I couldn't come up and I'm afraid I was rather rude to her.'

She gave a little chuckle. 'Really?'

'Yes. I asked her if she knew there was a war on and that people were fighting for the likes of her and she wasn't going to stop me from coming up when I might never see you again. That shut her up.' He kissed her cheek. 'I didn't mean that, of course; it was a small white lie.' He looked down at her. 'In fact, Lucy, there's a chance that we might meet again sooner than you expect.'

'What do you mean? We're leaving now. I don't know when I'll be home again.'

'You'll be mad at me when I tell you!' He gave her a bashful grin. 'I've enlisted. I'm joining the RAMC.'

'What! But you're needed here – your research!'

'My research will be just as important over there. I'll see at first hand what's required and can report back. I've done it, Lucy: there's no going back, and no arguing.' He gave her a wry grin. 'Because I'll probably have the rank of an officer.'

'And I won't, of course, being a female doctor! But I don't understand why, Oswald.'

'I've said for long enough that I was unsure about whether to enlist, but by joining the RAMC I don't have to carry a weapon, or at least if I do I'll only be expected to use it in self-defence. You know that I'm a pacifist. I could never kill anyone.'

He gazed at her so pleadingly, clearly desperate for her to understand his reasoning, that she was relieved in a way, because she had had the fleeting thought that perhaps he was doing it in order to be near her, to protect her.

'But what will you do? You haven't had any medical training.'

'I've had some,' he admitted. 'I did a quick course in first aid, but what I am able to do, Lucy, is use the X-ray machines. I've had extensive experience and these machines are invaluable for checking injuries. And I'll be a stretcher bearer too if necessary!'

Rose knocked and looked in through the open door. 'We ought to be off, Lucy.'

'Yes, of course. This is my cousin, Oswald Thornbury,' Lucy said. 'He's come to tell me that we might meet in France.'

'It's a big country,' Rose commented wryly as they shook hands. 'We don't know yet where in France we'll be.'

'Wherever there's fighting there'll be a CCS,' Oswald said, looking at Lucy. 'I'll find you.'

The journey to Boulogne was a rough one, with high seas that lashed over the deck. Lucy and Rose kept to their shared cabin, both aware not only of the danger of the heavy seas but also of the fact that beneath them there might be mines lying in wait.

'I've always wanted to ask, but there has never been much time for conversation,' Lucy said as they sat on their bunks. 'What do you remember about my mother? What was she like? I don't have a proper picture of her or my father in my head.'

'No photographs?'

'N-no, at least I don't remember seeing any.' Did she? A distant hazy memory came sidling back of someone packing boxes; were there photographs? 'Mama was dark-haired like me, and Papa was too, so my uncle told me.'

'You only need to look in the mirror to see your mother,' Rose smiled. 'You are the very image of her. She was much younger than you are now when she left the medical school. She was extremely clever, destined for great things if they hadn't—' She stopped and shrugged. 'There's no knowing what love can do,' she said softly. 'Or how it can change lives.'

'No,' Lucy murmured, lost in thoughts of her own.

'Your cousin, Mr Thornbury,' Rose said. 'Which side of the family is he from? He's not dark-haired like you.'

'No, he isn't. It's rather complicated. My aunt had been married before, to Oswald's father, and after his death she and my uncle met and married; a few years later Uncle William adopted Oswald and he became a Thornbury. So even though we were brought up together and have the same name, we're not actually related.'

'Ah,' her companion murmured perceptively. 'I see.'

Lucy glanced at her. Should she read something into those few words, or was she only imagining that something more was implied?

It was an early dawn, cold, wet and cloudy when the passengers disembarked and were rushed to horse-drawn wagons which took them along an unlit main road until they reached some railway sidings. There they showed their travel documents, and Lucy and Rose and several nurses and other personnel were hurried on to a railway train on a single track where the engine

258

was already huffing out short bursts of steam. Once they were aboard the wheels started to turn and with a great gush of steam and smoke but with no whistles or shouts the train moved off.

I hate trains when it's dark, Lucy thought. I hate the sound of the wheels clattering as they turn on the track and the smell from the engine, and the smoke; they bring back such uneasy memories. She and Rose sat close together and turned their faces to each other; they didn't speak, but Rose took Lucy's hands and clasped them within hers, which was very comforting. This is it, Lucy thought. We're on our way. There's no turning back.

CHAPTER THIRTY-SEVEN

'You all right, sergeant?'

'Yes, thank you, sir. You?'

Henry nodded. 'Think so. You've got a few scratches. Better get them treated before it all kicks off again.'

'Oh, they'll be all right, sir.' Josh brushed a hand over his left eye and felt the stickiness of dirt and blood.

'No, come on, down to the medic and that's an order.'

Reluctantly Josh followed the captain down the trench to the first-aid post where there was already a queue of men, some limping, some with blood streaming down their faces, others holding their arms as tenderly as if holding a baby. These were the lucky ones. Josh knew that they had lost a lot of men in the battle, but hadn't yet dared to ask just how many.

Henry was bypassing the queue and Josh followed him, but drew up short when the captain halted.

'Are you all right, private?' He'd stopped by a soldier who was bent almost double and holding his stomach.

'Don't know, sir.' The soldier's words were practically inaudible and he tried to straighten up. He suddenly retched and clutched his abdomen again. When he looked up both Henry and Josh saw that his face was white as chalk. They each took an arm.

'Make way!' Henry called out and the other men moved to the side of the narrow trench as the captain and the sergeant manoeuvred the injured man forward.

'Stretcher bearer!' Josh called, but not so loudly that his voice could be heard over the top, though he reckoned that the enemy would be attending to their dead and injured too. This had been another bloody battle.

Two stretcher bearers arrived and within a few minutes they had the soldier on the stretcher and were hurrying as fast as they could towards the first-aid post, where a medical officer took over. To call it a first-aid post was a play on words, Josh thought grimly, although the medics did a good job in dire conditions. The space was no more than a dugout, lined and topped with boards which wouldn't withstand an artillery or grenade attack; but it was equipped with a makeshift planked table for the injured, and boxes of blankets, bandages, carbolic soap, antiseptic and anti-tetanus that the medics could use to make the men fit to be sent back to the trench or down to the next dressing station.

Josh sat down on a folding stool to await his turn to be cleaned up, and the captain stood with his arms folded as he watched the injured man being attended to.

'Have to send him down the line, sir,' the medic told him. 'He's been hit by shrapnel by the look of it. He'll need a surgeon to take it all out.'

Henry nodded. It was as he expected. The soldier's tunic was ripped and bloody, but with a bit of luck and medical expertise he'd recover and come back. Poor devil, he thought, but at least he was still alive and not lying in a bloody heap as so many of his other men were.

He turned to his sergeant, who was sitting with his head held back whilst his face and eyes were washed with cold water and carbolic soap, dried, and anointed with an antiseptic cream. 'It's nowt,' Josh said through gritted teeth.

'You're right, sarge,' the medic said. 'You'll live to see another day, but as a precaution for now I'm going to put on an eye shield just to keep out any dust or dirt. You can take it off in the morning, unless of course you're called elsewhere during the night.' He turned to search in a medical box to find what he wanted.

'Have you heard from your sister since she came over?' Henry asked in a low voice.

'Edie? Yeh, she was on her way to a hospital near to Calais. Wimereux I think it was. I've lost my bearings,' Josh admitted with a laugh. 'We've moved on such a lot.'

'We have,' Henry agreed. 'I met her by chance on my last leave; she told me she was coming out.'

'She's a rare girl is our Edie,' Josh said as he submitted to the indignity of an eye patch. He stood up. 'Though there are many brave women coming over. Lucy Thornbury is one of them.' He swapped places with the captain as Henry sat to have his bleeding hand washed and bandaged. 'She's a doctor now.'

'Yes, Edie told me. I didn't know she was coming over too.' He grimaced as the antiseptic stung. 'We should hope that we don't meet up with them.'

'Amen to that, sir,' Josh said grimly.

'Thanks for waiting,' Henry said to the soldiers standing in line as they made their way back. 'Take some rest when you're done.'

'Aye,' Josh echoed. 'Get some shut-eye while you can, lads.'

He followed the captain into the officers' dugout. 'Just wanted to ask how many men we've lost, sir?'

'Quite a few,' Henry said.

'I know that already, sir,' Josh said prosaically. 'How many's a few?'

'A hundred at least,' Henry admitted. 'The Northern Division have lost more than we have. They were a lot closer than we were.'

Josh nodded. 'Did they use gas?'

'No, not this time, thank God,' Henry answered. 'But it's on the cards that they will. Make sure the men have their respirators on them at all times.'

It was true that Josh had lost his bearings, having been moved from one ridge to the next and then alongside the Ypres canal to where they were now dug in somewhere near the village of Hollebeke in Flanders. Beyond this the German front line awaited them, unless they were moved again. Everywhere looked the same, he thought, it didn't matter where they were; what would once have been a green and pleasant landscape was now a sea of mud.

A hundred men, he mused. One hundred letters to be written home to say that someone's husband, father, son, would not be coming home to a joyful reunion. And what of the enemy? The same would apply; some mother or wife would be waiting. How did they get their news delivered? Did they watch out for the post as all the Allied families did?

He never swore, he'd never been allowed to. There were always strict rules at home when he was a lad and any indiscretions the boys committed were at the risk of having to scrub their tongues with soap. But his mother wasn't listening now and he swore beneath his breath. What a gory *blood-spattered* awful war this was.

I can't believe I'm still alive. Stanley began a letter to Joshua. It was months since they had met and that was by chance as they were being transferred from one area to another. They had both been marching their men, following a line of wagons, water carts, forage carts filled with medical supplies, cooks' wagons and wagons with stores. They were to be given a three-day respite in the same village, which contained nothing but half a dozen empty cottages; these might serve the officers as places to write letters or communicate with others further down the line or be given orders.

The infantry section to which he and Josh belonged would make camp in the least muddy field that they could find. He'd been wondering, as they'd marched, about battles that had been fought in earlier centuries and how communication would be managed, musing that it would have been by a mounted soldier bearing a letter and not by field telephone as it was now, although the messages were often garbled and incomprehensible. Then he'd spotted his brother.

When they were lads they had often laid their arms across each other's shoulders as they walked, but were never outwardly affectionate. It wasn't a lad thing to do; though it was different with their brothers. Bob being the eldest and Charlie being the baby, a show of affection with them was allowed, like giving your mam a kiss goodnight. But he and Josh did everything together; everything that Stanley did Josh had to do too, just to show that he could.

When they had issued orders to their men they went in search of one another, and first they saluted and then spontaneously put out their arms to embrace.

It was a good three days, Stanley pondered now. They'd had a chance to catch up on letters home and discuss the family, but never the fighting and only rarely the men they had lost, and then only when they had both known the person they were speaking of.

But he sighed now; he didn't really want to write of the terrible battle they had had earlier that day, and to no avail: they hadn't gained an inch of ground. Half his unit was decimated, including some of the officers, and there had been many soldiers with serious injuries; they'd been carried across the battlefield to the medics and if they'd survived that journey would now be on their way by wagon to the nearest CCS, which was why he couldn't believe that he was still in one piece, apart from a small segment of shrapnel that was lodged in the fleshy part of his arm. Not worth bothering about, he'd decided; it'll work its way out and if it doesn't I'll get it seen to tomorrow.

Dusk was falling as he made his way down the trench to speak to the men. It was well built as trenches went, with sandbags lining some of the walls where they overlooked the enemy line and partially laid with wooden footboards, but the weather hadn't helped that morning; where there were no footboards the rain had increased the depth of mud that sucked on his already wet and claggy boots. His feet itched. He stretched his toes inside his wet socks and determined to change them as soon as he'd spoken to the men.

'Try to get some sleep, lads,' he repeated as he passed them. 'We're almost there, we're making good headway,' which was a downright lie. 'Don't forget to say your prayers now,' and some of the young lads, eighteen or nineteen years old, obediently put their hands together and muttered, 'Our Father who art in Heaven, hallowed be thy name . . .' Some went on to ask for blessings on those at home, mothers, fathers, brothers, sisters and every other relation they could think of.

The older men, those in their late twenties and early thirties, were writing in notebooks or on scraps of paper, perhaps to their wives, mothers or children. They looked up as he passed them and he nodded, not wanting to disturb them in their thinking. They have old eyes, Stanley noticed, just like mine. I feel as if I have seen the whole of my life pass by and that I'm an old man, older than my father or even the grandfather that I can barely remember.

It wasn't as if they spent the whole of their soldiering stretch in the trenches; it just seemed like it, and it couldn't be right, he pondered, that men had to spend any time at all dug into a hole in the ground like the rats who shared the space with them.

He reached the dugout where his commander was sifting through a pile of paperwork. Draped round his neck was the Geo phone or listening device that was used to detect any enemy tunnellers beneath them; above his head was a hanging lantern and his whistle on a length of string, and the gas bell to warn of impending gas clouds; on the small wooden table a heap of dog tags belonging to only some of the casualties. 'How many men down, sir?'

The captain pushed his cap back and wearily rubbed his fore-head. Stanley reckoned that he was a year or two younger than him, a regular soldier just as he was, not a recent enlister.

'Don't ask,' he said bitterly. 'Too many to count. I feel sick to my stomach when I think of the number I have to report in the morning. I just can't face it tonight.'

'Get some shut-eye then, sir,' Stanley said. 'It'll keep till 'morning.'

'Are you on guard duty?'

'Aye, I am. I'll not sleep anyway. I'm past sleeping. I don't think I'll ever sleep again.'

'No, me neither,' the captain admitted.

Stanley went back to his post and felt in his sack for clean dry socks and a towel, then leaned on the trench wall to take off his wet footgear. He dried his toes though the towel was soggy, powdered them and put on the dry socks, and finally folded up some sheets of thin lavatory paper and put them inside his boots to soak up the damp before putting them on again.

He stretched and shrugged his shoulders to ease the stiffness and looked about him. The younger lads were curled up sleeping like babes in their func holes; of the others, some were sitting with their eyes closed, others were still writing. There was, he thought, a kind of calm. He patted his waist and chest to check that his field dressing packs were in place; these had saved the lives of many a soldier hit by a bullet or shrapnel and he was eternally grateful that there was a plentiful supply of them, made in Hull by the T. J. Smith and Nephew company.

He climbed the short ladder up to a ledge a few feet below the top of the sandbagged wall with his box periscope in his hand and his rifle strapped over his shoulder.

The periscope was wrapped in shredded muddy sacking that wouldn't be noticed from the other side and he slowly and carefully placed it on a flattened shelf that had been scooped out for the purpose between the sandbags, so that it protruded a mere few inches above the top. Then he positioned his rifle on the sniper ledge and made himself comfortable, half lying on the ledge so that he could look through the bottom of the periscope.

The sun was almost down, dropping below the horizon leaving streaks of gold and purple in the sky, a backdrop to a clump of stunted blackened trees that had almost escaped the shelling and a building with its roof blown off that hadn't. The land was empty, although only a few hours ago it had been littered with hundreds of bodies, both British and German. There had been a mutual truce whilst both sides gathered up their injured and the almost living, brought back to die with their own countrymen. Both sides were counting their losses.

Stanley closed his eyes for a second, seeing it all again as if it were imprinted in his brain, and felt . . . stoical. What would be would be. He had no influence on what the morning would bring, whether he would live to see yet another brutal day, or die. He was a soldier sent to war, to fight; that was what regular soldiers did. It was the young men, boys merely, singing and swaggering in ill-assorted caps and clothing, full of bravado as they joined the line of volunteers, that he was sorry for. He, as a recruiting sergeant in his smart uniform, had painted a picture of the honour and glory they could achieve and had instead given them a bloody battle with no victors. Guilt, he thought. It's written all over me.

CHAPTER THIRTY-EIGHT

The train stopped several times to allow passengers to get on or off and finally it was time for Lucy and Rose to get off too. It was still raining and very cold, and Lucy was glad that she'd packed warm scarves and stockings. Over her plain buttoned jacket and skirt she wore a woollen cloak, and she had a fur hat on her head.

An official called out their names and asked them to follow him and led them towards an army truck and helped them aboard to sit next to the army driver. 'Good luck, ladies,' he said, before dashing away again.

'Where are you taking us?' Rose asked the driver once they were under way.

'I'm taking you to a military base hospital a few miles from here, ma'am,' he said, 'and then I expect you'll be given details of your next place, if you're moving on, that is; or perhaps you'll be staying there? I don't know, as I'm not given information. Doctors are you, ma'am?'

'We are,' Rose said crisply. 'Come to do our bit.'

He grinned at them both. 'And very welcome you'll be, believe me.' Then his grin slid away and he became solemn and grave as he added, 'Very welcome indeed.'

After nearly an hour, the cloud lifted and the sun made an effort to shine, and after passing through a woodland road where they heard the sweet sound of birdsong and saw squirrels scurrying in front of them, he turned off and drove through a pair of large iron gates and along a sweeping drive with lawns on either side, where in front of them was a large lake with a bridge over which they drove to arrive at a very grand chateau.

They both drew in a breath; the chateau was of grey stone, and twin towers, each with six floor-length windows and three tall chimneys on its peaked roof, stood at each end of a very fine house. A white-painted double door set in the centre of the main building had a crisp white awning stretched over the length of it and two French windows on either side, whilst on the upper floor were six more windows set beneath a grey slate roof which bore a single tall chimney and an attic window.

'Just look at that,' Lucy breathed. 'Isn't that wonderful?'

'Not bad, is it, miss?' The driver grinned and immediately corrected himself. 'Sorry. Doctor.'

Lucy smiled. She knew she looked young. Was young; but probably not much younger than him.

He pointed. 'Tents make it look very jolly, don't they?' he said. 'Like having a summer party in your front garden.' He became serious again. 'Except we know that it's not.'

The lawns in front of the house were filled by four large white tents or marquees and several smaller ones. She could see nurses coming and going in their crisp white uniforms and headdresses, many of them wearing the cape of the QAIMNS, some with the white cap closely fitted and the veil tied in a knot at the back of the neck and others with it loose, indicating that there were Red Cross nurses here as well as QAIMNS and VADs.

'We're in good company,' Rose commented. 'So many women here, all determined to do what they can.'

The driver got out of the truck to come round and help them jump down and then took out their bags. 'I'll show you the way in,' he said, and led them as far as the white door which he opened to put their bags inside. He touched his peaked cap. 'Good luck,' he said. 'It's quite safe here. The Germans don't drop their bombs this far; at least, they haven't done yet.'

'Let's hope they never do,' Lucy murmured. 'Thank you very much. What's your name?'

'Green, ma'am. Private Arthur Green.'

'Well, thank you, Private Green,' she said. 'Perhaps we'll see you again. Keep safe.'

He touched his hat. 'I'll certainly try, miss – doctor,' he said, and walked away, and as he did she noticed he had a very pronounced limp. A war injury, she wondered, or something else that hadn't stopped him from joining the military.

They were greeted inside by a man in a lieutenant's uniform who stood up from his desk and took them along to a room off the great hall where he asked them to be seated whilst he went for the RAMC medical administrator. They'd glanced around them as they'd walked down the hall and noticed that the doors of some of the rooms were firmly closed, but two rooms were open, revealing beds and a nurses' work station by the door.

A grand oak staircase in the centre of the hall swept upwards before it divided off two ways, presumably one to the west wing and one to the east.

'Whoever could have owned this?' Lucy whispered. 'It has to be someone very grand. Are there still titled people in France? A nobleman? A duke perhaps?'

Rose shook her head, she didn't know either, and they whispered possibilities as they waited, counts and countesses, dukes and duchesses, marquesses and marchionesses. 'A baron?' Lucy giggled and Rose put her hand over her mouth to hide her laughter.

The administrator was wearing the uniform of a major and he greeted them warmly. 'Major Dobson,' he said. 'So very pleased to meet you, so good that you could come. Two of our doctors urgently need to go on leave; they're just about worn out. Perhaps you could unpack and find your way around today and start tomorrow? They'll show you the ropes in the morning before they go.'

'Are we staying here?' Rose asked. 'We understood that we'd be going to a casualty clearing station.'

'That is what we've been told,' he said. 'It's usually RAMC personnel who go up there, but we are very short of doctors and surgeons here and so . . .' The question of their being women doctors and therefore unsuitable for the CCS they both felt was left hanging in the air.

'I am an experienced surgeon,' Rose said firmly. 'I've operated on both men and women for over twenty years. Dr Thornbury has worked by my side for a considerable time in Endell Street hospital; you need have no fear that we will faint at the sight of a severed limb.' She looked at him unwaveringly. 'I understand that female nurses are routinely recruited to go to casualty clearing stations. We are here to save lives, Major Dobson.'

His face cleared. 'Thank you, Dr Mason,' he said. 'I'm quite sure you will be sent to one of the units eventually, but if you would stay with us for a short time we'd be most grateful and you'll also see how we run things. Here at this base hospital we take the badly injured transferred from the CCS, or those on their way back home. At full stretch we can take five hundred patients; at present we have twenty doctors, some of them surgeons, some ward doctors. We do not differentiate between male and female, not in this hospital at any rate, even though word has it that the War Office does – or did,' he added. 'Happily they are coming to their senses now that they see the need of all experienced medical staff.'

He gave them the number of the room they were to share and where to find it on the first floor. 'We don't have access to the whole house,' he explained, 'but we do have the use of the bedrooms. The nurses are on the top floor, all the male medical staff are in the east tower block, the military in the west. When you've unpacked, if you come down I'll ask an orderly to show you round and perhaps you'd like a pot of tea or coffee and something to eat?'

'Oh, thank you, yes please,' Lucy said, beaming at him. 'That would be most welcome.'

They found their room, which was huge with a battered but very large wardrobe and two single beds with a chest of drawers at each side. A cast iron radiator stood beneath the window, which looked over a terrace and lawns, the lawns being filled with white tents just as the front one was. On opening a door

271

they discovered a large bathroom with a rolltop bath with brass taps and a washbasin with a mirror above it.

'Oh, do you think the water is hot? I'd do anything for a soak in a bath,' Rose said, and ran a tap in the washbasin to test it. 'Mm, only tepid. Perhaps it will be on later.'

'We'll ask when we go down,' Lucy said. 'Perhaps it's only on for a short time each day.'

'Will you ask, Lucy?' Rose said. 'You do it much more sweetly than I can. You'll have everyone eating out of your hand before the end of the day.'

Lucy laughed. 'I'm sure that's not true!'

'Oh, but it is,' Rose said, taking off her jacket and then her shirt and rummaging in her bag for a clean one. 'That truck driver was most taken by you.'

'That's only because he was young.'

'And I'm old enough to be his mother. Had you realized that, Lucy? I could be your mother too.' She looked tenderly at the younger woman. 'Except that I'm not the motherly kind.'

Lucy sat on the bed to unfasten her boots. 'I hadn't thought about it,' she admitted, 'but of course you could be. You were my mother's friend.' She looked at her companion. She always seemed to be so strong and efficient, never stood any nonsense from anybody, but Lucy sensed that she had a vulnerable spot that she was yet to find. 'I hope you will be my friend too,' she said softly.

Rose patted the top of her head. 'I hope I already am,' she answered. 'We all need friendship.'

They were downstairs ten minutes later and found the orderly who was to show them round, but he took them first to the refectory, which was set out with tables and chairs and a long counter laid out with cups, saucers and very large teapots, with portable ovens set behind it. In the far corner were large stone sinks where young soldiers were scrubbing vegetables and a work table where army cooks were rolling pastry and chopping meat.

'There'll be hot food ready at five o'clock,' the orderly said,

272

'but in the meantime I can rustle up a pot of tea and a sandwich if you'd like. You must have had a long day.'

'We have,' Lucy said. 'We left England last night and have been travelling ever since, so we are ready for a bath and bed to perk us up for tomorrow. Is there any chance of hot water?' She looked up at him sweetly.

He nodded. 'The boiler goes on at five o'clock of an afternoon and then again at about four or five in the morning.' He glanced at the clock on the wall. It was half past four. 'There's an old coal and wood boiler out at the back of the house,' he said. 'The men who stoke it call it the Black Pig; if they don't look after it it goes out. They run it low during the day and then fuel it up again at about this time. I'd give it an hour to heat up, so if you start to run your bath at about six it should be nice 'n' hot.'

'Wonderful,' she murmured. 'Thank you so much.'

They drank their tea and ate a ham sandwich and then he took them off on a brief tour of the house. Of the two open rooms in the hall that they had previously noticed, one was a fever ward for those with trench fever or other infectious or skin diseases, and a nurse handed them a face mask and indicated a washbasin where they could wash their hands before entering; the other was an anteroom holding a dozen beds, all of them occupied by patients, which led towards another room used as an operating theatre.

There was a notice hanging on the door which said *Surgery in Progress* so they didn't attempt to enter, but there was a small window cut into the top of the door so that they were able to see inside. Rose went first and said, 'It looks well equipped,' as if she were pleased, and then stood back for Lucy to see.

She stood on tiptoe and saw two narrow operating tables, one of which was in use by a surgeon who had his back to them. On the far wall were several gas and oxygen cylinders and a large trolley with surgical instruments on the top shelf and face masks, bandages and padding underneath; a second trolley contained knives and saws and beneath were several deep metal containers, from one of which a bloody limb protruded. A deep

273

white sink was on another wall, with a shelf of towels above it.

She nodded and murmured to Rose that it seemed to be as well resourced as Endell Street. The other doctor agreed that it did.

'If you'd like to look outside at the hospital beds, ma'am,' the orderly said as they came back into the hall, 'do feel free to wander, but I must ask you to excuse me as I have other duties to perform.'

'Of course; we mustn't hold you up,' Rose said. 'Thank you very much indeed for your help. What is your name?' she added, taking a leaf from Lucy's book. 'So that we know who to ask for another time.'

'Rymer, ma'am, Private Herbert Rymer, and you're Dr Mason and Dr Thornbury.' He turned to Lucy as he spoke. 'Pleased to make your acquaintance.' He touched his forelock with his finger as if he were wearing his cap, which he wasn't, as it was tucked beneath his arm, and marched away.

'A very nice young man,' Rose murmured. 'I think you'll have to watch out, Lucy, or you'll be breaking a few hearts whilst we're here.'

Lucy just laughed. 'I'm practically an old maid. I'll be twenty-three in August.'

'Oh, dear!' Rose gave a great sigh as they went outside. 'Poor you. Indeed, you'd be considered to be on the shelf if you were at home leading a normal life.'

They inspected the outside wards in the marquees and again they appeared to be run very efficiently by the nursing sisters, with doctors in attendance. Then, as it was getting close to six o'clock, they went inside the chateau again. A good smell of food was coming from the refectory but both agreed that they were almost too tired to eat and were not so hungry after eating the sandwich. As they approached the stairway, two men came out of the anteroom, one in his forties, one in his late twenties, the older man still in his blood-spattered white coat. 'Ladies,' the older man proclaimed. 'May I be of assistance?'

274

'Dr Mason,' Rose said briskly. 'Surgeon. And my colleague Dr Thornbury. And you are?' she asked pertinently.

He stared at her for a moment. 'Oh, erm, Dr Staples – and, erm,' he loosely indicated his younger colleague, 'Dr Howard. I had no idea that we were expecting, erm, more members of the fairer sex to take over our role. No one said.'

Rose didn't blink an eyelid as she answered, 'The fairer sex? Who might they be? Did we see anyone of that description as we journeyed here, Dr Thornbury?'

Lucy kept a straight face. 'I don't believe so, Dr Mason, although I wasn't looking out for anyone of that sort. I've only seen doctors, nurses and soldiers.'

She saw a flicker of amusement on Dr Howard's lips before he looked away.

'Well, ladies – erm, doctors,' Dr Staples blustered, and didn't appear to notice the anger on their faces or the consternation written on Dr Howard's. 'I suppose, seeing as you're here, do you wish me to show you the operating theatre before we leave? Show you the ropes and how we like things to be done? It can be a bit bloody, you know. Probably not at all what you expect, or have come across before.'

'No, thank you,' Rose replied, her voice tight as steel. 'We are quite familiar with operating theatres and equipment. As long as it has been left clean and scrubbed down ready for use,' she looked pointedly at his stained coat, 'we can manage perfectly well. Are you the only surgeons on duty today?'

Dr Howard was about to speak when Dr Staples interrupted. 'Ward doctors,' he said. 'Women, some of them. But they don't operate, they tend the injured as they come in.' He frowned. 'Well, if you're sure you can cope, we'll leave you to it. I hope you've got strong stomachs. It's not like midwifery, you know!' He gave a gruff laugh.

'Have you ever attended a birth, Dr Staples?' Rose asked, and Lucy could hear the ice in her voice.

'Good heavens no!' he said heartily. 'I leave that to the midwives.'

'So you've never seen a woman with a ruptured womb, or

attended a home birth where the mother is delivered of a child by caesarean section?'

He paled and began to look uncomfortable and shook his head.

'Well, thank goodness for that,' Rose said vehemently. 'For without that experience, no woman would want you near her. Good evening, *doctors!*' she emphasized, and turning on her heel she walked upstairs.

Lucy gave her a few minutes to calm down, going into the refectory before following her up to their room. Rose was discreetly undressing, about to put on her dressing gown. 'Don't get upset over that silly man,' Lucy said quietly.

'Sometimes it still gets to me,' Rose said bitterly. 'The male prejudice. Even after such a long time in medicine. But anyway, it doesn't matter! I'm running a bath,' she said, changing the subject. 'Would you like to take yours first, Lucy, and then I can linger? Leave the water. I know you're clean and it's wasteful not to.'

'All right,' Lucy agreed. 'I'll take a quick dip. One of the maids from the refectory is bringing us a tray of tea and biscuits. I asked if we might have one and she said she'd bring it up. Wasn't that good of her?'

She bathed; the water was hot and soothing and she closed her eyes and thought if she wasn't careful she'd fall asleep. She was drying and putting on her dressing gown when she heard a knock on the bedroom door and Rose speaking to someone.

'There you are,' she said, coming into the bedroom. 'There's still plenty of hot water if you want to top it up.'

'Oh, bliss! Thank you, Lucy, you're a dear.' Rose had her cup of tea and a biscuit in her hand and took them into the bathroom with her.

When she came out half an hour later, pink and warm and ready to climb into her bed, she smiled when she saw Lucy fast asleep on her pillow, a half-eaten biscuit in her hand and a half-drunk cup of tea on the table beside her.

She leaned over and gently took the biscuit from Lucy's fingers. Still looking down at her, she murmured, 'How proud you would have been, Alice, of your beautiful, talented daughter. I'll try to watch over her as you would have done, and love her as I once loved you.' Gently she stroked Lucy's cheek. 'Goodnight, Alice. Sleep well, dear Lucy.'

CHAPTER THIRTY-NINE

She was on the train again. She heard the screech of brakes, men shouting, the shrieks of women and children screaming, the squealing of metal on metal and the sensation of falling as with a series of heavy thuds the carriages toppled off the iron rails. She opened her mouth and gave a long silent scream and felt the press of protective arms and warm bodies above her. Someone was knocking; was someone coming to rescue her? She felt warm tears on her cheek. Someone was knocking; *Tell them to stop, Mama*, she sobbed.

Someone was knocking. Lucy sat up in bed. A hospital bed; was she still there? Her mama lay in the bed next to hers, her dark brown hair in a long plait stretched across her pillow. But no; she'd been dreaming again. It wasn't her mother, it was Rose, her friend, and they were in France. She slipped out of bed, put on her dressing gown and went to the door. 'Just a minute.'

An orderly stood there, a Red Cross band on his arm. 'Dr Mason? Sorry to disturb you, ma'am.'

'Thornbury,' she said huskily. 'I'm Dr Thornbury. Sorry, I was fast asleep.'

'That's all right, ma'am. It's very early, but Major Dobson requests that you and Dr Mason kindly meet him in the refectory in half an hour. We're expecting a big influx of injured men within the next few hours and he wants to discuss procedure.'

'Of course.' She cleared her throat. 'We'll be down

immediately.' Behind him she saw nurses scurrying up and down the stairs, coming off or going on duty, some of those going down still pinning on their caps. 'Thank you.'

'What is it?' Rose was sitting up, leaning on her elbow. 'Is it an emergency?'

'Yes,' Lucy said throatily. 'It is. Or it will be.' She went to the window and drew back the curtains; for a second she was confused. It wasn't night, was it? It wasn't the sunset that she could see? No, it was the dawn, but a dawn such as she had never seen before, with vivid red streaks and black smoke-filled clouds above the layer of lightening sky. Was that the noise she had heard in her dream, which was now rapidly dissolving? Had she heard explosions of gunfire and not of a train coming off its tracks?

They hurriedly dressed and went downstairs, joining the throng of nurses queuing up for breakfast. An orderly came towards them. 'Good morning,' he said. 'Dr Mason and Dr Thornbury?' When they said they were, he asked them to follow him to a table at the side, next to one where Major Dobson and the lieutenant who had shown them in were having breakfast.

They both stood up as they approached, standing until Lucy and Rose were seated.

'I hope you slept well?' the major asked. 'There'll be a busy day in front of us. The coffee is excellent, by the way,' he said, as the orderly waited for them to choose an option for breakfast.

'I heard gunfire,' Lucy said, choosing coffee, boiled eggs and bread and butter. 'Has there been a big battle?'

'I'm afraid so,' he said. 'Jackson here received the news early in the morning and came to wake me, but I was already awake and dressed. Blighters didn't even wait until dawn before setting off their artillery.'

'But you won't know yet how many injured will be arriving, will you?' Rose asked.

'No,' he replied, taking a sip of coffee. 'We don't, and we'll probably get some from the CCS who are being moved out to make room. You'll know about the triage system, I expect?'

'We do,' Rose said. 'We used a similar practice at Endell Street.'

The major went on to say they would expect to receive the injured from the second group and as they were speaking other doctors arrived for breakfast. Major Dobson introduced Dr Mason as their new senior surgeon and Dr Thornbury as her assistant, to replace Dr Staples and Dr Howard. Lucy counted ten including Rose and herself and two others were women, one of whom Rose had clearly met before. Four women, six men, not a bad mix of male and female, she thought. I hope we all get on. She had never worked with male doctors before and she saw a couple of the younger ones eyeing her curiously.

'I'd like to make some changes, unless Major Dobson has any objection,' Rose said when she had finished her meal, addressing those sitting at the two adjacent tables. 'Could we meet after Dr Thornbury and I have had a proper look at the theatre and before any casualties arrive? I won't keep anyone from their duties longer than necessary, and it will be an opportunity for you to make any suggestions for improvements that you think might be useful. Shall we say twenty minutes? Unless anyone is going off duty, and then we can speak later if you wish.' Twenty minutes would allow them to eat breakfast but without too much chat. She turned to Major Dobson. 'I'd also like to meet Matron and the senior nursing staff,' she said. 'A good hospital can't run without them.'

She thought that he looked a little put out, so she added, 'I'm quite sure that it runs well already, major, but I need to be guided by what you have already put in place.'

Lucy saw a few raised eyebrows, mainly among the young male doctors, and a wry smile and a twinkle in the eyes of the two women. Two of the men said they were about to go off duty but would stay behind to hear what she had to say.

The major came with them to the theatre. 'What was it that you didn't like in the theatre?' he asked.

'Oh, no, please don't misunderstand me,' Rose said quickly. 'It's just that when we looked through the window yesterday we saw that the surgeon and his assistant were working at one operating table and I wondered why there wasn't a senior nurse assisting so that Dr Howard could be dealing with other patients, either on the wards or, if necessary, on the other table.'

'Ah, well, yes, I see. Dr Staples liked to have the theatre to himself when operating. Dr Howard was perfectly capable of carrying out other surgical tasks, but Dr Staples insisted he helped him.'

'Which meant that another patient had to wait longer than he needed to.'

'I'm afraid so. I'd be quite happy for you to change that arrangement.' Major Dobson looked at them both with a degree of relief written on his rather florid features.

'Well, then,' Rose said, 'if you would kindly send me two orderlies to move the tables and the gas canisters, what I suggest is that I use one table for amputations or other serious injuries, and Dr Thornbury has the other, to either stitch up surgical wounds or limbs that have sustained amputation, or to attend other injuries such as broken limbs that need resetting, or burns that require dressing. I'll need a large lined limb basket and a table to contain the knives, saws, swabs and antiseptic.'

Lucy could tell that Rose was in her professional element. What she was saying made perfect sense.

'To assist us we will need either a doctor or a senior nurse,' Rose continued. 'I will speak to them, which is why I asked to meet the senior nurses. We only want those who understand surgical procedure; this way, I feel sure we can move more swiftly and see more patients.'

Major Dobson positively beamed at her. 'Excellent,' he said. 'I'll send two orderlies right away.'

'And two people to scrub everything within an inch of its life, if you please, major,' she called after him as he headed for the door. 'So I hope you have plenty of carbolic soap and antiseptic!'

He simply lifted a hand as he went out of the door, and Lucy laughed. 'There's one very relieved administrator,' she said. 'I believe he thought you were going to upset his whole system.'

'It's a perfectly good system he's running,' Rose acknowledged. 'It was the previous surgeon who didn't want anyone else in the theatre with him, or at least not anyone who knew as much or more than he did, that was the difficulty; and he relegated the women to the wards, you notice. It shouldn't have been about him and his self-esteem; what it's about is getting these injured men attended to as fast as possible in order to give them another chance in life.' She gazed at Lucy. 'Do you understand what I mean, Dr Thornbury?'

'Yes, Dr Mason,' Lucy responded; she knew perfectly well that Rose's prime purpose was to attend her patients as quickly and efficiently as possible. 'I understand exactly what you mean.'

Rose had other measures in mind. Whilst the theatre was being cleaned and rearranged to her satisfaction, she spoke to the other doctors in the refectory, asking who was able to assist at surgery. There were several, including Dr Dorothy Lawson, whom she had met many years ago, and Dr George Rutherford, who said he had been very disappointed to be demoted, as he put it, to ward doctor by Dr Staples when he was well trained in theatre procedures.

'Well, in that case,' Rose said, 'if you will assist me with the first surgery, then providing everything goes well I'll appoint you as the second in seniority, assisted by Dr Lawson when you're on duty. We'll ask Major Dobson to have a duty rota implemented. Dr Thornbury will be senior assistant attended by a senior nurse once I have found someone suitable.'

If Lucy was disappointed not to be the first to assist Rose she didn't show it; there would be plenty of opportunities for that, she was certain.

'The other thing I would like to do,' Rose went on, 'if Matron and the major have no objections, is to move the fever ward outside to one of the hospital tents. Those with trench fever and those with venereal disease should be kept separate if they're not already, and being outside in the tents with plenty of blankets will not harm them in the least, and the same nurses can go with them. I realize how a sense of trust is built up between patients and staff.'

She looked around to see if she had everyone's attention, and she had: Rose in full flow was very compelling. 'Those coming in from the CCS with fresh injuries can go straight to the inside ward, once it has been scrubbed out from top to bottom, so that they can be assessed. I trust they will feel safer inside after the trauma they have been through on the battlefields. Any patients who are waiting inside to go back to England for further treatment, or to convalesce, can also be transferred to a separate outside ward, well away from the fever ward. Dr Thornbury, perhaps you will inform Major Dobson of these requirements and ask if they could be implemented immediately, before the newly injured arrive?'

Everyone, apart from those going off duty, was galvanized into action. Rose went off to find Matron to gain permission to interview the sisters and staff nurses and find those with strong stomachs to help in surgery. As she expected, there were many who were able; these she asked to give their names to Major Dobson or his assistant to add to the duty rota.

Lucy talked to Major Dobson and found that he was satisfied with the proposed changes, and pleased to think that the injured would be seen much faster than previously. She had also asked for more aprons and gloves to be left in theatre and a separate basket for the used apparel. She enquired about laundry facilities and the major was pleased to tell her that they had excellent amenities run by the RAMC.

She went into the refectory to find Rose to tell her that everything was in hand, but she wasn't there, so she walked towards the front door to take another look at the tented wards. She introduced herself to a ward nurse who walked with her alongside the patients, who were lying in hospital beds as pristine as any in a normal hospital. Only the slight flapping of the canvas gave away the fact that it wasn't.

'Some of these patients are waiting to be taken to surgery,' she told Lucy. 'Their injuries are not considered to be urgent or life-threatening; they're mostly broken limbs waiting to be set, or head injuries, but painful nevertheless. When they have been attended to they can be sent back to England to convalesce.

We're so pleased that you are here. We've been very short of surgeons.'

We should see them as quickly as possible, Lucy thought. They're holding up beds that could be used for more urgent cases, and I'm sure they'd like to be sent back to England. I'll speak to Rose about it.

Rose had come to the same conclusion and had called for an urgent meeting in an hour with all the doctors, the senior nurses and Major Dobson. 'The theatre is ready for use,' she said. 'That is the quickest turnaround that I have ever seen. Congratulations, major.' She gave him a quick approving smile. 'What I suggest is that we have a light lunch now and then all those attending surgery should scrub up. Major Dobson has arranged for the patients to be swapped over immediately, the head injuries and broken limbs to be brought into the ante-room ready to be sedated and attended to. After treatment they'll be taken to a new ward that is being assembled as we speak.'

She turned to the major for confirmation, and when he nodded she said, 'Come along then. Let's do what we are here for.'

She's so passionate, Lucy thought, and looked at the other medical staff; they too seemed energized and uplifted. This was what they had been trained for; they had come to treat the sick and injured. She thought of all the years of examination and study that they had had to undergo to reach the level of expertise and qualification that had eventually brought them to this foreign land, and they were ready and eager.

When they emerged from theatre and the surgical wards, having attended to most of the waiting patients who were now sleeping comfortably in their fresh beds in the new marquee, it was well into the afternoon. Lucy stood on the steps of the chateau and felt a great degree of satisfaction; she had cleaned up the head injuries, removed pieces of shrapnel from arms, chest and backs, asked the staff nurse to bathe and bandage sore, reddened, dust-filled eyes and assisted Dr Lawson to

284

tranquillize patients in order to reset broken legs, arms and ankles.

She had done all of this before at Endell Street, but never with such a sense of urgency as she had felt here in the midst of war. She had brought a cup of coffee out with her so that she could clear her mind and thoughts, and as she sipped she gazed beyond the lines of white tents towards the long drive and the bridge that they had crossed only the previous day. Her eyes suddenly widened. A long cavalcade of horse-drawn wagons, followed by several motorized military vehicles, was crossing the bridge.

The newly injured; she put her hand to her mouth. They're here! She took a deep breath. And we're ready.

CHAPTER FORTY

Since the first bombs on an unprepared Hull that had pulled Nora, William and Eleanor from their beds and out into the streets, and another unexpected raid early in 1916 when much damage was done and many citizens were killed and injured, the furious inhabitants quite rightly complained, with the result that within a matter of weeks a contingent of civil defence personnel arrived to put in place anti-aircraft guns and powerful searchlights.

In April the city was visited again but this time it was ready and waiting, with the Big Lizzie warning buzzer blaring and guns set. The Zeppelin was caught in the searchlights and hit, dropping thousands of feet and releasing only one bomb, which caused devastation among buildings but no fatalities, before it moved off over the Humber and out to sea. Everyone breathed a sigh of relief; perhaps now that Germany had been given a warning there would be no more bombings.

But that uneasy peace didn't last very long and another aircraft crept in again during the darkened hours before an early dawn, returning from a mission raid elsewhere and spitting out its remaining cargo on outlying roads, railway lines and buildings, causing death and destruction and terrifying the vulnerable inhabitants.

'Whatever can we do?' Nora complained as they sat down for supper. 'There's nowhere to shelter. I've heard that some people are spending nights out in the fields outside the city because they don't feel safe within it.'

'I've heard that too,' William said. 'We've also had more customers coming into the bank and drawing out their savings in case the bank is hit and they can't access their money. They'd always get it back, of course, but perhaps not immediately!'

Nora looked at him in dismay. 'Oh, my word! Perhaps we should think of going to Pearson Park after all?'

William sighed. 'We might give it some consideration, I think. We could put in extra security for this house and not tell anyone what we're doing, because there have been vandals entering empty property; perhaps leave a light on overnight, as long as it doesn't show outside; and buy camping beds and spend the nights at the park house. At least you'll never be late for work, Eleanor,' he said, in the vain hope of lifting their spirits.

'If we had a dog, Sally and I would feel perfectly safe to be left on our own,' Eleanor suggested, 'and maybe Mary and Daisy would stay too sometimes. We could share a bedroom; we wouldn't mind.'

'We'll see about the dog,' Nora said vaguely. 'It's just something else to think about. And Mary won't want to stay; she has a husband, don't forget.'

Eleanor went up to bed just after nine as she always did, as she had an early morning start. William turned to Nora. 'So what's worrying you, m'dear? Are you thinking about Oswald?'

'I am, as a matter of fact,' she said in a low voice. 'We haven't had a letter for a month, nor a telephone call.'

She had been pleased when William had had the telephone installed but now she worried when she didn't hear from Oswald or Lucy, and although William frequently pointed out that very few places would have private telephones they could use, it didn't lessen her anxiety.

'He said he'd be moving off at a minute's notice, didn't he? He'll be in touch when he reaches a base, I expect. Remember, he might be at a military training camp without access to a telephone.'

287

'Or even pen and paper,' she said ironically. But he had no answer to that.

Oswald had been waiting for his orders to leave for France for months and was growing increasingly impatient, even though he was heavily involved in important scientific work. The eminent scientist John Haldane, having reached an agreement with Lord Kitchener over the type of respirator needed to keep the troops safe during a gas attack, had been overruled by the First Lord of the Admiralty, Winston Churchill, who had had previous experience of another type of mask used by the Navy which in the scientist's opinion was useless and gave no protection whatsoever. Now the race was on to invent a more efficient mask and to discover the root and effects of the different types of lethal gases.

Oswald had been moved several times to various laboratories in the London area and was now preparing for the transport of the mobile X-ray machine, therefore assuming that his posting to France or Flanders was imminent. He wrote another letter home, reflecting that he hadn't received one from his mother or William for a few weeks, even though he had written to them; he'd placed the last one on the desk of one of his colleagues asking him to post it for him with other laboratory letters as he had to rush to catch a train. There was never time to find an office telephone that wasn't in use.

In the letter he told them that his journey might be imminent, and asked them if they'd heard from Lucy. He wanted her address urgently, if they knew it. *No one seems to know the whereabouts of anyone*, he wrote. *Life is in a state of flux.*

The next morning when he arrived at the laboratory, his immediate superior gave him his instructions. He was leaving that night on a troop ship. Although a biomedical scientist, he had specifically asked to serve as a combat medical technician or operator of the mobile X-ray machine in a medical unit attached to the RAMC.

The use of these machines had been pioneered by Marie Curie and the French, who had been at the forefront of developing the motor-driven units; the intrepid and fearless scientist Marie Curie had driven one of the wagons to the front herself, and by so doing had given Oswald the opportunity to go anywhere to assist and support. This, he'd thought, was his way of serving his country without raising a rifle to kill.

For quite some time he had worn a badge on his coat lapel to show that he was engaged on important war work, but somehow it didn't seem enough and he had often felt hostile eyes upon him, especially those of women old enough to be his mother, as if querying why he wasn't in uniform as their sons were. Now he would be. It had already been issued and was hanging in his wardrobe at his lodgings waiting for him to wear.

He shook hands with his white-coated colleagues. Some of them thought he was mad, leaving important scientific laboratory work to risk death or injury; his reply was that to learn by knowledge and experience on the battlefield might be more effective than experimenting in a research laboratory. He admitted only to himself that there was another reason.

He arrived back at his lodgings by lunchtime to change and pack the few belongings he would require, notably the gas respirator, encased in a satchel, several field dressing packs that he put in his breast pockets, warm socks knitted by his mother, handkerchiefs from Eleanor – and something from Lucy; he looked about him and picked up her last letter, though it had arrived several weeks ago.

He had been provided with a large rucksack for his greatcoat, which he packed as it wasn't a cold day, and at the last minute he put in a woollen scarf and gloves; winter, he thought, might be back before he was. Finally he dressed in full uniform, putting on vest, shirt, trousers, socks, puttees, and leather boots, then the jacket with the red-cross patches on each shoulder, the leather belt, and last of all the stiffened peaked cap with the badge of the RAMC.

He opened the wardrobe and looked in the long mirror behind the door and blinked. It wasn't him. Couldn't be him. He was the lanky, floppy-haired, myopic boffin. Abstractedly he pushed his spectacles up his nose; this fellow with the shorter haircut – for he'd called into a barber's shop on his way back – in an itchy khaki uniform and a cap that hid half his forehead was someone he didn't know, but whom he had seen many times out on the streets, marching in formation with his comrades, whistling or singing patriotic songs to the cheers of flag-flying onlookers.

Instinctively he straightened his shoulders and lifted his chin, and then, putting his gas satchel over his shoulder and his rucksack on his back, he went downstairs. He'd already paid his rent to the landlady and left her his parents' address in case of any letters, although what he meant was in case she should hear that anything had happened to him, so he didn't expect to see her again before he left, but she came out of her room at the end of the hall when she heard his booted footsteps.

'Oh.' She put her hand to her chest. 'Dr Thornbury – erm, captain? I hardly recognized you.'

'I don't recognize myself, Mrs Thompson,' he admitted. 'And it will be lieutenant for the moment, although we are not officially given a rank in the RAMC. I'm a medical technician and not carrying arms, but only medical supplies.'

'Oh, that's good,' she observed. 'So we'll see you back in one piece when this awful war is over?'

'I certainly hope so,' he said, seeing no point in telling her that anyone out on the battlefields could be at risk of a stray bullet or a dose of gas to choke them to death. 'If there's any post—'

'Oh! Yes, a letter came in the afternoon delivery. Here you are.' She turned to the hall table where a solitary letter was waiting on the polished surface.

He took it from her and, glancing at the handwriting, put it safely in his pocket to read on the train journey to the ship where he would join his fellow travellers and collect his medical equipment.

'Thank you, Mrs Thompson. I've been waiting for this, and hoping it would arrive before I left.'

He put out his hand to shake hers, but she leaned forward

and kissed his cheek. 'You take great care now,' she murmured, with a catch in her voice.

'You too, Mrs Thompson,' he said, moved by her reaction to his departure. 'No going out dancing on a moonlit night; and head for the pantry if you hear those Zeppelins above you.'

'I will,' she nodded, as if now guided by someone in authority. She opened the front door for him and he stepped jauntily down the steps to the footpath, hitched the rucksack higher up on his shoulders, and began to whistle.

CHAPTER FORTY-ONE

Edie and Milly Thomas rushed to catch the train that was to carry them towards the base hospital close to Boulogne; since moving from Wimereux they had teamed up, nursing sister and staff nurse, to work together in several casualty clearing stations, and recently had spent their leave in a small hotel in Boulogne where they had rested before moving on once more. Boulogne was heaving with military personnel, ambulances and medical aid wagons, both petrol and horse driven, and hundreds of nurses in transit.

Edie wore the grey woollen dress of QAIMNS with the high white collar and deep cuffs, her sleeves adorned on the lower arm with two scarlet bands signifying a nursing sister. Staff Nurse Thomas was in a similar uniform but with plain sleeves and a badge on her cape to show she was in the TFNS.

They didn't expect to stay more than a month at the base hospital; only long enough to give the existing nursing staff a chance of a break from the difficult and draining assignment of caring for the injured. For Edie and her companion it would be a respite from the challenges of a CCS and both felt refreshed after their stay in Boulogne.

On leaving the train they were put on board an army truck and driven by a cheerful driver who told them something about the hospital, which was situated in a chateau. 'Lovely, it is, the building I mean; you'd need plenty of money to be able to afford to buy it.'

'Where do you think the owners have gone?' Milly asked him.

'Dunno,' he said. 'But I reckon they saw the signs of war coming and got out whilst they could. It's made a good hospital anyway, and is run really well by the RAMC and QAIMNS. I took a couple of women doctors there a while back. One was a bit spiky, but the other one, younger she was, was a right cracker. I thought she might be put off by what she'd see but she's still there. I've seen her a few times since, when I've dropped off other medical staff.'

'She obviously made an impression on you,' Milly giggled, and the driver winked.

'Too classy for the likes o' me,' he admitted.

'What did she look like?' Edie asked.

'Aw, right pretty. Dark hair, sweet face. Nice, too, I should think. She asked my name when I dropped them off and she remembered it when I last saw her out on the lawns.'

Edie smiled. 'Did she tell you hers?'

'No she didn't and I didn't like to ask. Wish I had,' he said regretfully. 'Mebbe I'll ask one of the nurses next time I come.'

'Is this your regular job?'

'Aye, bringing staff in or taking them on elsewhere. I was invalided out of my regiment; got injured in the first couple of weeks after coming over. Took a bullet that smashed up my leg. I was that mad to be missing it that as soon as I was able to move about I asked to come back, said I'd do anything that didn't involve too much walking. So here I am!'

'Good for you,' they both said. 'Well done!'

They were both impressed not only by the beautiful chateau but by the apparently well organized array of hospital tents on the front lawns. Edie sought out the matron and reported them both for duty, and an orderly took them up to the two top-floor rooms that they'd be sharing with other sisters and staff nurses.

In Edie's room there were three beds, two already occupied, one by clean laundry and the other by a sleeping nurse who had kept on her uniform but taken off her cap and let her hair down.

Edie tiptoed to the single bed by the window and placed her bag on it. There was a washbasin against the wall and she washed her hands and face, brushed her hair, put on her white cap and apron and silently left the room. She knew how important sleep was when you were too tired to finish undressing before falling asleep.

As she came down the flight of stairs to the first floor a door opened and she automatically looked towards it. It was Lucy!

They both gasped and rushed towards each other, gathering one another up in a great embrace.

'Oh, Edie!' Lucy cried. 'I've been hoping and longing that we'd meet. I'm going for something to eat. Can you come too, or are you on duty?'

'Matron said we can eat first seeing as we've been travelling. I don't have to be on the wards until six.'

'Oh, good! I want to know all about where you've been and who you're with. You said "we". Are you with a unit?'

'I go wherever I'm needed,' Edie said. 'Wherever there's an emergency and nurses are required. I've made friends with a staff nurse with TFNS; she's very cheerful and we work well together. We've been all over, Lucy, I can't believe how far we've travelled and yet remained in France. You know I was in Wimereux to begin with? They were given orders to close; can't think why, because there's such a desperate need for hospital beds and nurses.'

They went into the refectory for an early supper. 'Is it all right for us to eat together?' Edie asked. 'In some of 'hospitals doctors and nurses eat separately.'

Lucy shrugged. 'Don't know, but don't care either. We'll eat together, Edie. Why not?'

'I don't care either,' Edie laughed. 'Oh, it's so good to see you, Lucy. It's been so long!'

When they sat down again with their food, Edie went on, 'From Wimereux I first went to Villeneuve-St-Georges; it's a railway junction close to Paris and there are some very large railway sheds, and it was there that I got my first taste of what war was really like. The sheds were filled with beds and sick and dying men. We were only allowed to work for three months and then had to take an enforced break. But then I was asked if I'd move on and Milly came too, to a church somewhere near Versailles, and then we went on again to an abandoned school; it seemed that wherever there was an empty space it was filled up with beds ready for the next battle and the injured.' She shook her head and closed her eyes for a second. 'It's a living nightmare, Lucy,' she said with a break in her voice, 'and I dread each day that one of those injured might be one or both of my brothers.'

Lucy listened quietly, and then said, 'These are the casualty clearing stations you're talking about, are they not?' When Edie nodded in reply, Lucy lowered her voice. 'When you go again, Edie, I'm coming with you.'

Lucy had decided some weeks ago that it was time for her to move on. It wasn't that the work here wasn't important. It was. It was one of the busiest and most efficient of base hospitals. Doctors Rose, Rutherford and Lawson were all senior to her in age as well as experience, and soon Dr Howard would be returning, and as many of the sisters and staff nurses were skilled and qualified in surgery procedure, Lucy increasingly found herself doing the rounds of men in recovery. Which was all good and worthwhile, she thought, but she needed to gain more experience in theatre work and for this she felt that she should move to a casualty clearing station. When she had mentioned this to Rose, she had realized by her reply that Rose had found her niche here and would be reluctant to leave.

After supper with Edie, she was introduced to Milly; they remembered each other in spite of the years in between.

'We met on a train to London!' Lucy said. 'You were hoping to be a governess or a school teacher and I was going to an interview.'

'Yes,' Milly agreed. 'And I don't suppose you'll recall, Dr Thornbury, but that day I was on my way to see my uncle to ask if he could help my mother out financially, and he said no, he couldn't; so I got work in a shop and brought in a small amount of money and was still able to help Mother when she wasn't very well.' She looked sad for a moment. 'She got worse over the following year and eventually died, but my brother managed to get me a grant and I began a nursing course.'

'I'm so pleased that everything worked out for you after all,' Lucy murmured. 'But very sorry about your mother.'

She went along to speak to Major Dobson after Edie and Milly had left to go on the wards, and made it clear to him that she would like her name to be put forward for transferral to a casualty clearing station. He seemed anxious, rubbing his hand over his chin and glancing frequently at a dossier on his desk.

He cleared his throat. 'You will be aware, Dr Thornbury, that there was a large-scale German attack on the Verdun front at the beginning of the year, with many British casualties. We had only a capful of those who were injured; I believe you and Dr Mason had arrived the previous day?'

Lucy nodded. She had never seen such a huge number of injured soldiers arriving in carts, wagons and lorries, all desperately in need of urgent attention, and they were the lucky ones.

He looked at her closely. 'The British Fourth Army has taken over the battle plan on the Somme river, and although I cannot reveal more to you I can say that more doctors and nurses will be needed there before this summer is out.' He sighed. 'You won't like it when I say that you are young, Dr Thornbury, but there is great danger involved in working in a CCS, so much nearer to the front than we are now—'

'Am I in greater danger because of my youth than the older doctors or nurses?' she interrupted.

'Mm, well, no,' he agreed with a slight smile. 'I don't suppose the enemy would target you specifically, but I feel I should warn you.'

'I know a nurse younger than me who has already worked in several casualty stations and has lived to tell the tale.' She was thinking of Staff Nurse Milly Thomas. 'I'm almost twenty-three,' she told him. 'A responsible adult and an experienced doctor.'

He sighed again. 'Very well. I'll add your name to the list. There will be a group of medical personnel going out in a matter of weeks to set up the stations.'

'Thank you.' She gave him a big smile. 'Where will we be going?'

He shook his head. 'That, I'm afraid, I can't disclose. But you will be informed.'

'Thank you,' she said. 'Thank you very much.'

All she had to do now, she thought, was to inform Rose. She wondered if she would be displeased.

Oswald had located the X-ray equipment, which had been safely locked in a shed at the embarkation port along with the army vehicle that would house it. The vehicle had been stripped out in readiness and he was able to say what he would require: a narrow bed for the patient, a screen to protect the injured from curious eyes, a neck collar to hold the head still for head and skull injuries, rubber protective aprons for the operatives, a large space to contain the machine and, most important of all, a dynamo to attach to the motor's engine to power it.

He had been allocated an army driver, experienced in motors and electrical equipment, and within a few days of landing in France they would be arriving at the first casualty clearing station and setting up in readiness for the expected injured once further battles commenced. Oswald's role was to identify shrapnel and shattered bullet fragments that might create infection and subsequent death and pass on the information to the surgeon, thus saving the lives of many. The pity was, Oswald considered as he surveyed the neat unit, that there were very few of these life-saving machines and so many hospitals crying out for them. Nevertheless, he thought, we must do what we can.

CHAPTER FORTY-TWO

July 1916

Had anyone had the time or inclination or even the courage to put an ear to the ground beneath them they would have felt and heard the ground of France shake. The heavy tread of thousands of boots, the rumble of wagons, the stamp and plod of horses' hooves turned the once quiet meadows and peaceful river banks into a quivering mass of mud as opposing armies gathered on each side of the River Somme for what was becoming known as the Big Push or the Somme Offensive.

1916 had been a terrible year and it was only halfway through. There had been much headshaking as if to say that life was bad enough without the news of the Irish uprising outside Dublin's General Post Office during March; in May came the devastating news of the battle of Jutland in which both the Royal Navy and the German navy claimed victory, both with the loss of thousands of lives.

Lucy had arrived at a casualty clearing station just outside the town of Albert in northern France, replacing one of the doctors who had gone back to England on sick leave, and was delighted to find that Edie and Milly were also there. It was a large unit, mostly tented and adjacent to a church hall that had been requisitioned by the British army. A large contingent of English doctors and nurses were already busy with casualties from the spring offensive on the Somme battlefield behind the British and French line.

Here, no one questioned her age or said she was young, though she felt that some of the older male doctors looked at her sceptically and spoke condescendingly and she knew she would have to prove her worth; most of the medical staff were exhausted by the demands made on them and were just pleased that others were coming in to help relieve the situation which, Lucy gathered from the rumours that were flying around and the thousands of marching troops she had seen for herself, was going to become very much worse.

The explosions began before dawn on the first day of July and Lucy was awakened from a deep sleep in which she dreamed again that she was on a train. The deafening crashes, blasts and detonations were much worse than she remembered them and she cowered like a child again between the sheets. Then she remembered where she was and that she was safe, but that there would be others who were not. Daylight began to light up the canvas of the tent she shared with another doctor. She slid out of her camp bed and poured water from a bucket into a bowl to quickly swill her hands and face before she dressed. Her companion was still sleeping and she gently shook her shoulder before unfastening the door flap and stepping outside.

People were moving, running even, doctors, nurses, orderlies and messengers. She made her way to the main tent where the casualties would be taken, made it known that she was on duty, and then slipped across to the canteen tent for a cup of coffee and porridge for breakfast.

By midday the casualties were being brought in, first in their tens, then fifties, until after that they became uncountable and many had to wait in the lorries and wagons that had brought them from the battlefield before room could be found. Nurses ran to those waiting outside to administer immediate first aid. Church and chapel ministers hurried to give spiritual help, and those needing urgent amputation to save their lives were brought straight into surgery.

Lucy swilled her hands and arms in the deep sink in the

theatre and then scrubbed with carbolic soap before treating each patient. She had been by a senior surgeon's side for most of the afternoon before he had suddenly turned nauseous and had to go outside for air. When he came back she had amputated a soldier's limb from above the knee. His leg had been blown apart and he was bleeding profusely, and to remove the lower leg was the only way to save his life.

The soldier had already been given a dose of morphine to calm him, but when she had explained what she was going to do his eyes filled with terror and he shook his head. 'Do you want to live?' she'd asked softly. 'Do you want to go home to England and your family?'

Tears streamed down his cheeks. 'Aye,' he cried, 'I do. I've got a young bairn and – me wife – what'll she do without me?'

'You won't feel pain,' she assured him. 'Not during the surgery, but afterwards you will, I'm afraid. But think of them and you'll survive. Do you want to take the chance?' She hovered with the chloroform mask, and when he agreed she gently placed it over his face and nodded to the anaesthetist to turn on the gas machine.

By ten o'clock in the evening she could barely stand, her hands were shaking and she was ordered off duty by the duty officer. She was positive that she had demonstrated to anyone who had any doubts, and to herself, that she had earned her place. This day, she discovered a month later when moving to another CCS, had been the first day of the battle of the Somme, beginning with the battle of Albert on the first of July. It had been one of the largest battles and the worst day in the history of the British army, with twenty thousand British killed and forty thousand injured or captured on the first day, but as the driver of the vehicle that transported her reported bitterly, it wasn't over yet.

There was no X-ray unit at the next CCS and Lucy asked the duty officer if they had yet had the use of one.

'We did, but they moved on,' the officer said. 'There are so few of them that they have to share them out.'

'Do you remember the name of the radiographer?' she asked.

300

'My cousin is out here working as one, but I haven't been able to catch up with him yet.' In all the months she had been in France she had not heard from Oswald, and she was becoming anxious.

'I remember the last one we had. The boffin the lads called him. When he wasn't required on his machine he went off to the battlefield to become a stretcher bearer, then he came back, washed and got changed and became a boffin again. I can't recall his name though. Oh, wait a minute. I think the lads called him Oz.'

'Oh, yes! That's him.' She put her fingers to her mouth and hid a gasp of relief. 'Thank goodness.'

'Come to think of it,' he added, 'he said he was looking for his cousin – that would be you then?'

'Yes.' She gave a choking laugh. 'That's me. His cousin. Where was he going next?'

'Who knows?' he said. 'Wherever it is, the battlefields all look the same. A sea of mud, trenches and barbed wire and bodies scattered like poppy seeds.' He lit a tab end of cigarette and drew on it heavily. 'Do you know how many we lost on the first day of the Somme, and do the bleeding top dogs care?' She nodded, but he went on. 'Fifty-eight thousand lads,' he said harshly, and gazed blankly out across the line of white tents, seeing who knew what. 'Some mother's son, some wife's husband, some child's father, and who gives a toss? It's sheer slaughter, and all for a bit of land that won't be fit for owt by the time this is over – if it ever is. Haig,' he said bitterly, speaking of the top commander, and nipping out his cigarette he stamped on it on the ground. 'I'd shoot him myself if ever I saw him.'

He drew in a deep breath. 'You should go home, miss – doctor,' he said. 'This hellhole is no place for such as you.'

Lucy heard that many men had been lost from various pals battalions and she wondered about Stanley and Joshua and if they were still safe. As the year wore on she eventually caught up with Edie when they both were taking a break from their duties away from the front.

'They're all right,' Edie told her when Lucy asked about her brothers. 'I heard from home that they'd had a letter. The post is very erratic. It's cos we keep moving about and 'post can't keep up with us. I don't know how they're surviving. I've heard that a million men have been killed or injured, and some of 'em are Hull lads. That can't be right, can it? A million!'

Lucy didn't answer. She'd heard that too. She had also received an outdated letter from home which said that Oswald still hadn't been in touch.

She and Edie and Milly, who were all due leave, agreed to spend Christmas together in a guest house in a village near Arras, which was under British control although fairly close to the German lines. There had been some severe bombing in the town but there was a military presence so they felt fairly safe. Lucy and Edie wrote letters home telling everyone that everything was fine and that they hoped to be home soon. Lucy included a note to say that although she hadn't met up with Oswald she had heard word of him.

In January 1917 Lucy was given leave to go to England; this was a general procedure to allow the medical staff to take some proper rest. She agreed that she would and wrote to Rose to say that she would call to see her on her way home, but there was no reply and she wondered if perhaps she had gone on leave too. A few days later she received an envelope in an unfamiliar hand and opened it to find it was from Dr Dorothy Lawson, to tell her that Rose was very ill and was asking for her.

She asked for immediate leave of absence and by truck and train she arrived back at the base hospital within two days. There were several new faces amongst the medical staff but Dr Lawson came immediately to greet her.

'I'm so sorry, my dear,' she said quietly. 'Dr Mason is very sick. She caught influenza and it has turned to pneumonia. She keeps asking for you. There's something she wants you to do for her.'

'Take me to her, please.' Lucy was distraught. Of all the dreadful things she had seen, this was the worst possible news.

Rose was in a small room that had been converted into a sickroom, lying still with the blinds drawn to keep out the light.

Lucy sat in the chair by the bed and placed her hand over her friend's.

'Are you asleep, Rose?' she whispered. 'It's Lucy.'

Rose turned her head. 'You came.' She breathed shallowly. 'I'm dying, Lucy. There's no other word for it.'

'Please don't, Rose. I should miss you so much.' Lucy felt tears gathering and her throat tightened. She had seen so much death and had kept her emotions under control, but she couldn't contain this. 'Try to rest,' she murmured. 'It's the finest cure.'

Rose gave the slightest of smiles. 'I want you to go and see Olga,' she whispered. 'I want you to tell her – as I have never told her often enough – how much I have loved her. She – she was always jealous of your mother, you know; she thought – thought that I had loved Alice more than her.'

Lucy licked her lips. 'My mother?' she said, thinking that Rose's mind was wandering. 'But—'

'Alice didn't love me.' Rose took a gasping breath. 'It was always one-sided; she only ever loved your father, but she was very beautiful – just as you are – and I was besotted by her.' She gently squeezed Lucy's hand. 'But I love Olga and I want you to tell her after I'm gone. *Please*,' she beseeched her. 'I can trust no one else but you. No one else will understand.'

'I will tell her,' Lucy said brokenly. 'But I'm going to nurse you back to health and then you can tell her yourself.'

She sat with the sick woman every day; she washed her down with cool water then wrapped her in blankets, she gave her sips of boiled water and spoonfuls of chicken broth and occasionally, when she could obtain it, she gave her a glass of hot water laced with a drop of French brandy and a few grains of sugar. After a week Rose's breathing improved and she sat up in bed with several pillows behind her back and was able to take more soup with a few small pieces of chicken in it. After two weeks she was talking about getting up.

Lucy sat on the bed beside her. 'Are you still threatening to die?' she asked.

Rose smiled. She was still very pale and weak, but she shook her head and said huskily, 'I think I might have changed my mind over that. Thank you, Lucy.' Her mouth trembled. 'I really thought my life was over.'

A slight knock came on the door and Dr Lawson looked in. 'Is the patient able to receive visitors?'

'Oh, I don't think just yet—' Rose began, but Lucy interrupted.

'I think you might like to see this visitor for a few minutes,' she said, and couldn't conceal the big smile that covered her face.

Olga, or Olive, came into the room and for a moment looked shocked as she saw Rose's pale, thin face. Then she hurried to her friend's side. 'Oh, my poor Rose,' she wept. 'They said you were very ill and I was – I was—'

Lucy and Dr Lawson silently left the room and Lucy breathed out a huge breath. 'She's going to be all right now, isn't she?'

Dr Lawson nodded and said, 'Apparently so, though I would never have thought it just a few weeks ago. You did well, doctor.'

'She was one of my mother's best friends,' she said softly. 'One of only a few who remember her. I couldn't let her go.'

CHAPTER FORTY-THREE

Passchendaele, 1917

It was too late for Lucy to go home, having spent so much time with Rose, and she resumed her duties, going wherever she was sent. In July, she, Edie, Milly Thomas, two other doctors and several nurses, replacements for other medical staff who were going on leave, were travelling by train and army lorry towards Ypres in west Flanders and an advanced dressing station outside the town of Potijze, a place name that no one could pronounce.

In May there had been a vicious battle in what became known as Oppy Wood where many pals battalions, including the Hull units, were casualties. The Germans were holding the defensive line in a wooded area that was filled with barbed trenches, and held their nerve whilst under severe attack. The wood itself, though by now sparsely treed, was still very dark. Then came a moonlit night and by its light the Allies were seen advancing and another onslaught began. Some men got through the line but many were either killed in doing so or taken prisoner.

Artillery attacks began again in July, but then came the heaviest rain in thirty years and on the Passchendaele battle-fields of what had now become the third battle of Ypres tanks sank into the churned-up mud and couldn't be moved, men were stuck up to their waists in quagmires unable to use their rifles or artillery, and both men and horses drowned. In August, when the weather improved, heavy artillery attacks began again that brought in more casualties, and yet again in September and October, and it seemed as if the commanders and the generals wouldn't give up the fight until everyone, allies and enemy alike, was totally obliterated.

Lucy still hadn't heard from Oswald, nor did she expect to; no one had the time or inclination to write letters. The injured men who were brought in, those who would survive, were patched up and either sent back to the front for another session on the art of survival or sent on to base hospital. Life for the doctors and nurses was a constant loop of treating mangled limbs, mopping up blood and gore and giving succour to the dying.

Many men of the pals divisions were brought in, including the Grimsby Chums and the Hull Pals, and Lucy or Edie, who was working alongside her, would always ask if anyone had news of Stanley or Josh or Captain Warrington. Sometimes they had been seen and it was comforting to know they were still surviving. If Lucy was able to catch any of the stretcher bearers she would ask if they knew anything of Oswald, but rarely did they know him.

Then one afternoon, Oswald turned up in theatre, complete with his mobile X-ray machine, as she was attending a soldier who was riddled with shrapnel.

She wanted to put out her arms and hug him, but all she could do was stand and stare. She was wearing a bloodstained gown and her gloved hands were bloody too. The other surgeon present, who was dealing with a head wound on another bed, looked at Oswald and said, 'About time! Where in hell have you been?'

Oswald looked at him laconically, pushed his wonky spectacles with their cracked lens up the bridge of his nose and said, 'Just taking a walk in the park, don't you know?'

A few miles outside the village of Passchendaele, Stanley was instructing his men, including the special unit of 'bombers' armed with grenades. 'Helmets and gas masks on as soon as you hear 'whistle or 'gas bell. Bombers, be armed and ready. Things are really hotting up, lads, and if you're not prepared you're a goner.'

'We'll be goners anyway, sarge,' somebody interrupted, 'if we're hit by artillery fire or a gas shell.'

'You might be wounded, that's true,' Stanley replied. 'And to avoid being hit you keep running, ducking and dodging, never in a straight line, and keep on firing. Avoid any shell holes, not only because there might be unexploded bombs in them but also cos they're full o' water and you might drown.'

'And I haven't brought my swimming togs, sarge,' a wag from up the trench said wryly.

'I'm glad that you're all in such a good mood.' The captain came out of the dugout. 'We've lost a lot of men and we don't want to lose anybody else. Do as the sergeant says and we'll come through it. The Allies are taking more ground, we've got the Canadians and the Aussies with us, and now the Americans have come in we're bound to succeed.'

He dismissed the men and Stanley suggested they got some shut-eye. This was a very wet trench, although it had been well built originally with plenty of sandbags and duckboards, but after the torrential rain it was filled with sludge again. It took all his energy to keep up the men's spirits. It seemed to him that the war was never-ending; they were living in a land of mud and filth and there were bodies out there that would never be recovered. In spite of what the captain had said, the amount of ground they had gained was minuscule. The battle of Broodseinde at the beginning of October had given the Allied forces possession of the ridge east of Ypres, but since then nothing had changed. General Haig had a lot to answer for was his opinion, and continuing this third battle of Ypres and the attempt to take the village of Passchendaele, which was still held by the enemy, Stanley considered a fruitless endeavour that had led to the death of thousands of Allies and Germans. There was little of the village left and the church tower was no longer visible on the horizon.

It was bitterly cold and he huddled inside his greatcoat as

he pencilled a short letter home, telling them that he was fine and that he would soon be taking some leave and was looking forward to a hot bath and some good grub. *Don't worry about me,* he said finally. *The powers that be say this will soon be over and we'll be home sweet home again. Keep the Home-Fires Burning, as they say in the song. Much love from your son Stanley.*

He folded the letter, and unbuttoning the top pocket of his tunic he slipped it inside. He touched his dog tag with his army number on it for luck, positioned himself against the trench wall and looked through the periscope towards Passchendaele village. All was quiet, and the setting sun was glistening on the muddy landscape, turning the mire to myriad rainbow colours: blue, green and purple. He leaned back against the sandbags, folding his arms, and closed his eyes.

When he opened them again it was dark and he'd lost track of the time, but he sensed that something was amiss. He looked about him down the short trench and saw the captain in the dugout, the listening device hanging loose round his neck and his head lolling on his chest. Most of the men were asleep. He turned over and looked through the periscope. The sky had darkened except for long silver streaks on the skyline.

I must have nodded off, he thought. Is this still night or another day dawning? He screwed up his eyes, blinked and looked again. Was there movement or was he imagining it? Were there human forms slithering over the wet ground and were those stumps of blackened bushes really crouching men holding rifles, and – he twitched his nose – could he smell something?

Yes! He shouted and blew his whistle, pulled on his helmet and heaved on his mask as he'd told the men to do. The captain woke and rang the gas bell even though as yet he was unaware of the fast approaching gas cloud, and the men were instantly on their feet and in position.

Stanley blew his whistle again. 'Ready, men! Let's get at them. Up and over.'

They rushed as one, all yelling and shouting, guns blazing, the bomber unit hurling grenades straight into the line of the enemy that was advancing towards them. Some of the German soldiers went down as the projectiles found their target, but there were more of them, hordes of them, and with their armaments prepared they had been patiently waiting several hours for dawn to break. With the field guns firing and tear gas canisters and shrapnel-filled shells landing in the heart of the British advance, all resistance crumbled in their path. As Stanley's rifle slipped from his grasp he pressed his hand to his chest to keep safe his letter home, and left behind the war and the battlefield for ever.

CHAPTER FORTY-FOUR

Mary closed her door in Grotto Square but didn't lock it. No one locked their doors in this part of Hull for few people had anything worth stealing, and besides, the neighbours would notice if anyone went into the wrong house. She was on her way to Baker Street and patted her coat pocket to make sure she had her keys; the Thornburys' door would be locked for there was plenty that was worth stealing there, even though Mrs Thornbury had packed quite a few of their valuables away because of the war and Mr Thornbury had taken some to the bank for safe keeping.

But first she must call on Dolly and find out if she'd heard anything from Josh or Stanley; Ada too was waiting to hear from her husband Isaac as she hadn't received a letter in weeks. Ada rented a room further down Mason Street which she and Isaac had taken in readiness for their wedding day, but he had only spent a week in it before being called up and sent off immediately for training. Ada had kept it, as she was earning enough to pay the rent; she liked being mistress of her own place even though it was just one room, as she could come and go as she pleased, something she had never been able to do before.

Mary came through the archway and turned right, looking about her. There was a woman ahead of her standing in the middle of the footpath as if she were looking at something or someone. Mary paused. People were constantly on edge, looking in the sky for enemy aircraft, seeing spies everywhere, throwing bricks through the windows of shops with a German name. Oh, no. She drew in a breath; the woman was looking at a telegraph boy cycling towards them.

It was one of the worst things of the war, Mary thought, the waiting and watching for news, and the poor young lads carrying telegrams must have hated their jobs, for inevitably they were bringing bad news to someone.

I'll just wait a minute, she considered. He's passed Ada's house already. I'll wait for him to pass our Dolly's. The woman in front of her crossed over the road and walked on; she must have been doing the same thing as Mary and had now decided that it was safe to go home. Thank goodness we had daughters and not lads, she thought. I'd not have a minute's peace if my bairns were abroad like Dolly's.

Then she heard screaming and someone, a woman, hurtled down the steps of one of the dwellings. It was her niece Ada, and she was running towards her mother's house. Mary hurried towards her, calling, 'Ada, Ada!' but Ada took no heed and almost knocked over the telegraph boy, who was dismounting from his bicycle.

Finally hearing her aunt's calls, Ada turned to Mary. 'Aunt Mary!' she shrieked, waving an opened telegram in her hand. 'It's Isaac! He's missing, believed killed in action.'

'Come inside.' Mary took Ada's arm and led her up the steps towards Dolly's rooms. 'Try to keep calm; come on, come on.'

They were halfway up the stairs when the doorbell rang and she turned and saw the telegraph boy standing on the doorstep looking through the open door.

'Mrs Morris?' he said. 'I'm looking for Mr and Mrs Morris.' He held out an envelope. 'I've got a telegram for 'em.'

Mary grabbed the banister rail and muttered under her breath. Not another blow! How will they cope? She looked up the stairs; Ada had paused and was standing with her lips parted and her hands clutched to her chest, then Mary slowly lifted her head and looked up to the next landing to see her sister Dolly staring down at them.

'I can't take it, Dolly,' she said. 'You'll have to come down.'

Dolly slowly descended, shaking her head. She patted Ada's cheek as she passed and it was as if she were sleepwalking as she continued down the stairs. 'I'm going to collect 'washing,' she mumbled. 'I shouldn't be here really. I'm late.'

'It doesn't matter,' Mary said softly. 'Everybody'll understand.'

Dolly looked at the telegram and her lips moved as she silently mouthed their name and address.

'Is it you, missus?' the boy asked.

Dolly nodded and he touched his cap and turned away, and Mary thought again that it wasn't the right kind of job for such a young boy.

They sat down in Dolly's neat as a pin room and Ada looked at her and mumbled. 'It's Isaac, Mam. He's been killed at a place near – Yp—'

'Ypres, is it, lovey?' Mary asked and Ada nodded, tears rolling down her face.

'Thing is,' Ada murmured, her voice thick with grief, 'I feel as if I hardly knew him. I should've married him afore, when he first asked me.'

Dolly sat with the telegram in her hand and looked down at it. 'Should I wait till your da gets home?' she asked Ada.

Ada shook her head. 'You need to know, Mam. Mebbe one of 'lads is injured and coming home. Open it.'

Dolly's fingers trembled as she tried to slit the thin paper, and then read the message inside. She handed it to Mary, who took it reluctantly.

She read it and swallowed hard. 'It's Stanley,' she whispered. 'And he's not coming home.'

Mary had the painful task of breaking the news of Stanley's death to Dolly's husband Tom and their sons Bob and Charlie; they were all at work. First of all, though, she went to Baker Street and left a note for Nora Thornbury to say that her family had received bad news from abroad and she was informing the other relations and would be in later. They would understand, she knew, but nevertheless she didn't want them to come back to a cold house and no dinner.

What a dreadful time, she grieved as she walked across to the Paragon railway station; bombings by Zeppelins, families killed in their beds and lately the endless casualty lists in the newspapers; and now, she sighed, there would be two more to add to the number.

She left messages to be given to Bob and Charlie, who were both elsewhere on trains, and then she called at Bob's house and spoke to his wife Iris, who was expecting their second child fairly soon. 'Ask him to go and see his mam when he comes home, will you, love? And our Ada.'

Iris knew how important families were at this time and how upset Bob would be to lose his brother. 'What about Josh?' she asked. 'Has owt been heard about him?'

Mary shook her head. 'Let's hope that no news is good news, eh, love? Now, you go and have a sit down. Shall I mek you a cup of tea?'

'I'm expecting my mam to call in,' Iris said, 'she'll mek one. But you can stop if you like.'

Mary thanked her but said she'd better get off. She had yet to locate Stanley's father, who, Dolly had told her, was working in one of the warehouses at the town docks that week, and Mary wasn't relishing breaking the news to him. Tom was a man of few words – mainly because with a wife like Dolly it wasn't always possible to get a word in edgeways – but she also knew he would hold in his grief and that wasn't a good thing to do.

She was directed towards the back of one of the warehouses off Princes Dock, where she found him shifting large crates ready for loading on to a ship. He looked up and she knew she didn't have to say anything. The news was etched on her stricken face.

'Which one is it?' he asked huskily.

'Stanley.'

'Gone? Or injured?'

Mary put her fingers to her lips to still them. 'Gone,' she choked. 'I'm so sorry, Tom. Can you go home to our Dolly?' She gulped down tears. 'There's more,' she said. 'Isaac, our Ada's man. He's gone too.'

He put down a crowbar he was clenching and reached for his jacket, which was hooked on a wall close by. 'Come on then. We'd better get home.'

They walked in silence across the town; it was a calm late autumn day with the sun bright but not warm, as if winter were hovering near. Many women were wearing black and some men had black armbands and Mary wondered how many bright young lads who had gone singing and whistling from the city with a sense of adventure and derring-do, prepared to fight for their country, would be coming home. And if they did, how much would this dreadful war have changed them?

She remembered how proud Dolly and Tom had been when they had seen Stanley, the recruiting sergeant, outside the city hall telling the queue of men who were waiting to sign up what a wonderful life soldiering was. And mebbe it was once, she thought, and this war, so it was said, was the war to end all wars. I hope that's right, she mused, and then our children's children, and their children's children, can sleep safe in their beds at night.

CHAPTER FORTY-FIVE

Josh had been resting for five days. It had been good to relax and chat of normal things; he'd seen Oswald, who told him he'd met Edie and Lucy recently, and then he'd shot off somewhere in a hurry. He'd had hot meals from the canteen, bought cigarettes and tobacco and had a good scrub down and washed his clothes to get rid of the lice. He was bothered about his feet, which felt spongy, but the nurse who looked at them just said try to keep them dry. He'd laughed at that and remarked easier said than done; she'd agreed that it was and given him some extra talcum powder to put inside his socks. But he felt in better spirits for being clean and fed and wrote a letter home to tell them everything was fine and that a rumour was going round that the enemy was losing heavily.

He *had* heard that the British army, including the Canadians, had lost a lot of men over the summer and early autumn during the earlier Ypres battles, though he didn't mention that. It also worsened his concern over Stanley. The Germans had massacred a British line near Passchendaele; there had been several battles in that region over the last few months and he knew that Stanley's battalion had been heading in that direction. It was shortly to be his platoon's destination too, as soon as they received their orders.

The command came sooner than expected; the next day they were directed on to lorries on the first stage of their journey to the battlegrounds where, they were told, the ultimate prize

– capturing the village of Passchendaele – would be waiting.

They were directed towards the trenches only recently vacated; most of them had been blown apart by shells and needed to be repacked with sandbags and duckboards. Many of the working party, the trencher men, were sickened by what they found and could be heard retching as they dug their spades into the wet ground, even though stretcher bearers and working parties had been there before them to rescue who or what they could find.

'I think this might be the final battle of Ypres, sergeant.' Henry Warrington came to speak quietly to Josh. 'I gather that Haig will pull back whether we take Passchendaele or not. I . . . erm, I've written a letter home.' He tapped an envelope in his hand. 'If I give it to you – you know, in case I don't make it – will you post it for me? I sent one from the canteen, but . . .'

Josh nodded. 'Yeh, course I will, sir.' He took it from him and slipped it into his top pocket. 'I'll give it back to you when we're done here.'

Henry grinned back at him and put out his hand to shake. 'I've been glad to have you by my side, Josh, and not fighting me as you once suggested we might.'

'Did I?' Josh laughed. 'I wanted to fight everybody when I was a lad,' he admitted. Then he became serious and his grin slipped. 'But now I've had a bellyful and I'm done wi' fighting for ever if we get out of here in one piece.'

Henry tightened his grip. 'Me too,' he said. 'Let's be sure that we make it.'

Oswald had a regular driver, Corporal Tommy Morris of the RAMC. When he first met him and enquired if he knew Stanley and Josh Morris, Tommy told him he was a cousin: his father was one of the brothers of their father Tom.

The two of them got on well together. Tommy was not only an expert on motor engines and dynamos but also a fearless driver, and took many shortcuts over land instead of roads in order to reach either a field ambulance station or a CCS in half the time it would normally take, so that Oswald could quickly set up the X-ray machine to locate the broken fragments of bullets or shrapnel lodged inside the injured men, and the medical officer would then direct them to the nearest place where they had more surgeons and facilities to remove them.

Both of them had an unerring instinct to turn up where they were needed and both also acted as stretcher bearers when necessary. Now, though, they were in the middle of an argument and rank didn't immediately play a part.

'We're not needed in Passchendaele,' Corporal Morris complained. 'It'll be too bloody, too messy and too muddy. I'll never get 'lorry through and you don't want us to turn it over and lose your precious machine, do you? We'd be better going to a base hospital.'

'It's not *my* machine,' Oswald roared back. 'If it belongs to anybody it belongs to Marie Curie and I defy *you* to tell *her* that we must take it where it's needed!'

Corporal Morris continued to argue but Oswald would have none of it. In the end he shouted at him. 'Right! I'll drive the damned lorry myself,' and proceeded to climb into the cab. 'It's not that far from here.'

'You don't know how to drive,' Morris claimed, 'and besides, I've got 'keys.' He patted his pocket triumphantly.

Oswald jumped down from the lorry. 'I'll know how by the time I get there. Give me the keys and that's an order. I'm pulling rank, corporal, and I'll put you on a charge if you refuse.'

Corporal Morris's mouth dropped open and he handed over the keys. 'You wouldn't.'

'Probably not,' Oswald admitted. 'I wouldn't want to see you in front of a firing squad.' He looked at him squarely. 'Are you coming or not?'

'Yeah, I suppose so.' Tommy Morris took back the keys. 'Somebody's got to look after you. I was warned you were a nutty boffin, and now I know it's true.'

Oswald glared at him but hid a grin. It was true he probably would have turned the lorry over, and as they lurched over ruts and rubble and wrecked roads towards the outskirts of the village and he saw the boggy land with its deep potholes and craters where men and horses could lose their heavy gun carriers, he knew that the corporal's concerns were justified.

It was dark by the time they reached the canteen that had been set up in a small wood, well away from the front line but within sound of any battle that was expected. General Haig wanted the prestige of finally wresting the Passchendaele Ridge away from the Germans and this, it seemed, might be his last chance. He had brought in the Canadians under General Sir Arthur Currie, who had his own ideas of a battle strategy; Currie was a commander who stayed with his men out in the field and knew of the obstacles that had to be overcome.

The canteen was being run by the YMCA and they were given hot soup and sausages and hoped for a quiet night, though they both doubted that would be possible, which was confirmed by a Canadian soldier with an injured foot in a temporary splint who had been left behind by his division.

'Our units are up there on the western flank with the French,' he said. 'You'll hear fireworks before long. I wish I could have been there with them.'

You might find you were pleased not to be, Oswald thought. Not everyone will come out unscathed. There had been thousands killed in the battles across Flanders and the bombardment of Ypres had been going on since July; they were now at the beginning of November. Three months, he considered, and for what?

They slept in a hut until early morning and as a cold dawn was beginning to show across the horizon Oswald heard the first explosions of the artillery offensive; he looked out of the door and saw the sky redden and then turn black and then yellow. He sniffed. No smell as yet, but he was almost sure the yellow was a gas cloud.

'Come on, corporal.' He shook Tommy Morris by the shoulder. 'Time we were off.'

'No breakfast again,' Tommy mumbled. 'I'm going to complain to my quartermaster about unfair working conditions.'

Oswald smiled. What was it about the Morris clan that kept them so cheerful?

318

The canteen was open and they grabbed a bacon sandwich and a cup of hot coffee that they gulped down before moving off. The reverberations of explosions and artillery gunfire were deafening, and they knew that they would be more useful in this battle as stretcher bearers and first-aiders than endeavouring to use the X-ray machine. 'We can use the lorry as an ambulance to get the injured to a hospital,' Oswald said. 'This is going to be another almighty gruesome battle.'

An hour later they were approaching the immense battle area. The British field guns were firing, as were the Canadians'; the Passchendaele Ridge was being assaulted from all sides and yet the enemy in a final desperate attempt to save their line were answering back. The ferocious gunfire, the shouts of armed men and the barrage and clamour of explosives was overwhelming.

'It's sheer slaughter.' Oswald couldn't keep the anguish from his voice as Corporal Morris parked. 'So many men. Such carnage.' He went to the rear of the vehicle and pulled out the folded canvas stretcher that had been allocated to them. The X-ray machine was of no use here. It was physical help that was needed now.

Henry rang the gas bell violently and insistently. He'd seen the insidious yellow cloud released from the enemy's gas cylinders heading towards them before he'd heard the gunfire, and he prayed that the masks and respirators would suffice to help them breathe and that the toxic substances would not penetrate. The medics and officers had been warned that German scientists were constantly working on various poison gases, and their British counterparts were working to find a deterrent. One of the suggestions put forward was that the soldiers should make a flat pack of mud, something that was readily available, wrap it in a cotton handkerchief and place it inside their respirators, so that if attacked by gas they would be able to breathe through the mud. Not all the soldiers complied, but many did, including Henry and Josh.

The unit had already endured hours of artillery fire, yet

in the latest communication Henry had been told this would be the final Allied offensive against the German stronghold of Passchendaele, the highest point of the Salient; the Canadians were in position and they were prepared to risk all to take it.

So this was it: now or never, do or die, the final assault. Each of them with his own thoughts, fears and palpitations, Captain Henry Warrington and Sergeant Joshua Morris simultaneously blew their whistles, and at the signal the combatants, no longer men and boys, charged, yelling, shouting and guns blazing, over the top.

Oswald and Corporal Morris joined the stretcher bearers and RAMC men to assist the injured and carry them to the first-aid post that was built within a trench; some of the men were past requiring any assistance, and those who were barely alive had to be left behind as orderlies, stretcher bearers and uninjured men moved across the stricken ground. Those with lesser injuries were prioritized. Others, with minor injuries, dragged themselves and their comrades to a safer place where they would wait for assistance.

Some of the men were screaming that they couldn't see and that they were on fire and Oswald made them his priority. 'Swill them down with water,' he yelled to the orderlies in the first-aid post. 'Wash their eyes and take off their jackets in case they're contaminated. And wear your gloves; don't touch them with your bare hands.'

He didn't know what kind of poison gas had been used; chlorine laced with phosgene that attacked the lungs, or mustard gas that burned, or a combination of both, but whatever it was it could soak through garments and burn the skin beneath. It was worth the risk of catching a chill in the November air to avoid the blisters and pus that would come later if contaminated clothes were left on. If the respirators had worked the soldiers would avoid the agonizing effects of having their lungs stripped apart and their eyes blinded. The soldiers who were not injured ran towards them to help lead them towards the medics.

All the stretcher bearers ran with their masks firmly in place and their heads down to collect the injured; they were all at risk from the bouts of artillery and sniper fire that was still coming from the ridge. Oswald wondered if the German soldiers were as sick of the war as the Allies were and wanted to go home as badly. He guessed that they were, and did; and the dying would be leaving behind families and loved ones just as the Allies were.

By the afternoon the guns had stopped but for some occasional sporadic sniper fire; both sides of the conflict were collecting their dead and injured. It was starting to rain again, making bad conditions even worse.

An injured soldier with a head wound was being carried back for attention and called out to Oswald and Tommy, 'There's an officer over yonder trying to find his way,' he shouted. 'He's not from my trench. I think he's been blinded.'

Oswald looked towards where he was pointing. The stretcher bearers had been over that area and he thought they'd picked up everyone alive, but the soldier was right: a figure was staggering and struggling to right his mask and heading towards a deep shell hole full of water.

'I reckon he's been blinded,' Corporal Morris said, starting to run. 'He's disorientated.'

They ran towards him. 'Keep your gloves on,' Oswald said again to Corporal Morris as they approached. 'Hang on, soldier,' he shouted. 'We're coming.'

The officer turned towards his voice. He was covered in mud from falling, his mask had slipped and his hands were shaking violently.

'Captain,' Oswald said, 'let's get you back to first aid.' He fumbled to adjust the officer's mask to protect his eyes and larynx though he feared some damage had already been done, then took hold of his elbow with his gloved hands. 'Take off your coat, sir, and then we'll get your injuries seen to.'

'What! I can't. I can't see. It's the gas!'

'I know.' Oswald carefully unbuttoned the officer's greatcoat, helped him off with it and trailed it by his fingertips through the mud. 'Have you any other injuries, sir? Can you walk?'

'No. Yes. I can walk.' He reached out for Oswald's arm to guide him. 'Help me to get back to my men. I'm Captain Warrington. I must see – find out – if they're injured or killed. What hell is this? The shells. Have you seen my sergeant? Will you find him? Find my sergeant. The gas. I can't see.' His speech was jumbled and incoherent.

Oswald led him back towards the first aid post whilst the corporal ran towards another injured soldier. How could they help them all? There were men crying out for assistance whilst crawling across rubble and out of potholes towards their dead comrades and how, in all things miraculous, he pondered, did he chance upon Henry Warrington when there had been hundreds of men swarming out of the trenches to fight for their lives? He looked back towards the ridge that had been fought for and it was all but flattened. There was no church spire either. But there was a British flag fluttering there. Passchendaele had been captured; but at what cost.

CHAPTER FORTY-SIX

Lucy glanced down at her bloody gloves. Another life saved, another limb for the limb basket. The fiery incinerator outside the CCS was constantly working overtime. She was following Rose's organized method of using two operating tables in the theatre, only now she was the surgeon with an assistant doctor; Sister Edie Morris and Staff Nurse Milly Thomas worked on the other table, stitching a patient's wounds or treating stumps of arms and legs; in an anteroom a senior nurse dealt with serious cuts and head injuries. The three of them, she, Edie and Milly, worked as a team, and when their duty rota expired others took their place.

Only occasionally did male doctors, young and opinionated, and older ones set in their bigoted and prejudiced ways say she shouldn't be here, but no one said she was too young. Sometimes at the end of the day she felt as if she were a hundred years old. They all did, doctors, nurses, orderlies, administrators alike. They were all exhausted, but none more so than the injured men who were brought in.

There was a constant turnover of doctors and nurses when those on the point of collapse were replaced by others who had been away for a well-earned rest, and this station would be Lucy's last before returning to a base hospital.

A medical orderly came to help lift her patient on to the other table. His left arm had been amputated to just above the elbow. Edie was waiting to stitch the wound in her neat hand and bandage it whilst the soldier was still unconscious. He would be put to bed on the ward and if he was well enough would be transferred in two days' time to a base hospital for a further check-up before being sent back to England for final treatment and a discharge.

Before his operation Lucy had asked him what had been his occupation before the war.

'I was a carpenter,' he said, his eyes creased with pain.

'You'll still have one hand,' she said softly. 'Will you be able to manage?'

'What's the alternative, doctor?' he'd asked.

When she said there wasn't one, he simply answered, 'So be it.'

How brave they were, these men, she'd thought as she held his good hand and waited for the anaesthetic to take effect. So stoic and fearless. Nothing, she thought, could be any worse than what they had already been through.

She'd removed her bloody apron and was scrubbing her hands when a nurse put her head round the door. 'Dr Thornbury. There's someone asking for you. He says it's urgent.'

They're all urgent, Lucy sighed, every one of them, but before she could answer the nurse added, 'He says his name is Dr Thornbury.'

'Oh!' Then it must be urgent. Oswald never gave his professional designation if he could help it; he used to joke that people expected to see him with a stethoscope round his neck if he did. 'My cousin,' she said. 'I'll be out in a moment.'

'Oswald!' He was sitting outside the theatre with his elbows on his knees and his head in his hands. When he looked up she could tell that he was troubled. 'What is it? Are you all right?'

'Yes, yes.' He shook his head as if to wake himself up and clumsily stood up. 'It's not me. I'm so sorry, and I know we shouldn't claim priority when there are so many injured, but the thing is, darling Lucy, I don't think he'll survive the night.' His voice cracked. 'If he doesn't lose his leg he'll lose his life.'

She pushed him back on to the chair. 'Who are you talking about?'

'Why – Josh, didn't I say? Henry's all right, well, he's not, but he's not going to die or at least not immediately as long as his lungs aren't affected, but Josh—' His words rushed out spontaneously, incomplete and confused. 'I couldn't stop the bleeding and neither could the medics; there's a doctor with him now, but he needs immediate surgery—'

'Take me to him; where is he?' She took his arm and they followed the nurse, who had waited while they talked.

There was a long line of beds where the most urgent cases had been taken and two doctors and several nursing sisters were already in attendance. Oswald led her to where Dr Rutherford was examining a patient. He looked up at Lucy and then at Oswald.

'This soldier is a friend, I gather? He's in a bad way. We can try surgery, but he's lost a lot of blood.'

Lucy bent over Josh. He was conscious, but only just. His right leg was a mangled mass of flesh, blood and splintered bone.

'We can amputate above the knee, can't we?'

'Yes, but it must be immediately. Aren't you going off duty?'

'Not now I'm not,' she said, letting out a gasp of breath that she'd been holding since seeing Josh.

George Rutherford looked seriously at her. 'Sure you want to do this?' he asked. 'If he's a friend?'

'I do,' she answered. 'Will you help me?' When he nodded, she said, 'Let's get on now, but will you make sure that Sister Morris doesn't hear of this? He's her brother. She can come in later.'

Edie and Milly were coming off duty, and after transferring the patient they had been attending Edie came looking for Lucy and found her as she was about to enter theatre.

'Did I hear that Oswald was here?' she asked. 'Is he staying?'

'Erm, he didn't say, but I expect he will until tomorrow.'

'Maybe I'll go and find him,' Edie said eagerly. 'Are you coming?' She frowned, 'I thought you were off duty now.'

Lucy swallowed. 'I'm helping Dr Rutherford with an urgent case that can't wait.'

'Oh, well in that case—' She too turned to return to the theatre.

'No, no, it's all right; you get off to bed,' Lucy said quickly, but apparently she insisted too vehemently, for Edie immediately eyed her suspiciously.

'What kind of injury?'

When Lucy stuttered over the details of amputation, Edie said, tight-lipped, 'Who is it? Is it one of our lads? Stanley? Or Josh?' When Lucy reluctantly admitted that it was Josh, Edie said, 'I have to be there, Lucy. I have to help him.'

'No.' Lucy spoke firmly. An orderly was trundling a patient's trolley towards them. 'I promise that you can come in once we've prepared him for surgery, Edie, but you're not being there during it, so don't argue. You can ask Milly to be there. She doesn't know Josh. Go and fetch her now.'

Lucy had never seen her strong and resilient friend, who had stayed fast at her side as they'd fought for so many soldiers' lives, fill up with tears and show such emotion, and she knew that she was doing the right thing. It would be hard enough for her, and she was pleased that George Rutherford was going to be there too. A few years older than her, and an excellent surgeon, he was always grateful that Dr Mason had given him his rightful place as a senior doctor rather than an underling to Dr Staples, who, so they had heard, had gone back to England.

When Josh was ready for surgery, Lucy asked Milly to bring Edie in for a few minutes only so that she might speak to her brother. She'd calmed herself and stood steadily beside his bed. He was almost unconscious, for he'd been given morphine, but she touched his cheek with her scrubbed hand and whispered, 'Now then, our Josh. What's all this about? You've been fighting again, haven't you?'

His lips worked and she leaned to hear. 'S-sorry, Mam,' he faltered. 'Won't do it – again.'

Her lips trembled as she realized that he thought she was

his mother, and she kissed his forehead and turned away. She nodded at Lucy and Dr Rutherford, acknowledging that they had been right to insist that she shouldn't be there, and left the theatre, going to join Oswald whom she had found in the canteen fast asleep with his head on a table.

He was sitting now with a cup of coffee in front of him and he stood up as she came to join him and asked if he could get her anything. She said not.

'I've been to see Josh,' she said.

'Ah, you were allowed in after all?'

'For a moment only. Lucy was right; she put on her doctor's hat and said no.'

'If you don't intend going to bed,' he said, 'and I can't imagine that you will until you know how Josh is—'

'I won't,' she interrupted. 'I'll stay up all night if necessary, but I wanted to ask you. How did you find him in that massacre out there, one soldier amongst thousands?'

'Sheer luck,' he said. 'We'd picked up so many, including Henry Warrington, who has been gassed—'

'Henry! Henry Warrington? He's here?'

'Yes, yes.' He waved vaguely over his shoulder. 'We brought him in with Josh and a couple of others in the lorry. We couldn't get many in because of the machine taking up so much room; I'm leaving it here now and then going back first thing in the morning.'

'But,' she interrupted again, 'how did you find Josh?'

'It was Henry who alerted us. He said he couldn't find his sergeant and then when I'd taken him for treatment at the ADS the penny dropped that he meant Josh, so I went back to look for him.' Oswald ran his hands over his face. 'I thought he was dead,' he muttered, 'and I didn't know it was him, not at first. My driver, Corporal Morris – he's a relative of yours, seemingly – had gone off with the stretcher to help another first-aider. It was mayhem, Edie, total mayhem, but anyway, I went back to where we'd found Captain Warrington and found some more men who I assume were from his trench. They were Hull Pals, at any rate, and none of them looking good, but alive. I

327

whistled for some assistance and a couple of stretcher bearers came running and took them.'

His account was jumbled and out of sequence and he couldn't recall in what order anything had taken place, but he ploughed on.

'I could hear someone. I've got good hearing,' he mumbled. 'Making up for my poor eyesight. And it was such a low cry, like a cat or some other injured animal, and when I went to look where it was coming from, I found him. I didn't know it was Josh,' he repeated, 'not at first, but I saw that he was breathing so I carried him back.'

Edie looked up to see a soldier coming towards them. 'Looking for you, sir,' Corporal Morris said. 'Captain Warrington is asking for you.'

'Hello, Tommy,' Edie said. 'Remember me?'

Tommy Morris shook his head. 'Don't think so, Sister. Have we met?'

Then he looked again and put his head on one side. 'Though you do look familiar – you're not – by heavens, it's Edie Morris. Well, by all that's wonderful. Fancy seeing you here.'

She stood up and they hugged. 'Thank you for bringing Josh in,' she said, and took her handkerchief from her pocket to blow her nose.

'Not me,' he disclosed. 'It was 'mad boffin here,'' and Oswald muttered something about no respect. 'It was him who brought him in on his back, as we'd run out of stretchers. Me and another first-aider took his legs, what's left of 'em,' he blundered on, not realizing that Edie didn't yet know how serious Josh's injuries were, 'and got him to ADS. They tried to stop 'bleed- ing, but—'

'That's enough, corporal.' Oswald stood up. 'Would you like to come over and see Captain Warrington, Edie? With luck he'll probably be transferred tomorrow.'

'Yes, I would,' she said, more worried now than ever over Josh, but realizing that seeing Henry might take her mind away from it.

Henry was in a tented ward with other gas victims. He'd

sustained some injuries to his hands but nothing that required any more than cleansing, antiseptic cream and bandaging, but his eyes were covered in a bandage strip and he lay on his bed silent and comatose.

'Captain Warrington,' Oswald said, 'I've brought someone to see you; an old friend from our childhood.' He patted Edie on the shoulder before moving off to his waiting position by the theatre door.

'There's no one here that I know from my childhood, only my sergeant,' Henry said to his retreating back. 'I need to get back to my men,' he said croakily. 'They'll need their orders.'

Edie patted his arm. 'You know me, captain,' she said softly, 'although you were a lieutenant last time we met. Edie Morris, Josh's sister. We have a mutual friend in Dr Lucy Thornbury.'

'Edie.' He reached for her with his bandaged hand. 'Oh, I don't want you to see me like this.' He turned his head away.

'I've seen worse, captain,' she said bluntly. 'Much worse. You haven't had your face blown apart like some.'

'I know. I know,' he said brokenly. 'But what am I going to do without my sight? I'm finished in the army.'

'You and many others,' she said. 'Including Josh.'

'Oswald found him,' he said. 'He went back into all that mire and found him. He would have died if he hadn't, might still,' he muttered. 'I heard him arguing with someone that he must get him straight to surgery or he might not make it. That's why he insisted on bringing him back here himself— Oh, God, I'm so sorry, Edie. Josh is your brother, isn't he? I'm confused. I've lost so many of my men.'

'It's all right,' she said soothingly, knowing that he was suffering from the shock waves of what had happened. 'He's being cared for now; they're doing what they can.'

Henry began to weep. Below the bandage covering his eyes, his cheeks were wet. 'Edie, can I touch your face? I won't ever see it again. You were so lovely that day, do you remember, outside my parents' house? And I thought, I thought, that if I survived the war I'd ask if we could meet. I really wanted to. But now what use will I be to anyone? No use at all,' he said numbly.

'But you've survived, Henry. There are thousands who haven't, but you're still here, living and breathing.' She touched his damp cheek. 'But if you're not going to stand up and get on with life, whatever or however it is, then there'll be no place for you in mine.'

'Do you mean it?' he said, reaching for her, his bandaged hands fumbling for her face where with his fingertips he traced her cheekbones and down to her lips. 'Would I stand a chance, Edie? You wouldn't be put off if my sight doesn't return?'

She put her hand gently over his. 'I wouldn't be put off, Henry,' she murmured. 'I'll not be your nursemaid, but we could perhaps get through this together?'

He put his head back against the pillow and smiled, though tears still poured down his cheeks. 'I've dreamed of you, Edie. Dreamed of having a life with you. Never really believing but always hoping that it might happen. Do you think that I might kiss you?'

She looked round the ward. The lights were low and there was only one nurse in attendance by the workstation. She leaned towards him and kissed his lips and he gently stroked her face. 'Not a word to Matron,' she breathed.

CHAPTER FORTY-SEVEN

Many scientists and expert surgeons had arrived at the war zones since the beginning of the war, when it became known how many injuries were occurring, and had freely given their advice on the use of anaesthetics and surgery including amputation, and both Lucy and Dr Rutherford had been pleased to take their guidance and instruction.

Dr Rutherford had agreed to attend Josh and like Lucy he preferred not to use the guillotine which, though swift and clean, had been discovered on occasion to cut the nerves so severely that the patient was left with paralysing pain in the phantom limb that never went away. Instead they both preferred using surgical knives and saws for amputation and packing the open wound with antiseptic and carbolic until they could be transferred for further treatment.

Dr Rutherford was laying out his equipment and Lucy was cleaning up Josh's wounds ready for surgery when she suddenly said, 'Wait! I can feel that there are broken pieces of explosive bullets in the calf and the shin bone, but I wonder – is Dr Thornbury still here with the X-ray machine?'

'He's too far gone for that. We must operate now.'

'The bleeding isn't as intense as it was. I think we should examine under X-ray and take out what we can find. If we can stem the bleeding further, the surgeon at base can decide whether or not to amputate. Nurse,' she called. 'Ah! Staff, will you send someone running to find Dr Oswald Thornbury and ask him to bring the X-ray machine urgently, please, if it's not in use.'

Milly Thomas sent someone immediately to look for Oswald. Dr Rutherford was not pleased but Lucy insisted. 'If we find there are too many to remove we'll amputate, but if there's the slenderest chance—'

'We'll patch him up and send him back to the trenches again, is that what you're saying?' Lucy could see that her colleague was angry that his judgement was being questioned.

'You know it's not,' she said brusquely. 'He won't be going back with injuries such as this, but two limbs are better than one if we can save it. I'll bow to the results of the X-ray and then we'll make an instant decision.'

Oswald arrived within ten minutes; Lucy was getting anxious in case Josh's condition worsened, but the X-ray revealed that most of the fragments were not too deep and that it would be possible to remove them. There were also some embedded in his right shoulder.

'Worth a try,' Oswald agreed when they examined the plates. 'And it will get him back to base. It's no fun travelling by lorry or train with severe injuries, and even after amputation soldiers can die.' Oswald's face was white. 'I hate the sight of blood,' he muttered.

'Let's do it then,' Lucy said firmly. 'Staff Thomas, you can help. You've got small neat hands.'

Dr Rutherford finally, though reluctantly, agreed, and as he constantly checked Josh's condition Lucy and Milly, armed with fine surgical tweezers and sharp knives, carefully cut into skin and flesh to reveal and remove the fragments beneath.

Edie was able to see Josh once he was back in the recovery ward, where Milly was looking after him. Milly told her what had happened in theatre and said they'd been able to remove all or nearly all the shrapnel. Josh was still under the effect of the anaesthetic but Edie kissed his forehead and knew that he had a fighting chance. She spent an hour sitting by his bed once he was back on the tented ward, and at midnight she, Lucy and

Milly went wearily off to bed and asked an orderly to wake them at six the next morning.

In spite of being tired when she'd climbed into bed Lucy didn't sleep immediately, and when she did, her dreams were jumbled with images of Josh and Oswald and bloody shattered limbs, and she kept calling to Oswald to ask him what he'd said, because there was something she didn't understand.

When she sat up, startled by the early morning call the following morning, she remembered. 'The thing is, darling Lucy,' he'd said. It was a brotherly expression, wasn't it? Or cousinly, or friendly even. Didn't Pa say it too sometimes?

On reaching the orderly desk she asked where he was and was told that he and Corporal Morris had returned to Passchendaele and would be back in two or three days.

'Dr Thornbury appears to be a law unto himself,' she said to the RAMC orderly who gave her Oswald's message.

'That's what we thought, doctor.' He shrugged. 'He's attached to us but he seems to go wherever he pleases.'

The dream was just a frivolous matter brought on by the events of the gruelling day, and she dismissed it, or thought she had, but throughout the morning his words kept returning, and she was also worried about him. He was tired, she thought; exhausted even. He shouldn't have gone back to Passchendaele; he wasn't a soldier and his scientific skills were of no use there. The war wasn't over. There was still danger ahead.

Josh was doing well though he wasn't yet out of danger and was unaware of the trauma of decision-making on his behalf. Edie had gone immediately to his bedside as soon as she had come on the ward and was sitting with him before going on duty. When Lucy came in to check on him, Edie stood up.

'Dr Thornbury,' she said formally. 'I'm due for a transfer. I'm going to speak to Matron and tell her I'd like to take it and accompany my brother to the next base hospital and then on to England.'

'Very well, Sister,' Lucy replied in the same correct manner. 'In the circumstances I would do exactly the same. If Sergeant Morris is fit enough to be moved tomorrow, perhaps you'd arrange transport? There'll be many others going too, so make sure he's on the list.'

Edie breathed out. 'Thank you, Lucy. I've been awake most of the night thinking of what I'd tell my mother if anything should happen to him, and there's still no news of our Stanley.'

'Josh is going to need a lot of care,' Lucy said softly. 'You know that as well as anyone, and there's still the chance that he might lose his leg. I'm going to recommend that he's transferred to Endell Street hospital when he gets to England if it's possible. He'll need more treatment than we can give him here.'

There were many more injured soldiers waiting for treatment and the medical staff had worked through the night on the urgent cases; the station could take five hundred patients and they were almost full and searching for beds. It was imperative that some of the patients were moved as quickly as possible to make room.

Another contingent of doctors and nurses arrived at midday and the staff huts and tents were almost as full as the wards. Edie put Josh on the list for transfer and then went back to find Henry. He too was being transferred, he told her, and seemed to be more stoic over his blindness that he had been.

'I'm still alive, Edie,' he said. 'Did I talk foolishly when I was brought in? I felt desperate, so many of my men killed and thinking that my life was over too until I realized how many had injuries far worse than mine and how many had died.'

She had a sinking feeling that the personal things he had said to her were only uttered in anguish and that he hadn't meant them, like a man in drink declaring his passion; she'd met a few of those, she thought, and their desires were soon forgotten and not to be taken seriously.

He asked about Josh and she told him that he would be transferred the next day. 'They've tried to save his leg, though he might need further surgery.'

'He's got a chance then,' he said. 'I'm so relieved. I'm leaving tomorrow too, or so I was told. Do you think he and I could travel together? We're in the same regiment, after all.'

She said she didn't know, she didn't deal with the

administration, and he remained silent for a moment, and then clumsily reached out to find and hold her hand.

'Is there anyone close enough to hear us, Edie?' he whispered, and she answered that there wasn't. 'Because you probably think I was off my head yesterday and talking nonsense, which I undoubtedly was, but what I said about you and me was true. I did – that time back home – and still do want to be with you again. Is that possible? Will you consider it? I loved your smile and your joyfulness and when this dratted war is over . . .'

She smiled, even though he couldn't see it, and put a finger to his lips. 'Ssh,' she murmured. 'Yes, I think it's possible, but let's give it time, shall we? No promises yet.'

He sat back, and still holding her hand said softly, 'All right. But I'm happy to think that there are still some good things left in life after all.'

Edie was given permission to be transferred and Milly was too; they had both gone well over their permitted time and both, with other QAIMNS and TFNS staff, were to travel with and take care of the injured personnel by ambulance and rail towards Boulogne. She bade a teary goodbye to Lucy. 'I'm going to ask for a transfer back to England,' she said. 'Before that, I must care for Josh and try to find out where Stanley is. I've got a bad feeling about him, Lucy; something's telling me that all is not well.'

'I feel for you, my dear friend,' Lucy said softly. 'Such a worry. But take care of yourself too. Don't overwork. You've done more than your share.'

Edie hugged her. 'Listen who's talking,' she said. 'We'll meet in dear old Blighty before too long, won't we?'

'Yes, of course we will,' Lucy said. 'You can depend on it.' But first, she thought as she turned away and went back on duty, I must find Oswald. I have something to tell him.

Lucy was officially called back to the base hospital near Boulogne, the same one she had served at on arrival. She hadn't been given a date but was expected to be there as soon as possible. She asked the administration officer if she could leave in the next few days, when most of the Passchendaele injuries had been attended to. It was only a lull, she realized; the end of the war was not yet in sight. Troop movement towards Cambrai signalled there were yet more battles to come, and this CCS might be moved nearer to another battlefield.

It was almost a week later that she packed her bag when transport and a driver who was going back to base were allocated to her. No one else was travelling that day. She said goodbye to her colleagues and Dr Rutherford shook her hand.

'No hard feelings?' She smiled.

'None,' he answered. 'Let me know how Corporal Morris gets on, will you, if you hear from his sister? I understand she's a friend of yours.'

'The very best of friends. I've known her and her brothers since we were children.'

'I wonder – erm, when this damned war is over.' He paused and gazed at her. 'Might there be a chance of our meeting up again? I'll be going back to London.'

'I very much doubt it, George,' she hedged. 'I'll be going back to my home town.'

'Which is?'

'Hull, on the east coast. Kingston upon Hull, to give it its proper name.'

'Oh.' He grimaced. 'Cold and wet.'

'Sometimes it is,' she agreed. 'But we don't live there for the weather. We live there because of the people. They're honest and kind, and reliable, and . . .' She hesitated, pondering. Do I mean what I'm going to say? 'I'm probably going to set up a medical practice there.'

'Really? Are you going to set a trend as the first woman doctor?' His tone was jocular.

'Too late for that,' she replied seriously, realizing by his manner that there was still a hint of lingering prejudice in spite of their having worked side by side. 'It's been done already. Dr Mary Murdoch pioneered that role and Dr Louisa

336

Martindale was her assistant. I shall simply follow in their footsteps.'

'Oh!' His face gave away the fact that he was astonished. 'Well, good luck,' he said. 'Erm, yes, good luck indeed.'

She went to where an army truck and its driver were waiting for her. The driver turned and they instantly recognized each other. He was the one who had first brought her and Rose to the base hospital. 'Private Green,' she said. 'I remember you.'

'And I remember you, doctor,' he grinned. 'Except that I'm Corporal Green now. I've been promoted; driving whilst under fire,' he said bashfully. 'I was taking nurses to a CCS when we were fired on by an aircraft.'

'Goodness! Really?' she said as he took her bag and helped her up the high step into the lorry. 'What did you do?'

'Drove into a wood where the pilot couldn't see us. It was nothing, but the nurses were terrified and reported back that I'd saved their lives.'

'Which you did!' she said approvingly. 'Well done you. I feel very safe now that I know I'm in such good hands.'

He grinned and started up the engine. 'Back to base hospital, is it?'

'Y-yes, but would we have time for a short detour?' She gazed pleadingly as she spoke. 'I don't think it will take long.' She was guessing, of course; she didn't know how long it would take.

He raised his eyebrows. 'I suppose so. Where do you want to go?'

'Passchendaele,' she said. 'I want to catch up with a friend. And send him home.'

CHAPTER FORTY-EIGHT

As they approached Passchendaele there were dozens of army vehicles, gun carriers, ambulances and a slow-moving tank coming towards them.

'Look at that,' Green muttered. 'I've not seen one o' them before. Mark One tank; there aren't many of them. That lot are all being transferred elsewhere. To another battleground. Just because one battle is over doesn't mean there isn't another being planned.' He turned to her. 'You say your friend isn't a soldier? So what's he doing out here?'

'He's a scientist,' she said. 'He brought over a mobile X-ray machine, and he volunteers as a stretcher bearer for when the X-ray equipment isn't needed, which it isn't during battle, but only afterwards.'

The land around them leading to the village was desolate, looking as if it had been ripped apart by a brutal giant hand. Everywhere they looked were scorched crooked stumps that had once been trees; the pitted earth was black from explosions from ground attack aircraft as well as grenades and machine gun fire, and rutted with deep water-filled tracks from tanks and gun carriers; cavernous open pits were full of muddy water, abandoned enemy guns and broken duckboards. Here too were the remains of trenches and dugouts, blown to pieces by mines and flamethrowers.

Lucy wept, tears running down her face that she didn't wipe away. She felt as if she could hear the distant resonance of gunfire and the echo of the combatants' cries. This was where the injured men she had treated had been and in spite of their wounds she had never heard them grumble. True, some had called out for their mothers, wives and children, but not once had she heard anyone rail against the madness of sending them out to fight in a war that was not of their making.

Corporal Green pulled off the track to give the convoy room to pass. He was muttering beneath his breath, and finally said, 'If I hadn't copped a bullet in my first battle, this is where I'd have been and probably never lived to tell the tale.'

He moved off again and hadn't gone far when a lorry appeared travelling towards them, being carefully driven over the rutted track. Green lifted his hand in acknowledgement and Lucy glanced at the driver and passenger as they passed, and then shouted, 'Stop! It's Oswald. Sound your horn! Can you turn round?'

'Not without getting bogged down I can't.' He sounded his horn, long and loud and they saw the other vehicle slow and then stop.

Lucy began to open the door. 'Hang on! Where 'you going?' Corporal Green protested. 'You'll get stuck in the mud.'

'I'll be careful. If they see me the driver will back up,' Lucy said.

He went on objecting as she jumped down and he was right, the road was thick with mud and her boots sank into it. 'Make sure it's him,' he said, 'and then I'll find somewhere to turn. I gather you don't want to go any further?'

'No,' she said, slamming the door. 'I don't.'

She waved her arms above her head, and shouted, 'Oswald! It's me.'

The passenger door in the lorry opened and a soldier wearing a peaked hat and a white band on his tunic sleeve jumped down and began to run towards her.

'Lucy! What on earth!' Oswald gathered her up in his arms. 'What are you *doing* out here?'

'Looking for you,' she said tearfully. 'You disappeared.'

'I was coming back,' he said, and cradled her face in his hands. 'I left a message to say I was coming back.'

'But you said a few days,' she insisted, 'and it's been over a week. I was worried, and besides,' she said feebly, 'I'm being moved back to Boulogne.'

He smiled and his eyes crinkled. 'You're going the wrong way if you're heading for Boulogne. You should have asked for a driver who can read a map!'

Corporal Green had managed to turn the lorry round and was chugging back towards them. He turned off the engine and got out of the vehicle and shook his head when he saw them standing so close. He looked Oswald over and saluted. 'Well, sir,' he grinned. 'I hope one day there'll be somebody willing to chase for miles over a battleground for me.'

Corporal Morris leaned out of the cab of his lorry. 'Is that you, Private Green? Trust you to find 'best-looking doctor this side of 'Channel.'

Corporal Green strolled over to the lorry, shouting back, 'Best doctor too from what I've heard,' and then something about his being a corporal now.

Oswald took her hand. 'Why did you really come, Lucy? Not just because you were going to Boulogne? I'd have found you, you know. I wouldn't have lost you.'

'But I was worried,' she said. 'I thought you'd go off to another battle.'

He nodded. 'I perhaps would have done,' he said softly. 'But I've been recalled to England. That's why I shot off back to Passchendaele, to see if there was anything else I could do before leaving. There are thousands of injured men, Lucy. Allied and German, and we located so many hidden injuries with this incredible machine; but there's a technician arriving to take my place and I'm leaving it at the base hospital for him until it's needed again somewhere else – which it will be,' he added.

Lucy reached up and kissed his cheek. 'I'm still glad that I came,' she said. 'I've seen now just what it was like for our soldiers.'

He took off his hat and bent towards her. 'I love you, Lucy,' he said.

'I know,' she murmured.

'Do you know for how long?'

She shook her head.

'Since that day when I took you to London for your hospital interview and we went out for supper.' He grinned. 'And the Italian waiter said—'

'And for your beautiful wife?' she laughed. 'I knew something had changed between us that day.' She lowered her voice. 'I didn't know what, but recently I've been thinking about the poetry book you gave me such a long time ago and the poems that you chose – and I wondered if perhaps . . .' she hesitated, 'and then, when you brought Josh in last week and you were so exhausted you didn't know what you were talking about, you said *"the thing is, darling Lucy"*. . .'

He nodded and bent to kiss her lips. 'That's how I always think of you,' he said softly. 'And the poems reminded me of you. *She was a phantom of delight when first she gleaned upon my sight* . . .' He smiled. 'But what now, Lucy?'

'The thing is, *darling* Oswald, I have to go back to base and you have to go to England,' Lucy murmured. 'So, will you wait for me until I return?'

Corporal Green was walking back towards them. It was time for them to move on.

'I've already waited a long time, Lucy,' he said softly. 'I'm a very patient man; I can wait a little longer.'

In May of 1918 two former soldiers were walking along Albion Street in Hull. It was the first time they had ventured out alone; at least, they were not quite alone although it felt like it: their first try at independence. Josh, with a very awkward swing to his right leg, had a walking stick in one hand and the other on the shoulder of his companion and former captain, Henry Warrington. Ostensibly, it was Henry who considered he was assisting his friend in their walk, as the injuries and pain in Josh's leg had been so appalling that it had taken weeks before he could stand; some surgeons had recommended amputation of the limb, but he had insisted that he would put up with the pain for as long as he could. But it was still an option open to him.

Josh, however, considered that he was surreptitiously supporting Henry, by accompanying him to the Hull Blind Institute that was situated in Kingston Square, a mere stone's throw from Henry's home.

Walking at a discreet distance behind the two men were two nursing sisters, Sister Morris and Sister Thomas, both of whom, apart from keeping a medical eye on their patients, had personal reasons for being there.

When Edie had first heard of the loss of her brother Stanley she was devastated, and her initial response was to come home immediately to comfort her parents and siblings, especially Ada, who had received confirmation that her husband had been killed in action and would be awarded a small pension; but on reading her mother's letter for a second time Edie saw that her postscript said that she must keep on doing what she could *for them other poor lads who needed her.*

Dolly Morris didn't know then that Josh had been injured, and Edie decided that she would delay her return to English shores until Josh was transferred back for further treatment; and there was Henry to consider. He was being relocated to St Dunstan's Lodge in Regent's Park, where he would be rehabilitated as a blind veteran, so she knew she could see them both if she went back to work at St Thomas's Hospital.

Sister Milly Thomas, having nursed Josh during his initial surgery, had resolved to continue to care for him, especially as she had fallen in love with his humour and his cheeky grin which had survived in spite of his pain, and knew that she would love to be part of the large family that Edie had told her about. Her own brother had been injured, and when he wrote to her to tell her that he had been discharged, he also told her that he had met a young lady and they were going to be married. Hearing what had once been her worst fear, she had heaved a great sigh of relief at the news that she didn't have to be responsible to him, but was free to live her own life.

'I don't want to be confined to basket making,' Henry was saying to Josh. 'Not that I'm criticizing it, everybody needs a shopping basket. I just feel that I could do more. At St Dunstan's it was suggested that I could train as a physical therapist or a reconstruction aide. It's the kind of treatment that might help you, Josh.'

'Your father would be pleased about that, wouldn't he?' Josh said. 'What did he say?'

Henry's father, Dr Warrington, had been very positive, and it was through him that this meeting at the Institute had been arranged now that Henry was home. He had also taken Josh as a patient at the Hull Infirmary. Henry's mother, however, had gone to pieces on hearing of Henry's blindness; she was still suffering from the trauma of Elizabeth's becoming a widow, although Elizabeth herself was proving to be more of a stoic than her mother, and had decided to stay with her husband's parents so that they might enjoy the company of her father-less children, unlike her own mother who had said she couldn't possibly cope with small children in her time of grief.

'My father says that I'll manage fine,' Henry answered. 'It was St Dunstan's who recommended that I should begin training as a massage therapist, and when Father came to see me there he agreed with them. They all said that life doesn't stop after losing your sight and that thousands of soldiers will have to get on with their lives. The aim of the Hull Blind Institute, just like St Dunstan's, is to get blind people back to work or business. The founder of the Institute, Alderman Lambert, was himself blind. I reckon I'm lucky,' he said with feeling. 'I might have blisters – I don't know, I can't see them – but my larynx and lungs haven't been affected. But you know what, old chap?' He lowered his voice, although the two nurses were out of earshot. 'I want to become independent before I ask Edie to marry me. Do you think she'll have me?'

'Ooh, I don't know about that. You don't know our Edie like I do,' Josh joked. 'She allus did have a life of her own. I wonder, though,' he added seriously, 'will she have to give up nursing if she marries?'

'I don't know,' Henry said. 'But we won't have any money worries. I was given an inheritance from my grandfather when I was twenty-one and I haven't touched it.'

'I wasn't thinking of money,' Josh said bluntly. 'I was thinking of our Edie and if she'd ever want to give up nursing.'

Edie intended signing up at a local Hull hospital; many had been set up during the war years to nurse and rehabilitate injured soldiers. She also intended marrying Henry when he got round to asking her, but here was the dilemma: how could she do both when there was still the ridiculous notion that nurses should give up their profession once they married?

I'll not have it, she decided. I'll find a way round it, though I'll not live in sin either. Whatever would my mother say? And as for Henry's mother, she'd die of apoplexy! Even though I think that in spite of not being part of her social circle, she's relieved that Henry cares for me. She won't make any objection anyway; not that she can. Henry and I are both of an age when we can do whatever we want without asking anyone's permission.

She thought too of her mother and father. She was staying with them until she obtained a nursing position, and only a week ago she had answered the door to the postwoman bearing a registered letter. She had signed for it and taken it through to them. Her father had been unwell since the news of Stanley's death and hadn't been back to work, spending most of his days hunched by the fire; and although her mother was putting a brave face on their loss, she hadn't come to terms with it either. They were both relieved to have Edie home in one piece, and Josh, despite the seriousness of his injuries, was much the same as always.

Her mother had taken the letter with trembling fingers. 'I can't open it, Edie,' she'd muttered, 'though I can't think there can be any worse news than we've had already.'

Edie had offered to read it and pulled out two sheets of paper, one carefully placed between thin cardboard. 'It's from a chaplain,' she'd said, and proceeded to read aloud the message, which explained that the sender had been given the enclosed

344

letter by an orderly who in turn had been given it by a stretcher bearer who had been at Passchendaele.

I took the letter to the authorities, the writer told them, *and asked if they would check the details, and then I asked if I might send it to you, the people to whom it was addressed. I hoped that you might find some comfort in the knowledge that he was thinking of you to the end.*

Edie had carefully taken out the stained and torn letter and read it. 'Stanley says he's fine and looking forward to coming home . . .' She couldn't read any more, her voice was so choked by unshed tears, and she handed the paper to her mother. Josh had just walked into the room and looked from one to another. 'What?' he said. 'What's happened?'

Edie shook her head. 'It's Stanley's last letter home,' she said, tears at last beginning to fall. 'Somebody found it, and 'minister's sent it on.'

And somehow, she thought now as they turned towards Kingston Square, they had that day all found some peace, a release of emotion that they had all kept firmly sealed, as the minister ended by saying that perhaps a memorial stone could be erected in Stanley's name so that he would never be forgotten.

I wish Lucy would come home, she thought now. I miss not seeing her, and although I'm very fond of Milly and hope that Josh asks her to marry him, as I know she hopes too, I want to talk to Lucy. We've shared so much in our lives. I also want to ask her if she realizes that Oswald loves her, has always loved her but never dared to tell her. She gave a little smile. That significant moment during Lucy's twenty-first birthday lunch when Mr Thornbury gave a speech. I saw the way Oswald looked at her. If that wasn't love in his eyes then I don't know what it was.

They reached the Institute and Henry and Josh, with a companion on either side, negotiated the half dozen or so steps up to the door that stood wide open to welcome them.

CHAPTER FORTY NINE

June 1918

Oswald stood on the Southampton dockside as the troop ship slowly came into berth. He'd been waiting, shivering, for hours. Shivering, not because he was cold – it was a beautiful June morning – but because he was anxious. There was still a danger to shipping and Lucy would be on this ship; German submarines had been seen in United States waters during May just before launching yet a third offensive in France. There had been rumours of an enemy retreat, but most of those who had been in the middle of the conflict viewed that news with some scepticism. They had heard it all before.

It was a full ship; full of injured soldiers and nurses bringing them home, the nurses' uniforms a bright shining symbol of purity against the soldiers' khaki. He would, he thought, have difficulty in picking out Lucy in her doctor's sombre and practical jacket and skirt of grey.

He was tempted to run and give a helping hand to those who were disembarking the gangplank, but he resisted; he didn't want to miss Lucy in the melee.

But she saw him first; there she was halfway down in the crowd, waving one arm, the other clutching her two bags. He let out a breath and waved back. Thank heavens, he thought. At last! I hope she's all right.

She was fine, she said, when he greeted her with a hug, but he commented on her looking tired.

'Been up all night,' she admitted. 'There were a lot of serious injuries on board.' She smiled brightly at him. 'But now here I am back on English soil . . .'

She was nervous, apprehensive that he might have changed; that when he had spoken those words of love, it was because of the precarious circumstances and the threat of death and injury hanging over them; and she worried too that she had also changed. It was inevitable. She wasn't the young girl she had been; she was a woman now who had seen terrible things. This dreadful war had scarred everyone.

'I've missed you, Lucy,' he murmured. 'The time you've been away has been endless.'

She nodded. 'It has,' she agreed. 'And I've missed you too,' she said softly.

'How much?' he asked, catching hold of her by her shoulders.

She looked at him, into the soft grey eyes behind his new spectacles. 'More than I can say,' she whispered. 'You've been in my life for ever, and when you're not there' – she lifted her shoulders – 'there's something missing. It's taken a war for me to realize that.'

'And now?' He was asking the same question he had asked her after Passchendaele.

'Can we go home?' Her voice cracked with emotion. 'It's been so long.'

He picked up her bags, and with his arm draped around her shoulder they walked away from the quayside towards the rows of coaches, ambulances and cabs waiting to transport travellers to hospital or home. But he steered her away from the public vehicles and led her towards a motor car.

'What's this!' she exclaimed. 'Is this yours?'

'No! I've hired it,' he laughed. 'I'll drive it to London. I've booked a hotel for tonight and I thought we could get the train home to Hull tomorrow, when you're rested.'

Lucy turned to look at him, a question on her lips.

347

'Two rooms.' He raised his eyebrows and gave a whimsical smile. 'Suitable for cousins!'

There were few passengers on the morning train and he found an empty carriage so they were able to catch up on news of home without speaking in whispers. Oswald had been back to Hull several times, and he'd seen Henry and Josh and Edie too.

'Edie's longing to see you,' he said. 'She says she has things to tell you.' He grinned. 'I think they'll be about Henry, who, incidentally, is training to be a physical therapist. Edie says he has wonderfully sensitive hands.'

Lucy smiled and Oswald, raising his voice over the whistle, the shriek of escaping steam and the clatter of wheels, went on, 'Henry's asked her to marry him and she wants to, but she doesn't want to give up nursing.'

Lucy considered that. 'She could go into private nursing, but maybe she doesn't want to; she's very experienced and will want to use her knowledge.'

She thought of the people she had said goodbye to – Dr Lawson, George Rutherford who had wanted to see her again, Major Dobson who had been kind and wise, Corporal Green, intent on doing what he could in spite of his injuries – and wondered what role they would all play once the war was over. Their lives would undoubtedly be changed.

She asked Oswald what he had been doing since he came home and he told her that he had again refused to work on poison gases or any means of destroying an enemy, but that he had been able to apply his observations after Henry's respirator mask had slipped to his work on ways of refining them, and that he had also been involved in research into improving medications and testing new ones. He was, he said, intent on choosing a role which would enable lives to be saved and not destroyed.

It was right for him, she thought as she listened. He had always said that he would not kill another man.

'Lucy.' His quiet voice broke into her thoughts. 'I wanted to tell you that Pa said they were going to write to you to tell you

348

something, but I suggested they wait until you get home before they broached the subject.'

'Oh, what? They're going to move to Pearson Park, aren't they?' Her expression fell. 'They haven't gone already?'

'No, of course not. They wouldn't without consulting you first, but Pa says that it's time. That when you come home you might have other plans.'

Lucy put her hands to her face. 'I can't bear to think that I'd be going back to an empty house,' she whispered. 'I have this memory of once before . . .'

He took her hands away from her cheeks and held them clasped within his. 'Lucy,' he said, 'you don't have to be alone. I have told you that I love you. I will never leave your side, but I don't want to be your cousin or your brother or your companion, I want to be part of your life for ever; to be married to you, but only if you love me too.'

'But of course I do.' Her eyes brimmed with tears. 'I have never loved anyone but you, Oswald. I cried once when we were children because you wouldn't play games with me, and—' She gave a hiccuping laugh. 'At school a girl once commented on your lovely eyes and I was annoyed because I didn't want anyone else thinking of you in that way.'

He laughed. 'Really? Who was she?'

She pulled her hands away and gave him a reproving tap. Then she said softly, 'Do you really want to marry me, Oswald? I'll still want to be a doctor; can I be a doctor and a wife? That's the only thing that's holding me back from saying how much I want to be your wife and mother to our children. Is it too much to ask?'

He was silent for a moment; how hard it must be for women, he thought. They have been alongside men in the most distressing of situations and for many of them, once the war is over, they will have to go back to how things were before and find that for them, nothing has changed.

'Not too much for me, Lucy. You should know me better than that. Who encouraged you first to speak to your headmistress? Who went with you for your first interview?'

349

She began to smile. Of course, it was Oswald who did those things; he was the one who had seen her potential. 'You've always seen the best in me, Oswald; you've been influential in making me what I am. I could never doubt that you'd always be by my side.'

They were pulling into Leeds railway station and they got to their feet to catch their connection to Hull. Oswald put his arms round her and kissed her gently on the lips. 'Next stop home, Dr Thornbury. Everyone's waiting for you. Shall we tell them our news?'

She returned his kiss. 'I think perhaps we should, Dr Thornbury. Will they be surprised?'

'Not in the slightest, I shouldn't think. They'll guess as soon as we walk through the door.'

It seemed such a long time since she had been at home. Everything looked much the same except that the house was full of flowers brought in especially for her return, and yet there was something different that she couldn't quite put her finger on. They were all thrilled to see her again and she felt their love enveloping her. Uncle William and Aunt Nora were both emotional and Eleanor, who was now a fashionable young lady with a shorter hair style and shorter skirts, cried when she saw her; and as for Mary, she was quite overcome. Lucy gave her a great hug and said that the house wouldn't be the same without her.

It was whilst they were eating their supper and Lucy was looking speculatively around the room that she realized what the difference was.

'You've moved the ornaments from the mantelpiece,' she said. 'And the mirror and paintings from the wall. Why is that?'

'Because of the bombing, my dear,' Nora said. 'I was so afraid that our precious belongings would be damaged. There was another Zeppelin attack in March this year over east Hull, you know. Fortunately no one was hurt, except of course everyone was very frightened.'

'I think we tended to forget,' Lucy murmured, 'that whilst we were abroad you were also suffering at home.'

350

Oswald nodded in agreement. 'An enemy in the skies wasn't something that anyone had bargained for.'

'So where have you put everything?' Lucy asked. 'Where is a safe place?'

Nora looked rueful. 'Well, heavy items like the mirror and the paintings in a cupboard under the stairs and the lighter ones in the loft with the other things, which as Pa pointed out wasn't at all sensible because if a bomb had fallen on the house the roof would have collapsed! But after the effort of putting them up there we decided to leave them.'

Lucy smiled at the irony of it, and asked, 'What other things in the loft?'

Eleanor and Oswald also looked questioningly at their mother.

'Why, yours, my dear. Don't you remember?' Then Nora seemed taken aback. 'Oh! No. Of course you wouldn't.' She flushed. 'I was going to bring them down when you were twenty-one, but then what with the war starting – and then after you went away I thought we'd better leave it until it was ended, and before we – well,' she said, floundering a little and looking at William for support, 'it's not something we've properly discussed yet.'

'You mean the possibility that you might move to the house in the park?' Lucy said quietly, helping her out. 'Perhaps we could speak of that another day? But what things of mine? I don't have anything in the loft, do I?' A vague recollection came back to her of someone packing boxes.

William lifted his hands negatively. He didn't know.

Nora gazed at Lucy and swallowed. 'Your parents' possessions. Silver photograph frames, candlesticks, cut glass bowls and vases. I was so afraid of breaking them; I had never possessed such beautiful things and – it was such a sad and difficult time,' she said in a low voice. 'I was coming to live in someone else's home and was fearful that they'd be a constant reminder to all of us, but to you most of all, dear Lucy, so that you would never get over your parents' loss.'

They might have been a comfort to me, Lucy thought, but I

351

was only a child then and they were material things. Aunt Nora did right and yet she did wrong too, because I forgot that they were there.' Her own childhood self now recalled saying, 'Those are Mama's things.'

She reached across and took Nora's hand. 'Don't be upset,' she said softly, for she could see that her aunt was distressed. 'You did what you thought was right. Perhaps tomorrow we could get the ladder and take a look at what's up there?'

The next morning Nora stood at the bottom of the ladder whilst Lucy and Oswald climbed up into the loft. They took a candle with them as there was no light. Huge cobwebs draped from the joists and there was a strong smell of soot, and the boxes which they easily found were covered in dust.

'Mater!' Oswald shouted down. 'Can you throw up an old duster or cloth? Everything's filthy.'

Nora sent Mary off to fetch one, not wanting to leave her post at the bottom of the ladder, and Mary was about to climb up to give it to them when William appeared and insisted that he should be the one to go. He climbed halfway up whilst Oswald reached down, and the duster changed hands.

'I wish I'd known about this space when I was little,' Oswald observed. 'I'd have made a den up here.'

'So would I,' Lucy said. 'I suppose we never looked up at the ceiling, and I'd completely forgotten about the packing of ornaments until your mother mentioned it.' She hesitated, biting her lip. 'I'm not sure how I'm going to feel about seeing them again. Or maybe I won't remember them.'

'You'll be all right,' he murmured. 'Considering what you've seen in the last few years, your parents' possessions can only bring back good memories.'

He opened one of the boxes. 'This has silverware in it,' he said, holding out a box of silver cutlery. 'And this,' he began to unwrap a picture frame, 'and this . . .' He paused as he looked at the photograph, and handed it to Lucy. 'Is you getting married to someone else.'

She held up the candle to see it. It was indeed her very image; a dark-haired, very young woman sitting in a chair wearing a wedding gown with a white lace and gauze draped bodice, long full sleeves, and a satin skirt that hung in dark folds to her feet. On her head she wore a simple coronet of flowers and a flowing veil. At her side stood her new husband, smiling and handsome in a morning suit and cravat, and wearing a rose in his buttonhole.

Mama and *Papa*; she couldn't even whisper their names. She didn't know them then, of course, couldn't recall them dressed in such finery, but she was undoubtedly there, hidden behind the huge bouquet of lilies and roses that her mother carried.

When she regained control of her voice she murmured, 'What else?'

Without speaking, Oswald handed her another silver photograph frame; the photograph was of her mother and father and baby Lucy draped in a lace christening gown on her mother's knee.

'Will you bring them down for me, Oswald?' she whispered. 'I'd like to put them back on the mantelpiece.'

She climbed down the ladder and Nora viewed her anxiously. 'Did you find them?' Her face crumpled and she faltered. 'I'm so sorry, Lucy, if I did wrong to put them up there.'

Lucy kissed her. 'You didn't do wrong, Aunt, you did what you thought was right. I do understand; you were coming to a place that wasn't your home, although I hope that you now feel it is, and I understand too that you were expected to look after a child who wasn't your own.'

She led her into the sitting room where William was reading the morning newspaper. He looked up as if he was going to tell them the latest news, but he saw his wife's distressed expression and immediately got up from his chair. 'My dear!' he said to her, drawing her to him. Lucy hid a tearful smile; some things never change, she thought, and Pa's beloved expression that covered all ills clearly hadn't.

Oswald didn't come down immediately, and just as Lucy was about to go and look for him he opened the door. 'I'm a bit dusty,' he said, and indeed he was, with cobwebs in his hair and soot on his face. He was carrying a long flat box that he placed on the floor.

'Don't open it yet until I've washed my hands,' he said, and dashed away.

'Did you know that he was called the mad boffin whilst he was abroad?' Lucy said in an attempt to lighten Nora's mood. 'He was forever turning up somewhere with his X-ray machine and then disappearing to go elsewhere.'

William smiled. 'That's my boy.' He nudged Nora and she gave a weepy laugh.

Oswald came in again; he'd washed his hands and face, brushed away the cobwebs and combed his hair. He knelt down on the floor by the box and carefully opened it to reveal layers of white paper. 'I've looked already,' he admitted, 'so I know what's inside. Will you all close your eyes for a moment please?' They did, and heard the rustle of paper. Then Oswald gave the word and they opened their eyes.

Lucy got up from her chair. Oswald was holding up her mother's wedding gown. The white lace and gauze were flimsy as cobwebs, and the skirt was shiny folds of indigo satin. He came towards her and held it against her; she took it from him and buried her face in it, breathing in its old aromas, images of her mother.

Tears ran down her cheeks, as they did down Nora's and William's too, but Oswald took the dress from her and draped it across the back of the sofa. Then he turned to her, and taking her hand he dropped to one knee.

'Lucy. I'm asking you now, when my very dear parents are present to witness my proposal . . .' He gave a deep intake of breath. 'Will you marry me? Please,' he added. 'You already know that I love you and now you have the wedding dress, and inside the box is another little gown waiting for another little Thornbury, so there's really no need for us to wait for anything except for you to say yes!'

She laughed and cried and put her arms about him, then kissed him and whispered so that only he could hear, '*Yes.*'

CONCLUSION

During the early hours of 5 August 1918 Lucy awoke in her top-floor childhood bedroom, startled by the wailing alarm of the Big Lizzie siren and the pounding of feet on the stairs. Oswald, who was home for a week's summer holiday, knocked and then opened the door.

'Get up, Lucy,' he said urgently. 'It must be a raid.'

She heard him knocking on Eleanor's door and then his parents' as she hurried into her dressing gown and slippers and ran down after him. He was standing at his parents' door having an urgent conversation, which turned out to be them refusing to get up, assuring him that it was probably a false alarm; there had been so many, and where would they go for safety? They were as safe in their beds as out on the streets. Eleanor went back to bed.

Lucy and Oswald went down to the kitchen and made tea. 'Perhaps they're right,' he said gloomily. 'I confess I'm the same during a raid on London. We are so unprepared for war at home.'

They had opened the front door and looked out. There was no sound, though there were one or two people outside, looking up at the moonlit sky.

'I'm angry,' she said as they sipped their tea. 'Out on the battlefields soldiers expect to be shot at, but it's so cowardly to bring the war to innocent people.'

That was the last of the Zeppelin raids on Hull; they

discovered later that the aircraft had been caught in the searchlight and beaten a hasty retreat, dropping only a smoke bomb that did no damage.

When the end of the war and declaration of armistice came on 11 November at eleven o'clock it brought the citizens of Britain on to the streets to celebrate.

In Hull, as in the rest of the country, there was no rejoicing for some, like Dolly and her family, her daughter Ada, and Max's parents, who were left bereft that their men wouldn't be returning home, that all they had were memories to console them.

Lucy and Oswald married in the spring of 1919 with Lucy wearing her mother's wedding gown, coronet and veil. William gave her away, and Edie and Eleanor were her attendants, whilst Henry and Josh were joint best men for Oswald. He didn't believe in convention, he'd said when he'd asked them, and he wouldn't like to choose between them.

In May of the following year Lucy gave birth to their daughter Alice. Edie, although not a midwife, assisted in the delivery and became Alice's godmother along with Eleanor; her godfather was Edie's newly-wed husband Henry.

Lucy's desire to enjoy her baby daughter replaced the earlier plan of incorporating a surgery in the Baker Street house, using the study as a consulting room, as she and Oswald had previously discussed. Oswald was now working in a research laboratory attached to the Infirmary. They were, though, still talking about future possibilities, and during a walk one cold but sunny day early that winter, with a proud Oswald pushing the bassinet and making cooing noises to a chortling Alice, they noticed a vacant building further down Baker Street with a *To Let* sign outside. They stopped and peered through the dusty windows into the empty rooms and then turned to look at each other.

'A clinic!' Lucy said. 'Research laboratory!' Oswald returned.

They both laughed and Alice squealed a toothy grin back at

them. 'Yes, my darling Alice,' Oswald leaned over his daughter and gently squeezed her dimpled cheek. 'A mini hospital,' he told her, and she blew bubbles at him. 'Where minor injuries can be attended to—'

'With a physical therapy section, run by Henry,' Lucy added. 'And a senior nurse – two nurses,' she said, thinking of Milly. 'Shall we ask for an appointment and take a look? On the other hand, how will we pay for it? My inheritance?'

'Or a bank loan,' Oswald suggested. 'Set against my salary.' He grinned. 'I know a friendly bank manager.'

By the summer of 1923 they had obtained grants and the clinic was up and running with a waiting list of patients. Edie was the senior nurse with Milly her second in command; Henry had finished his training as a physical therapist and would join them shortly when a room had been fitted out to his requirements; his father had agreed to give one day a fortnight as a senior consultant. Lucy had written to Rose, who had set up her own London practice with Olive, who had decided to keep her new name as there was still some anti-German vilification, and asked her if she could recommend a qualified junior doctor who would be willing to work in Hull.

A reply came immediately; Olive Spence's niece was newly qualified and looking for a position.

'Perfect,' Lucy said after interviewing her and offering her the post. 'Now I can spend more time at home.'

Oswald wagged a finger at her. 'I should think so too.'

She was now occasionally using the home consulting room for people who wished only to see her. Several of them were men from the Hull Pals whom she had treated in Flanders and France. She didn't always remember them – there had been so many, after all – but there was one she did remember. He rang the doorbell one September morning and Alice had run to get there before Mary, who came early every morning and went home after lunch, after giving the young maid, Dora, one of her many great-nieces, her instructions.

'Would you like to see Dr Mama Thornbury or Dr Papa

357

Thornbury?' was Alice's usual mantra to a stranger at the door.

This man had given her a big grin as he bent down and said, 'Dr Mama please.'

Lucy was hurrying down the stairs as Mary crossed the hall. There was the chortling cry of a young baby from the upper floor.

'I fink this gentleman needs a new arm, Mama,' Alice said in a loud whisper. 'Shall I ask him to come in?'

'No thank you, darling,' Lucy said. 'I'll do it. You go with Mary.'

She ushered the man into the consulting room, which was now fully shelved and filled with medical books, a desk with her chair behind it and two chairs in front.

'Please take a seat,' she said, but noted that he waited for her to be seated first. 'How can I help you?'

'You won't remember me, Dr Lucy,' he began as many of them did, and she raised her eyebrows. A former soldier then. A Hull Pal. He lifted his empty sleeve. 'You took my arm off during 'war . . .'

'I'm sorry,' she began, but he broke in, 'and saved my life.'

There was a glimmer of recognition. 'Were you the carpenter?'

'I was!' he said, as if astonished that she'd remember. 'And I've only just discovered that you've opened a surgery here in Hull. I keep in touch wi' some of 'Hull Pals, those that are left, and one of 'em told me about this young woman doctor who'd served in 'war. I couldn't believe that it might be you. We all called you Dr Lucy, you know,' he continued, and his voice cracked. 'And we all fell in love with you, and said that out there was no place for someone like you. But,' he went on, 'we're all glad that you were.'

He took out a handkerchief from his pocket and wiped his moist eyes and blew his nose. 'Really glad.' He took a breath, and said, 'Can you put me and my family down on your panel, please? I don't want anybody else looking after us but you.'

*

358

It was only a few weeks later and Lucy had put baby Joseph down for his afternoon sleep when the doorbell rang and she heard Alice's voice calling to Dora that she would go. She loved to answer the door and would run to be first and turn the key to open it, but Lucy never wanted her to. There could be anybody there who might take advantage of the child, or someone who had had an injury that she shouldn't see and she vowed to remind Oswald again to have a chain put on the door that Alice couldn't reach.

'Wait, Alice,' she called down. 'Wait. Leave the door.'

But it was too late, and the little girl was already spouting her usual question before she hesitated and turned to her mother, putting her fingers to her mouth. 'Mama,' she said, 'I fink this lady's not very well.'

Lucy hurried towards her and put her hand on her shoulder. This was just the sort of thing that she had feared; someone ill on her doorstep. 'Go inside,' she murmured, but Alice clung to her skirt. 'The lady knows me,' she whispered.

Beneath her hat the elderly woman who stood on the doorstep had white hair streaked with dark strands, and was well dressed in a plain neat fashion.

She looked at Lucy and clutched her chest, moaning and catching her breath, and reached to hold on to the door frame.

'Go inside, Alice,' Lucy said again, and to the woman, 'Are you unwell?' She called to Dora, who came hurrying towards her and picked up Alice.

'No,' the woman gasped. 'I'm not ill. I'm – I'm just – it is Alice, isn't it?' But she was gazing at Lucy as she spoke and not at her daughter.

'You'd better come inside,' Lucy said, and led the woman into the consulting room where she sat her down and poured a glass of water from the jug she kept on her desk.

'Take a sip of water,' she said quietly. 'Just a little,' and then taking the glass from her asked her to lower her head if she was feeling dizzy.

'It's all right,' the woman muttered, and rubbed her forehead with her fingers. 'I've – I've had a shock. I'm not ill.'

'Have you had an accident? Lucy asked her. 'Or seen one? Is that why you are upset?'

The woman shook her head and then began to weep. Lucy sat on the chair next to her and held her hand. 'Rest for a moment and take a deep breath, and then tell me about it. Would you like a cup of tea?'

'Yes, please.' Her hands trembled as she opened her handbag for a handkerchief. 'I'm sorry – so sorry to be a nuisance.'

'You're not a nuisance,' Lucy said, and went to call Dora again to bring a cup of hot sweet tea.

'You don't know me, do you?' the woman said.

Lucy said she didn't and asked her name.

'Maria Alice Masters,' she said, and gazed at Lucy as if waiting for a response. When none came, she said tearfully, 'I'm your grandmother, Dr Thornbury. Your mother's mother.'

Lucy felt faint. Black spots appeared before her eyes and her ears thrummed. She heard the front door open and knew it was Oswald returning home. She willed him to come in, which he did, knocking first and slowly opening the door in case she was with a patient.

'Come in, darling,' she whispered.

'Is something wrong?' She heard the concern in his voice.

She lifted a hand to indicate Mrs Masters. 'This – this lady says she is my grandmother.'

Oswald pulled the chair from behind the desk and placed it next to Mrs Masters. Leaning towards her, he quietly teased the information out of her; when Dora brought tea for Mrs Masters he asked her to bring in a fresh pot for all of them.

Mrs Masters explained that her husband had died in 1917. He had been adamant from the day he had banned their daughter from her home that there should be no contact between them; but although her husband had ordered her to destroy it, his wife had kept the letter that Alice had written to them to tell them she was married and had a daughter of her own.

'After he died, I wanted to look for Alice and her family, but I didn't dare go out alone because of the bombing and it wasn't until after the end of the war that I plucked up courage to travel to London and begin the search of the records. We had always lived a quiet life and I had no friends that I could ask to come with me.

'I'd never been allowed to go anywhere unless Mr Masters was with me,' she continued. 'I think he realized that I would attempt to find Alice, and I would have done.' She began to sob, and through her tears she mumbled, 'And then I found that I was too late; that she and her husband had both died many years before.'

But after returning home with her grief she had remembered the child, and when she felt strong enough she began the search again. 'It took such a long time,' she wept, 'and then it took me even longer to dare to travel here, to a place I didn't know, and when – when I rang your doorbell and the little girl answered the door—' She heaved a sobbing breath. 'It was like looking at my child again – I was so confused, and then you came to the door.' She gazed at Lucy with tear-filled eyes. 'And I saw Alice again, as a grown woman – or how she would have been; she was only eighteen when I last saw her – and I thought my heart would break!'

'Lucy's guardian, her uncle, said that he'd tried to trace you when her parents died,' Oswald said softly. 'They were killed in a train crash, but Lucy survived. She knew nothing about her grandparents until she was grown up, when her uncle told her that her mother had been banned from her parents' home.'

The door slowly opened and Alice stood half in and half out of the opening, her fingers to her mouth and her gentle eyes, so like Oswald's, looking anxiously from one to another. Oswald held out his hand to her and she came to him and sat on his knee.

'Alice,' he whispered in her ear. 'You'll never guess who this is.'

Alice looked at Mrs Masters and then her mother and then up at her father and murmured into his ear, 'She looks very sad. I fink she made Mama cry.'

361

'She has been very sad,' Oswald said gently. 'But now I think she might be happy again, and Mama will be very happy too.'

Alice slipped down from her father's knee and leaning in towards her great-grandmother whispered confidentially, 'I've got a baby brother. He's called Joseph Oswald Thornbury. Papa calls him Jot because he's only little.' She laughed and put her thumb in her mouth, and then she took it out and said, 'Perhaps you'd like to see him and that might make you happy?'

Maria Masters, her eyes streaming, looked at Lucy, and when Lucy, her own eyes wet and too choked to speak, nodded, she said, 'I would. It would make me very happy indeed.'

In his usual intrepid manner Oswald gathered everyone together, ushering Lucy and her grandmother and Alice into the sitting room where there was a warm fire burning and asking the nursery maid to bring a sleepy Joseph down to be introduced before being taken back to his cot again. He asked Dora to make more tea and bring cake, and told her that if anyone else should ask for Dr Lucy she should say that she was unavailable. Then he set about telephoning his mother at her Pearson Park home to say that as soon as Pa arrived from the bank would they please come over straight away and bring Eleanor too if possible as something momentous and wonderful had happened and they should be here to share it.

Lucy wiped her eyes and gazed at her grandmother sitting next to her on the sofa; she had taken off her hat and coat and was having a conversation with Alice who was showing her one of her dolls; she could hardly take it in. How this poor gentle woman must have suffered for so many years. Hard enough for me as a child to lose my parents, but my loss has been lessened by the love that Uncle William and then Aunt Nora have shown me. Grandmother Masters had had no one with whom to share her grief of losing a daughter, not just once but twice.

The door quietly opened and Oswald stood half in half out, just as Alice had done earlier. Lucy stretched out her hand to him, to bring him to her side, into the fold.

I am so lucky; I have my dearest Oswald whom I love so much,

William and Nora, Eleanor who is a sister to me, my good friends, and now I have my beautiful children. I have been blessed, she thought, and felt Oswald's tender touch on her shoulder, and I must restore and make amends for the hurt that has been done.

'Dearest Grandmother,' she murmured, reaching to take up the veined hand and pressing it to her cheek. Here was her very own flesh and blood. They would need time to get to know one another: so many questions to be asked and answered. 'You must come back into my life, and that of my husband and children.'

Grandmother Masters brushed away her tears. 'I would like that very much, Lucy dear,' she said huskily. 'So many years have been wasted and I would like to make up for that lost time.'

'We can't forget the past,' Lucy told her. 'It is part of who we are.' She smiled and blinked away her own tears. 'But we can at last look forward to a brighter future.'

ACKNOWLEDGEMENTS AND SOURCES

I have used many websites and independent sources for information on the First World War and for general reading. These include:

Hull and East Riding Institute for the Blind (HERIB), www.herib.co.uk

Kingston Upon Hull War Memorial 1914–1918 – The Story of Hull in World War One, www.ww1hull.org.uk: website for details of the Hull Pals and Zeppelins over Hull.

The Hull People's Memorial, www.hull-peoples-memorial. co.uk: with thanks to Alan Brigham for valued information on aspects of the First World War and the memorabilia in the remarkable Hull People's Memorial Gift Shop and Museum.

Blind Veterans UK, www.blindveterans.org.uk: with thanks to Robert Baker, information and archives officer.

BBC World War One at Home, *Endell Street, London: Only All-female Run Military Hospital* [audio], 3 Feb 2014, www.bbc.co.uk/ programmes/p01rjcsv: deeds and words of the suffrage military hospital in Endell Street, London.

EyeWitness to History, www.eyewitnesstohistory.com: gas attack.

Scarlet Finders, www.scarletfinders.co.uk: British military nurses, QAIMNS and TFNS.

The Long, Long Trail – The British Army in the Great War of 1914–1918, www.longlongtrail.co.uk

Firstworldwar.com – A Multimedia History of World War One, www.firstworldwar.com

My grateful thanks to Professor Martin Goodman for allowing me to use details from his excellent and informative book *Suffer and Survive: The Extreme Life of J. S. Haldane* (London, Simon and Schuster UK Ltd, 2007).

Thanks are also due to Tony Kaye of T. S. Kaye and Sons, Yorkshire tool merchants, for permission to use details from his company's archives.

And my grateful thanks, as always, for the guiding hands of my efficient and supportive team at Transworld Publishers.

This is a work of fiction and any inconsistencies or inaccuracies contained within it are mine.

ABOUT THE AUTHOR

Since winning the Catherine Cookson Prize for Fiction for her first novel, *The Hungry Tide*, Val Wood has published twenty-two novels and become one of the most popular authors in the UK.

Born in the mining town of Castleford, Val came to East Yorkshire as a child and has lived in Hull and rural Holderness where many of her novels are set. She now lives in the market town of Beverley.

When she is not writing, Val is busy promoting libraries and supporting many charities.

Find out more about Val Wood's novels by visiting her website at www.valeriewood.co.uk

N